Take Flight

TAKE FLIGHT

T. E. Price

NEW YORK

LONDON • NASHVILLE • MELBOURNE • VANCOUVER

Take Flight

Published in New York, New York, by Morgan James Publishing. Morgan James is a trademark of Morgan James, LLC. www.MorganJamesPublishing.com

ISBN 9781631952906 paperback
ISBN 9781631952913 eBook
Library of Congress Control Number: 2020943107

Cover and Interior Design by:
Chris Treccani
www.3dogcreative.net

To our fawn.
You are so much stronger than you know.

"The pen heals. Preserves. Remembers. Forgives in time, by necessity."
—Bryan Thao Worra, *"Pen/Sword"*

Contents

Acknowledgments

I would like to thank my husband, Matt, who has always championed my writing and encouraged me to follow my dreams.

Thank you to my parents: Mary-Lynn, who instilled in me a love for reading and writing at a young age and who has played a pivotal role in my writing from day one—thank you for your countless hours spent on my manuscripts and for believing in me; and Bob, who has been inspirational in my spiritual journey since I was a child and who is constantly encouraging me to honor God in all areas of my life, including my writing.

To my sisters, April and Chanelle, along with the rest of the McRae clan, thank you for being my biggest cheerleaders.

A big thank you goes to Chad and Mindy Babcock for providing endless details of Oklahoma culture and terrain.

I would also like to thank Erin Unger, Ruth Buchanan, and Janine Rosche—your coaching, editing, insights, and encouragement have been paramount in the publication of this novel.

The entire Morgan James Publishing team has been phenomenal throughout the publication process—thank you to each and every one of you for making this dream come true.

Finally, all thanks and honor be unto God, for "I can do all things through Christ who strengthens me." (Philippians 4:13, NKJV)

CHAPTER 1

He told me I would never have the strength to leave. But look at me now. I did it. I got out. Just hours earlier, I was frantically packing my personal belongings, praying he wouldn't return home in the midst of my escape. My brother flew in to help—this decision I've made sets my stomach in a constant state of churning, but it had to be done, and Harrison understood why. All the memories I have of him have haunted me these past three years. When I finally mustered up the courage to tell Harrison what my life had come to, he didn't hesitate. He booked a flight from Michigan to Oklahoma and came to my rescue. We managed to escape while he was still at work. Now the question remains—am I safe here?

I rise from the leather couch positioned in front of the big, bay window and walk beside the fireplace to glance outside. The hairs on my arms stand on end. Should I hang curtains? I feel so vulnerable with my life on display through these naked windows. Maybe I'll run the idea by Ainsley.

Checkered sunlight peeks through the mid-October leaves that paint the thick grove of trees surrounding this place. In simpler days, the scene would have called for a pumpkin spice latte and an oversized, cable-knit sweater. But now, I see only a hedge of protection . . . or camouflage for a trespasser. A shudder courses up my spine. He won't find me here, Ainsley had convinced me of that. But my best friend doesn't know what he's capable of. Still, the pale blue lake house is better than where I came from. At least here I can gather my thoughts and decide where life is taking me.

I meander past the circular table that sits a few feet from the front door as I move to the small kitchen. My best friend and I share almost everything, but it is now clear why Ainsley didn't share this one thing with me as I focus my gaze on the huge family portrait positioned on the back, kitchen wall. This little cabin was designed for the three in the photo—no one else. In the still frame, Ainsley's husband, Will, has one arm wrapped around Ainsley's thin waist and the other arm is holding their newborn son, Miles. Will's brown hair is swept to one side, and his clean-shaven face highlights the dimples that Ainsley fell in love with. Ainsley's pin-straight, shoulder-length hair is blown back by the Oklahoma winds we're all too familiar with. Her bright smile is a brilliant contrast to her dark features, but in this photo, her smile doesn't quite reach her eyes. Will and Ainsley met right out of college, and everything moved quickly. She was married in no time, only to discover she was pregnant within months. Then life happened, and now, an inch of dust has formed on the border of the frame. This lake house has been abandoned for some time now. It's crazy how quickly the inside can collect billowing dust balls and tangled spider webs, even if this place was built only a few years back. Which reminds me, I still need to clean.

Sighing deeply, I move to the fridge and survey the empty shelves. There is a grocery store farther up the road. Do I have it in me to go? If I did, what would I buy? I press a palm into one eye. It's not like I'm hungry. I'd rather take a nap—all thanks to my escape earlier today. In a few short hours, Harrison helped me move out of the house that had trapped me in my pain and misery. I've done what I thought was impossible. I've finally left *him*.

My eyes don't take in much—a stick of butter, store brand maple syrup whose overflow has crystalized on the top shelf, and old salad dressing—so I shut the fridge and lean back on the counter. I close my eyes, let my head fall back, and exhale to the point where my lungs burn. *Screech.* My eyes fly open as my quick inhale sparks my adrenaline. My body starts trembling. *What was that?* It came from the front porch.

Frozen in place, only feet away from the front door, I listen intently. There it is—another scratch. Everything inside me aches to run, and yet my feet remain rooted to the floorboards. My heart thuds heavily in my chest. *Is there something outside? Someone?*

I wait where I am for a few more seconds, unable to be seen from the bay window, but I don't hear anything. Has he discovered I've left him by now? His office is just down the road from the house that held me prisoner. Did he somehow follow me here? Has he waited until Harrison left to attack? *Slow it down, Hallie.* The hair on the back of my neck raises as I slide open the drawer next to the fridge and reach for a knife. I edge closer to check the front door. But opening that door to see what could be outside threatens everything—my resolve, my escape, my safety.

Holding my chin high, I press my ear against the door and listen with all my might. Another light scrape vibrates through the wooden structure, and in a flash, I unlock the deadbolt and fling it open.

A wooden plaque, hanging from thick twine, goes flying, clatters across the front porch, and down the three stairs into the hard dirt. Blinking rapidly, I quickly survey the flat, open terrain edged by the forest, then peer down the long dirt drive. The wind blows through the trees, releasing a deluge of red and orange leaves that flutter to the ground. I pause just a moment longer. I'm all alone. I let out a long, shaky breath as I descend the steps and retrieve the plaque. My fingers trace over the words, *The Bakers*, and I hesitate. Now that I'm here, it's not technically The Bakers' lake house anymore. But then, what if he finds me here? Wouldn't it be best for him to think this is still their exclusive vacation home?

Nodding my head, I hang it back on the nail. Besides, I'm not going to change it out for one that reads "Hallie McClain," or even just "Hallie." Every bone in my body wants to drop my last name forever, but that will take a while. When I made the decision to leave him, it was for good, and the state of Oklahoma could legalize that divorce in ten short days. But thanks to a *little promise* I made, it's going to take longer than that.

One thing's for sure. I'm not going back. Standing in the breeze, I wrap both arms around my shoulders. This next year is going to be tough. Do I have to keep that stupid name all year long? I shiver as my last name echoes again and again in my mind, alongside the memory of what *he* did...of what he said he'd do.

Pressing my free hand to my stomach, I steal one last look around, then walk into the lake house and let the door click quietly behind me. I twist the deadbolt and lean back on the door. It's quiet out here—in the middle of nowhere, with no one to keep me company. Did Harrison really have to catch that flight? My chin dips to my chest, if only I had the dogs—*his* dogs—with me right now. Those dogs were always there when I needed them, when things got tough. Whether I was outside in the pens loving on them, or they were kissing on me, one thing remained true . . . we were all drowning in the reality of being hurt by *him.* Tears threaten as I lower my gaze. There's no way I could have saved the dogs, too.

The tightness in my throat thumps. *Ugh!* I need to distract myself. Thrusting my back off the door, I turn to the far-corner bedroom of this simple, rectangular structure, intent on unloading my clothes. As I stride between the table and leather armchair that matches the couch, I pause, step back, then lay the knife on the table. There's no harm in keeping it out, at least for the rest of the day. I tear my eyes away from the shiny blade and lift my head as I continue across the house. This open floorplan isn't expansive, but I don't need anything extravagant. A big house with nice things isn't worth it if it comes at a cost—the cost of freedom . . . the cost of safety.

As I enter the hallway alcove, I peek into a little boy's room to the right, and then flick on the lights to the bathroom in front of me. My eyes narrow, and I tiptoe toward the shower curtain. I bite my lip, then throw back the curtain. *Whew.* Empty . . . just as I guessed it would be. But I had to check. I let out a laugh as I exit the bathroom shaking my head. Swinging open the door to the bedroom that was Ainsley and Will's, I glance around. My shoulders draw farther down my back as my mouth settles into a half-smile. The room holds a queen-size bed, two nightstands, and a dresser directly across from the centered bedframe. It's not much, but it's perfect for me.

Moving over to a big, black trash bag full of clothes, I start to sift through the contents with a firm nod of my head. It's time to get settled in my new home. I rustle around for a second, looking from bag to bag, hoping to find a good starting point, when my blood freezes in my veins. A noise from the front of the house sends my mind racing. I wait—*maybe it's the plaque on the front door again.* It's not. *Thump-thump.* Footsteps thud up the front porch. Someone is here.

CHAPTER 2

My mind reels. Maybe it's Harrison—did his flight get delayed? My shaking hand grabs for my phone in my back pocket to check the time. As my breaths shorten, I punch at my blank home screen. Harrison's flight is long gone. *Who's here?*

A knock on the front door slices through the pulse of my heart beating against my temples like a drum. I crouch beside the trash bag of clothes and wait. Maybe it's a mistake—someone who isn't looking for me. A neighbor? I didn't see any other houses on the drive in. What if someone broke down nearby and needs some help*? Whoever it is, they just need to go away!*

Another impatient knock hits me square in the chest, and my body tenses for a fight. I gulp and rise. *If he's found me, it's all over.* My legs threaten to hold me upright as I stumble out of the bedroom and slink toward the bay window. No matter how I crane my neck, the front porch isn't in sight. Pressing my face against the cold pane, I spy the front grill of a familiar car. Uttering a cry of relief, I rush to the front door and fling it open. Ainsley's brow creases. She studies me as I place a hand over my heart, unable to catch my breath. Her head juts past me, she winces with the shine of the setting sun glinting off the blade still on the table behind me, then her face melts.

"*Hallie! I should have called to let you know I was coming,*" she exclaims as she rushes inside. She flings her purse on the hardwood floor and wraps her arms around me. I haven't regained enough strength to speak, but I don't have to. Ainsley squeezes me closer and says, "I got my parents to watch

Miles so I could come help you unpack. I didn't feel right just giving you the key…I need to be here to support you through this."

I pull back, and with a relieved smile, I say, "I'm just glad it's you. For a second, I thought—" and my voice tails off.

"I should have guessed," she says. "Does he know yet? Does he know you've left?"

Picking at a hangnail, I shrug, "Dunno. I've blocked him, so if he's trying to get in touch with me, he won't be able to."

"That's good." She glances over my shoulder at the clock on the stove. "He should be getting home from work any minute now, so he'll know soon enough."

I nod, take a shaky breath, then start moving back to the bedroom again. Those bags have to get unpacked if I'm going to get any rest tonight. "I was just going to organize my clothes, wanna help?"

"Sure," Ainsley says. She follows in my wake as I glance back at her. She rips her eyes away from the family portrait as her face blushes. Biting her bottom lip, she says with a pointed finger, "Maybe you should snag that family picture hanging in your parents' hallway to replace that one while you're staying here." With a quick chuckle, she adds, "You know the one… where you and Harrison look like a younger version of your mom and dad."

Harrison is built exactly like my dad—tall and muscular with dark hair and brown eyes. His frame is quite the opposite of my petite build, which I got from my mother. I also inherited my mother's green eyes and dirty blonde hair. The joke's always been that we are the cookie-cutters of our parents. Offering a tight-lipped smile, I say, "We'll see." I'm not ready to have my parents' faces staring at me all day. I shake my head, then pause in the doorway of the bedroom.

Ainsley approaches my side, exhales slowly, then says, "It's been a while since I've been here."

I clench my jaw, then clear my throat, "Thank you so much for letting me use this place, Ainsley. You have no idea how much it means to me knowing I don't have to move back in with my parents—that I have someplace to go where *he* can't find me." I lay my head on my friend's shoulder in appreciation.

Ainsley rests her head on top of mine, "No problem. I'm just glad *someone* is going to use it." She turns to face me, "It's been empty for a while. And you were right—this is the perfect place for you."

We move inside the room and start rummaging through the bags. "So, how did it go with Harrison here? I'm assuming you got out without any difficulty."

I shudder at the thought of my early morning escape strategically planned long before *he* returned home from work. "Yeah," my heart thumps hard in my chest, "I just can't believe I did it, Ainsley. I'm *finally* out." My heart soars with my newfound freedom as I add, "Harrison was great. He really helped with moving all the big stuff and renting the truck. I'm shocked he was willing to leave Isabel and the twins in Ann Arbor to help, especially with my parents in town." A heavy sigh escapes as I add, "They just don't understand why I've left *him*, so I didn't feel right asking for their help." My jaw tightens. It's not that I *need* anyone's help. I can do this on my own—the hard part's already over. Then my shoulders ease. It's nice to have company, though, and this *is* the only place I can go in all of Oklahoma where *he* won't find me.

Turning slowly, Ainsley moves to the dresser with a bag in her hand. Her silence brings me back to the conversation we had when I told her what had happened in my marriage and why I had to leave—when I told her about that *one night* . . . when I knew it was over for good. "What's this?" she asks, spinning back in my direction.

My eyes land on *his* box of cigars, that dreadful red and black wrapper visible from the glass pane framed by Ainsley's hands. My chest tightens as the painful memory of how I got my haunting scar burns vividly in my mind. "*Gosh*—how did that get in there?" Without expecting an answer, I refocus my attention on my clothes and say, "Harrison must have accidently packed that in the rush of it all. Please take them home to Will." My stomach does a summersault. The thought of ever smelling a Davidoff Yamasa cigar again is more than I can handle.

Ainsley sets the cigar box down on the dresser and begins unloading some other things. "Hey, check this out," she says, pivoting again in my direction, but this time holding a picture frame of us in Key West. "What a great time, huh? We always have a good time when we travel together."

Our smiling faces stare back at me from the frame as my memories ricochet to the night I had returned from that trip. It had been a rough one. One of many I endured in that marriage. Ainsley moves around the bed to place the picture frame on the far bedside table. "Yeah, we have great memories together," and with a chuckle, I add, "I'm glad you sat next to me in that English class years ago—college was shaping up to be a lonely time." A hanger slips through my grip and falls to my feet. I bend to pick it up as I continue, "I thought I was going to be all alone again once you found Will, so when you introduced me to . . . to *him*—well, I figured it all made sense. You would get married, I would get married, we would both live happily ever after."

Ainsley averts her eyes. "So much for that." She looks back at the picture, then says, "I wish I had known how bad it was for you. I can't believe I didn't pick up on it."

I grab a dress from the bag at my feet and hang it up, pushing the hangers down to create more space in the closet. Ainsley's phone rings in her purse that is still on the floor in the kitchen. She makes a run for it, leaving me behind to finish setting up the room. "It's probably Will," she yells over her shoulder as she jogs toward the phone. The ringing stops and the front door slams as Ainsley exits to take her husband's call.

For a few moments, I stand still, my mind tethered to our conversation. I must have been good at hiding it…all the signs. Ainsley didn't know, Harrison didn't know, and my parents still don't know.

Isabel knew, though. Harrison told me earlier today while we were unloading the moving truck how she had wanted to tell me just how awful she thought *he* was. Isabel's never been good at hiding her emotions. That's been true since the day my brother and she started dating in high school. When Isabel transferred to the private school for her senior year, that's when she first met *him.* Harrison told me today that Isabel wanted to warn me about him—that she wanted to tell me how he had tried to date her all those years ago, and how she could tell he was a jerk. Harrison cautioned her to keep that from me. Everyone tried to convince Isabel that *he* had changed.

And it was convincing—the guy was serving in the church, my parents liked him, and my best friend introduced us—he couldn't have been *that* bad. But Isabel wasn't convinced . . . *why was I?*

Why did I make the decision to marry him? It shouldn't have mattered that he made good money. And yet, that *private school, country boy meets business man* persona always intrigued me. He was a bit of a mystery, and I found that exciting. He was an impressive golfer and had a good reputation in the community. He was going to church with me at the beginning, and he seemed to have it all together. My arms drop to my sides. "I got sucked in, like I always do," I whisper to the empty room.

The front door slams again as Ainsley rushes toward me, her cell phone still in her hand. "Jonathan knows," she says, her face ashen. I freeze at the sound of *his* name. She gulps as her eyes lower for a moment, then she looks back at me, "I guess word travels fast in a small town, and Will knows one of the wellhead pumpers that works for Jona—" She licks her lips, "For him," she corrects. "Will said that this guy was supposed to go over for a drink after work, but when the guy drove past the house, *he* was outside. And I guess he was pretty upset because the door was left open, and the inside of the house looked a mess. The guy said the hunting dogs were going mad in the backyard pens, and there was a ton of broken glass and things littering the front lawn where he was pacing. He must have destroyed y'alls' picture frames."

Ainsley chews her lip. However, my thoughts jump to the various hunting rifles lining his gun safe, and that image makes my breath come to a screeching halt. I force a slow inhale. "I'm safe now," I reassure both of us. "He can't get me here."

Right?

Chapter 3

The water sparkles as sunlight dances across the surface of the rippling lake barely visible through all the trees. Settled in the rocking chair on the back deck of the lake house, I breath in my surroundings, processing all that has taken place over the past few days while trying to determine what is to come. I can't believe I actually had the courage to leave him. But could I really stay in that marriage forever? No . . . and I didn't want anyone to tell me I had to.

There was a time when I was nervous about my brother's reaction—worried that he would encourage me to stay in the marriage, to work through our problems, to keep praying until God made a difference. Yet, when I unloaded the shameful truth, there was no deliberation…he wanted to get me out of there just as badly as I wanted to leave.

My head drops against the back of the rocker as I fixate on that moment when I revealed the darkest secrets of my terror-filled marriage to my brother. *Crunch!* I jerk my head forward. The rustling of leaves to my left has me fighting for air. Something is moving in the woods. My skin crawls as my eyes pierce the spot where the noise originated. The trees move ever so slightly as a fawn at the edge of the wood patters into view. I exhale while my grip on the arm of the rocking chair loosens. Every muscle momentarily poised for a sprint relaxes, and I smile at the spindly-legged creature.

Harrison always says I remind him of a fawn, so innocent and timid. Much like this fawn, I'm naïve, clumsy, easily distracted, and fairly forgetful. I wish I could process the unknown well, but instead, I'm just like this poor, little thing, skirting the edge of the forest all alone. The fawn leaps quickly out of sight in reaction to a movement from the woods. Is the little deer running toward its mother, fearful of its surroundings, unsure of the world, unwilling to venture too far from safety? I shake my head as I clench my teeth. That's not me—*I don't have to run to anyone*—and certainly not my parents. They don't get me, anyway. They're always pushing me to be stronger, and yet, they disagree with the strongest decision I've ever made… to leave *him.*

The wind rustles the leaves of the forest that secures this hiding place of mine, and I shiver in response. I am all alone, there isn't a neighbor for miles. Harrison landed safely in Michigan yesterday, and Ainsley is currently getting ready for church…something I should be doing myself. But could I really fathom facing anyone right now? Going grocery shopping yesterday was one thing—I needed to do that—but putting on a show for the church goers is different.

My heart thumps hard in my chest at the reality of being truly alone. In the first few days after the wedding, I kept telling myself that I had Jonathan, but it didn't take long for me to realize I was alone in my marriage. Alone, just days after I married him, alone in trying to improve our marriage, alone in my dreams and desires for a romance that would never flourish. Alone—with terror serving as my constant, sickening companion. If it's possible, I felt lonelier then than I do now, sitting here beside this isolated lake, rocking back and forth, with only my thoughts for company.

The cool morning breeze loosens a few strands of hair that I quickly tuck behind my ear. I lift the hood of my high school's cross-country team sweatshirt to protect me from the chill of the fall air as I reach for my mug and take another sip of my coffee. The heat of the brew warms me as I hug my mug closer to my chest where my team logo is, testifying to my only potential reprieve from loneliness during my high school years. It's not like being alone is a new feeling for me. Unlike Harrison, who has always been outgoing, I struggled to make friends when my parents moved the family from Michigan to Oklahoma all those years ago. I made plenty of acquaintances—sure, and there were a lot of guys who tried asking me out, but I didn't have any real friends. So, I joined the cross-country team, even though *team* didn't reflect the reality I experienced since I ran with earphones during practice, my music taking the place of comradery. I developed the habit of running with my head down, something my coach tried to correct given that I could only see a few steps in front of me. Perhaps this running ritual of mine was an omen, a hint of what was to come in my adult years. I went through college, graduated with an Associates in Business, but had no idea what I wanted to do with it. I struggled losing Ainsley to Will, so I dove blindly into a relationship with Jonathan, oblivious of where that would take me. It seems like my whole life I've had my head down, always running away from something instead of toward something.

The alarm on my phone nestled inside the front pocket of my hoodie begins to jingle, breaking the silence. The church service starts in ten minutes—time to turn on my laptop and watch the live recording. I reach for my phone to turn off the dinging as I rise from the rocking chair, taking one last survey of the beautiful view. If I have to be alone, I couldn't think of a prettier place to be.

I amble around the right corner of the deck and enter through the side door, greeted by the lit fire, welcoming me to my comfy domain where I can lounge in sweats while still enjoying the church service from their online feed. I flip open my laptop and cuddle into the leather couch. The seat has been warmed by the fire, and I sink deeper into the folds that cushion my body. With a blanket tucked around me, I wait for the music to begin.

The screen shows the masses starting to filter in from the foyer. I smile. Connect Church is my safety net. It's been three long years of attending services alone, trying to hide my tears. The members and leaders knew I needed them from day one, although they didn't *exactly* know why. Before our wedding, he filled the seat beside me, but after the honeymoon was over, the seat was vacated, and my heart was broken.

I squint toward the front row where Ainsley and I sit after singing on the worship team. We usually sing together, and I grimace at the thought of leaving her alone up there today. The stage stands empty while the clock at the corner of my screen counts down to the start of the service. My heart lifts at the memory of Harrison and I singing together on that stage; he was the Worship Leader, serving as the lead guitarist and vocalist at that church before he and a very pregnant Isabel took the job in Ann Arbor. My brother is the one who encouraged me to start going to church after I stopped attending my parents' church years prior. Eventually, he led me to understand what was lacking in my life. There was a hole in my world that couldn't be filled by distractions or relationships. Thankfully, Ainsley supported my decision to give my life over to Christ, and she was quick to follow in the same path. Once we both graduated from college, we settled in the same area and began attending and serving at Connect Church together.

A large shadow crosses in front of the camera and my breath catches in my chest. Is that *him?* Would he show up at church trying to find me? It's been years since he attended Connect Church, he wouldn't go now that I left him . . . or would he?

The tall figure walks toward a seat in the middle row, and I exhale sharply. It isn't him. I shake my head as the timer on the screen continues to count down. The one thing I can depend on is his determination to maintain a good public image. He would never show up at church and make a scene. He's always had this undeniable desire to come across as respectable to those in the community. When he took over his father's position as supervisor of the wellhead pumping company, his *good-guy* act increased double-fold. He wouldn't do anything irrational to taint his reputation. He has the county fooled, just as he had me fooled before we were married. He wouldn't sacrifice his image just to get back at me. So, how *is* he handling my departure? Has he told anyone? Does his family know yet? Maybe he'll keep going on with his life, as if nothing has changed.

The music begins, jolting me out of my downward spiral. The thin frame of Chip Catcher, the worship leader that replaced Harrison, fills the screen. His hipster attire is countered by his shiny, shaved head and burly beard, but his style works for him as his music and stage presence seem to draw in a crowd. Ainsley finds her place on the stage beside Chip, and the familiar melody of today's opening worship song eases my heart. My eyes are drawn back to the aging bass player standing in the spot where Jonathan used to play while we were dating. Tugging on the blanket, drawing it closer to my chin, I breathe in a slow, calculated breath. He can't find me here, and he won't do anything in public to ruin his coddled reputation.

The service today is about baptism. Bile rises in the back of my throat and my stomach tightens. I'm still not baptized, despite my faith in Christ. But could I really stand before all those people and share my testimony, especially now that I've left my husband? Pastor Noah's introduction sends my wandering eyes back to the screen as he challenges our willingness to trust Christ. The camera focuses on his pale features and cleft chin as he directs us to a passage in the Psalms. He reads to the congregation from chapter thirteen verse five: "But I trust in your unfailing love; my heart rejoices in your salvation." He places the Bible on the podium and scratches at the edge of his short, silver hair as his pale blue eyes penetrate the audience. "Have you placed your trust in Christ?" he asks, his voice just above a whisper. "Do you have reason to rejoice in your salvation? If so, why don't you proclaim that trust proudly today?"

Pastor Noah continues with his sermon, but his voice drowns in a sea of thoughts. That's it, that's my problem. *I don't really trust God*—not enough to publicly proclaim that trust. Biting my bottom lip, I lean my cheek into one hand. Can I really trust God after he led me into such a terrible marriage? And just after I became a Christian, no less.

My cell phone buzzes on the coffee table beside me. My hand flies from my face as I lean forward. It's my mom. I glance back at the screen and see people lining up to get baptized. Maybe I'll take her call instead of watching this. I exit the live feed and pick up my cell.

"Hi, Mom," I somewhat screech. Clearing my throat, I drop my voice back to my normal pitch, "I thought you agreed not to call on Sunday mornings. I'm usually in church."

"Oh, yes," she greets matter-of-factly. "Well, your father and I were just driving home from *our church*, and we thought we would call to check in on you. All settled at that lake house now?" She doesn't bother to ask why I'm not in church this morning. No surprise there.

I roll my eyes at the sound of her tone. My parents are creatures of habit, they retired years ago when they moved the family to Oklahoma, seeking a simple, country life away from the cold temperatures and city life Michigan had to offer. Since then, my mother's hair appointments and the small, country church services remain pretty much the only two activities that get her out of the single story, outdated house where I spent my middle and high school years. "Yep," I reply, then quickly add, "and please don't tell anyone where I am. I need to stay—" I hesitate, weighing every word, "—away from the public. That includes the hair salon, Mom. It's just down the road from my gym, and I don't want people knowing I've left *him*." Silence follows on her end. "How was church?" I throw in. I've said what I needed to say, no point in opening the conversation just to hear, yet again, my parents' theories on my broken marriage.

"It was good," my mother sighs, "but you would know if you went with us every now and then." She pauses, letting the sting of her retort hang between us.

I cast my eyes downward and pull my knees to my chest. I should let the comment pass, but I can't seem to help myself. "Your church just isn't for me, Mom," I begin. "It's a great church, and the people are really nice, but I just...I really like Connect Church." My mother doesn't respond. There it is—another moment for a daughter and her mother to bond . . . gone. This is our reality, we just don't know how to relate to one another. I hype up my pitch, my words projecting through my constricted throat, "But I'm glad you and Dad still enjoy it." The conversation of church is never an easy one. My parents use church as a ruse. They attend the service on Sundays as if the practice will erase the sins they've committed throughout the week. Ever since I was young, I knew this side of religion wasn't for me. I need a real, day-to-day relationship with Christ, even though I still have some trust issues. Perhaps the trust issues stem from my parents. Or maybe from Jonathan.

"Well," my mother clears her throat, bringing me back to our conversation, "did you do *anything* this morning?"

"I watched the service online," I say, sitting up a little taller. "The sermon was on baptism." I glance at the sleeping laptop sitting on the coffee table. I should have just ignored her call, like I usually do. Would it have really been that bad to watch the people in the service do what I still can't bring myself to do?

"Oh, that's nice." My mother is at a loss for words again. Muffled whispers fill the background. "Your father wants to talk to you."

"Could we just—" I interject, but it's too late. My dad's dominant tone rings through every syllable of his brusque greeting.

"Hallie," he starts, "I saw Jonathan's car circling our house yesterday, and I thought I should tell you." I grip fistfuls of the blanket as a shudder passes straight through me. My lungs inflate, but I can't bring myself to say anything. Of course he went by my parents' house, that's where he expects me to be. The silence stands for a moment, but my father doesn't wait to hear my response, "I wanted to talk with him, but—"

"*No!*" I take a quick, steadying breath. "Just don't let him in or try to talk to him, Dad," I beg. "It's over between us, and I don't want to complicate things with useless conversation." That would be something my dad would do. Chat away to the monster who has stolen so much from me...as if nothing has changed. But my parents don't know what happened. And I couldn't tell them. It was hard enough sharing those shameful details with Harrison and Ainsley.

"Hallie, now you listen to me," my father punches back, "Jonathan left a note on the front porch saying that he just wanted to talk with you, and he deserves to hear from you. That man took care of you. He placed a roof over your head, and you never went hungry. He may not have been the best at showing it, but he was a good husband."

My eyes flutter closed as a tear escapes down my face. My dad couldn't be more wrong. My parents don't have the slightest clue what took place in that marriage, and my dad's harsh accusations confirm that I made the right decision in keeping my secrets from them. I try to answer, but I stumble over my words. I don't have it in me to defend myself, and my dad knows it. His disappointment is more than I can stand.

"People will find out you two are no longer together, and we don't want word of your *divorce* getting out at our church." He sighs heavily. "Why can't you be more like your brother? He and Isabel are happy," he states, as if he knows what it takes to have a healthy marriage. But he doesn't. He never looks at Mom the way Harrison looks at Isabel. "And I am sure they have had their problems," he continues, "but they don't walk away from their marriage."

My chin begins to quiver. Harrison and Isabel have a great marriage, a marriage that I have longed for since the day I returned from my honeymoon. It's not my fault that my marriage didn't end up the way I intended. I did everything I could to stay in that marriage, but my efforts didn't sway *him* in the least. Besides, I had to get out, my safety depended on it. Refusing to let my parents know I'm on the verge of tears, I steady my breathing long enough to say good-bye.

"I have to go—" I manage, my face burns from my father's blustering.

"Fine," my dad retorts, "but you *will* honor our request, Hallie. Do not file those divorce papers for at least a year. All your mother and I need right now is a *divorced* daughter on our hands. People will be talking about this for years in our small town. Maybe after a year of contemplation, you'll see the depth of this terrible decision and return to Jonathan."

The line goes dead. So much for a *good-bye*. I throw my phone to the opposite end of the couch. It bounces off the cushioned arm and lands beside my bundled feet. I dive face first into the leather cushions, beating my fist against the couch. I don't care about my parents' disappointment—they may not see it, but I *am* strong. I had it in me to get out, and I have it in me to do so much more with my life than I was ever allowed to when I was with *him*. I'll show them. I push myself upright and set my jaw. *I'm not a little fawn anymore.*

Chapter 4

My nightmare takes form the moment I find myself rounding the corner of my parents' one-story home, keeping my eyes fixed on the outdated, shag carpet that leads to the dining room table. "Hallie," my mother's voice calls from the dining room. "Dinner's ready. Let's eat while it's hot." The wall of the narrow hallway opens to the small, dining space. A harsh gasp escapes as I see Jonathan sitting at the table with my parents. I stumble back into the hallway. *Why is he here?*

Leaning against my parents' tacky wallpaper, I steady my shaking legs in the shadows that keep me hidden from his sight. "Don't be rude, Hallie," my dad demands from his seat at the head of the table. "Come here and sit down, the food's getting cold."

I obey my father, just as I always have, even if I disagree. Somehow, my legs carry me to the table where I pull out the chair opposite Jonathan. His beady, black eyes narrow like a hawk closing in on its prey, as if he's already determined how I would react to this situation, playing into the reality that I don't have it in me to disregard my parents' commands.

"No, not there," my dad says, shaking his head as he redirects me with a swift gesture of his hand to the open chair beside Jonathan. I hesitate, then cower and comply under my father's stern gaze. "Hurry up, Hallie, your mother has worked hard to prepare this meal, and we're all hungry."

I sit down, every fiber of my being shaking with my slow descent. Refusing to look at Jonathan seated to my left, my throat constricts as my dad asks him to say the blessing. "Let's bow our heads," Jonathan says, his deep voice sends a chill that seeps into my bones. I glance around the table while my parents calmly lower their heads. As I squeeze my eyes shut, I feel the weight of Jonathan's heavy hand on the back of my neck. My mind aches with the urge to escape as Jonathan begins his prayer. With his first words, he tightens his grip—his long fingers edging closer to my throat—and I scream.

The sound of my shriek wakes me, and I sit straight up in the lake house bed that I now claim as my own. My eyes dart around in the darkness as if every shadow is concealing Jonathan. I wipe my hair off my damp face as I flop back on my pillow—what an awful nightmare. Rubbing my eyes, I roll to the other side of the bed and pick up my phone to check the time. It's 5:36, the sun won't rise for another hour. With a heavy sigh, I try to close my eyes again. What are the odds that I could go back to sleep now? I roll and twist around for a few minutes, but images of Jonathan sitting at my parents' table wearing that familiar, smug grin haunts me. *Hmph!* I won't be getting any more rest.

I swing my legs over the side of the bed and shuffle my feet around trying to find my slippers. I trudge out of the bedroom, tucking my phone away in the pocket of my jogger pants while making a beeline for the fireplace. As the flames flicker to life, I watch the dance of light fill the room. Will I ever stop dreaming about *him?* It's not fair—I've left him, yet he still has a stronghold on me. He can still manipulate my mood and sense of safety, even now, as I stay hidden away in these woods. Will I still dream about him after the divorce? Will I always be looking over my shoulder?

Stepping back from the fire, the memory of his hand on my neck sends a shudder down my back, and I shrug my shoulders closer to my ears, as if to protect my exposed skin. I run my fingers through my hair, adjusting the bulk of it to one side. A cup of coffee is just what I need to lift my spirits. As I move to the kitchen, my hand pauses on the light switch. My arm hair stands on end at the idea of drawing attention to the inside of this secluded cabin. *Nah,* I don't need the lights on, the glow from the fireplace is enough to help me navigate in the kitchen. I shuffle over to the counter and power up the Keurig. I'm not a big coffee drinker, but I do indulge in the occasional cup. Although I'm aware of the calories that accompany my flavored creamer and whipped cream, I welcome the splurge. My diet usually consists of fruits and veggies, protein powder, and the occasional complex carb alongside a portioned serving of meat. Working as a personal trainer, I have to live up to it all. But I can't complain. I like what I eat.

I mosey over to the fridge, pour a generous portion of creamer into my coffee, and find the can of whipped cream, shaking it before topping off my mug. For the first time since awakening, I smile, making my way over to the couch with my cup of caffeine and sugar—offerings of a promising start to my day. The next hour is spent on the couch with intermittent prayers and some reading from my Bible app. My dream about Jonathan must have some significance, and I pray about that for a bit. My parents' invitation to Jonathan for dinner mirrors my growing lack of trust in them. And what's with Jonathan saying the blessing, just as my dad had asked in the dream? It's as if my subconscious is punching me with the reminder that Jonathan is the master of manipulation—he's always been great at playing to his audience. Whether it's praying or feeding the crowd the right line, he works his angle to keep them eating out of his hand, believing his every move and word without question. He's always in control, and he knows the power that accompanies it. The last sip of my coffee is cold, and I grudgingly accept that it's time to get off the couch and get ready for work.

My slippers make scuffling noises across the hardwood floors as I drag my feet back to my bedroom. I grab my gym bag from the closet and fill it with all the items needed for my workday. The thin, white curtains that frame the bedroom window glint with the muted morning hues, suggesting I have enough time to workout at the gym, shower, then clock in for work. *Ugh!* I've got another late shift tonight. Guess I should pack some meal supplements to get me through my twelve-hour shift. I zoom to the kitchen and come back with enough protein bars to pack out the front zipper of my gym bag. Making my way over to the dresser, I sift through my drawer of leggings. I lift a black spandex pair that should do for my workout and yank out the gray cotton pair folded beneath it for the remainder of my day. I toss the cotton pair into my bag and pull on a pink and black, spandex tank top with a built-in bra and crisscross straps across the back. The sleek material pulls tightly across my torso, and I run my hand over my stomach. My head falls as my fingers brush over the circular scar on my lower abdomen. Biting my bottom lip, I shake my head, willing myself to move past the horrific memory of *his* cruelty. But this scar will never let me forget. Inhaling, I draw myself up to my full height and find a high-neck, coral tank to pair with my gray pants. *I can't dwell on it.* I shove the shirt into my gym bag, packing it in next to my protein powder and protein shake bottle, then zip up the bag and leave it on my bed as I hastily finish my morning routine.

As I exit the front door, a cool breeze sends me right back inside, dashing to the back of the lake house for my black jacket hanging in my closet. I lock up behind me and rub at my hip as I walk the dirt path to my car. *Ouch!* Maybe I can make time in between clients to stretch my hip flexors.

I throw the gym bag into the cluttered backseat of my car and shut the door as I shiver. I shove the keys into the ignition, hold for a few seconds before my engine catches, sigh as my car rumbles to life, then cringe as I travel down the dirt drive leading to the main road. My long drive to work in my struggling car hasn't changed with the move to the lake house, but Jonathan still makes that short drive every day in his new, black Audi. When we were still living together, my complaints about my car fell on deaf ears. Instead of buying me a vehicle, he had a last-minute change of mind to trade his former car for the sleek Audi, and I was still stuck with my white, outdated Chevy Cavalier. My car groans as I pull onto the paved road. To add insult to injury, even Jonathan's red, hunting truck would have been better to drive than this piece of junk I'm traveling in. But he would *never* have agreed to that.

Swerving to avoid a pot-hole in the semi-abandoned strip mall that holds my small gym, I find a spot, jam the car into park, turn the key, and pat the dash as it jostles still. My eyes land on the red brick building and glass door reading "Jim's Gym," and I look heavenward for a moment, then slump my head forward again. I grab my bag, slam the car door shut, and wish for the hundredth time that I worked at a place that paid better.

"Hallie, you're here early," Jim calls out as the bell on the glass door draws the old man's gaze up from the scattered papers strewn across the welcome desk.

"Hi, Jim. I figured I'd get my workout in before I start work today." I avoid touching on the conversation of my sleep deprivation. I would rather workout after my shift, like I usually do, but what's the point? I'll be exhausted after my late shift tonight anyway. I hide my thoughts behind a quick wave and push open the women's locker room door to drop off my bag before I start my workout.

Whew—glad that hour's over with. I wipe my sweaty brow and check my heart rate while walking back to the locker room. As I count the pumps of my rapid pulse, a voice near the front desk makes me grimace and throws off my counting. Sure enough, Danny, who is crossing the threshold of the gym entrance, has seen me before I can disappear beyond the locker room door.

"What's up, shorty," he gibes, as he always does. The irony found in this nickname he's pegged me with has grown old given Danny is not much taller than I am. His chest juts out preparing for another taunt as his eyes run the length of my body. Danny's muscular frame leaves a box-like impression that makes me crinkle my nose, and his assessing gaze doesn't help. "You hear Tricia wants to train with me now?" I offer a quizzical look in reply. "Yeah, she said you did a good job getting her toned-up, but she wants to create some bulk . . . guess she knows who she needs to go to for that," he finishes as he squeezes both hands together in front of him and sinks his neck back in a flex designed to show off his traps.

Fighting the urge to roll my eyes at one of the other personal trainers who mans this gym, I glower back at Danny who has just stolen another one of my clients. It seems like I lose all of the young ones to him. "Well, I still have Georgina," I retort, immediately regretting the only quip that came to mind.

With a smirk, Danny asks, "Who . . . Wrinkles?" He jeers, slapping his knee in jest. "Georgina comes by her nickname honestly—you can't really enjoy training the *oldies*."

Waving him off, I push open the women's locker room door, abruptly ending our conversation. I can hear Danny laughing on the other side of the door as I throw back the farthest curtain, enter the spacious stall and turn on the shower. Ripping at my clothes, I tug and pull as if I'm wrestling with my doleful reality. How is it that the one thing that drives me in this job keeps getting lost to a meathead like Danny?

In record time, I'm out of the locker room and clocking in. Jim walks by me with an anti-bacterial spray bottle and a rag, making his way to the back wall where the cardio machines stand. I grab a bottle and cloth from the stand near the front of the room and follow him. I don't have a client for another half hour, and I need something to keep me busy. We walk past Danny who has just begun a training session with a tall brunette. He holds her waist as she sinks down into a squat, but the ten-pound plates on each side of the bar suggests she doesn't need a spotter. I almost gag at the sight of his greedy face as he watches the brunette sink lower and lower.

"You alright, Hallie?" A tone of concern threads Jim's question.

I tear my eyes away from the scene in front of the squat rack and plaster a smile across my face. "Yes, absolutely," I reassure Jim with a nod.

"If you say so," Jim says with a raised eyebrow. He moves to the closest bike, angled to face the back wall where the televisions hang, and sprays the surface of the seat. I begin cleaning the first of many treadmills lined up directly behind the bikes. This gym may be old, but it is well organized and perfectly sectioned with the rows of cardio machines near the back wall, weight machines to the left and free weights to the right. We clean silently for a moment as the sound from the weather forecaster from one TV clashes with the ESPN announcer's voice from another. A man in his late fifties climbs slowly off the elliptical at the other end of the row. He and Danny's brunette bring the grand total of guests to two. "You don't seem like yourself, you know," Jim says as if he's been contemplating my behavior since the moment we started wiping down the machines.

I gulp. Maybe all Jim needs to know is that I haven't been sleeping. He doesn't have to know *why*. "I haven't been sleeping all that well lately," I begin, my tone so low it sends me scrambling. "But it's not going to affect my work," I quickly chirp.

Jim chuckles as he moves to the next bike, "I wouldn't let you go, even if it did." He smiles while continuing with the familiar routine. "I knew when I hired you I had struck gold. The other trainers don't pick up a rag to help me clean without being told to," he adds, lifting his cloth only long enough to motion at my efforts. "And that bozo over there," he indicates toward Danny, "I can do without the arrogance and perverted stares. No one has complained yet, but I know I'm just biding my time with that one." Jim resumes his cleaning, "He's always in competition with the other trainers, as if he gets a medal for collecting more clients." I grin as I move to the next machine in my row. "And what's with all the nicknames?" he asks, "I don't want to know what he calls me behind my back—probably something like *senile Jim* or *decrepit boss-man.*"

With a laugh, I add, "You're not senile or decrepit."

"My Halloween costume this year suggests otherwise," Jim replies with a smirk. "On that note, I'm thinking about having a small gathering with all the trainers on Halloween night. I could close the gym early that night and get the crew together."

"Sounds fun, let me know if you plan on doing it." A lonely lake house awaits me on Halloween night. Without a neighbor in sight, I won't be decorating or handing out candy anyway. This possible party might not be such a bad idea. I glance back at Danny…then again, maybe not.

"Well, it's still up in the air," Jim says. "But, if we do it, you could bring Jonathan, too."

My eyes widen like a child caught in a lie as I fix my attention on cleaning, avoiding Jim's gaze. Did he catch my reaction? "Yeah, I think Jonathan will probably be busy that night," I assure Jim with a steady tone. My dream and the memory of *his* hand on my neck flash into my mind, and my skin crawls. I've got to keep my escape a secret. No one can know . . . at least not yet.

"I figured as much. Jonathan has only made it to one of our parties. He seems like a pretty busy guy."

"Mmm-hmm," I respond behind closed lips.

Perhaps sensing that I don't want to get into it, Jim runs the cloth over the final bike and straightens up. "Well, I'm going to get a coffee from Java. Want one?" Jim has always been a supporter of the small businesses still trying to make a go of it in our tired strip mall. Most businesses have relocated two blocks east, away from this forgotten area and into our quaint downtown, lined with restaurants and clothing boutiques, providing the only semblance of class this small town has to offer.

"No, I'm fine," I say with a half-smile, "thanks though." As Jim leaves, I transition to the free weights. *Man,* I really hate this small town. Businesses fall apart, people never leave and no one new moves to the area…that is, apart from my parents. *Ugh . . .* my parents. I'm due for our weekly visit—it's hard to avoid when my work is so close to their home. Why did I promise to visit *tonight*? What with my dream and this long shift ahead of me, I might lose my mind if I have to spend an hour with them. Yawning, I give a final swipe to the bench and nod my head. My lack of sleep can suffice as an excuse for the second time today. I speed walk to the locker room; I'd better make this call to my mom quick before my 9:30 arrives.

* * *

The minute hand on the big, round clock finally hits 9:00 p.m., and I drag myself to the locker room. I survived another twelve-hour workday. A few of the other trainers are still wiping down the equipment now that all the gym members have departed, but they urged me to call it a day after witnessing my many yawns. My heart lifts, thankful I canceled my visit with my parents as I revel in the thought of collapsing in my bed the moment I get back to the lake house. Slinging my gym bag over my shoulder, I amble out of the locker room door and make for the exit. Thank God I grabbed my jacket on the way out this morning. I huddle against the building for a second, momentarily protected from the wind as I zip it up. Red lights to my left distract me as I feel for my keys. I lift my gaze, squinting at the taillights of the sleek, black car that has caught my attention. I stumble back, my tired body igniting as I refuse to believe what I'm seeing. The all-too familiar Audi melts into the shadows beside Java. *He's here.* Without another thought, I race back inside the gym, my body trembling from a sight I was too exhausted to expect.

CHAPTER 5

I fumble for my phone and call Ainsley. I can't go back to the lake house—he will follow me. I need to be somewhere safe. The moment our lines connect, I whisper in panic that Jonathan is waiting outside for me—that he *can't* follow me home. No hesitation—I'm ordered to her house. And Will is going to wait in the driveway for me.

My hands tremble as I end the call. How should I leave the building? *Do I let him know I'm on to him, or do I play it stupid?*

"What are you doing?" A deep voice coming from the area of the men's locker room startles me so severely that I yelp. Danny eyes me suspiciously as I locate him standing in the scarcely lit hall. "Are you okay?"

"Yeah, I uh—" with a redirected gaze, I fumble around the desk, looking for an excuse as to why I'm huddled behind the counter. It's not time, yet, for others to know about my situation. "I forgot to clock out—just looking for a pen to initial the mistake." I grab for a pen, but try as I may to steady my hand, the pen shakes in my grip. Danny shrugs and pushes open the men's locker room door. "Wait, Danny," he glances back at me over his shoulder, "are you, um . . . leaving soon?"

"Yeah."

"I'll just walk out with you, then," I say, trying to manage my cracking voice as if this is routine. Danny cocks his head, narrowing his eyes that are now shining with eager lust.

"Sure, let me just grab my bag," and he disappears behind the door, focusing on his confident strut rather than my visible trepidation.

TAKE FLIGHT

The moment he's out of sight, my hands drop to my quivering knees. I need to play it cool, but every muscle of my body threatens to send me collapsing in a heap on the floor. I hear the locker room door swing open, and I straighten in a flash. Slapping a plastic smile on my face, I realize it's too forced. *You can do better than this!* I need to hide my fear, but at what cost? I don't want Danny to think I'm interested in him. Apparently oblivious to my state, Danny begins bragging about his day as we exit the building, but my ears don't take in a word he's saying.

My head fixes forward, but my eyes dart in all directions in desperate search for Jonathan's car. Is he near? Is he watching? I force my pace to slow down and match Danny's lethargic saunter, my quaking stride leaving me wobbly, like I'm walking a tightrope. At my car, Danny offers a suggestive good-bye, but I respond with a distracted wave as my eyes try to slice through the shadows. In a flurried instant, I shove my keys into the lock, open the door, and dive in. Jamming the key into the ignition, I forget about my seatbelt as the car groans for a second. *Rmm-rmm.* Come on! *START!*

The engine catches to life, and I shift into drive, hitting the gas pedal hard. I shoot out of the parking lot, cutting Danny off, but I don't care. The underbelly of my car clangs over the pot holes that I'm not bothering to swerve. My eyes stay glued on the rearview mirror once I turn onto the street. *Nothing.* I drive around the bend of the street, preparing to navigate down a one-way. But there's still no Audi. It doesn't matter, my rapid heart rate urges me to race on. One turn, then another. Still nothing. *I think I've lost him!* The light I'm approaching turns red, and I slam on my brakes, my eyes are so fixed on the rearview mirror that I missed the light turning yellow. Inhaling slowly, I drop my face into my clammy hands and rub my temples. I guess he didn't see me leave the parking lot. I guess I dodged him.

The green hue of the light on this empty street lifts my gaze, but just as I'm about to accelerate, I see the Audi idling silently behind me. My heart lurches into my throat like a bullet leaving a gun. I squeal my tires as my foot slams on the gas. I don't care what the speed limit is, I have to get away. The Audi follows, keeping speed. There's no way I'm going to outrun him in this crappy car, but I have to try. I gain speed as I approach another stoplight ahead. It turns yellow. *I can make it.* I speed through just in time to see it turn red, but Jonathan doesn't stop for the red light. And now I know. He won't stop for anything.

How will I lose him? My mind spins with the options that lay ahead. Maybe I can lose him on the highway—he doesn't know where I'm going. My heart slams against my ribs. Is there any chance I can outrace him on the highway? The merge to get on the highway approaches. *Phlunk-phlunk.* My car can barely handle this speed. *I can't do it!* I speed past the on-route. *What now?* A familiar one-way street speeds into view. Is this the one with the laundry mat, or the one with the Chinese restaurant that circles back around to this road? *Too late.* I yank the steering wheel, and for a moment, it feels like my car tilts on two tires. As I race down the winding one-way, Jonathan flies by the turn. I see his brake lights in my rearview mirror; he's turning around in the adjacent parking lot. It won't be long until he's on the same street. A stop sign approaches, I turn right without touching my brakes. The speed of my turn shoots me dangerously close to the graveled edge of the road. Swerving the car back into my lane, I take the next left. If I can make enough turns, maybe I'll lose him. *Grumph!* My car groans with the acceleration. *Don't die on me now!* I turn right, then another right. The road that will take me to the highway is just up ahead, and I don't see the Audi behind me. The last stop sign in my way to freedom zooms into view, and I fly right through it.

Headlights only feet away flash in the driver's side window as I hurl across the two perpendicular lanes. The driver swerves, barely missing the back end of my car. He lays on the horn, calling attention to my dangerous driving… alerting Jonathan. Adrenaline blinds me for a moment as I straighten out my swerving car and race to the highway. My eyes dash between the empty rearview mirror and the left turn that will catapult me into the safety of highway traffic. In a flash, I speed into the turn. The Audi is nowhere in sight.

* * *

Trying to ignore the sunlight drifting through the blinds of the windows that line Ainsley's large guest room, I fight back tears, roll out of the king-size bed, and trudge to the huge guest bathroom, exhausted from the sleepless night I just spent at my best friend's house. I turn on the faucet in one of the double sinks, rinse my hands in the cool water, then splash my face in hopes of bringing some life to my weary body. I don't need Ainsley, I can do life on my own. Heck, I got out, didn't I? I'm strong enough to make it alone. But my stomach eases ever so slightly while thinking back to how Will stood in the driveway for me last night . . . to how Ainsley handed me a change of clothes and hugged me goodnight.

I fumble for a towel as a high-pitched bark distracts me from the thoughts swirling in my mind. "Sasha," I greet as I turn off the water. The black, teacup poodle wags her tail as she prances in the door frame, happy to welcome a guest into her domain. "What are you doing in here?" I dry my face, place the towel back on the gray, granite countertop that matches the neutral colors of the guest room perfectly, then peer around the corner to find the pajama-clad culprit standing innocently in the open guest room door. "Well hello, Miles," I greet while walking toward him. A grin spreads across the toddler's round cheeks, and his dimples immediately remind me of his dad.

"Hi, Hallie," he mumbles, half covering his face as he side-shuffles in my direction. Sasha runs ahead of me to meet Miles. She jumps all over his tiny body, sending him, in a fit of giggles, to the lush, gray carpet, his pacifier dropping from his tiny grip with the fall. Instantly feeling weightless, I run over to join the fun, rolling on the carpet and tickling Miles as Sasha dodges back and forth between the two of us, licking our faces and nuzzling us with her wet nose.

"Oh, no," Ainsley groans as she rubs at her eyes while entering the room. "Miles, how did you get in here?" She plants a mothering fist on her hip. Her sweet boy shrugs his shoulders as he gets up, grabs his pacifier, and chases after Sasha, who is now licking Ainsley's feet. "Oh, Hallie—I hope they didn't wake you. They were playing in the living room when I left to make a pot of coffee."

"No, no," I say as I lift myself off the carpet. "I was already up when they came in. Honestly, they were the perfect wake-up call. Couldn't think of a better scene to lift my spirits." I miss my dogs...well, *his* dogs. If only they were allowed inside. Maybe I could have had some happier mornings like this if Jonathan had a heart. I force a smile to my sagging cheeks as I watch Miles follow Sasha to the living room where the sunlight is streaming through the skylight window in the cathedral ceiling, kissing the cushions of the large, L-shaped couch that stands in the middle of the enormous space. I shuffle across the bedroom and flop down on the bed as Ainsley settles into the Victorian chair situated in the corner. She crosses her tanned legs and shifts her weight. "Thanks for letting me stay here last night," I say, hugging my knees close to my chest as my head leans back against the antique, wooden headboard.

"No problem, I have about a zillion pairs of yoga pants and t-shirts for any night of the week. So, whenever you need a safe place to stay, you know you can come here."

"Thanks," I mumble, my gaze dropping. "I can't believe he was waiting for me after work. I mean, I should have expected it. Apparently, he did loops around my parents' house after I left him, so why wouldn't he try to follow me home from work?"

"Yeah, I bet he's angry you left. I just hope he doesn't want revenge."

My insides tighten as I skirt over the many possibilities of what his version of revenge might look like. "I was so distracted and exhausted last night, I just wasn't prepared to see his car. I dunno if he's told anyone about me leaving, and I can't control what he says, but I'm still keeping it quiet at the gym." I squeeze my eyes shut, "*Ugh*! What if I had led him back to the lake house last night?" Jonathan *can't* know where I live. My eyes fly open and I rock slightly, grabbing for the gray and white floral duvet, desperate for its warmth and protection. "Will was great to wait for me in the driveway just in case Jonathan figured out where I was heading and somehow got past the coded gate. It was nice to have a male presence."

Ainsley shrinks into her chair as her knee begins to bounce at the mention of her husband, "I'm just glad he was here and awake." She opens her mouth and closes it again, then says, "You know, it might not be a bad thing if you let another man know about your situation, like maybe someone from church." She hesitates, "It's just that Will is hardly around anymore." After a moment's pause, she continues, "I just don't get it. When Will is home, he's constantly on his laptop or his phone. I basically have to force him to spend time with his son, who absolutely adores him. It won't be long before Miles is old enough to remember all this crap. And as for me," she shakes her head, "I'm just that pretty girl he married. He doesn't have time for me. Sometimes when we lay in bed at night, I feel like I'm lying next to a stranger. I don't even know who he is anymore . . . maybe I never did." She sighs, throwing both hands up as if to say, *why me?* "I'm sorry—I don't mean to be over here griping about all my problems." Ainsley sits forward in her chair in order to lay eyes briefly on Miles. Content with his nearby presence, she settles back in the chair.

"It's fine," I reply. It's like Ainsley to direct the conversation onto herself, even after hearing about the chase from last night. This might bother others, but I don't mind. "I know other people don't have perfect lives and marriages, but I don't want them to end like mine will . . . in divorce." I sense the conversation has taken an uncomfortable turn, so I purse my lips, then add with a smirk, "Remember that couple from Cancun at the all-inclusive where we stayed?"

"The ones who spent the whole afternoon kissing and doting on each other?" Ainsley tilts her head and grins, embracing the change of subject. "They were all about their marriage, trying to shame us for leaving our husbands behind and taking a week's vacation, just the two of us."

"Yeah, but when we saw them at night, after a couple of drinks, they certainly seemed more interested in the single people around them than in each other. I think I caught her flirting with the hotel workers like two dozen times, and the husband was always at that one bar with the chesty bartender."

Ainsley laughs, but only for a moment before adding, "Yeah, *now that's the life.* We should take a trip like that again." She raises an eyebrow, "Will can't go with me." Her shoulders lift with a heavy sigh, "But you know my parents don't mind taking care of Miles and Sasha while I'm gone. I swear, every time we take a trip, they pack bags as if I live a state away rather than ten minutes down the road, then they settle into this room like they own the place."

I snicker as I fluff the pillow behind my back. "Didn't they stay here the whole time we were in Chicago?"

"Yeah—while we were weathering the rain, they were staying here like they were on vacation. I don't think our pool has ever gotten that much use. I wouldn't be surprised if my parents *actually* slept in the chaise lounge chairs of our cabana that whole week," Ainsley adds with a cackle. "I got a ton of texts and videos of Dad floating in the pool while Mom played with Miles in the shallow end. Meanwhile, we were hopping from one place to the next trying to get out of the cold."

Nodding, I add, "I got a text or two myself that week, remember?" I flinch. Jonathan hated it when I traveled, and yet he never took me anywhere. Not that I would have wanted to go with him anyway. Ainsley was the only chance I had to momentarily escape, and it was better for me if I gave him little-to-no warning of my departure. It didn't matter that I saved up my own money or that Ainsley helped pay for the costs, he would simmer in his anger for the entire duration I was gone, and I paid for it when I finally returned.

Ainsley presses a finger to her lips, then says, "Maybe you shouldn't have gone on all those trips with me."

"No, I wanted to go," I say, my voice rising. Our trips were my only reprieve. "It was like my heart started to lift the closer we got to the airport. And when the plane took off, I felt weightless, soaring high above all my troubles thousands of feet below."

"Yeah, Lord knows I needed to escape, too." She peeks again at her son playing quietly in the living room. "Miles is such a great kid—well-behaved, quiet, polite . . ." she sighs. "I just didn't expect to get pregnant so soon after the wedding. My parents help so much, but I still feel like a single parent most of the time. I guess I just get overwhelmed with my life and how things turned out—I never would have predicted that I would be a parent at this age." With a shrug she adds, "Life didn't pan out the way I expected it would."

I wrinkle my forehead. "Me either. I mean, at least your family's still intact. I'm getting a divorce, and I'm twenty-five years old." We both remain quite for a moment, contemplating the changes that have taken place in the few years since we graduated from college. "Sometimes life isn't fair," I conclude.

Miles teeters into the room and crawls onto his mom's lap. "You ready for some breakfast, little man?" she asks as she squeezes him tight.

"Yeaahhhh," he squeals, the prospect of food creating a simple joy.

I slide out of the guest bed as Ainsley stands with Miles wiggling in her arms. "What should I do with the sheets?" I ask, "I can strip the bed and—"

"Oh, don't worry about it," Ainsley interrupts, "the cleaning lady will be here in two days and she can do it then." She waves her hand nonchalantly, as if to establish the normalcy of hiring a cleaner. But Ainsley didn't come into money until she married Will, and the humble home she grew up in is nothing compared to this sprawling mansion where she now resides. I quickly arrange the duvet and pillows, reassembling the room into the magazine-cover suite it resembled before I spent a sleepless night in it. Grabbing my gym bag by the door, I follow Ainsley into the living room, past the front door, down the hall, and into her large kitchen. Ainsley places Miles in his deluxe high chair.

"So, what are you doing today?" I ask as Ainsley secures Miles in the high chair and moves around the island to her fridge.

"Not much," she shrugs in response as she pulls out a container of applesauce, closes the fridge, and opens the white cabinet door to grab the baby cereal. The cleanliness of this professionally designed and decorated kitchen makes a high chair seem out of place. The white marble countertops, white appliances, and tan colored accent of this space look like a vision out of a home renovation TV show, not a breakfast nook for a toddler. "I was thinking about going to the mall this afternoon, wanna come?" Ainsley asks while Sasha paws at the sliding glass door that leads to the strip of grass beside their heated pool.

"I can't, I should actually go now if I wanna slip back to the lake house before work today," I reply. "Thanks though," I add, my tone lifting as if my enthusiasm will follow. Ainsley shuffles over to Sasha and checks to see if the black iron gate enclosing her back yard is locked. She nods, slides open the glass door, then navigates around the high-top table to hug me good-bye.

"Thank you so much for letting me crash here last night," I say as she wraps her arms around me.

"Any time. Can you let yourself out? Miles won't be this happy for much longer," she says as she steals a glance at her son before rushing back to the breakfast prep.

"Yeah, I'll call you later," I say with a quick wave. "Bye-bye little man," I add.

Shifting the weight of my gym bag on my shoulder as I walk through the house, I close the front door and breath in the fresh air. I walk down the expansive steps onto the cement path and make my way to my car that sits awkwardly in front of their three-car garage, seriously out of place in a gated neighborhood of mansions. While backing out of their curved driveway, I observe the aesthetically pleasing sight of the Bakers' well-manicured lawn and how the grass offers a pleasant contrast against the white stone home.

Shifting my car into drive, I rumble down the twisted roads. A little voice in the back of my head tells me to look for Jonathan's car. But there's no sign of him as I survey my surroundings.

The houses are all so beautiful and evenly spaced, offering enough land to feel separated from the neighbors, but not enough for complete isolation, like the lake house. As I come to a stop at the end of the street, I catch sight of a Scissor-tailed Flycatcher perched on the iron fence of a nearby home. The gorgeous, gray and salmon-pink coloring of our state bird captures my attention. When will this fellow find friends and navigate south? Winter will be here any day now.

Hiss! My car idles at the stop, scaring the bird into flight, his absurdly long tail fluttering as he soars upward. Watching through my windshield as the bird rises higher and higher, my heart pangs with the longing to take flight like this wondrous creature. He comes and goes as he pleases, his wings carrying him from frightening moments to the safety of the sky. Nothing is tying him down, he's free to escape as he sees fit. The bird disappears behind the tall pines in the distance, and I linger at the stop sign for a moment to rest my head on my steering wheel. "God," I whisper in prayer, "I just want to escape, but I have no idea where to go. I can't keep dodging Jonathan like this." With a sigh, I raise my head as if it weighs a ton. I don't have the money to move. And where would I go? It took me almost ten years to find a friend like Ainsley. Do I even have it in me to start all over again? My hands slide loosely down the steering wheel and into my lap. Can I ever trust God with my future, especially if I'm always looking over my shoulder?

* * *

"Great practice, everyone. Let's take twenty before the church service starts," Chip Catcher says to the worship team as he runs a hand over his bald head, straightens his plaid shirt and walks to the far end of the black stage to place his guitar in its stand. "Hallie, can I chat with you for a moment in my office?" he asks just as I'm walking down the left side of the stage to follow Ainsley into the brightly lit foyer. With a quick nod, I hang back as Ainsley, deep in conversation with the keyboard player, continues down the aisle. I follow Chip toward the small office just around the corner from the stage, squinting against the reflection of the bright spotlights as they bounce off the back-drop decorating the wall directly behind the stage. The bronze plate on the office door flashes Chip's title, "Worship Leader," with the Connect Church logo situated in the corner, indicating the office and the job that used to be Harrison's.

I settle in the seat opposite Chip's desk trying to hide my curiosity as he pulls out his chair. He adjusts the pant legs of his skinny jeans as he gets comfortable. "Is everything okay? I hope Becca's alright," I add, pointing to the picture frame sitting on the corner of his desk, capturing the smiling faces of Chip and his wife at Disney World.

"No, she's fine," Chip assures me as he reaches for the picture frame and turns it out of sight. "Little bit of a cough, so she didn't feel like she could carry a tune this morning." I nod. Becca can sing on key, but her voice is not very strong—singing with a sore throat could draw some unwanted attention. "Thanks for stepping in last minute, Hallie," he adds. "I hope my text this morning didn't wake you."

"Not at all, I tend to be an early riser these days," I chuckle. The office gets quiet, so I clasp my hands together in my lap and chew at the inside of my mouth.

"I've been noticing you aren't volunteering to sing on the worship team as much anymore," he states, stroking his long beard as he talks. "Not that I'm trying to pry, but something's off with you."

I look down at my shoes, my toes wiggling against the material. What do I say? My throat tightens. This conversation could erode the protective walls I've worked so hard to build. "Yeah, I'm definitely up for serving more now. But I…uh," I cough, trying to steady my shaky voice. Was Ainsley right? Should I let another man know about my situation? I pick up my head, and with a sturdy tone, I say "I've left Jonathan." Chip's hand stops, mid-stroke, and his eyebrows raise high enough to disappear into his hairline—if he chose to have one.

"Wow, Hallie," he starts, rolling the chair closer to the desk and leaning into the conversation, "I had no idea it was that bad."

"I um…I just couldn't stay," I finish. He doesn't have to know about the secrets I've been keeping from the church all these years, especially that *one* in particular. My hands begin to tremble in the silence that follows. I can't meet his gaze. Is Chip about to dismiss me from the worship team? Am I going to have to wear the scarlet letter—a "D" replacing the "A"—screaming the reality of my failed marriage to the entire congregation?

"Good for you," Chip finally replies, startling me from my blaring thoughts. "I think it's great you've finally made a decision for yourself. I don't know what happened in your marriage, but that guy never shows up to church with you, he didn't come to hear you sing on Sunday mornings, it just seems like he was really holding you back." I squirm in my seat. Jeez, I knew it was bad, but does he have to point out all this? Was it that obvious just how bad it was? "Do you think this is permanent?" Chip asks. Is that accusation I hear? Maybe not, maybe it's just me.

"Yes." My fists tighten as my face flushes. "Look, I really don't want to get into the details, but it's over. Jonathan is a good guy, and I wish him well." I flinch. Why do my lies for him surface so easily? It's my desire to keep his reputation unblemished; a desire I can't explain…and I hate it. Did this habit build out of a need to hide my reality from the world? Or have I told this lie to myself enough that I'm actually convinced there's truth to it?

"Well, I'm sorry that your marriage has ended this way," he says, his brow furrowing as his eyes lock with the keyboard in front of the monitor. "But maybe this is a good thing that you'll have some free time, because I think I need your help with some changes I'd like to make with the worship team." Chip clears his throat, "Hallie, I need you to sing on Team B as well. I need you to be the *lead* singer on Team B."

My palms begin to sweat. I rub them down my jeans, then say, "I thought Becca was the lead singer on that team."

Chip leans back quickly and squirms in his seat as his eyes move to the floor. "I think she'll be okay with this change," he adds, waving a hand in the direction of the picture frame without looking at it. Checking the time on his watch, he springs from his chair as he says, "Let's discuss the details later, I just wanted you to start thinking about it before I make any permanent changes. We should probably get out there."

I follow him toward the door, but just as we are about to exit the office, I add, "Chip, if you could just keep my . . . *situation* to yourself for now, I'd really appreciate it." I shove my hands into my front pockets, then say, "I know word will eventually get out, I guess I just want to control the way it's shared. *Divorce* usually doesn't sit right with the church."

Chip turns from the partially cracked door just long enough to acknowledge me, but he avoids my eyes. "Your secret's safe with me." He wavers in his step, still turned enough in my direction, then adds, "Maybe it's best if we keep everything we discussed in here quiet, at least until I can work out the logistics of it all." And although I feel like a weight has plunked down on my heart, I nod in agreement.

CHAPTER 6

My favorite worship song, a rendition of the hymn "It Is Well," fades as Ainsley flicks her car blinker on to leave her neighborhood already decorated for the Christmas holiday. The passenger's seat heater of her Toyota Highlander warms me as I contemplate the words of the song. It isn't well with my soul—there's so much unknown in my future. I want to trust God. I really do. But how can I when I don't know where my life is going? Even as I'm getting things done—working longer hours, filling out paperwork for a new bank account, applying for health insurance—this past month hasn't provided any reassurance or clear direction.

"What a great song. Let's suggest it to Chip for next week's worship. You will be perfect for that harmony," Ainsley says as she angles her rearview mirror to get a better glimpse of Miles in his car seat behind us.

I blink and shake my head. It's funny how easy it is for me to get lost in my thoughts. "Mmm-hmm," I offer behind closed lips. This song would be a good fit, but I don't think I could get through it without crying. Soft music draws my attention back to the radio as the announcer on our local Christian music station starts to read Scripture, "Shout for joy to the Lord, all the earth. Worship the Lord . . . Enter his gates with thanksgiving and his courts with praise; give thanks to him and praise his name. For the Lord is good and his love endures forever . . ." I drop my gaze as I re-adjust my seatbelt. *Love.* What does it mean to feel loved by God? Yeah, sure—he loves me. So, why don't I feel it? "You've just heard some verses from Psalm one hundred," the announcer continues, "and what a reassurance it is for us, to trust in a God whose love and faithfulness endures forever. We are to give thanks to him for all that he provides."

Ainsley leans forward in her seat, muting the volume. "With all this talk about *giving thanks*—how was Thanksgiving at your parents' last week?"

"Oh," I start, slumping my body on the door as I turn toward her, "boring, really. We ate, Dad watched football, Mom tried to bring up Jonathan and how lonely he must be during Thanksgiving. It was awkward, so I went back to the lake house early."

"You don't think he went to his parents' house for Thanksgiving?"

"You know, I figure he probably did. But then again, he may have made an excuse and skipped it. I haven't heard anything from his parents or his brother. They haven't contacted me, so I don't think they know I've left him. They aren't shy—his dad would certainly have something to say, which makes me think he hasn't told them."

"You blocked his number, but did you block his parents too? Maybe they did try to get in touch with you."

I sigh as Ainsley makes another turn, navigating to my work where my car is still parked. "No, I didn't block them. I figure I owe them something, at least a small explanation, although I definitely won't tell them everything." One thing's for sure, I definitely won't tell them about *that* night.

"Hallie, you gotta tell his dad what he was doing at work. Don't you think his dad oughta know what went on behind the scenes, I mean, especially because *he* took over when his dad retired?"

My face twitches as I rub at my neck. What if someone could hear this conversation now? We slow down for a stoplight. In my silence, Ainsley turns to study me. "I can't tell his dad that," I confess. "It would ruin him . . ." Ainsley purses her lips as if to say, *and?* I shake my head. There's nothing more to say about that. "Anyway, tell me how the Christmas party went last night—I'm sorry I didn't go. I guess I'm just not feeling up to that kinda stuff these days. Miles and I cuddled on the couch and watched a few YouTube clips on my phone just after you and Will left. He went down after that, no problem."

Ainsley grabs her head and moans just as the light turns green. Miles screams in glee, causing Ainsley to wince. "Well, I think I drank too much…

but I had to," she defends. "*What a dull bunch.*" I roll my eyes, the hint of a smirk tickling my cheeks. This is my best friend. Whenever things get boring, she knows how to liven things up. Before you know it, she's chatting with everyone and anyone. Once the life of the party, always the life of the party…that is, if there's enough alcohol in her system. "You know, Rita was there with Andrew—I haven't seen him since we graduated from college." She runs her fingers over the smooth leather of the steering wheel, "Remember when he had a crush on you back in college?" She chortles, "Man, he would have done anything to be with you. He would chase us around from party to party, always by your side in case you ever got too drunk. I was wondering when the guy would catch on," she nudges me across the center console, "I mean, getting drunk was never your thing—it's mine." She tips her head back and holds her hand above her mouth, pretending to down a drink, then laughs.

I avoid the conversation of over-drinking with a shrug and refocus on Andrew, "Yeah, he's not my type. He is a nice guy, though. Did it look like he was having a good time with Rita?"

Ainsley chuckles, "Maybe. He definitely was spending a lot of money on her at the bar. But you know Rita, she was lapping it up—getting spoiled by him while flirting with the singles around her the moment Andrew left to buy her another cocktail." Her tone lowers while adding, "I really dunno why she came over to talk to me if she was having such a *good time* flirting."

"What did she want to talk to you about?" I ask, just as we pull down the street leading to my work.

Ainsley looks out her window at the vast emptiness that surrounds the decrepit strip mall and gulps. "Oh . . . uh," she starts, her voice jumping several octaves, "well, she just wanted to gossip, you know." Ainsley yanks her hair off her neck. "She just told me about a bunch of people in town and what they were doing—who got fat, who got married, who had a baby… that kinda stuff."

"Oh," I say, trying to catch my best friend's eyes just as she pulls into the parking lot, her large tires managing the pot holes better than my car. Silence follows as she pulls into a parking spot. I clear my throat, "Well, thanks for driving me to work," I finish, moving my gaze to my gym bag on the floor. Why does it feel like the air has left the car?

"No problem," Ainsley squeaks. She shifts her car into park then adds, "And thanks for watching Miles last night—you gave my parents a night off from babysitting." She waves her hand across the parking lot, "And I guess it's only right that I pick my babysitter up and drop her back off at her car." Her smile is set by the time she finally faces me, but then her lips slide downward. "Is that Rita's Jeep?" she points to the Connect Church sticker visible on the back windshield of a vehicle parked a few spots away.

"Yep," I say with a shrug. "She started working out here not too long ago."

"She's probably working off all the alcohol she drank last night."

I chew the inside of my mouth. It's not right to talk about people like this, and I don't want to keep caving to gossip like I do when conversations take an awkward turn. But I'm in no position to give a lecture—especially when my best friend is struggling to make eye contact, for whatever reason. "She comes in often enough, not just after a night out."

"Ah, she's probably here for all the guys. I mean, that woman is desperate," Ainsley tilts her head. "I swear, she flirts with all the single men, even at church." My gaze flits between my shoes and my friend. This all might be true, but I don't need to hear all the details. "She seems eager to find a *daddy* replacement for her kid. You know, she's always looking for ways to make herself out to be the victim…sharing all the sorry details at church of how that guy got her pregnant eight years ago and then left." Jutting her neck out, Ainsley adds, "But luckily she *found God.*" Ainsley's fingers form quotation marks in mock disapproval. "More like she found a room full of potential dating options."

I squirm in my seat, glance at the clock on the large screen of the Highlander, and make for a quick departure. I grab for my gym bag on the floor, and we say our good-byes as I close the passenger's side door. *That was weird.*

Rita's shrill laugh bombards me as I enter the front door of Jim's Gym. My eyes dart to the scene at the front desk. Rita is leaning on the desk with one leg crossed behind the other. Does she know she's giving Danny, who's seated in the office chair behind the desk, an eyeful of cleavage right now? *Ding-ding.* The bell dangling on the door draws their attention toward me. *Ugh!* Better make a run for it. Too late, they're both staring at me now.

"Hi Hallie," Rita sneers. Is it just me, or is she upset at me, as if I've just interrupted something? I acknowledge her greeting with a quick wave and a closed-lip smile as I try to speed past the scene. Why does the locker room have to be beyond the front desk? Danny pulls his gaze away from Rita's chest long enough to give me a seductive smirk and nod of the head. I quicken my pace to reach the women's locker room. Once I'm behind the closed door, I lean against the inside wall, glad to get away from whatever's going down at the desk. With my ear positioned close to the crack of the door, I hear hushed whispers. In an attempt to catch a couple of words, I open the door an inch and strain to listen to whatever Rita is rambling on about. It must be juicy. Usually, her loud voice would easily carry all the way in here.

"Hallie?" a voice from behind startles me, and the door slams closed as I swing around. Caught in the act.

"Hi Georgina," I greet with a slapped smile across my face as I join her in the short, L-shaped hall that turns left toward my locker. Checking the clock on the wall opposite the showers, I add, "You're here early, I wasn't expecting you for another fifteen minutes."

Georgina props one leg up on the wooden bench that sits between the walls lined with lockers and re-ties her shoelace. "I thought I'd ask you about some stretches before we get started today," she adds, then leans back to glance at the barely visible edge of the locker room door, like a lurker curious at what prompted my eavesdropping only moments earlier.

I burst out laughing in an obvious attempt to draw the old woman's attention back in my direction. "Our work out from the other day must have been intense, huh?" I tease, shoving my gym bag in the locker with fidgety hands. I slam the locker shut. *Oh great.* I forgot to clock-in. There's no way I'm going back out to Danny and Rita to fix my time card now. "You're my first client today, so I haven't even clocked-in yet. But no worries, we can stretch now, and I'll manually fill in my time card later if you'll vouch for me."

Despite the prickling of my scalp, I grin as she drops her foot from the bench, rubs her leathery arms, and follows me out of the locker room with her overly agreeable reply, "Of course. I'll gladly talk to Jim anytime." I wince as we leave the locker room. Is every woman at this gym dying for male attention?

An hour later, I find myself counting down the last ten reps of Georgina's upper body workout. With a motion for a high-five, I exclaim, "Great work—*you're done.*" She lightly taps my hand while I use the other to grab a towel. I hand it to Georgina as she places her five-pound weight on the floor.

The old lady takes the towel from me and wipes her brow as she stands up from the bench. "Thanks, Hallie. You always push me," she says as she makes her way to the locker room like she's wading in knee-high water.

"No problem," I announce in her wake. Without turning her body, Georgina waves farewell above her head. Bending to pick up her weights, my face crumbles, the five-pound dumbbells offering a gut-wrenching visual of my doleful reality. I want to be transforming bodies in this job, but I seem to be drowning in a sea of old women and meager workouts.

"What's-up, beautiful," I spin around to meet Danny's greeting as I watch him spray the bench that Georgina was just on, then carelessly wipe at the surface without looking, his eyes never leaving my body.

"Uh…what happened to my *shorty* nickname?" I ask, keeping my distance as I move away to pick up some scattered dumbbells. Can't he just shrug and walk away? *Wishful thinking.*

"I just thought you should know how beautiful you are. Isn't it nice to hear every once in a while?" he retorts. "Oh hey, let me grab those for you." He abandons his spray bottle and cloth and lunges toward the thirty-pound dumbbells I'm currently reaching for. I move back and frown. This guy's never this helpful. My fists tighten. Does he think I can't handle that weight? I contemplate moving around some heavier dumbbells in an obvious effort to make my point, but I slouch my shoulders and turn away instead. How come I can't tell him how frustrated this makes me? I'm a qualified trainer—I can put away the big weights by myself. Although I'm punished by my missed opportunity to speak my mind, Danny doesn't let me dwell on it for long as he adds. "Uh, I noticed you weren't wearing your wedding ring," he points at my hand.

Cringing, I quickly unhitch my furrowed brow before swiveling in his direction. "I never wear my ring to the gym," I reply. *Phew!* The truth saved me from having to devise an excuse on the spot.

"Oh, yeah...yeah I know," he sputters. "I guess I forgot." His distant gaze is evident for only a split second before he adds, "That's probably best, cuz of all the equipment." He struts off in the other direction while muttering something to himself.

My head rears as I turn toward the locker room. What was that all about? I pause and look back at Danny for a second. Who cares. *Grrll!* My stomach growls as I lay a hand over it. When was the last time I ate? There's got to be a protein bar in the front of my gym bag. But as I make my way to the front half of the building, I can't seem to shake that conversation with Danny. What *should* I do with my wedding ring? I'll never wear it again—so what's the point of keeping it? I slide into the locker room, find the protein bar, and grab for my phone in the side pocket of my gym bag. It wouldn't hurt to do some quick research. There's got to be some private jewelry sales online. But I don't make it to the internet browser as I see Andrew's number in a message icon on my lock screen. I open my messages and my body tenses as I read:

> Hey Hallie—it's Andrew. I have been thinking about you a lot lately and all the parties we went to in college. If you're free sometime, we should catch up over a cup of coffee.

My mind races as I read the text over and over. Why is Andrew texting me after all these years? Did seeing Ainsley at the Christmas party last night spark some memories? *Ugh!* He knows I'm married. That's not okay—he shouldn't be texting a married woman to meet up for coffee, even if we used to be friends.

Suddenly, the pieces snap together. Word has gotten out about Jonathan and me. That's why Rita was whispering at the front desk. It's why Danny has all of a sudden taken his flirting to a whole new level, mentioning my ring and all. It must be why Andrew has texted me.

I throw my phone down on top of my gym bag and pace the empty locker room. Grasping the sides of my head, I filter through the strange events that have taken place since I stepped into work this morning. My mind is spinning faster than I can keep up, so I plop down on the wooden bench and steady my breathing. *I have to get away from all this.*

I grab for my phone again, bringing up Harrison's name in my messages. My thumbs tap with furious speed, offering a quick greeting then requesting a trip to Michigan for the Christmas holiday. I don't want to stay here and try to explain my failed marriage. To anyone. I open a new window to search for flights. *Ahh!* I can't afford these prices. Why is it always so ridiculously expensive to travel around Christmas? My chin trembles. I drop my head into my left hand as my right hand grips my phone, new prices popping up, one by one, none of them in an affordable price range. My eyes burn as I squeeze them closed. I drag my hand down my face. Wait a minute . . . *ahah!* My empty ring finger offers an instant solution. That's exactly what I'll do—I'll sell my ring to help pay for my flight. In perfect timing, Harrison's text lights up the top of my screen saying, "*Come on! I can't wait!*" Taking a deep breath, my shoulders lift as I open the text message window. I'll be booking my flight today.

CHAPTER 7

The dual engines of the plane rumble to life as I buckle my seatbelt and prepare for take-off. The flight-attendant has just finished the instructions at the front of the aircraft. During her presentation, I watched a man in a business suit, seated in the front row, wipe the sweat off his brow at the mention of oxygen masks dropping. Passengers' nervous habits always leave me trying to mask my giggles. He and I are exact opposites. The movement of the plane and the feeling of lifting off the ground brings me nothing but peace and excitement. Here I am again, reveling in my chance to escape. As we race down the runway for Michigan, the comfort of freedom floods my mind, and I settle into my aisle seat, smirking as I witness the same sweaty man grip the armrest, his knuckles turning whiter as the aircraft picks up speed.

The ring sold quickly online, providing the funds for my spontaneous trip to Michigan over the Christmas holiday. The memory of Jonathan's cruelty and lack of affection sends a chill up my spine—he made sure my ring finger screamed his ownership while using the façade of love and generosity to aggressively mark his territory. The single, three carat stone set on a white-gold band did not sell online for the same price it was sold to him. But when it came time to sell, I chose to sacrifice the money in order to make this trip happen. Besides, I purchased this flight on my credit card. I've got to boost my non-existent credit line, and what better way to pay for this escape than with a symbol that kept me prisoner. *Good-bye wedding ring, hello family time.* As I fly higher and higher in the sky, leaving behind the Oklahoma gossip and date requests far below, a smile spreads from ear-to-ear.

The two-and-a-half-hour flight direct to Detroit goes by quickly, and I exit the gate to find a welcoming group of short, strawberry-blondes waiting for my arrival. Branson and Bailey have taken on most of their mother's features. With their curly hair and blue eyes, it would be hard to tell that Harrison was their father if it wasn't for their long, lean build. Wheeling my carry-on luggage up to my sister-in-law and the twins, Branson jumps at the sight of my familiar face and bounds toward me.

"Aunt Hallie," he screams, leaping into my open arms.

"Buddy! I'm so happy to see you," I greet, kissing his soft cheek before placing him down. He runs back to his mother and sister, his arms pumping faster than his legs can carry him.

Her son's excitement sparks a twinkle in Isabel's big, blue eyes as she pulls me into an embrace, holding on as I gladly accept the warm welcome. "We're so happy you're here, Hallie. I wanted to fly there with Harrison when I heard what was happening, but I just couldn't with the kids," she muffles through our hug.

Pulling back, I offer an understanding smile and nod. Eager to avoid conversation about Jonathan, I bend down to greet my niece who is clinging to Isabel's leg. Running a hand down Bailey's soft curls, I coo, "Well hello, beautiful. You act like I'm a stranger." Bailey turns shyly into Isabel's arm, hiding her face with a hint of a grin.

"Don't worry about her, she'll warm up like she always does," Isabel reassures me as I reach for my suitcase. We all turn and walk toward the exit where the long line of vehicles moves slowly through the curbside pick-up of this busy airport. "Branson, wait for us," Isabel yells as her son runs ahead, dodging travelers and their luggage, surging toward the door with dauntless independence. "I swear, these two couldn't be more opposite," she laughs, nodding at her son who has acknowledged her call, but waits impatiently, tapping his foot with his arms folded across his small chest. "They may have shared my womb, but as they get older, they become more and more like Jekyll and Hyde."

"Mooommm," Branson whines from just inside the automatic sliding doors, "We gotta hurry cuz Dad's waiting in the car."

Isabel nods, "Okay, Mr. Hyde," she says, throwing a quick wink in my direction. We pick up our pace, and Isabel's curls threaten to escape from her loose clip as Bailey drags behind us, a shy grin warming her porcelain complexion. "Harrison thought it would be best to use the curb-side pick-up. The airport is so busy this time of day, so I figured I would meet you at the exit while he inched his way up the line. As it turns out, neither one of these munchkins wanted to wait for you in the car," she snickers. "But it isn't easy getting four-year-olds in and out of their car seats, let alone keeping *both* of them safely by my side." Isabel flashes a beautiful smile as we approach Branson, who lunges for my hand.

"Well, I've got him, so maybe that'll make it easier," I joke.

"What would make it easier is if I was born with lovely, long limbs, just like these two and their daddy. Then I would be able to keep up." We laugh as Bailey does a little skip to show-off. Branson and I fall behind, treading down the long line until we locate the tan, Hyundai Santa Fe idling at the far end. Harrison jumps out of the SUV at the sight of us, and the back hatch opens automatically as he closes his driver-side door.

Isabel takes over with the twins as I move around back to greet my brother who is shuffling around a few items in the hatch, trying to make room for my bag. "Well, if it isn't my awesome, little sister," he says while pulling me in for a hug.

"I hope you'll still be saying that at the end of this long stay," I retort with a laugh as Harrison reaches for my suitcase and hauls it into the small space behind the third row.

Harrison playfully narrows his eyes at me, then adds, "The length of your stay isn't the issue—trying to find space for your suitcase is. We usually don't use the third bench, so it's gunna be a tight fit." He wrestles with the suitcase, his muscles flexing as he tries to determine the best way for it to fit. "I think I got it, though," he says, backing up and lowering the hatch. Clapping his hands together in an accomplished *task-complete* fashion, he says, "That's the hardest work I've done all week. Now let's get a move-on; it's almost five o'clock, and Friday evening traffic is the worst."

As I squeeze into the back seat, Harrison shuts my door then slips behind the wheel. Searching around for my seatbelt, I buckle in and remove a half-eaten cracker from a crevice, dropping it in the nearby cup-holder with just my forefinger and thumb. *How long has that been there?* I shake my head. "So, you were able to take off work to come pick me up, then?" I target Harrison as he checks over his shoulder trying to nose his way out of the line and into the far lanes of slowly moving traffic.

"Yeah, university students really don't want a whole lot to do with a college pastor any time after lunch on a Friday," Harrison says with a chuckle. "Today was especially slow, what with the Christmas holiday and all, so I was home before lunch." He flashes a smile at his wife and reaches over the center console to hold her hand.

"December will be a slow month, so we all should have plenty of time to spend with you," Isabel chimes. "Harrison has booked a skiing trip with a group of college students who stay around here for the Christmas break, so I figured we would all tag along."

"Oh—yessss," Branson adds to the conversation at the mention of skiing. "Only this time, I wanna snowboard like Daddy!"

"We'll see," Isabel says as she shifts in her seat to catch sight of her babies. "What about you, Bailey? Are you excited to ski?"

Bailey places the Barbie she has been silently playing with on her lap as she looks up at her mom with exceptionally wide eyes, "Uh-huh—and I want Aunt Hallie to come, too." *Aww—melt my heart, why don't ya?* Isabel seems to have read my mind, and she meets my eyes, smiling, as if to say, *I told you she would warm up.*

"I'll be there," I reassure my niece, her round eyes swiveling in my direction, although she still avoids making full eye contact. "It's been a while since I've skied though," I add as I start to pick at my fingernail. "I don't know if it will come back to me that easily."

Harrison laughs, "You'll be fine. It's just like riding a bike. Once you get the hang of it again, you'll be hitting moguls at top speed." The blinker ticks, indicating Harrison's merge onto the highway as we follow the flow of cars leading us into Ann Arbor.

"You guys still liking the apartment?"

Isabel groans, steals a quick glance at Harrison, then says, "It works for now, but we will be outgrowing the space soon, I imagine. The kids can only share a room for so long, and we always like to keep a guest room available for visits like these." She gestures at me before adding, "All that to say, it would be better if we could move into a house with four bedrooms instead of the three we have now in the apartment."

"But that won't happen for a while," Harrison interjects. He nudges his wife who likes to push her opinion, then offers her a grin in an effort to bring her back to reality.

"Yeah," she sighs after a moment of silence, "Ann Arbor is just so expensive, and Harrison needs to stay in the area for his work with the U of M students, so we are trying to save up. Since Harrison is raising funds for his work, it's hard to ask people to give more when all our immediate needs are being met." The struggle that Isabel has with Harrison's fund-raising for his job is evidenced in her tone, but she keeps a reassuring smile etched on her face as if to acknowledge that parachurch ministry jobs don't tend to fund a luxurious lifestyle.

"Mom, I could get a job," Branson suggests, his youthful voice tinged with all the enthusiasm a four-year-old can muster. I love how my nephew is eager to follow adult conversations while my niece remains content to quietly play with her dolls.

"You could?" Isabel responds over Harrison's laughter.

"That's my little man," Harrison cheers. "The men can work while Princess Bailey and Queen Mama relax at home."

"*Actually,*" Isabel retorts as she stares daggers toward the driver's side, "*Queen Mama* is planning to go back to teaching once the kiddos get enrolled in school."

"Really?" Surprise marks my tone. But in all honesty, this news shouldn't shock me. Isabel has always been head-strong, unwilling to let gender stereotypes or traditional beliefs interfere with her life goals. She was an extraordinary elementary school teacher before she got pregnant with the twins, but she felt like transitioning out of the school system was a good idea during their move to Michigan. When the twins were born, she was able to pour her passion into the education and development of her own children, which has certainly paid off.

Isabel smiles back at me huddled in the rear of the car, "Yeah, I've been missing teaching a lot lately, and we could really use the extra money. I just have such fond memories of my teaching days . . ." and we get lost in a conversation about her success stories and funny episodes for the remainder of the car ride.

* * *

"Home sweet home," Harrison declares as he shifts the vehicle into park under the protective aluminum carport that covers the assigned parking spaces of their apartment complex. We all clamber out of the vehicle, thankful that the neighbors have yet to return home from work where they park dangerously close to the already confining lines of each space. Harrison moves to the back of the vehicle to grab my bag, I help Bailey out of her car seat and Isabel wrestles Branson out the other side. We finally meet at the bottom of the apartment complex stairs, all of us slightly out of breath.

"If you think that's bad, imagine what this was like when the twins were newborns. Although the outdoor flight of stairs leading up to their front door isn't necessarily daunting, I know they have another flight of stairs to tackle once we enter the apartment. "Yeah," Isabel starts, following my gaze and predicting my thoughts, "it's a good thing Harrison does a lot of his work from home—this is a workout in and of itself."

Harrison brushes past us with my bag. "Come on people, it's cold out here—only getting colder as the sun sets." We climb the stairs behind him, the vapor from our breath validating Harrison's statement about the dropping temperature. Oklahoma is one thing, but this Michigan, winter weather is a whole different ball game. It's no wonder my parents left Michigan. The front door swings open to reveal a small foyer where Harrison kicks off his boots and quickly makes his way up the inside flight of stairs. The kids follow, throwing off their winter jackets as Isabel and I shiver, inching our way into the warm space while the gang moves up the stairs.

"I don't know who designed this apartment, but they could have added more space in this entryway," Isabel grunts as we finish hanging the discarded coats and begin our own climb in the chilly enclave. Both kids run full speed down the hall to their room, Isabel beelines for the fireplace on the back wall of the open dining and living room space, and I set my purse down on the dining room table.

Harrison exits the first door on the left in the little L-shaped hall. "Your bag is in your room," he tells me. "I just have to use the bathroom, then I'll be right out." He crosses the hall to the master bedroom and disappears behind the closed door.

Isabel grabs a toy off the worn, brown couch next to the fireplace and says, "I'll just make sure the twins are okay." She trudges down the hall and disappears around the corner of the L, just past the second bathroom that I will be sharing with the twins while I'm here. "Help yourself to anything in the kitchen," Isabel shouts from the kids' room.

For a moment, the apartment is silent. Breathing in deeply, I roll my neck around trying to work out the kinks that the plane ride and cramped backseat have produced. I glance through the sliding glass doors to the patio. Although none of the furniture inside the small apartment has changed since my last visit, they've added a new outdoor set to the once empty balcony. A thin dusting of snow covers the patio table, and I sigh. The set hasn't been used in a while and probably won't be for another couple of months. Turning to my left, I enter the kitchen and open the fridge. I grab a bottle of water, close the door, and let my eyes wander over the children's art work decorating the fridge door.

"We should frame some of that stuff," Harrison says from behind me, and I jump at the sound of his voice. He chuckles, "We could use some updates to this place, wouldn't you say?"

"I think it's great, you guys have such a cozy, little home," I reply, twisting the cap off my bottle and taking a swig.

"Hmmm," he starts in agreement, then adds, "Isabel's right though, this place is starting to get old. I want to give her a house, but we just can't afford it right now." He drops his head, but immediately picks it up as he hears his wife's footsteps approaching.

"Okay—now to get dinner started," Isabel says, rubbing her hands together. "If you give me my space, the food will be on the table within thirty minutes."

"Not a problem," Harrison says, raising both hands in surrender. "Just let me grab a beer, and Hallie and I will take our conversation to the living room." He sidles up beside me in the enclosed kitchen, opens the fridge, grabs a beer and pries the top open with a special magnet designed to do the trick. I begin to follow Harrison out of the kitchen, but he halts, pivots toward Isabel who is turning on the oven and kisses her gently, running the thumb of his free hand gently down her cheek.

"Come on—at least wait till I leave the room," I grimace, but my heart throbs with the loving gesture just witnessed between my brother and sister-in-law. Their relationship epitomizes everything I ever wanted with Jonathan, but never experienced. Harrison laughs while leaving the kitchen, walking past the dining room table to the cozy living room space, warmed by flickering flames. I settle in the corner of the couch closest to the fireplace, my Oklahoma skin still covered with goosebumps from the outdoor chill. Harrison drops into the creaky recliner beside the couch, leans back, then stretches out with noises that give testimony to the age of the chair.

He sips his beer, then places his free hand behind his head and says, "Now this is the life."

I nod, staring down at my water bottle. Could my life be any more different from Harrison's? The reality of my past and the mood that would shift the moment Jonathan took a beer out of the fridge pounds against my skull. My memories stand in stark contrast to the love just witnessed in the kitchen, radiating to every corner of this apartment. "You really love her, don't you?"

Harrison looks at me, his eyebrows pulled down in concentration, and takes a moment before saying, "Apart from God, that woman is the best thing that ever happened to me." With a sigh, he continues, "I want to treat her with the respect she deserves while loving her in all the ways she needs. I want to provide everything for her. I want to be the husband and father I said I would be in my wedding vows." He takes another drink. "I want to be all of that for her, but I know I fall short—probably more often than I can imagine—and that is where Christ comes in. When I fail, *He* reminds me of the promises I made before God as I took her as my wife, and *He* gets me through the highs and lows of this rollercoaster journey called life."

My chin begins to quiver. *No, be strong!* You're not a little fawn anymore. But I can't help it, my sorrow takes over. I would have given anything to hear Jonathan say something like that about me. Instead, he left me fighting to believe my worth—he left me terrified…a hollowed-out version of the woman I've always wanted to be. Harrison lets me cry quietly for a while, then with his head lowered, he whispers, "I'm sorry, Hallie. I should have known what he was doing to you from the start. I should have saved you earlier." My crying continues until I can reduce it to a sniffle. Harrison reaches over to the box of tissues on the side table that separates the recliner from the couch and tosses it in my direction. As the box sails toward me, I fumble and miss it.

We both giggle. It doesn't get much more uncoordinated than *that*. Again, another stark difference between my brother and me. Dabbing at my damp face, I take in a deep, shaky breath. What would I do without Harrison? He lets me be myself, even when my attempt to stay strong crumbles. "Sorry, I'm just—" I start.

"You don't have to apologize, Hallie," Harrison says with a raised hand and a shake of his head. "What you have been through is unthinkable. I'm still wondering how you keep it together. No woman should have to endure what you went through with Jonathan." My head shoots up in warning, and he corrects himself. "With *him*, I mean." He twists to glance down the hall behind the recliner, just in case either of his children have snuck out of their room to eavesdrop. Before this trip, we all decided we weren't going to use *his* name anymore, especially around the twins. Some things should be forgotten, and the twins are young enough to forget. I just wish I could. Harrison's shoulders drop—the coast is clear. He turns back toward me and adds, "When you told me all that he had done to you, how he had—"

"*No, don't,*" I interrupt as vivid scenes flash through my mind and send an icy shiver down my spine. I can't relive *that* again—not here, not now. Harrison draws his head back quickly, but with his next breath, his questioning eyes soften. "Let's talk about happier things," I suggest, plunking the tissue box down beside the couch. My emotions can't handle anymore, for now—I don't intend to spend my precious vacation time on the horrendous recounts of my failed marriage.

"Sounds good to me," Harrison says as he raises his bottle with a side nod. I raise my water bottle in an awkward attempt to *cheers* from across the space, and in an instant, we are both laughing.

* * *

"Wow, Hallie," Harrison exclaims as we slide to a stop at the bottom of a slope. "You're catching on faster than I imagined. I'm impressed." Harrison snaps one boot out of his snowboard as I start shuffling toward the line for the lift. "How long has it been since you've skied?"

I tap a gloved finger to my cheek, then say, "Must have been five years, at least." Some guy on a snowboard zooms by us. *Whoa!* Did this showoff have to get so close to the tips of my skis? Both Harrison and I cock our heads back. That was a bit much. I shake my head, then catch a glimpse of Isabel in her bright blue jacket on the bunny hill with the twins. "The kids are really doing well," I exclaim as both Harrison and I move into the long line for the lift.

"Yeah," Harrison starts, "they get better every time we come. Bailey always takes a while to get the hang of it, but Branson is ready to take on a black diamond—at least in his mind he is."

We laugh just as a group of college kids kicking back on a bench near the lodge yell for Harrison. Harrison waves, "I should go check on them. You good to do the next run on your own?"

"Sure, no problem," I say, my chest lifting. Harrison nudges me in the shoulder with a playful fist as he snaps his other boot out, picks up the snowboard and leaves the line, making his way to the rowdy college group. I shuffle along with the moving line. *Ouch.* My shins are killing me. I bend down to click my boot out of my ski. My hips tighten with the movement and I cringe. If I could just get a little lower. *Ugh!* Why do they have to make these snaps so difficult to reach?

"Here, let me get that for you," a voice offers from behind. The showoff on the snowboard leans down and pops my ski boot out.

"Thanks," I mumble while shifting my foot around in the boot. Taking off my gloves, I wiggle around the top clamp. These things don't cushion against the shin-bone like they should. I keep my eyes on the task long enough to avoid conversation with the stranger, but as I pick up my head, I meet his pink, drooping eyes for a brief moment. The deep lines forming around his lazy smile suggest he's older than the teenager I pegged him for while speeding dangerously close to me earlier.

He extends a flirty greeting, and he looks like he is going to shake my hand, so I lower my gaze and fumble to put my gloves back on while clicking back into my ski. "What's your name?"

"I'm Hallie," I mumble. Pinching my lips, I turn quickly to advance in the line that is inching toward the lift. Will he take a hint already?

"Do you mind if we ride the lift together? All my friends went up without me and the line's kinda long."

"Um," I start, glancing at the ever-growing line behind us. "Yeah, that's fine, I guess." I meet his eyes once more. His cloudy stare leaves me wriggling in my jacket. Shifting from his gaze, I chew my lip as a knot forms in my gut from these all-too familiar signs. I've been here before. Three, long years of Jonathan's bloodshot eyes and irrational behavior…I can recognize the signs a mile away. But truth be told, his pot smoking habit proved to be the least of my worries.

Neither of us says anything until we finally get up to the lift. As the machine sweeps us off our feet and we pull the bar across our waists, I grimace. Why did I have to let him ride with me? I could have easily said how uncomfortable this all made me feel, but no—as always, I keep my opinions to myself.

"Come here often?" He tugs off his beanie—his shaggy hair falling in tufts around his thin, stubbly face.

I clear my throat, turning my gaze straight ahead as I say, "Actually, no. I'm just visiting my brother and sister-in-law for the holiday."

"Nice," he says. He's trying to spur our conversation, but I'm not making it easy. I hate awkward conversation with strangers. I mean, how high do you have to be to not pick-up the vibes I'm sending? "You gotta boyfriend?" I shudder and scoot away. Now that I'm pressed against the far side of the lift, there's no way he isn't catching on. But his lazy grin suggests otherwise. *Feel free to cut to the chase, pal.*

"Yes," I lie. Is that what it takes to end our conversation? Bile creeps into the back of my throat from the smell of marijuana clinging to his jacket. But at least it's not the smell of a Davidoff cigar. That smell will haunt me forever.

The stranger shifts listlessly in the swinging chair, "Well, he isn't here, and I didn't see a ring on your hand, so it can't be that serious."

My lips part in response to this guy's advances. *Wow.* Blunt, rude, crass—*you got anything else up your sleeve, buddy?* I gulp—this guy's an idiot, so why do his words sting so bad? "It is," I retort through gritted teeth. My chin lifts as my eyes narrow. I have never been this stern to a complete stranger, or anyone else, for that matter.

He throws both of his hands up as if pleading *not-guilty* and shrinks back. With a shrug of his shoulders, he lets his eyes wander the snowy terrain. The landing for a green trail comes into view. Finally—a chance to escape. Indicating my departure without a word, I lift my skis off the foothold and push up on the bar. By the time my skis hit the snow, I'm fighting back tears. It doesn't seem to matter that I was triumphantly firm with him minutes before…he got to me. It's not that this stranger reminds me of Jonathan; he's far too laid back to parallel the aggression evidenced in Jonathan's simplest, day-to-day moments, even if they did share the same *recreational* habits. But did he have to mention the lack of commitment from my made-up boyfriend? I slide down the slope—one easy hill, then another. What is it about me that invites noncommittal relationships—whether it's my husband or a fake boyfriend? Am I not worth anything more? Can I ever fight my way out of Jonathan's grip? Will he be coming for me, searching our small town until he finds me?

My anguished questions punish my thoughts as I shift my weight back and forth between my skis. *Clack!* I hit a patch of ice and go tumbling to a quick stop. My hips ache with the fall. I slowly pick my head up, unable to hold back the tears that melt the snow beneath me. Another skier races past me, but I'm too far off the beaten path for them to stop. Resting on my side, I take a moment to cry…out of embarrassment from falling, out of pain from my hips, out of fear for my future, out of terror from my past. *Oh God, how can my life be such a mess? I thought things would get better once I left him. I thought I would be on a journey to healing and freedom, but I'm still desperate to escape it all.* I swipe at my tear-streaked cheeks with the back of my scratchy glove. If I wait here much longer, people will begin to wonder. I sniffle, turn over on my skis that are thankfully still in place, and begin making my way down the slope, once again. It's time for a break…and maybe a peppermint mocha.

This time, I don't care how much it hurts my hips to bend at an angle—with great difficulty, I pop my skis boots out, place them on the rack and clunk up the stairs to the lodge. As I enter the heated, open space, I spy Isabel and the twins seated by one of the large fireplaces, taking a break from the bunny hill.

Navigating between the tables, I slump down in the rocking chair beside Isabel. Her smile quickly slides to pursed lips. "What's wrong? Did you hurt yourself?" Does she mean physically, or emotionally? Doesn't matter, I divulge the full events of the last twenty minutes anyway. When I am finally through, I take a couple of deep breaths, thankful the twins are playing with each other farther away from the fire.

With the children out of earshot, Isabel takes the first opportunity she has had to speak openly about the man I have just left—the monster who has tormented me since our honeymoon. "Hallie, it's okay to feel all this. Of course you're overwhelmed—you have just gotten out of a difficult, three-year marriage." She sighs, "Harrison shared with me everything that you told him a few months ago, and I don't know if I could have endured all that. I never liked the guy. I thought he was a scumbag back in high school, and although he put on a good front for your family, *he never fooled me.*" Isabel pulls her beautiful curls over to one side of her shoulder and leans in, "Jonathan was terrible to do all that he did to you…he should be sitting in prison right now, and although Harrison has told me to stay out of it, I think you should take him to court. He deserves to rot in jail."

My chest thumps, "He wasn't *that* bad." I take another breath, preparing to go on, but Isabel interrupts me before I can make any more excuses for that man—as if the excuses could protect me from the stupidity of marrying him in the first place.

"He was, though." Isabel gently floats her hand onto my shoulder. Can she see my struggle to protect the image of a man I have worked so hard to defend in the past? *Thunk!* Isabel's rocking chair gets bumped from behind, and we both glance back to find Branson listening intently to our conversation. With a groan, Isabel quickly redirects, "Hey buddy, have you been here long?"

Branson walks slowly around the rocking chairs, leaving his sister playing behind him, and climbs into my lap. "I heard you talking about Uncle Jon, Mommy," he says slowly, trying to understand what he has just heard. "Uncle Jon said he was going to take me hunting when I got older… will he?"

"Oh, baby," Isabel starts, sending an apologetic glance in my direction. "Uncle Jon isn't going to be a part of our lives anymore."

"But what about hunting?" Branson's wide eyes question his mother as his face falls.

Isabel opens and closes her mouth, like a fish out of water, then finally says, "Uncle Jon was a bad man, and he hurt Aunt Hallie. I'm sorry sweetie, but Uncle Jon will never be part of this family again. There won't be a hunting trip."

I gulp back tears and swivel to look at Bailey playing behind us. It's better to avoid Branson's questioning eyes, looking up at me for answers. But I find Bailey with her head turned, staring right at us. Hands frozen in the air, still holding her boot she's been playing with. She's been listening too. She meets my gaze, and her eyes dart downward. There was something about *Uncle Jon* that caught her ear. In the silence that follows the finality of Isabel's last comment, I turn my head back. It's unlike Bailey to listen to adult conversation. Branson heaves a sigh. He's heard all the answers he'll be getting today. And at that, he lifts his tiny hand to stroke it down my face. My eyes glisten. He can't go hunting, but he's still siding with *me.* Branson leaves my lap and runs back to Bailey. For a moment, Isabel and I watch them play together.

Isabel finally breaks the silence, "You know, I never would have let Branson go on that hunting trip. I didn't trust Jonathan with the twins. I would never have told you that at the time. I couldn't tell you what it was about him that caused such an extreme reaction inside me, but I would never have let Bailey or Branson go off alone with that man."

I lower my gaze. My stomach knots to the point where I think I might double over. My sister-in-law was correct in her assessment of the man I had married. It was why I secretively got the IUD put in shortly after our honeymoon. It didn't take long for me to realize I could never bring children into that situation. I'll never forget the day he found out about my IUD. It was the same day I got my scar.

Chapter 8

"Oh Bailey, look at your pretty, new doll," I exclaim as Bailey timidly tugs at the last piece of red and green tissue paper, revealing the baby doll I bought her for Christmas. The wrapping gets tossed to the side as Bailey coos excitedly, hugging the box to her chest while her ringlets create a beautiful halo dropping to her shoulders.

"What do you say to Aunt Hallie?" Isabel prompts, inclining her head.

Bailey gingerly places the box down and tiptoes like a dainty ballerina around the various gifts strewn across the floor, making her way over to where I am seated on the couch beside the warm fireplace. "Thank you," she almost whispers, falling into my embrace.

"Merry Christmas, gorgeous," I reply as she kisses my cheek before running back to her doll. Tightening my housecoat around me, I huddle into the corner of the couch. *Brrr!* Snowflakes kiss the sliding glass doors and melt instantly, creating a dancing glimmer of lights bouncing off the Christmas tree we decorated last week. I take another sip of my peppermint coffee and revel in the warmth of being inside. What would I do without family? What would my Christmas look like this year if I wasn't sitting here, drawing this morning to a close with the few remaining gifts sitting under the tree.

"This one's for Hallie," Harrison says as he carries a silver and red box over to where I am in the corner of the living room. "Ho-ho-ho," he adds jubilantly as the Santa hat slides further down the side of his head.

My fingers graze my parted lips. "*Guys*—you already got me that verse in a frame, which was more than enough." Harrison and Isabel's funds are tight. They weren't supposed to buy me anything this Christmas. We agreed upon that before I arrived.

Isabel waves her hand nonchalantly as I take the gift from Harrison. I open the box to find a silk, off-the-shoulder blouse. "It's beautiful—this blush shade of pink is gorgeous. Thanks, y'all," my southern drawl catches me off guard. *Hmph.* My words have been slipping between the nasally, mid-west accent connected to my upbringing in Michigan and the southern twang brought on by my marriage to an Oklahoma country boy. When my accent takes a southern turn, I'm reminded of *him*. In a desperate attempt to hide my shudder, I lift the shirt out of the box.

"I was thinking you could wear it for our New Year's Eve party next week," Isabel starts. "I know you fly out the first, and you don't have to stay up till midnight, but I figured it would be something to wear while we have a few friends over for the evening."

"*It's perfect.* You guys are so thoughtful—*thank you!* I'm gunna put my gifts in the guest room." I start to rise from the couch, then my eyes take in the boxes, gifts and wrapping paper scattered in disarray, leaving the off-white carpet barely visible. "Never mind," I laugh, settling back in, "I'll do it later."

"Well, Branson and I picked out that shirt, isn't that right, bud?" Harrison says to his son who is busy wielding his new Star Wars lightsaber, completely oblivious to the comment. Isabel rolls her eyes and giggles at the fallacious statement; we all know the boys in this family get their style from Isabel's fashionable eye. "Whoa, little man, not so close to the tree," Harrison lurches from the recliner in an effort to redirect his son away from the Christmas tree sitting between the sliding glass door and the TV mounted on the wall, a disastrous location to slash around a lightsaber, on all accounts. The rest of the gifts are eventually opened as the kids bounce around from one new toy to the next, asking Isabel and me to help open boxes or put in batteries while Harrison attempts to tidy-up behind them.

Yawning, Isabel asks me what time it is. I pick up my phone from the empty cushion beside me and check the time. "It's nearly noon," I reply.

What a relaxing morning. No rush, no bitterness . . . just bliss. My lock screen goes black. This morning has been so different from my last few Christmases. It used to be thirty minutes of grunts and closed-lip smiles. The morning never failed to disappoint me—always one gift, something bought last minute, no thought put into the haphazardly wrapped item. Christmases with him were a bust. But what did I expect?

My depressing thoughts are put on hold as my phone buzzes in my hand. I glance at the screen and my heart leaps into my throat as I see Jonathan's mother's name appear. I gulp. This day was bound to come. There's no escaping it now. My trembling finger swipes to accept the call. "Hello?" I answer, but the sound of muffled, angry voices sends me reeling. Do I really owe this family I used to be a part of an explanation?

A deep voice replies to my shaky greeting. "Well," Jonathan's father starts, "if it isn't the little home-wrecker." I flinch and my eyes water. That was harsh. I shoot a panicked look in the direction of Isabel and Harrison only to find them frozen in place. Pushing up from the couch, I fumble for my gifts. This isn't a conversation I need to have in front of the kids. As I hustle back to the guest bedroom, my arms full, I let Jonathan's father continue, "You could have told us you were leaving our son, Hallie. So, what's your plan—going after his money?"

"No, I . . . I," comes my stammering response. Why didn't I rehearse this? My insides lurch from the anger that slices through each of his words. They should have picked up on all the signs of our strained marriage. My in-laws are smart people—couldn't they piece it together for themselves?

"You what?" He continues, "You got bored? You *fell out of love*? You met another man? Which is it, Hallie? Take your pick . . . I'll tell you one thing. You've ruined Jonathan." My chin quivers as I plop down on the small, double bed situated in the corner of the tiny guest room. *Don't cry, don't cry.* I unload my armful on the mattress and stifle a quite sob as I roll to the edge. The sharp edge of the picture frame gifted to me earlier this morning bites into my leg. I wince and move the frame to the end of the bed as his father grunts, then says, "He showed up drunk to our Christmas meal, and it's all your fault." These words sting more than the bruise forming on my leg. I begged Jonathan to stop with all the drugs. How was I to know he would start drinking instead? Maybe this is my fault. Jonathan may have let loose in the privacy of our home, but he never would've embarrassed his family like this. "Do you know what this town's going to say about him when the divorce is final?" he continues. "Do you understand what your selfish, little act will do to my son's respectable reputation?" I open my mouth in hopes of defending myself, but nothing comes out. In my silence, Jonathan's father persists, "No, you don't know what you've done to him because all you think about is yourself."

Grunts of muffled support in the background tell me my former father-in-law is not alone in his perception of me. A booming voice demands to speak with me. It's his brother. "Please, I didn't mean anything—" I start, but the phone has been passed to the next family member.

"Jonathan's a good man," his brother begins. I shudder. The lie sears my mind, but my mouth is unable to protest. "He gave you everything you ever dreamed of—the nice house, the big yard, *he even bought some of those hunting dogs for you*," Jonathan's brother bellows. I squeeze my eyes shut. This conversation is going nowhere. Time to hang-up. *You can do it, Hallie—just hang-up*. "And now he's been left alone in that big house, all by himself, with no one but the dogs to keep him company."

"It's not like that," I whimper, "We were . . . he was—" I can't do it. There's nothing I can offer the McClains.

Jonathan's brother snorts an angry chuckle into the phone, "Well, if that's all you have to say for yourself, then just know you're not getting a penny from him in the divorce. You're poor, stupid, and without a hope—*and it's going to stay that way*." The line goes dead, and I fall back on the bed in a heap of tormenting sobs. I don't want his money, I don't want the trouble of dividing assets in court—he can keep everything—all I want is to be free from his power and terrorizing acts forever. What has he said in his drunken stupor at his family's Christmas dinner? I bet he didn't tell them how things *actually* were during those three excruciating years. Clutching my phone in my hand, I cry hard into the pillow, devastated by the injustice I just faced. If I was bolder, I would have told them the truth. If I was better at confrontation, I would have defended myself like I deserve. But no, I don't have it in me to be upfront. I'm the same old *Hallie*, keeping my opinions to myself, holding it together until the next opportunity for escape comes along.

My foot bumps against the frame sitting at the bottom of my bed. I grab at it and draw it up to my face. *"For I know the plans I have for you," declares the Lord, "plans to prosper you and not to harm you, plans to give you hope and a future." Jeremiah 29:11.* If this is so true, why do I want to throw this frame across the room? My jaw aches from clenching it so tightly. *I told you I couldn't trust you, God. And now look what's happened!*

A new onslaught of sobs sends me rocking. I've done it again. I can get so angry at God instead of accepting my own responsibility. I can't keep blaming God every time something goes wrong. So what if the McClains hate me? That's not God's fault. I left Jonathan, I fled when a window of opportunity presented itself, I kept my mouth shut when I could've told his family *exactly* why I had to get out. Time to come clean. In a silent prayer, I beg God for this verse to be true in my life. Without the tiniest clue as to what my future holds, all I can do is pray that God has an amazing plan for me…even if I can't see it yet.

* * *

The doorbell rings as I adjust the shoulders of my new, pink blouse. "The first guest is here," Harrison announces as he bounds down the stairs to the front door of the apartment. The kids are fast asleep, like two hibernating bears. *Good thing.* The noise of the crowd coming from the front foyer suggests it will be a lively party. As the group filters in, Isabel greets everyone with an elated grin while Harrison volunteers to take their coats back to the master bedroom. The smiling faces of Isabel and Harrison's church friends all turn toward me, and Isabel goes through the crowd, introducing each person.

I offer a small smile and nod as Isabel continues, "And everyone, this is Hallie McClain, my wonderful sister-in-law."

Heat rises to my cheeks as the sound of my married name rings in my ears. I go to correct Isabel, but the words get caught in my throat. I can do this. I push my shoulders back and say, "Actually, I prefer to go by Hallie

Reed." Isabel flusters almost imperceptibly. She addresses the mistake with an effortless apology followed by an offhand joke, then redirects everyone's attention to the drinks and appetizers covering the dining room table.

"Hallie," Isabel whispers as she pulls up beside me, taking advantage of her distracted guests, "*I can't believe I just did that.*" She tucks a curl behind her slightly pink ear.

"It's fine," I insist. "You aren't the first to make the mistake, and you won't be the last." With a sigh, I add, "It sounds weird for me to hear, too. I mean, I still stumble over my last name when I make phone calls and stuff. I just thought here, I don't have to deal with who I was. These people don't need to know my past." A pretty woman with a creamy, dark complexion meanders toward us with her plate full and strikes up a conversation. Nothing about her tone or language insinuates that she's aware of the awkwardness that occurred only moments before. In fact, no one is lingering over the correction I just announced. *Well, that proved to be easier than I thought.* I want to pat myself on the back for the unusual gumption I just displayed. My chin lifts, and I immerse myself in the conversation. This is my chance to inch out of my shell.

Most of the people at this party serve in Isabel and Harrison's church. Too bad I didn't get the chance to visit Nations Church Ann Arbor during this stay—we had to make a few guest visits to other churches these past few weeks so Harrison could connect with some U of M students. *Ah well . . .* next time.

The soft jazz music plays in the background as the clock counts down to midnight. I yawn. Can I make it until the ball drops? I check the time and groan. I don't think I can do it, not with my early flight in the morning. Maybe just a little longer. The doorbell rings again, and Harrison leaves the room to welcome the new guests. Three heads immerge at the top of the stairs, and my eyes lock on the couple standing beside Harrison.

As Harrison gestures to take their coats, my eyes narrow. Could this couple be any more beautiful? The man, tall and dark, casts his studious gaze across the group as he re-adjusts his designer-framed glasses. He can conquer the world just by surveying what's before him. But yet, the stubble on his face and his stylish attire suggest he's anything but nerdy. If his air of confidence doesn't attest to this reality enough, then the beauty of his wife certainly does.

The woman beside him throws back her long, blonde hair as she slips out of her white, knee-length pea coat. Her perfect waves swing with the motion as she hands her coat to Harrison. She turns just as Isabel approaches her side. Is she even wearing make-up? How can she do that and still look ready to walk down the runway? *Oh no*—they're coming my way. Why didn't I go to bed when I still had the chance? My eyes shoot down to my shuffling feet as Isabel approaches my side with the couple in tow. Harrison emerges from the hallway no longer carrying their coats and moseys up next to us.

I gulp, my gaze rising to meet the couple Isabel is introducing. "Hallie, I want you to meet Tom and Sarah Romano. They have been going to our church for almost a year now."

I nod my head and take a shaky breath. "It's nice to meet you." My voice is high, so I quickly put the attention back on them, "What do you two do?"

Tom scratches the stubble on his face while glancing at his wife. They laugh, as if they have just had a silent conversation determining who would speak first. *Wow.* Their connection is effortless. It's as if they are one being, so evidently in-sync that it makes my stomach clench. "Well, I am a professor at the University of Michigan. And my wife—" he gestures in her direction.

"I'm a labor and delivery nurse at the university hospital," Sarah finishes, as if their conversation flows easily from one to the other on a regular basis.

"That's great," I say, my tone still high-pitched. Why do I feel about an inch-high right now? My ears begin to itch. There is nothing I have in common with this incredibly intelligent couple.

I scramble for an excuse to remove myself, but I'm re-engaged with Tom's question. "And what do you do?"

"I'm, uh—well," I start, fiddling with a hangnail, "I'm a physical trainer. I work at a gym." Heat prickles my neck. Who am I kidding? My profession and education pale in comparison to the people standing before me. Harrison and Isabel duck out of the conversation as someone pulls them aside. There's been a spill in the kitchen—someone needs paper towel. Harrison and Isabel excuse themselves and leave to deal with the mess. I nod, expecting Tom and Sarah to follow them. But they don't. They stay right here with me, their gentle eyes locked on mine. Are they honestly interested in what I have to say?

"A physical trainer—that's amazing," Sarah exclaims. "I've always wanted to do that, but I just don't have the coordination or strength to motivate people in the gym." My eyebrows raise. This woman's curves are perfectly accentuated by her high-waisted pencil skirt and flowing white and gold blouse. I'm sure she has what it takes. She giggles and puts a hand on my shoulder, as if we are close friends sharing an inside joke. "Seriously," she says, "if you only knew how often I made a fool of myself in the gym, you would understand."

I shake my head and smile, "I'm sure that's not the case. We all can be a little awkward when we are learning a new exercise for the first time, but I bet you could do my job, no problem." They both laugh, showcasing smiles that must have been perfected by an orthodontist—it wouldn't be fair if they were both born with so much natural beauty. "Do you work out at a gym here in Ann Arbor?"

"Yes," Tom says with a slow tilt of the head. "We did some searching around and found this great, local gym downtown. We live farther out of the city, so we wanted to find a place that's easy for us to access before and after our work hours."

"We work such different hours that it's difficult to find time to spend together *and* workout," Sarah adds without skipping a beat. "If we can manage, we try to link up together at the gym as often as possible. Tom teaches me so much about different training techniques—so it's best if we can do the workouts together." *Of course.* They are that pedestal couple who trains together in the gym. They're the ones who do partner push-ups, ab rotations, and unified squats.

"Well, I bet we can learn a lot from Hallie," Tom replies. Feeling smaller than a flea, my glance fleets between the carpet and his face. He's just being kind. But his eyes spark behind those round, black frames, and his smile is sincere as he says, "Harrison brags about you all the time—it sounds like you know what you're doing in the gym, and I think it's awesome you have dedicated your time and effort to instill that kind of confidence in others."

I somewhat rock back on my heels as I offer a nod of gratitude. Could this perfect couple really be as humble and down-to-earth as they seem?

In that moment, laughter erupts from the kitchen, and the crowd turns their attention toward the noise. This is my chance to excuse myself. I quickly gush about how nice it was to meet them, then dash to my room. Isabel and Harrison will understand my need to turn in early for the night. Behind the closed door, I start getting ready for bed while filtering through my confused thoughts. Tom and Sarah seem so intertwined, as if their lives are effortlessly bound by their marriage and love for one another. The world has handed them beauty, intelligence, and talent. It's almost not fair. This is all I've ever wanted in a marriage. Their bond is so intact that it's as if they can read each other's minds. My heart dips to my stomach. They've got what I want—a relationship with someone who is so in sync with me that mind reading is second nature.

With this desire burning in my heart, my mind snaps back to the fullness of my reality. My marriage is over. It'll end in a divorce in nine and a half months. And who's to say I'll be free from Jonathan even after the divorce? Will he ever stop haunting me? Could I ever find myself in a loving relationship like Tom and Sarah's? I stare down at my limp hands, then start shoving my belongings into my suitcase, packing for my flight back to Oklahoma...back to reality, back to my constant fear, back to looking over my shoulder, waiting for something to go wrong.

Picking up the frame I received for Christmas, I exhale slowly. *I've got to memorize these words.* Maybe I need to start turning my doubts into trust. Maybe if I pray this verse, I can learn how to completely rely on Christ, especially in my time of need and desperation for a brighter future. Maybe, just maybe.

CHAPTER 9

"Hallie McClain," the flight attendant says as she scans my boarding pass, "glad you're flying with us today, enjoy the flight." She directs me down the hall that leads to the aircraft. I accept my boarding pass from her and cringe. I can't wait for the day when I'm finally freed from that name. Hallie McClain is what I've known for the last several years, and the change to Reed is going to require some getting used to again, and yet, that day can't come soon enough. Yawning, I join the line of people waiting to board as if I'm trying to wade through water, one tired foot in front of the other. While inching forward, I check the time on my phone. The Connect Church worship team should be ending their run-through before the Sunday morning service starts.

The pit in my stomach grows as I navigate toward my seat, and my heart battles this return to Oklahoma, despite my obvious need to make money. The lake house is lonely, my job is floundering, and the gossip mill in our small town is busy *turning* about my current situation. I couldn't stop the news from leaking. Now, it's just a matter of managing the mess I've left behind these past two weeks.

I store my carry-on in the overhead compartment then shove my purse under the seat in front of me. *Tight squeeze.* I settle into my chair, tightening the seatbelt across my lap. We'll be taking off any minute, so I check my phone one last time. Is Ainsley prepared to pick me up at the airport? I smile at her final, reassuring text and turn off my phone. Ainsley's a good friend… the kind of friend who would normally be traveling with me. Sighing, I glance at the empty chair between my window seat and the middle-aged woman in the aisle seat. If Ainsley were here now, she would have been sitting *there*, distracting me from my negative thoughts regarding my return to Oklahoma. It was during our first long-distance trip together that she realized the drastic difference between my reaction to taking off and my emotions while returning home. She guessed my marriage was mediocre at best. Could she have guessed the ugly reality I faced each time I returned home?

The powerful jets propel us down the runway, and my mind travels at the same speed through all the moments I shared with Ainsley on our plane rides home. Ainsley would always relate colorful stories of the vacation while recounting the highs—and sometimes the lows—we experienced on each trip. Tucking my hair behind my ear, I look out the window at the buildings growing smaller and smaller below me. I loved having my friend on those trips, but why was she always caught in some kind of flirtatious moment? And why would she skirt over them on our flights home? I chew the inside of my cheek. Those flirtatious moments took a turn for the worse during our Key West getaway. Some guys bought us drinks while we were laying by the pool—they brought them over to us in an eager attempt to strike up a conversation. I had squirmed with discomfort at the gesture, so I thanked them briefly, but slipped into the pool to escape their pursuits and lingering eyes. They were staring at my scar.

Ainsley claimed both drinks, waved me off, and engaged in an animated conversation while I waded around in the water. We never talked about how she handled that situation, maybe because it was clear she enjoyed the guys' attention. Gulping, I close the window cover and grimace as my eyes stare at the seat back in front of me. After that trip, flirting became a central focus for Ainsley. We both had ulterior motives for our various vacations as the need to escape united us. Everyone faces the fight-or-flight instinct in a marriage, and our default was to literally take flight. It still is.

The seatbelt sign dings, indicating our ability to leave our seats and jolting my thoughts away from those prickly memories. It has been a while since Ainsley and I have escaped somewhere together, but I don't have to run away from my torturous marriage anymore—with my head down, reminiscent of my cross-country days, unwilling to take in my surroundings in an effort to respond appropriately to what lay ahead. As much as I miss my trips with Ainsley that provided a short reprieve, I don't miss the awkward situations created by Ainsley's flirting. *Ahh.* What does it matter now? I don't need to escape from *him*. I'm safely tucked away in the lake house, and as long as I'm careful, Jonathan won't find me there.

Looking down at my hands, I find a hangnail and begin picking at it. *Ugh!* I need to start trusting God if I'm ever going to make it through this divorce. I need to look where I'm going instead of running away blindly. My whole life I've been running. This is where it stops. I nod my head and take a deep breath. My New Year's resolutions are going to bring a change. This year is going to be the year that Hallie Reed becomes a *fighter*.

A child's ear-piercing cry from a few rows back startles me, and I jump. A chill runs down my spine. Why is it that every unexpected shriek from a child thrusts me into the sickening memory . . . of *him*? Of the night I came home early from work, and Jonathan wasn't expecting me. As I tiptoed up the stairs to our bedroom, I heard a child's wail from inside the room. In utter confusion, I opened the door to see Jonathan watching something on his laptop. I figured it was a scene from a movie, but my heart plummeted when I realized it was a live feed of a child being abused. Why would he watch such a wretched thing? But my questioning didn't impede him in the least. He wasn't remorseful—he told me I could leave if I didn't like it. I did . . . as fast as I could, retching the moment I made it into the bathroom down the hall. He didn't bother to check on me, to apologize, or even to offer an excuse that he *stumbled* upon the live feed. That was the day I realized the depth of his dark heart. That was the day I realized the issues I had experienced with him were deeply rooted and much uglier than I could've ever imagined. That was the day I knew having children with him was *never* an option.

Feeling the bile rise, I fight the urge to be sick. Wishing I could forget it all, I wipe the beads of sweat beginning to form on my brow and look for the flight-attendant inching her way down the aisle closer to my seat with the beverage cart. As I wait while massaging my temples, I focus on my breathing, trying to block the memories of *him*, of how I spent the night on the couch for the next week after that incident, of how I was fooled by such a monster. *Clunk-clunk.* The plane begins to jostle with some turbulence. I focus on the bouncing of the aircraft as I close my eyes and steady my breathing.

The flight-attendant asks what I would like to drink, and I tell her that water will be fine. The middle-aged woman in the aisle seat utters some sort of non-committal mention of *The Man Upstairs* as the plane takes another dip in the sky. Her nonchalant words spoken only in a time of need, as if God is only convenient when our lives are at stake, turns my thoughts around to my parents. I take a sip from the cup handed to me. Why do people depend on God only when it's convenient for them? Doesn't it seem better to always trust in an ever-dependent reliance on Christ and the salvation he offers through his death on the cross? If that were the case, then we could all find peace, even during turbulent times.

But do I really have this peace? My relationship with Christ still needs to grow; I need to become more dependent on him. Harrison mentioned this a lot during my time with them these past few weeks. My brother is good for me. He leads me to understand that my life, eternity, and everything that happens in between hinges on Christ alone.

The plane takes a sudden dive, and the middle-aged woman stifles a yelp. A little bit of water splashes out of my cup and onto my jeans. I take the napkin offered to me moments earlier and dab at my damp pant leg, but my thoughts are stuck on the differences between being a true Christian and being a church-goer. I'm a Christian . . . so why do I still resist getting baptized? Harrison was baptized shortly after he became a Christ follower. I was there. Our parents didn't go—they were at *their* church—but I wanted to be there when Harrison publicly declared his relationship with Jesus by symbolizing the death and resurrection of Christ through the act of baptism. I down the rest of my water. *Okay, God—I'll make a deal with you.* Who knows where my future is heading. But if I can trust you with my future, and if you show me you do have plans to prosper me and not to harm me—a plan to give me hope—then I will get baptized. I stuff the used napkin into my now-empty cup just as the pilot announces more expected turbulence. *How ironic.* Is this announcement prophetic—is this God answering my prayer, saying that things in my life might get worse before they get better?

* * *

Spying Ainsley's Highlander, I wheel my suitcase to her vehicle and throw my stuff into the back. Jumping into the passenger's side, I say a quick hello to Miles and shift my eyes to my best friend in the driver's seat. As I greet her, my hello gets swallowed up by shock. "*Whoa Ainsley, what did you do to your chest?*"

"Well, hello to you too," Ainsley jokes before adding, "what do you think of 'em?" She pulls her Connect Church t-shirt tighter across her body to show off her new additions, but she certainly doesn't have to draw attention to her former A cups that are now Ds. I offer a blank stare in response as Ainsley joins the moving line of cars. "I got them for Will as a Christmas present this year." Her smile wilts as she sarcastically adds, "Although, he barely noticed." My head reels at the implication of her gibe while she clarifies, "I mean, he noticed, but you know—" her voice trails off as she shrugs with a sigh. Eager to change the topic, she asks, "So, how was Michigan? Meet any cute guys?" She laughs as she quickly adds, "I'm just joking."

I clear my throat. I'm still married, and even the joke of meeting someone else while I'm going through a divorce makes me squirm in my seat. *She might be joking, but why would Ainsley be so insensitive?* "Well... Michigan was good," I say, my thoughts landing on the couple I met at the New Year's Eve party last night. Somehow, the memory of meeting Tom and Sarah has me clutching my stomach. But now's not the time to compare my current marital standing to their flawless marital connection, so I move the conversation along. "It's so cold there, though. I definitely didn't pack as many layers as I needed—I had to borrow Isabel's coats and stuff."

"Yeah, I bet," Ainsley says, oblivious to my shifting brought on by her query about cute guys. "How was Christmas morning? Did the twins love having their aunt there?"

I groan. "Christmas was great, but I finally heard from Jonathan's family."

Ainsley gasps, "Did they call? What happened? What did they say?"

"Yeah, they called. They weren't happy. Jonathan showed up drunk at his parents' house for their Christmas dinner, and I bet he gave them the perfect sob story about how I left him unexpectedly while he was at work one day."

I grimace as Ainsley shoots me a side glance. "Who knows exactly what he said to them, but somehow I was painted as an irresponsible wife who left him and is now trying to take all his money."

"Well, you should," Ainsley replies.

My eyes narrow. "You know I'm not in this for the money."

"I know, I know," she saves herself, "but he does owe you money for the car he never bought you." With a shrug of her shoulders, Ainsley asks, "What did his mom say? I mean, his mom has to at least know some of the crap you went through with him—didn't he treat her badly, too?"

I blink several times. He *better* not have treated his mom the way he treated me. I skip past the question. Ainsley can connect the dots if she pleases. I'm not going to gossip about it. "Actually, his mom didn't talk to me. Only his brother and his dad did." I massage the back of my neck, trying to rub out the tension that continues to build during this car ride back to the lake house. "I'm sure she didn't want to confront me. She's the only one in that family who truly accepted me. I know she loved me, she was probably just out-numbered with all the men in the room, each of them just as strong willed as the other." Ainsley nods her head as I continue, "I bet his mom knows something serious happened for me to leave him like I did, but she probably doesn't want to address it. I know she wanted me to be a positive influence in his life, so she's probably upset that I left, leaving her hopeless in a family full of men who refuse to change their ways." As I hug my arms across my chest, I drop my gaze. Jonathan certainly fooled us all in the beginning, trying to prove to everyone around him that he was ready for a change—that *love* made him realize how destructive he could be. Unfortunately, that façade faded, and I came to realize the destruction he was capable of.

"Well, forget about them," Ainsley says. "They probably know all they should—so it's best to just leave it at that." Ainsley takes another turn as she navigates toward the lake house. "If he's drunk all the time, he's probably sharing all the details, so you don't have to worry about it."

"Mmm-hmm," I absently respond. My stomach tightens at the mention of Jonathan's drinking habits. If only I had been firm from the start, then maybe I wouldn't have had to tolerate the ebb and flow of his destructive habits. It seemed simple enough. If I begged him to stop using drugs, he would change. How could I have known he would turn to alcohol like he has? In my mind, I had it all planned out. He would stop with the drugs and life would improve. *How naïve could I have been*?

Miles's whiney request for a snack draws my focus to the back half of the vehicle. "Hallie, will you grab that blue cup over there?" Ainsley requests. "I think there are some Goldfish in it." I reach into the backseat and hand the small container to Miles. "What do you say to Hallie?" Ainsley prompts.

A quiet *thank you* escapes Miles's half-full mouth as I take in his Sunday outfit. "He looks so cute today. That collared shirt makes him look even more like his dad." Pursing my lips ever so slightly, I ask, "Where is Will today? Did he go to church with you?"

"No," Ainsley starts, "Will is still missing church. He's so busy during the week that he makes excuses almost every Sunday morning."

"Oh, gotcha," I add in a voice that doesn't sound like my own. I don't want to create tension. "Well, he probably just needed to sleep-in today. If he's working late from home and has to get to the office early in the morning, then I bet he can use some extra sleep."

Ainsley hesitates, then caves to her frustration with a vent, "He's not sleeping. He actually went back into the city to look for an apartment." My bulging eyes swivel in Ainsley's direction. My mouth gapes. What does this mean for their marriage? Ainsley steals a glance in my direction, "*It's not like that!*" She darts her eyes around the car, looking everywhere but at me. "He's just sick of getting up early every morning and dealing with the traffic going into the city. He said if he had an apartment near his office, it would save him a lot of time, especially if he gets out of a meeting late and doesn't want to come all the way home." I pinch my lips together. It's not my place to speak my mind. Ainsley's marriage is her business. "He won't be using the apartment that often, just a few nights a week," Ainsley reassures, but the comment was meant more for her than me.

"Maybe you can stay with him a couple of those nights," I suggest through a constricted throat. If this is Will's plan, better make the best of it. "You can drop Miles off with me at the lake house or leave him with your parents. It might be nice to stay in the city some nights." Ainsley smiles, but it doesn't come close to reaching her eyes.

As we turn onto the dirt road leading up to the lake house, relief washes over me. "Chip Catcher was talking about you all morning at church," Ainsley puffs with a role of her eyes as the car jostles over the many ruts, "I think he's eager to get you singing again." She laughs, then adds, "His wife has been taking over your harmony, and you know Becca isn't a strong singer."

Although I agree with Ainsley, a desire to defend Becca surges through me as I reply, "She isn't too bad. Her voice sounds great when she sings that one song. What's it called?"

Ainsley shifts into park and swivels her eyes in my direction. She knows the one, and her head tilts in a *you gotta be kidding me* kind of way. Shrugging my shoulders, Ainsley finishes by saying, "Well, at any rate, I think Chip is excited to have you back next week."

With a nod and a stifled yawn, I thank Ainsley for picking me up, then head to the back to grab my suitcase. As I walk up the steps leading to the front door, I frown. I hope Chip hasn't made any announcement regarding me potentially serving on Team B. The key turns in the lock, and I open the door of the lake house, heading quickly to my bedroom for a much-needed nap. It's been a long day, and that car ride didn't help…neither will thinking about my early start to work tomorrow morning.

CHAPTER 10

My thoughts plow through the sermon Pastor Noah just delivered as I exit Connect Church and walk to my car. *Ugh!* Pastor Noah drilled into my issues surrounding trust and reliance on Christ this morning. At least his penetrating stare didn't rest on me sitting in the front row. That would have kept me squirming, but he couldn't have guessed his sermon would hit me square in the heart. I fumble for my keys as I approach my dilapidated car. *Gross.* All the rust around the tire rims and nicks on the windows point to exactly how used and run-down my car is. Resisting the temptation to rub at a smudge, a voice from behind startles me.

"You killed it again this morning, Hallie." I swivel to find Chip Catcher strolling toward me, his hipster outfit perfectly crafted for this dreary, mid-January day. "Man, we have been missing your voice on stage—it's good to have you back."

I offer a thin smile. "Thanks," I murmur, dropping my head ever so slightly to play with my keys, my eyes flitting between him and this preferred distraction.

Chip approaches, his head tilted. "Hey, you okay?"

"Yeah, I'm fine," I pick up my head and exhale into a smile. Now is not the time to get into a conversation concerning my finances and how I feel about my crappy car, or the tickle of fear constantly nagging somewhere in the back of my mind, as if I'm going to be forced to make a decision that may have a rippling effect on our worship team.

Chip lowers his voice to the point where his words are barely audible. "Have you given any thought to serving on Team B, especially now that we have you back?"

I shift from one foot to the other. "I don't know. I don't want to take Becca's spot—she seems really happy serving as the lead singer on Team B."

"You let me worry about Becca. I'll come up with some excuse that forces you to be in that position over her. I just really need you singing more up front." His deceit stabs at my heart, and my eyes drift away from his pinched face. In that instant, I catch Rita getting into her Jeep only a few cars down. Her sneer doesn't go unnoticed.

Like a lightning bolt jolting my body, I pivot back to my car as I say over my shoulder, "Let me think about it a little longer—thanks for leading worship this morning." Throwing him a nonchalant wave, I get into my car and shove the key into the ignition. *Phew!* I'm glad that conversation's over. I hit my rattling car into reverse, leaving behind Chip, who's rubbing his bald head in agitated circles. What lengths is Chip willing to go in order to remove his wife from the worship team…and why is Rita so intent on examining my every move? There's no way Rita could hear my chat with Chip, but was she capable of identifying my emotions during that brief conversation? *Jeez,* I'm in trouble. That woman is the town gossip. Speeding out of the parking lot, I shudder as I navigate onto the main road and duck down a side street to avoid the traffic that's building at the stoplight ahead.

Scurch! As I make my turn, my car suddenly lurches. Exasperated, I kick at the gas pedal, but the whole car shuts down. The steering wheel stiffens, and with great effort, I direct my car to a grassy patch on the side of the road. My vehicle coasts to a stop just as I release a frustrated cry. I turn my key again. *Come-on, you can do it.* Will you just start—please? *Click . . . click.* Nothing. Not even a small groan of life is left in the engine. I don't need this right now. I grab for my phone and call Ainsley. The line connects. "My car just broke down, and it's not starting again."

* * *

"I can't believe you're meeting with *him*," Ainsley says as she pulls into the parking lot of the strip mall. The Java Coffee House slowly comes into view as a pit forms in my stomach. My eyes quickly scan the parking lot in search for Jonathan's car. Is he already waiting inside?

"It's my only choice," I whisper. "My parents said they would only help me buy a car if I go back to Jonathan, and you can't keep carting me around like you have been all week—it's like you're my taxi driver." A small groan bubbles in the back of my throat as I add, "Since I'm refusing to move back in with *him*, the only option I had was to ask him to pay me the money he promised me years ago." I can't walk to work and my wage at Jim's Gym won't pay for a reliable car. *Without him, I'm screwed.* "He has the money to help, so I figured if I unblocked his number and asked to meet him at a public place, it might make him think he has a chance." I'm here—now it's up to him to give me the money.

"Well when you put it that way, I think you're doing the right thing—he owes you that money," Ainsley responds as my trembling fingers struggle to unbuckle my seatbelt. "But, I mean, what if he gets angry while you're in there alone with him?" She shifts into park. The truth is, his anger is the least of my concerns. It's whether he acts on it.

There's a weakness that radiates from my heart to my knees as I say, "That's why I'm meeting him in a public place. He won't do anything to ruin his reputation. And I have an excuse to make the conversation short: I have to be at work in fifteen minutes." I shake my head. Why couldn't my parents help me out just this once? Why do they have to put stipulations on *everything?*

"Okay—well I'm going shopping downtown. If you need anything, call me." She glances behind at Miles, then back to me. What did I expect? She shouldn't have to wait around and make sure I'm alright, especially not with a toddler in the car.

"It'll be fine," I reassure her through the pressure pulsing away at my temples. "I'll just walk down to the gym when it's all said and done."

She offers a curt nod as I exit the vehicle and walk toward Java, my legs shaking. This is the first time I will see Jonathan since I left him three months ago. I don't want this meeting, but I have no other choice. I order a tea and sit close to the window, away from the few Friday afternoon frequenters populating this dying business. The steam rises as I silently pray this meeting goes well. Jonathan sounded hopeful when I called him, and I didn't crush that hope. This is my chance to get the money he owes me—the money I need for a new car. If he's going to give it over, he needs to think there's hope for *us*.

Can I balance my reserve while offering this falsehood? There's risk that comes with dangling this hope—I'm playing with fire, and eventually, I will have to make my intentions clear. My stomach churns as I gulp back the sickness creeping into my throat. *Don't think about Jonathan's family.* This has nothing to do with the accusations they made about me going after his money. He made a promise to pay for my car years ago. I need that money. And I deserve it too. I take a deep breath as I brush the hair away from my face and sit up straight. *Time to pay-up, pal.*

The door opens, and my insides lurch as the six-foot-one man with buzzed, brown hair who haunts my dreams walks into the coffee shop. His beady, black eyes scan the room until he finds me, and in a split second, his fierce stare has me cowering in the corner. I fight against my nausea. *Dear God.* He's thin…much thinner than ever before. All it took was three, short months, now his polo shirt and khaki pants hang loose about his frame. He brushes aside the barista and strides toward me instead. He takes a seat across from me, his austere presence swallowing me whole. I look down at my steaming mug of tea. *Get right to the point. Ask for the money and leave.* But trepidation has struck my vocal chords, refusing to let me speak.

"Hallie," Jonathan greets with sheer dominance and a tone of belittlement, his deep voice reverberating through my entire body as I become rigid in my chair. My dread rises. He already has me locked in his invisible handcuffs. I lick my lips, but he doesn't wait for me to respond. "So, your car broke down?" He doesn't expect an answer. I nod anyway. "Why did you call *me*?"

My stomach tightens as I focus on the inflection of my voice and the purpose of this meeting. I have to calculate my best response before things take a turn for the worse. "I didn't have anywhere else to turn." I clear my throat. I have to feed his ego, but I still fight valiantly against what I'm about to say. "You've always provided for me, and I knew I couldn't depend on anyone else for what I need." A grin spreads slowly across his face. There, I did it. This is the response he was hoping for. My heart screams against this dangerous game I've begun. His bloodshot stare, accompanied with the dark bags under his eyes, the weight loss, and his scruffy face, evidence his return to hard drugs. My eyes flutter closed for a moment. He's going to be difficult to reason with in this state—he always was, but the drugs make it worse.

"I thought you would go to your parents for help," he accuses.

Biting my bottom lip, I answer, "I tried, but they had . . . um." I falter. He doesn't have to know the whole truth. "Well, they had certain stipulations—" I trail off. His eyes narrow anyway—he's too smart. The dots have already connected.

"Stipulations about me?" I don't answer, but that seems to be enough confirmation for him. "I knew your parents wanted us together—that's it, isn't it? Is that why you haven't filed for a divorce yet?" I turn away and sip my tea as the tension pulsates between us. Unable to respond, the fury in his voice, ripening with every word, echoes in my throbbing head. He bangs his fist on the table as he grunts an obscene word. I flinch and recoil. Tea spills from my mug and stings my skin. But I brace myself for something more painful. My eyes fly open. I blink rapidly and survey the people who are staring at us. They meet my gaze for a second, then quickly busy themselves in response.

Turning back to Jonathan, I reply in a low, trembling voice, "I've asked you not to use that kind of language around me." Too late. I regret my appeal as the veins in his arms become prominent with the tightening of his fists. This is about the time he starts to lose control. My skin prickles from my fingertips to my toes. I set my mug down and get up from my chair. This is done. I've got to leave, to escape, to get out while I still can. I'm indifferent to the money. Only my safety matters. In a sudden flash, Jonathan grabs my arm and yanks me to my seat. I crumble under his physical demand as my eyes clench shut. I swipe at an escaped tear. *Don't do this—don't cave! You're strong, Hallie—get up and leave!* I turn slowly toward the window and look out. I can't do it. I can't fight against this terrifying man. Another tear falls.

Jonathan runs both his hands angrily across his bristled head, "Look—I'm sorry. I just get so angry when I hear that everyone wants us back together—everyone but you. What about your friends, like the people at church, do they know?" I shake my head. He throws both hands in the air as I brush away my tears, pinching my quivering lips together. "Just move back home and I'll buy you a car."

My heart sinks. I've lost control of this conversation. I should've known this would happen. I should've been prepared for his manipulation. Heat rises to my cheeks through thick swallows as my face turns away from the window. This conversation is through, he's not going to give me the money unless I move back in with him, and I can't even pretend to agree to that. Then, Jonathan reaches across the table and strokes my shaky hand. My breath catches in my throat. I can count on one hand the times he's touched me gently in our marriage.

"Just think about it, Hallie," he says, his voice a low whisper. I look down at our hands. *The ring!* Has he noticed it's missing? Will he ask where it is? Can I lie? My breathing quickens as I give his hand a light squeeze. He releases his grip, and I slide my arm back across the table.

Phew! Bullet dodged. My face didn't give it away...my weak smile must have been his focus. He throws his weight to one side, takes a check out of his pocket, lays it next to my hand, then leans back in his chair. Was that all it took? One weak smile that was meant to cover up an empty ring-finger? I run my tongue slowly across my lips and reach for the check. *It's all here!* My heart leaps. I got what I came here for and without the violence I had expected only moments earlier. I get up to leave, but he puts up a hand, making sure he doesn't touch me this time, but stopping me in my stride nonetheless. "Before you go," he adds, "I just want you to know that I'm trying to make some changes. I've been waiting for your divorce papers, so when you called, I figured that you must want to work things out between us." Out of nowhere, he rubs at his nose. The drugs must be having a greater impact than I would have guessed—he's always been sketchy and somewhat unpredictable with his emotions, but the drugs seem to be taking their toll.

"I've got to go," I say, my heart thumping hard in my chest as I pinch the check between my finger and thumb. He can still change his mind. His eyes flash with the same blind fury that frightens me to the core of my being. "I have to work, remember?" I add with a shaky squeak.

"I just," he rasps through bared teeth. Then, he takes a deep breath and starts over, "I just want you to know that I'm going to get things right. It's part of my New Year's resolution." Somehow, his words puncture my heart, like a balloon deflating in my chest. It will take more than a lifetime of resolutions for this man to get his life back on track.

"I think that's a good place to start, but don't do it for me," I reply. His fists clench. He is teetering on losing control again. "All I'm saying," I add quickly, "is that you should get things right for your own sake." My mind goes blank. I have nothing else to encourage him with, so I walk toward the door, pausing for a moment, then offering my gratitude. "Thanks for the check," I mutter just loud enough for him to hear. "Maybe it would be good to go back to church, Jonathan. Not Connect Church, but your old church. Your family attends that church, and maybe they can help you get on the right track." With that, I exit the building. My grip tightens around the check that I had to sacrifice so much for, but my shallow breathing deepens with every step I take toward my work. *Thank you, God.* I got out of there safely.

***

I pull up to Connect Church in my new Toyota Corolla . . . or at least new to me. The dark gray body of this dependable car caught my eye while I was car shopping with Ainsley yesterday, and thankfully, Jonathan's check paid for it. With a smile glued to my face, I gingerly shift my car into park. Is there anything that can dampen my spirits today? To my dismay, Rita's Jeep pulls into the next parking spot. *Maybe so.* I take a moment to gather my belongings, my head ducked partially out of sight. She gets out of the car, wearing an obscenely tight shirt, as her seven-year-old son immerges from the back seat and races toward the entrance. *Go on—follow your son.* But she doesn't, my new car has apparently caught her attention. I fiddle with my keys for a moment. She's not going to leave—she's seen me, and now she's waiting to chat. *Ugh.* I reach for my Bible, open my door and offer a curt greeting. "Well," Rita taunts, "someone got a new car."

"Yep, I bought it yesterday," I reply, squinting in the sunlight as I click the lock button on the key fob and begin walking to the church building. Can this conversation be over, now?

"There's no way you could pay for that car with your measly job." My eyes widen. That wasn't fair—accurate, but unfair, nevertheless. Without waiting for my response, she adds, "So, did the church help you pay for that car? I saw the way you were talking with Pastor Chip last week. Was that because he agreed to help pay for this if you sing on the worship team more?" At this, my mouth falls open. *Now she's gone too far.* She snorts and rolls her eyes. "It's no secret that Pastor Chip likes your singing voice the best, although I don't know *why.*"

"Honestly, Rita," I bark. "I don't think it's any of your business how I paid for my new car." My voice begins to shake, but I continue anyway. I'm *going* to speak my mind. "Just so you know—the church didn't pay a penny for that car. And I have just as good of a voice as anyone else on the worship team. I use my gifts for God, not to get help with my personal circumstances," I throw back at her. If Rita is privy to Chip's preferences, does that mean Becca could be too?

Rita laughs, her shrill pitch drawing the attention of the welcome committee standing in the entrance of the church building. "Wow, you sound pretty defensive. If it wasn't the church helping you pay for that car, maybe you've got a *secret lover* who has deep pockets," she retorts with a playful tone. And yet, there's nothing playful about any of this. "But like you said, it's none of my business." Her nose crinkles with a smirk as she saunters off to find her son. My eyes narrow. I take a deep breath. What did she mean about this *secret lover* nonsense? I'm over it—what do I care if Rita thinks the worst of me? She's not *God.* I shake my head and stitch a smile on my face as I walk toward the auditorium. This morning was going so well. I'm not going to let that unwarranted conversation bring me down.

I make my way to the front row. *Whew.* I'm glad I'm not serving on the worship team today. Take that, Rita. There *are* others that sing on the worship team. I'm not the best...or the worst. Becca and Ainsley are already standing on stage with their mics in hand, preparing to start worship as the clock ticks down on the large screens positioned on either side of the stage.

Chip grabs for his guitar and scans the auditorium. His eyes land on me for a brief moment, then his gaze flits to his wife and slides down to the mic she's holding. The lump in my throat returns. Is it me, or have I somehow gotten myself into something so much deeper than simply volunteering to sing on Team B?

Swoosh. Somebody brushes my side as the seat next to me fills. *That's weird—no one should be . . .* the air leaves my lungs. My eyes bulge. *This can't be!* Jonathan stares back. A reckless smile spreads slowly across his dangerous face while he reaches for my hand and locks it in a death grip. The worship music begins.

CHAPTER 11

My heart thuds hard against my chest as my eyes drop to our clasped hands. Jonathan isn't loosening his grip. His chiseled resolve tells it all; he's determined to hold tight until the end of the service. I shudder as the congregation rises to their feet to sing. Thrust into a past I've been running from, I follow the lead of my husband.

But he's not my husband anymore! He's not! I blink several times, desperate to pull away from his grip. I could just leave—he wouldn't follow me. I could get in my car and drive off, he doesn't even know what my new car looks like. *But wait.* What if he hid in the parking lot before the service to see what I'm driving? What if he feels entitled to know what I drive now because he paid for it? Jonathan's always been a schemer. He plays this sort of twisted mind game only to prove he's one step ahead...is he? The sickening smell of a Davidoff Yamasa cigar wafting from his clothes is unmistakable. I clutch my stomach. This distinct smell is so closely linked to Jonathan and all he's done. My fingers move in slow circles around the scar he left all those years ago.

Focus! I can't drag myself down that road. My body tightens as my ears prick up. The worship music can serve as a distraction—it has to, I force it to. I steal a quick glance at Jonathan who is fixated on the stage. He is silent beside me, unfamiliar with the song we all know so well. My eyes travel down our arms to my imprisoned hand and my knees grow weak. He has complete control over me—I'm trapped.

My head drops in defeat as the battle inside me rages. *This year, Hallie is going to be a fighter. I have to be a fighter. I must fight against this.* But I can't. If I walk out now, the congregation standing behind me would realize there was something wrong. Everyone would wonder why I left my husband's side during church, especially after all these years of sitting alone, wishing he would make church and God a priority. It wouldn't take long for people to start whispering about us. *Ugh!* Then there's Rita, somewhere back there, eager to tell everyone that I was the one who left. That I want a *divorce*. My feet shuffle slightly, as if I'm ready to make a dash for it, but my body refuses to move. Without knowing my story, without knowing what this monster has done to me, the church would judge me. This is where I'll remain . . . frozen by his side. I can't wriggle my clammy hand out of his grip. I can't make a scene. I'm stuck.

I pick my head up, take a long breath, and fix my stare on the worship team. In that instant, my distracted gaze meets Chip's, who continues singing and playing his guitar, despite his tightly knit brow. *Ahh!* If he keeps staring at me like that, the whole congregation will look over here. I cower as my eyes dart to Ainsley. Her gaze flits between me and the crowd. She rubs at her chin as our eyes lock for a moment, and the urge to burst into tears consumes me.

After what seems like an eternity, the worship finally comes to a close. Pastor Noah walks across the stage and asks us to take a seat as he begins to pray. I lower my body, but I'm unable to close my eyes. *Is Jonathan wearing new clothes?* He is. His golf polo fits his thinning frame, his slim, khaki pants are neatly ironed, and his loafers are un-scuffed. His appearance is designed to communicate his collective behavior, as if he has a handle on his life, his marriage, and his relationship with God. My stomach lurches. He has gone to great lengths to impress his audience, and it's going to work.

My eyes drift back to Pastor Noah as the singers exit the stage. Silently, Chip claims Ainsley's seat beside me as his wife stops, mid-stride, wrinkles her forehead, then slowly redirects in order to sit on the other side of him. Ainsley slides into the seat at the end of the row, leaning forward to look down at me, her eyes wide and nostrils flared, then strains to lower her head in prayer.

Pastor Noah ends his prayer and asks the congregation to turn to Luke, chapter eight. My window of opportunity presents itself as I tug my hand out of Jonathan's relaxing grasp and reach for my Bible placed at my feet. Jonathan falters, then clenches his empty fist. I lean back with my Bible in my lap, stealing a glimpse at Jonathan's face. My heart races at the sight of his clenched jaw, pulsing with anger, and a sickening dread threatens to engulf me. With a resolve that only God can give, I force myself to focus on the message that has begun.

Pastor Noah reads, "A farmer went out to sow his seed. As he was scattering the seed, some fell along the path; it was trampled on and the birds ate it up. Some fell on rocky ground, and when it came up, the plants withered because they had no moisture. Other seed fell among thorns, which grew up with it and choked the plants. Still other seed fell on good soil. It came up and yielded a crop, a hundred times more than was sown." He scans the congregation as he asks which example resonates with us most.

He reads on to explain Jesus's words, and I follow along starting at verse eleven, "This is the meaning of the parable: The seed is the word of God. Those along the path are the ones who hear, and then the devil comes and takes away the word from their hearts so that they may not believe and be saved. Those on the rocky ground are the ones who receive the word with joy when they hear it, but they have no root. They believe for a while, but in the time of testing they fall away. The seed that fell among thorns stands for those who hear, but as they go on their way they are choked by life's worries, riches and pleasures, and they do not mature. But the seed on good soil stands for those with a noble and good heart, who hear the word, retain it, and by persevering produce a crop."

As Pastor Noah comes to the end of the passage, I witness Jonathan nodding his head in agreement, aligning himself with the *good soil.* My mouth gapes. Is this just a part of his *show*, or is he delusional enough to believe this is true of him? I close my mouth and gulp—he's anything but *good soil.* And my heart screams this truth with every fiber of my being.

The sermon continues as I roll out my shoulders, aching with the tension brought on by my surroundings. Jonathan is continuing to play the part, nodding at all the right times to show he's engaged. Chip periodically looks over at me, his rigid form seems to question what *this* might mean about my presence on the worship team. Ainsley's knee is bouncing, and Becca's fingertips are drumming. The front row is pulsating like a brewing storm.

My breath catches short as Pastor Noah finally finishes his sermon with a prayer. *Thank God—it's over.* I begin to collect my belongings, avoiding all eye contact like the plague. *Yikes.* Becca's darting eyes meet mine. Her head tilts as she surveys the bodies on the row, then stops on her husband. Her face tightens. I can't watch this—Becca's piecing the puzzle together. But what puzzle does she think this is? I lean closer to Jonathan and whisper tightly, "What are you doing here?"

He glares down at me with a plastic grin in place, like a snake ready to strike. "I'm going to church, just like you said I should the other day."

My brain rattles. "I said you should go back to *your* church," I hiss. "I deliberately told you not to come here."

Jonathan's eyes narrow, "But this is *my* church. I haven't been to my family's church in a very long time. And besides, you want to see God's word *sown,* don't you? Well, that's only going to happen here."

My lips part in disbelief. He knows he shouldn't be here, but he's making his case and defending it with scripture. "Everything okay over here, Hallie?" Chip questions from behind.

No, everything is not okay! I rage, but before I can respond, Jonathan leans past me and asks with a domineering smile, "What's your name again, man?"

"Uh, it's Chip."

"Chip, thanks for checking on my wife, but everything's fine." Then facing me, he lowers his voice and adds, "I guess I'll see you here next week." Coldness permeates the room and settles in my chest as he stands and walks out.

Next week? He can't come back here next week. All I want to do is turn and scream *nooo* across the auditorium, but I stare vacantly at the blank, auditorium wall instead. Somewhere behind me, Chip clears his throat then says, "I hope this doesn't mean that he's back in your life, Hallie." I lean forward in my seat and plop my elbows on my knees while I shake my head, unable to offer a verbal reply. "Good, because I still need you to be the lead female singer for Team B."

My head swivels as if to shoot a warning glare at him. *Oh dear.* Becca leans into view, her posture stiffening as her tongue pokes against her cheek. Chip flinches and slowly closes his eyes. With his back still turned, he's reminded his wife is seated next to him. I gulp against my constricting throat and refocus my eyes on the floor. Becca's lowered voice asks Chip to speak with him in his office. As their footsteps echo in my head, Chip's presence is replaced with an embrace from my best friend. I lean in to her as she says, "What the heck's Jonathan doing here?" *Ugh!* Jonathan. The reality of *his* presence here slams to the forefront of my brain. Don't cry—he's not worth the tears. I can't keep giving into *him* like this anymore. This is what he wants me to do, to cave to his will, to sit back and let him terrify me, just as he did while we were married. I form my hands into a steeple. I may not have been able to fight against him during the service, but I'm going to fight now.

"He told me he would see me here again next week, so I guess he's trying to make this his church again." I spit. *How dare he.* "This is my church, not his. He made that clear all those times I begged him to come to the service with me. And now he shows up, unexpected, and makes me sit through the whole thing *as if I'm still his wife*." I turn my head, as if I've been slapped, then add, "Yes, legally I *am* still his wife, but his chance to win me back withered long ago. I knew it was over when he . . . when he—"

"I know," Ainsley interrupts. I bite my bottom lip. *Thanks, Ainsley.* I didn't want to have to finish that sentence. She shrugs a shoulder and leans back. Neither of us wants to think about what he's done to me over the years…what he did to me that one night when I knew it was over for good. Or how he terrorized me afterwards. When I left him, I thought I was finally free. So what if his check paid for my car? I'm not going to repay him by pretending that everything is okay while he sits beside me at church. I can't handle his presence, his walk . . . his smell.

A shadow off to our right grows heavier as both Ainsley and I shift in our seats, only to find Rita approaching. *Ugh!* Not again. Can this morning get any worse? "Ainsley, Hallie," Rita greets as she tosses her jet-black hair then yanks her tight shirt down over her wide hips, "What did you think of the sermon?"

My head rears. What an odd question, coming from her. Ainsley cocks her head to the side, "It was good," she draws out. Is that the end to this encounter? Rita stands before us, crossing her arms. I guess not. Ainsley clears her throat, "And what about you?"

"Oh, I thought it was good, too," Rita responds. The piece of gum in her mouth doesn't stand a chance as she chomps harder and harder, her eyes flashing from Ainsley to me. "But I really enjoyed his Christmas series . . . you remember, Ainsley?"

Ainsley shifts in her seat, "Sure, that was a good series." Her voice has raised at least two octaves. "You're talking about the one just this past year?"

"Yeah, you remember—the one that started right after that Christmas party I went to with Andrew." *Chomp-chomp.* Rita raises an eyebrow, "You remember Andrew, don't you, Hallie? He went to college with you guys, right?" Rita leans her head forward as her eyes bare down on me. *Oh no!* Andrew's text about getting coffee. This is what she's after. But I never responded to him, nor would I . . . regardless of my marital status. I pick up my chin and nod with a tight smile.

Rita looms over me, then smirks. "Andrew and I are kinda hot and cold, but he always comes back around." What's her deal? If she knows he texted me months ago, then she should know I didn't respond. She looks to Ainsley with an ugly twist of her mouth, "Remember, I told you all about us at the Christmas party? How we date, on and off, and then you told me—" she starts to point at me with her long, pink fingernail.

"Oh yeah," Ainsley interrupts. Her cheeks flush as she waves a flighty hand, "I'm sure if you're off now, you'll be back on in no time. I mean, it's Andrew—he's always been like that. Even when we were in college." Her hollow laugh is followed with a flutter of her eyes. "Besides, we are all a little off beat at times, right Hallie? I mean, loneliness can do that." She nudges me with her elbow. Why is she drawing the attention back on me?

"Well, Hallie doesn't seem too lonely," Rita interjects with a sneer. My mouth parts. *You gotta be kidding me.* But my moment to defend myself for the second time this morning passes as she hastily adds, "Anyway, I have to get my son from the back. Kids' church will be closing soon. Guess I'll see y'all later."

Deafening silence sits between me and Ainsley, then she finally says, "That was super weird." I nod. *Yeah, it was.* Ainsley scans the vacating room. Apart from a group laughing in the back, and Pastor Noah and his wife chatting with an elderly man on the other side of the room, we are alone. "I should really go get Miles," she says. Ainsley stands, sighs, walks down the aisle, then skids to a stop. "Oh—and about Jonathan. Are you going to be okay?"

"Yeah, I'll be fine," I wave her on. "I just needed to vent." But I don't need to vent. I need to find a solution. I cannot afford a repeat of this morning—my nerves can't take it—it's enough that I'm always looking over my shoulder for him.

As Ainsley speeds toward the foyer, my eyes cloud in her wake. I shake my head. I just need to get out of here. Checking my surroundings, I count off the items in my arms. I've got everything—time to go. But the slam of a door off to my left startles me. Becca storms from Chip's office. Her head is down as she rushes up the aisle. Hesitating, I avert my gaze. Nope—no more drama for today . . . or any day, for that matter.

I take a deep, steadying breath against the brick forming in my stomach. Chip exits his office. His drooping eyes find me in no time. "Hallie, I'm glad you're still here." He glances back at his office with pursed lips, then forces a smile and lifts his shoulders as he meanders over and settles into the seat next to me. "I'm sorry if I interfered between you and Jonathan today, it's just that when I saw him arrive this morning, I—" and his voice trails off.

"No, it's fine, it was thoughtful of you to sit with me today," I reply, my toes wiggling inside of my shoes.

"Does that mean you're going to work things out in your marriage?"

"*Oh, no!*" I spit. "No, no—he just, uh, misunderstood a conversation we had earlier this week." Chip nods. "He said he'll be back next week, and I was too shaken to tell him not to return." A groan gurgles in the back of my throat as I add, "I've already made it clear he's not allowed to come here, but I don't know if he'll listen to me." I have to do something about the farewell promise he made to me today. *But what?* "Anyway, I should probably be going," I say as I stand with my things and survey the room. The auditorium is now completely empty.

"Actually," Chip says, "I, uh—" he runs a hand down his long beard as his eyes flit toward the auditorium doors, "I was hoping you would give me an answer about serving on Team B. I know I've been getting on you about this, but I really feel like this church could grow if you were singing more on stage, and if some people are removed from the worship team."

My mouth parts. After that episode with his wife, how does he have the nerve to ask me this now? The pit in my stomach flips. "Honestly," I start, "it seems like Becca was really upset with the news you shared just a few moments ago. I think this really needs to be more of a conversation between you and her rather than you and me."

Chip rolls his head to one side. "Listen, Hallie. I'm the worship leader, and I can deal with people who just aren't making the cut anymore. My wife will get over it." He pinches his lips together, then adds, "Yes, she wasn't all that thrilled that I talked to you about this change before I talked to her, but she will see my reasoning for it in the end, even if it might take a while for her to come around to it."

"Is she upset with me?" I blink slowly. *Don't say what I think you're about to say.*

"Ah, well," he clears his throat and studies his feet. "She's not happy, but she's talking out of pain. I know she doesn't *really* hate you, she just needs to get over this change and find another way to serve in the church."

The room begins to spin. *I never asked for this.* And now, I have to deal with another woman in the church who doesn't like me. "You should keep Becca. She's not a bad singer, and I should have never entertained this idea." I bite my bottom lip, and add, "Despite my circumstances, I don't want anyone else to deal with marital problems. I know how important it is to have a good marriage, and with the way Becca just stormed out of here, I think your focus should be on her, not on getting me to sing on stage more."

"Please, Hallie—"

I close my eyes and lift my eyebrows. "Chip, I'm not going to sing on Team B, especially with how Becca's feeling about this. My answer is no." Without another word, I race out of the auditorium to my car, desperate to leave this dreadful morning behind. I slam my car door shut and speed out of the parking lot. How can I come back here next week?

CHAPTER 12

B*uzz!* My eyes fly open, and I blink against the morning light. I lean over and hit snooze. Work can wait, especially on such little sleep. I pull the covers closer to my chin. *Just go back to sleep. Don't think about yesterday's church service.* Groaning, I roll into my pillow and pull the covers over my head. My dreams were tainted with visions of Jonathan searching all over town for me while Becca and Rita blame me for all the church's problems.

The jumbled scenes from my nightmares skirt my mind as I rub at my eyes. What would be the worst that could happen if I refuse to get ready for work? Am I even able to lift myself out of bed? The alarm goes off again. That's it . . . I'm calling in sick. I can't face work today, and I know Danny would gladly take on my clients for me. I pick up my cell and punch in the number. *Ugh.* I bet Rita will probably be at the gym today, too. All the more reason to call in sick—I don't want to face anyone who contributed to yesterday's experience.

Tossing aside my phone on the crumpled comforter, the lie I told Jim moments earlier appears to be inching toward truth as I try to massage away the massive headache building behind my eyes. I sink under my warm comforter. This is what I need. I can just sleep my Monday blues away. But my phone rings. Is it Jim calling me back? Did he change his mind? I grab for my phone. *Hmmm.* Unknown number.

"Hello?" I question, my voice still a little groggy.

"Hi Hallie, it's Noah Herald here." I spring to an upright position, grabbing at the sheets. *That's stupid.* It's not like he can see all this skin exposed from my scanty pajama top.

"Hi Pastor Noah," I greet, my pitch rising immediately. "How are you?"

Pastor Noah clears his throat, "Well, I'm actually calling because I'm a little concerned." In the pause that follows, a lump forms in my throat. What now? I wait for him to divulge details. I didn't tell anyone what had happened with Becca yesterday at church, not even Ainsley. I took the rest of the day to process it and found that I still couldn't come up with an immediate solution to smooth things over with Becca, so I decided to sleep on it. "I received a phone call this morning from a disgruntled church member," Pastor Noah continues. "This particular individual didn't feel like they could attend our church anymore because they didn't think it was right for you to serve on the worship team when you're having an affair."

My body goes completely still. *What's this about?* I stumble over my words. "An affair?" I squeak, "But I'm not having an affair. I . . . I don't understand."

"Listen, it's not my place to meddle in people's lives like this," he starts. "And you should know that I'm not calling to kick you off the worship team, but I am concerned about the claims that this church member has made. This person has a son who is *easily influenced*—their words, not mine—and they say that your presence on stage is sending a message to the congregation that we don't practice what we preach at Connect Church."

Rita. He doesn't have to say anything more. She made the call. Maybe Andrew is dropping her in hopes of pursuing something with me, even if I never texted him back. Is this her way of retaliating? "It's not true, Pastor Noah," I begin, "I don't know what was said, but I can tell you that I'm not having an affair." The lump in my throat makes it difficult to speak. Can he connect the dots by himself? *No.* I have to tell him about my pending divorce. "I, um—" I swallow against what feels like a bowling ball, but I continue, "I should probably come to the church and talk to you in person about what's been going on these past few months."

"Okay, that's fine," he replies. "Will today work?"

"Yes." A groan almost escapes. I run my tongue across my lips. Do I tell him about what happened between Chip and Becca too? Chip will be at the church when we meet. "Oh—ah . . . Pastor Noah," I clear my throat. "Can we meet while no one else is at the church?"

Pastor Noah hesitates, then says, "Well, I always ask my wife to stay in the building while I'm meeting with a woman. She'll work in the main office while we talk."

"That's not a problem."

"Why don't you come in at six?" he suggests. "Office hours end at five today, so that should give you plenty of time for the building to empty before we meet."

We agree, and I offer an awkward good-bye. Well, that's just great. Rita's talking again, and now it's forcing me to share all the prickly details of my messed-up life. I lay my phone beside me and look up at the ceiling. *Hmmm.* Perhaps this isn't the worst thing that could happen. I will plead my case against the ugly rumors, share the pressure I've been getting from Chip and how that could affect relationships on the worship team, and hopefully get some help with Jonathan's presence at church. Although there's a dark cloud hanging over me, maybe I can view this meeting as the silver lining. But for now, I need to take something for my slamming headache.

* * *

As I pull up to the church building, I begin to pulse with tremors. I have spent the entire day rehearsing what I should tell Pastor Noah. It won't take much to explain away the whole *Andrew* thing. But as the pastor of my church, he needs to know about Chip's request and how that has placed a wedge between me and his wife. And then there's the whole Jonathan thing. I should tell him what happened in our marriage. That's what it will take to understand why I've left that monster . . . and why I never want to see him again, especially not at *my* church. Can I handle all of this? My hands shake. What about that night? Should I tell Pastor Noah about *that*? My face starts to tingle. I shake my head, over and over, my breath hitching in my chest. I was barely able to share what happened with my brother and Ainsley, and they are the two closest friends I have in the whole world. How do I tell it now . . . to my *pastor*?

With my hand paused on the car door handle, I scan the parking lot one last time, checking for any vehicles other than Pastor Noah's. The coast is clear, it's just me and the Heralds. I want to run and hide. *Now would be the time.* But I will my legs to carry me inside the building. This is what I have to do . . . the new Hallie is a fighter.

I walk past the main office. Mrs. Herald is working away, her back to the door, so I don't bother with a greeting. I cross the hall and approach Pastor Noah's office. *Well, here goes nothing.* "Hey—come on in, Hallie." I smile through gritted teeth and walk through the door as Pastor Noah jumps from his office chair and rushes over to shake my hand. "Thanks for meeting with me," Pastor Noah says as he partially closes the door, all the while motioning with an open hand for me to sit in the black leather chair. He moves to the other side of the coffee table and settles in the matching loveseat positioned across from me in his spacious office lined with books. This nicely decorated office, spotted with pictures of the Herald family, is not a familiar space. I take a steadying breath. The confines of these four walls are incredibly daunting.

"Yeah, and thank you for agreeing to this meeting," I reply, my voice jagged.

"I need to start this meeting by reiterating that I am not here to penalize you, kick you off the worship team, or dig deep into your personal affairs." He shifts uncomfortably. Did he have to use *that* kind of language? His ears turn pink. "What I mean is, I want to offer pastoral guidance with whatever you're going through, but I'm not one to believe everything that's brought to my attention, and I'm not going to entertain the gossip that gets passed along to me, which is why I went directly to you after receiving that phone call this morning." I blink several times. *Are we going to get right into it?* "You suggested there are some things I should know, and I'm here to help you through whatever it is you're facing."

My pulse skyrockets as I prepare to share my rehearsed response. It's been a long time coming, but it's time to reveal my secrets. "I've left my husband," all I can manage is one short, quivering breath. "I guess I should start from the beginning, that way it will all make sense to you." He nods, his brow pulling tight, like a thread drawing his wrinkles together. *It's all or nothing.* "Ainsley introduced me to Jonathan shortly after we graduated from community college. She was my best friend and she had just begun her relationship with Will. Maybe she felt guilty over all the time she was spending with Will instead of me, I don't know, but she pursued a couple of Will's connections in order to set me up on a double date with Jonathan. The date went well, and it led to further dates. Before I knew it, I was in a relationship with a man who was older than me, treated me well, and had a great reputation in his community. He'd been attending his family's church, but since Ainsley, Will, and I were attending this church, he decided to go here with us instead. As you know, he began serving on the worship team. He's a talented bass player, and I really do think he appreciated this church back then."

I sigh, then whisper, "It was the only happy time in our whole relationship." Shaking my head, I re-cross my legs and lift my chest. "He proposed, I accepted, and we started planning our wedding. He didn't want to waste time, and Ainsley had just gotten married to Will, so I was okay with how fast things were moving, even if I was pretty young. But—" my mouth hangs open for a second. "The closer we got to the wedding, the angrier he became with some of the wedding details I was piecing together. I thought it was just the stress of planning a wedding in a short period of time. We were married within the year, and it didn't take me long to realize the mistake I had made. Once we were married, I discovered his anger was the truest part of his nature."

Pastor Noah's attentive gaze and respectful nod encourages me to continue. "We were on our honeymoon, and the wedding stress was behind us, so I figured his pre-wedding anger was behind us, too. But he became reactive to things that never bothered him while we were dating. Midway through our honeymoon, he became irrationally moody and explosive over things like my clothes, or my shyness . . . even the fact that I didn't have a drink with him at dinner. He knew all of that about me before we were married, but when I tried to find an answer to his irrational behavior, he would verbally lash out."

I gulp. I had cried myself to sleep that night. We only made it halfway through our honeymoon before I shed tears. It was the first of many tear-filled nights to come. "He told me I was boring. He yelled at me for a while, then got even more angry that I didn't yell back. The next day, he told me that marrying me was the worst decision he had ever made." Heat climbs up my neck as I add, "He looked at me as if he couldn't bear how revolting I was, and then he didn't speak to me the rest of the night."

My pastor's knowing nod and sad eyes testify to the bitter reality that he has heard stories like this before. "I guess the game was over, he *got the girl*, and he was stuck with me." My knuckles go white as I clasp my hands together. "Yelling became a way of life after that. It was like I couldn't do anything right. When I bought the groceries, it was the wrong brand, or I forgot something. When I made his food, it was never good enough. When I cleaned the house, it wasn't to his satisfaction. And when he tore me down, he would become furious that I didn't defend myself. But I didn't see the point—he'd made up his mind about me, and I wasn't going to change it."

My breath quickens, my mind teetering on the brink of a breakdown. Is this enough information for Pastor Noah to know why I left *him*? It can't be . . . not when there's so much more. "About a year into the marriage, I felt like I needed to get away. Ainsley and I had been going on brief, weekend getaways, here and there. Not too far, but far enough to feel like I could breathe a little. Miles was just old enough to be left behind, so we decided to fly to Key West for a week." I grimace. "Jonathan seemed like he was fine with the idea of the trip, but when I returned, his anger had reached a new level. That was the first time he hit me." The flash igniting Pastor Noah's eyes sends me backtracking, "He didn't hit me that often, and usually not hard enough to leave a mark. It wasn't that bad." I clench my teeth. I've done it again. Why do I do that, why do I still feel like I need to defend him? *I'm a fighter.* I don't have to defend him. He was wrong for what he did. Enough is enough, Pastor Noah has to know how evil Jonathan really is. I push forward. The fear that became my constant companion confirmed the mark he had left on my heart that night—the same fear that's causing the core of my whole being to shudder right now. "I, uh . . . I couldn't completely blame him because, not too long after, I realized he had been using some serious drugs. He became irrational. He started selling drugs at work, and with his position in the company, I knew he wasn't going to get fired. He'd been grandfathered in, and he was protected by his family's reputation. I asked him to stop, but he didn't respect me. He didn't even really love me. He made some promises, but it became clear that those promises were made because he wanted me to start having children." I lower my head. "By then, I knew I couldn't have children with that man. I couldn't bring children into that house."

I chew on my bottom lip. Pastor Noah doesn't need to know about the live feeds he was watching—how he enjoyed watching children being abused. He only wanted children so that he could establish more control—to appear to be that perfect family in the community. He wanted kids just to feed his power-hungry ego. I lift my head as my internal shaking takes control of my hands, "Eventually, I decided to take secretive precautions to make sure I wouldn't get pregnant. And Jonathan found the bill from the doctor." I squeeze my eyes shut, bile creeping into my throat. "He was smoking his favorite cigar," I shudder. "I noticed a paper in his hand, and when I approached him to see what he was holding, he yanked up my shirt and singed a ring onto my stomach, all the while yelling that if I didn't want to have kids with him, he would make sure I could never have kids." Pastor Noah's shoulders fall, but I don't give him the chance to respond as I continue, "You see, he would always rant that it was time I became a stay-at-home *mom*. I told him that I liked working. He would object, he wanted me at home—cooking, cleaning, and bearing his children. What women *were meant to do.* He told me we would keep having children until we had a boy to carry on the family name. After that night when he burned me, he never brought up kids again. But it's not like I was off the hook. He still made sure I was doing the all the chores…and to his standards too, like a *good woman* should."

I falter for a moment. *Ohh, those chores.* They were always there… waiting for me. My stomach flips. "One night," I close my dry mouth and try to swallow, "I came in from a late shift. Jonathan was high, and just as I laid down to go to sleep, he told me to fold the laundry in the dryer before it got too wrinkled. I was half asleep when I told him I would do it in the morning. Before I knew it, he had yanked me out of bed and shoved me into the doorframe. He said I would do it when he told me to do it." My heart twists from the agonizing pain of the memory. "I was tired of him using the drugs as an excuse for his behavior. I kept begging him to get off them, and he kept making empty promises. He told me he had stopped at several points in our marriage, but his unreasonable behavior suggested otherwise. One night, he left his phone on his bedside table while he was taking a shower. It buzzed, so I leaned over and saw a text from his ex-girlfriend on the lock screen. When I asked him about it, he freaked out. He threw me against the wall and told me that I should never snoop around on his phone. I started crying. It didn't make sense, so I asked if he was having an affair. He said I was ridiculous. His flimsy excuse was that Jessica was only contacting him because he was her dealer. He probably was her dealer, but if it was just that, then why did he freak out? I already knew he was dealing." I lightly shrug one shoulder and cast my eyes downward. "I didn't believe him about the affair, but I didn't have any proof, and I knew I couldn't push the issue and risk facing his wrath."

The pang of pure anguish punishes my insides as the magnitude of what's approaching hits me square in the chest. The air has left the room—it's left my lungs. *Is this enough for him to understand? Do I need to tell him about that night?* The old me is clawing at my resolve—I've already told him about Jessica—isn't that enough? My quivering state from what I know I need to share next charges me so violently that the room begins to spin. And as I ready myself to tell my pastor about the worst night of my life, the night I knew my marriage was over for good, the four walls of this office fade away, and it's as if I am reliving it all over again.

The hot air of the late-August evening has me fanning my neck, pulling the covers off. Should I venture downstairs to crank up the air conditioning? But I hear Jonathan ranting in the living room about something that's upset him on the TV. Better not risk it—I'll stay in bed, where it's safe, even if it is stifling hot. A glass shatters. I put my book down. What was that? Has Jonathan broken something? Must have, but was it on purpose? He slurs a slew of cuss words on his way to the refrigerator. My heart falls. He has had more than enough to drink. Ugh—*another one of those nights. I sigh heavily. He can get as drunk as he wants, I don't have it in me to plead with him tonight. Besides, the drugs were the real problem, and it seems like he's stopped using. Maybe it was my accusations about Jessica from a few months back when he almost got caught that forced him to stop. Yeah—that must be it. But why the heavy drinking? I lean forward in bed, listening fixedly. Silence. Maybe he'll just pass out on the couch, leaving me alone to read my book until I fall asleep.*

Loud thuds echo up the staircase marking Jonathan's clamber to the bedroom. Thump. *Pause.* Thunk-thunk. *Pause. He is far more drunk than I guessed. Squeezing my eyes closed, I repress my threatening tears. This is my life now, cowering in bed as my substance-abusing husband finds ways to terrify me. My eyes fly open as Jonathan slumps against the hallway wall, glowering at me through the open doorway with immense hatred radiating from his clouded glare. He heaves.* Oh-no! *He's going to be sick. He stumbles toward me, and I jump out of bed to guide him to our bathroom. If I'm going to get a good night's sleep, I can't spend the next hour washing vomit out of our sheets.*

"Don't touch me!" he slurs, shoving me to the side just as he leans over the toilet. My arm aches from the jab, but I wait by the sink in case he needs my help. His large frame straightens when he's finally done, as if his uneasy stomach has strengthened his willpower. He hates being weak, even if only for a moment. He shoots me a death stare while making his way toward me, and I recoil. The tension in the bathroom thickens. His face darkens…he's furious with my presence—watching him get sick, observing his momentary malaise. He reaches past me and turns on the faucet. Our eyes meet. The black depths of his pupils pulse. He's reached a new level tonight. It's like he's replaced the contempt he felt from his weakness with rage for mine.

As he rinses his mouth out, I hesitate beside him. I've got to placate his fury. I gently place a hand on his shoulder. In that instant, he snaps—straightening with such speed and determination that I'm blinded by his movements. He turns off the tap and grabs my wrist all in the same second. Slamming my arm into the wall and pinning me there, he leans in to kiss me. Through the stinging pain, I turn my head and stitch my eyes closed. I can't do this. His heavy breathing remains on my neck for several excruciating seconds. The putrid smell of alcohol sours my stomach. He stays there . . . heavy breaths, one after another. My body begins to wrack as I wait for whatever will come next. I have denied his kiss. There's no question now . . . I will pay for it.

"Jessica," he whispers dangerously in my ear, and my eyes fly open. "I will have you," he grunts menacingly, and in one swift move, his hands are around my throat.

I scream, but a silent screech is all I can force. His grip tightens as he rips me from the wall. I flail. Grab something . . . anything! *My fingertips skim the ceramic sink, but his strength is too much as he wrestles me out of the bathroom, smashing me into the door as it crashes against the wall. I push against him, fighting him as he thrusts me down on the bed, my eyes bulging with my constricting airway. He's going to kill me. His focused eyes that were blurry only minutes before lock with mine, and he smiles. He likes it.*

His hands leave my throat and I inhale sharply, drinking in the air like my life depends on it. But he begins to tear at my nightgown. "No . . . no!" *I gasp, through a constricted throat. He doesn't stop. I thrash away from his readying body.* Oh gosh—this can't be happening. *He hits me across the face. Hard. Harder than he's ever hit me before, and I go dizzy for a moment. A moment is all he needs. He's on top of me, forcing himself on me. I blink away the stars and push back at his massive body. This fight is exactly what he wanted, I can see it in his eyes, right before he hits me. Again. Then again.*

I have to escape! With each blow to my face, the evil of his excitement escalates, but it's not enough for him. His hands return to my aching throat. He will kill me if I don't get away…now. My eyesight fogs, stinging from sweat or blood, I'm not sure. I fumble down the headboard. There's got to be something that will help. My fingers meet the cold, iron lamp on the bedside table. With a burst of strength, I twist for the lamp and bring it down on Jonathan's head with all my might. The crash accompanies his release of my neck, and I break free as he crumples from the blow. Hastily gathering myself, I run into the hall just as my legs give out. I fall in a heap as I cough violently. The sound of glass breaking from the bedroom as the lamp shatters against the wall peaks my adrenaline, forcing me to jump up and race down the hall. His pounding footsteps race after me. I turn just in time to slam the bathroom door in his face. I fumble, then secure the lock just as he rattles the knob. He releases the most terrifying roar, like an animal raging in a fight to the death. The guttural sound of defeat, partnered with his persistent pounding against the door, sends me stumbling back. He could get in if he wanted. Is he really trying to kill me, or did he get lost in a moment of living out his darkest fantasies? I collapse on the bathroom floor, finally letting my husband's pure malice sink in. My sobbing turns to heaving as I reach for the toilet. His pounding stops, perhaps at the sound of my vomiting. Maybe he's sobering up, or maybe he's snapped out of the darkness. Does he know that he almost killed his wife? Whatever his reasons, he leaves me here, curled up in a ball on the cold bathroom floor. My tears continue to flow, mixing with the blood trickling down my head and collecting in pink droplets on the tiles beneath me. This is where I lay the rest of the night. This is when I know my marriage is over. I have to get out.

The walls of the office come back into focus, and I sit there with my pastor as silence fills the room. Pastor Noah rises from the loveseat and starts pacing. In the quiet that prevails, I sob uncontrollably. "How could . . . I just—" Pastor Noah stutters.

While I regain my composure, Pastor Noah hands me a Kleenex box and returns to his seat with unrest, then I quietly fumble to break the silence, "My plan to leave him began not long after that. I wanted to get out as soon as possible, but I needed to stash away money here and there without him noticing." I dab at my damp cheeks as my pulse begins to slow a little. "I needed help leaving, so although it took almost a month, I got up the courage to tell my brother and Ainsley. My brother decided to come as soon as he could, so he booked a flight for October. I kept out of Jonathan's way, doing what I needed to do until my brother arrived. Jonathan and I never talked about that night, but I knew it was only a matter of time before he would do it all again." I crumple the damp Kleenex in my hand. The worst is over now that I've shared what happened that night. It's all up-hill from here. I raise my chest and swipe at a stray tear. "I don't have proof that he was ever having an affair, so my biblical grounds for this divorce may seem unfounded, but I know I can't go back into that marriage. He made a lot of promises that he was going to change, but he never kept those promises. I know him too well—he isn't going to change. The evil look on his face that night will haunt me forever. The marriage is over for good. It took all the strength I had in me to leave him, and I will never go back."

Pastor Noah leans in, opens his mouth, pauses, then says, "Thank you for sharing, Hallie. I know how difficult that was for you." He sighs deeply. "You are so strong, stronger than you know. God's going to use your past to grow you in ways you didn't think possible, and I hope you can trust him for that."

Another tear slides down my face as I reply, "You know, not long into the marriage, I started praying that things would change. I prayed that Jonathan would realize how desperately he needed God—I prayed that God would save me. I've only been a Christian for a little under five years, but I know God is capable of the most beautiful miracles." I take a couple short breaths, then add, "I thought God would change Jonathan's heart, and maybe he still will, but I eventually realized that this change I was desperate for would only come if I left him. If I started over. And that's what I'm doing now. My parents are ashamed of me and my failed marriage. They've requested that I give it a year before I file for a divorce, and I'm going to honor that request. Honestly, they don't know everything that happened to me, and I don't think I have it in me to tell them." It's worth keeping the secret. My parents wouldn't believe me even if I did tell them. I press my tongue hard against the roof of my mouth. They will never know. I can't handle being re-victimized by their unwillingness to believe. I pinch my lips together, then add, "But for now, I just need to be rid of *him* for good."

Pastor Noah nods, rubs his face in his hands, shifts in his seat, then takes a deep breath to say, "I understand, Hallie. And I want to thank you for coming in here and telling me this when I know how hard that was for you."

I shift in my seat. "Well, I wanted to tell you all of this because I need your help," I squeeze the tissue balled up in my hand. "Jonathan showed up here yesterday morning. I've been keeping this whole thing quiet because I don't want people knowing about the divorce, but Jonathan has used my silence to his advantage, and he made me sit with him through the service knowing that I wouldn't make a scene." I clench my jaw. What I'm about to say jabs at my heart. But enough is enough. "I don't care anymore if people know about the divorce—I'm not sitting through another service with that . . . that *man*. I need your help to persuade him not to come back next week. I've told him not to, but he doesn't care what I say. I begged him to go to church for years—now he is using church just to get to me."

Pastor Noah glances down at his shoes, shakes his head, then looks back up at me. "I'm sorry you had to endure that, I didn't know that you had left him, and I can only imagine how difficult it was to see him again in church."

I tilt my head slowly. "I know that someone told you about an affair, and I think I know who did, but I'm not having an affair—I think she was just confused at seeing me with Jonathan at the service yesterday." I pause, "And maybe she's a little jealous too regarding a text sent to me that was really misleading—a text I never responded to."

Pastor Noah shakes a hand lightly at me, then says, "I don't need to know the details, Hallie. I don't know how reliable this woman's claims are, but I'm glad she made them simply because it led you here to share with me about your marriage. Does anyone else in the congregation know about your upcoming divorce?"

Oh gosh! Chip. I got so caught up in explaining everything that happened between Jonathan and me that I almost forgot about the whole thing with him and Becca. Butterflies fill my stomach as I clear my throat, "Ainsley knows, and she felt like I should tell a man in case anything serious happened." I quickly add, "And I'm confident nothing serious will happen—Jonathan's always been very conscious of his reputation, so I know he won't ever do anything in public." My gaze flits to the door, "But I did tell Pastor Chip, and I think he saw it as an opportunity for me to serve more on the worship team." My skin crawls with a tightness that reaches across my shoulders as heat courses through my veins. "But as it seems, he was wanting me to replace Becca, and that may have caused a problem, especially since Becca found out that was his plan when she overheard our conversation about it yesterday morning." My knee begins to bounce, "I didn't want to let Pastor Chip down, but I also didn't want Becca to feel badly about her singing. I just felt like I was stuck in the middle of it all when I should have just declined Chip's request and avoided the drama." My posture dips, "After yesterday, I left here wondering how I could come back next week if my safety net at Connect Church is gone. I don't feel like I can trust Chip, the women at church hate me, and I'm scared of Jonathan."

My proclamation hangs in the air for a few awkward moments while Pastor Noah curls his lips. *Ugh!* I would hate to be him right now, processing all I have just shared with him, trying to come up with a solution that will placate the masses. Finally, he nods his head and answers in a low voice, "I'm sorry that Pastor Chip put you in an awkward position. He, uh—he's confessed to some issues he's had with the worship team, and in turn, it seems like those issues are bleeding into his marriage. I should probably have a talk with him and Becca to make sure that they're working out their differences in a healthy manner."

Now look what I've done. My presence has created a bigger issue than just the problems with the worship team. How did I get myself caught up in such a mess? My chin starts to quiver. "I didn't mean to come here and get Pastor Chip in trouble. It's just, when Becca stormed out of here yesterday, I really felt like she was holding all this against me, and I never intended to get stuck in the middle of it. I told Pastor Chip that I wasn't going to sing on Team B . . . that I wasn't going to replace Becca on the stage. And I—"

Pastor Noah throws up a pulsing hand to stop me, "This is not your fault, Hallie. There are some other things that have contributed to this problem. I am just telling you this so you know you can come back to church next week without feeling like you need to explain yourself—to Becca or to Pastor Chip."

I take a few steadying breaths. Okay—so maybe *that* situation isn't as bad as it seems. "And what about Jonathan?"

Pastor Noah strokes his cleft chin and blinks slowly, "Unfortunately, Hallie, I cannot tell him to stop coming to church. We keep our doors open for those who want to draw closer to God. We extend grace, even in the darkest of situations. If Jonathan wants to repent of his behavior and develop his relationship with Jesus, then we want to help him. We realize how difficult it may be for you to see him week after week, but we can't close our doors to those who need Christ—if that were the case, no one would be allowed into our church. We all have sin in our life. We all need Jesus. I can't deny someone the opportunity to attend church unless something *happens* at church."

Well, what did I expect? He makes complete sense, and I respect his willingness to extend grace. This is what Christ does, time and time again—for everyone, no matter their past. Pastor Noah has said what he needed to say. But what do I do about Jonathan? He can put on a show with the best of 'em. I do want what's best for him. And wouldn't it be best if he were developing his relationship with God? That's his only hope for recovery. But what about the controlling clutch of his hand in church yesterday morning? That's confirmation he's attending church just to re-establish authority in my life. "I get it," I say with a begrudging shrug, "but I don't want him sitting beside me at church."

"That's fair," Pastor Noah says. "I'll have a talk with him next week. And if anything happens—anything serious, anything at all—I will tell him he cannot return to this church."

"Thanks," I mutter. But nothing will happen. He's playing his cards right. Sure, I've given up caring who becomes privy to our upcoming divorce. But that won't matter. He will work hard to convince the congregation that he's a changed man and that he deserves to have his wife back. There's nothing that can be done, I just have to deal with it. *Hmph.* I stand to leave.

"Just one last thing I need to address," Pastor Noah adds, "please don't share anything about Pastor Chip and Becca. I would appreciate if this information remains between us, even if the worship team does catch wind of some changes that Pastor Chip would like to make."

"Absolutely," I respond. Pastor Noah extends a gentle handshake, but his tired eyes say much more. As Pastor Noah says good-bye, he assures me that he will have a talk with the *disgruntled church member* about the rumors of my *alleged affair.* Whatever good that will do. Rita's a gossiper, and she may not get her way with the pastor, but she's a fighter, herself. If she went to the trouble to *tattle* on me to our pastor, then she will try to persuade others in the church that her tall-tale is true. *Ahh*—who cares? The reality of my life is complicated enough. I can't start worrying about her next rumor . . . at least not until it spreads.

Pastor Noah goes to close the door behind me, then swings it open again. "Oh, Hallie," he stays poised in the doorway, "This Sunday, I'll be announcing my upcoming sabbatical, so if you want to meet to talk more about this—about anything—let's plan on it soon." I open my mouth to decline his offer, but he stops me with the wave of his hand. "You don't have to decide if you want to now. Pray about it. It may be good to talk to someone about everything that has taken place during your marriage." I close my lips and offer a soft smile with a nod. *Hmm.* Today was rough, but now he has a better idea of my reality…who knows, maybe it would be good to take him up on that offer to talk more.

CHAPTER 13

I turn up the heat in my car as warm air blasts from the vents. *Brrr.* I hold one hand over the vents while my other stays glued to the steering wheel. What a pleasant contrast to the below freezing temperature and February winds outside. I navigate down some unfamiliar roads on this side of town as I follow the GPS to Noah Herald's home. When I didn't see Chip and Becca at church this past Sunday, I approached Pastor Noah to ask about their absence. He said they were taking a break to think over some things. It's none of my business really, so I turned the conversation back on me. Before long, I had booked a mid-week appointment with him, just to work through a few things I've been dwelling on since our meeting two weeks ago. The GPS keeps me on track as I cast a few side glances at the neighborhood of brick homes framed nicely with cement porches, modern pillars, and well-attended lawns. *Ahah.* There it is—the Herald's home…in the middle of *nowheresville.* I park on the road beside the drive and take a deep breath. Here goes nothing.

Exiting the car, I lean my shoulder into the wind and rush toward the front door that has the Herald's name on a decorated, wooden slab. As I approach the front entrance, my hand pauses briefly on the doorbell. My downcast look focuses on the two flower pots that frame the front door. These pots used to hold life, but now they are covered with dead leaves. *Humph.* Can there be a better depiction of my dismal reality? It's like the life has been sucked out of me. I don't have much more to give.

I shake my head. Can I go inside and discuss more details of my broken marriage? If I don't, does that mean I've lost my will to fight? I stand completely still, the counseling appointment looming like a cloud that won't stop following me. My mind plays a reel of all the demoralizing events that took place in my marriage, as if I'm watching jagged clips of a horror film. It'll get better if I talk about those events rather than keep them bottled up. Pastor Noah suggested as much . . . he even brought up the shame and lack of trust I carry from my past. He's right—I've got to talk through those problems. I also need to be free from the fear that stabs at me everywhere I go, as if Jonathan is lurking in the shadows, watching my every move. But will talking through those kinds of things help? When it comes to my safety, I'm not sure anything will.

I fill my lungs, lift my shoulders, and ring the doorbell. Footsteps approach, then the door swings wide. "Hallie, you made it," Pastor Noah greets. He ushers me through with an open palm. "I hope you don't mind meeting at my home office today. I like to change locations for some folks who prefer the comfort of a home. So many have appreciated the change of setting that most of my Wednesday work is done from home now." He leads me through the short, wide hall and into a spacious living room. The beige couch off to my left holds a few peach and navy-blue throw pillows. A side table, which has a few spiritual books lying across the surface, separates the couch and matching chair, creating an *L* in the center of the room. We head left toward an office space just off the living room when I hear Mrs. Herald's greeting from the other side of the room. I offer a friendly wave to the woman who has appeared in the frame of the kitchen entrance, then follow Pastor Noah into the office.

A large, black-and-white painting of the Eiffel Tower hangs opposite the loveseat. Pastor Noah motions toward the shabby-chic sitting area arranged in front of the rear, brick accent wall with a centered window. "If you can't tell, my wife decorated this space." Chuckling, he adds, "She said it would help women feel more comfortable, even though I meet with both men and women from the church here every Wednesday." I nod as I follow the gray carpet past a small bookshelf to my left and a wooden desk with a closed laptop and a stack of papers on my right. The light blue loveseat invites me as I move one of the two matching throw pillows to the other side, positioning myself close to the tiny, side table that holds a Kleenex box and a potted plant. Pastor Noah closes the door this time. He must be comfortable with his wife roaming freely about the house while wanting to protect the privacy of our session. He settles in the white armchair across from me and says, "At any rate, I'm glad you're here."

With a little chuckle, I reply, "I had to use a GPS to get here."

Pastor Noah tilts his head with a smirk as he lays his phone down on the waist-high filing cabinet next to the arm chair and says, "Most people do, there are really only neighborhoods on this side of town."

I hesitate for a moment as my stomach clenches. "I really do appreciate your willingness to meet. I told you the worst of it a couple weeks ago, but the conversation seems to have caused a reaction in me that I can't kick."

With a gentle incline of the head, Pastor Noah asks, "Why don't you tell me a little about what you've been working through since that meeting?"

Running a hand through my hair, I begin, "I haven't been sleeping, I've become progressively more nervous since I saw Jonathan at church. When I'm all alone or traveling in my car, I feel like I'm waiting for Jonathan to appear at any moment." Sighing, I add, "And I've been dealing with my shame." I bite my bottom lip, "I'm ashamed that I married him. I'm ashamed of what I let him do to me and how he manipulated me. I'm ashamed that I let it go on as long as it did . . . that I didn't get out sooner . . . before it got really bad."

Pastor Noah smooths the leg of his black slacks, giving me time to contemplate my thoughts before saying, "You know, Hallie, shame and fear are completely normal responses in matters like this. But I want you to understand that you don't have to be ashamed of your past. Christ has redeemed you from it, and you don't have to dwell on those emotions if you're willing to leave them in the past."

I breathe deeply. He can't be more right, so why do I still wrestle with my lack of trust in God? My shoulders slump. God led me to Jonathan. And Jonathan ruined me. I close my eyes, "You don't know how deep he had his claws hooked into me," I respond. "He controlled me in some of the worst ways possible . . . *and I let him*."

After a short pause, Pastor Noah asks, "Do you want to share some of the ways he would control you and how you felt about those actions?"

Not really! I don't want to share all that *stuff* only to be shamed by them all over again and then find myself even more fearful from the memories shared. But I'm here to get those thoughts out of my head, to stop dwelling on them. I want to be able to finally sleep without the fear that seeps into my subconscious. So, I nod and begin. "Well, one year, on our anniversary," I start, my gut tightening with a story I've been turning over and over in my head, "I booked a resort and spa for the weekend. I didn't tell him about it because I figured he would say no, but we didn't do anything the previous year to celebrate our anniversary, so I was hoping he would cave," I gulp. Of course, we never celebrated—Jonathan wouldn't have seen that date worthy of celebration. "Anyway, I surprised him that night and told him that our short, forty-five-minute drive to the hotel would be well worth it for the couples' massage and pampering. He didn't even waste a second to think it over. He just told me no. And that was that. We weren't going. It didn't matter that I had already spent the money and that it was non-refundable. It didn't matter that we were going to spend the weekend at the house doing nothing. He just made up his mind, and there was nothing I could do to convince him otherwise." I wrap one hand around my opposite thumb and squeeze it compulsively as I continue, "And I could've gone without him. I know it was our anniversary weekend, but that shouldn't have stopped me. If I was stronger, I would have just grabbed my already packed bag and left . . . but I didn't. Instead, I went upstairs and unpacked my bag without a word. I was scared of what he'd do if I made the decision to go without him."

"Did you do anything that weekend to celebrate? Did he take you out to dinner or buy you a gift?"

With a shake of my head, I feel a flush creeping up my neck as I say, "No, nothing. He ended up leaving that night to go hang out with a friend. I didn't want to be around him anyway, but his actions still stung. And forget the gift thing, he wouldn't even buy me a present for my birthday let alone our anniversary." I lower my gaze. Valentine's Day is coming up soon, and then my birthday. In a few weeks, I will celebrate with my parents and Ainsley, like I always have . . . he never had time for it.

"And how did that make you feel?"

With a sharp sigh, I lift my head. "Worthless. It was one thing to demand so much of me, but it was another to not even acknowledge our anniversary, Valentine's Day, or my birthday. I would always make him a special dinner on his birthday, buy him a gift, make him feel like a king—or at least try." With a heavy shrug, I say, "One of his birthdays, I made him a stir-fry. I had this new recipe that I was going to try out, and I knew he would like it . . . or at least I thought he would. I had taken my time finding the recipe, searching for all the ingredients in the grocery store and wanting to have it ready for when he came home from work." Shrinking into the corner of the loveseat, I grimace, "He walked through the door, asked me why dinner smelled so bad, yanked a beer out of the fridge, and turned on the TV. I tried to tell him happy birthday and lighten the mood with a joke about the food, but he mumbled something about me being stupid and then called me a few ugly names. By the time the food was ready, I was so frustrated with how he had treated me, especially after how much work went into making the night special, that I let my anger come out a little as I plopped the plate down in front of him. A little rice fell off the plate onto his dinner stand. He just looked at it for a second, then flipped the plate of hot rice into my face." I shudder. That rice had seared my skin, then the plate had broken around my bare feet. All I could do in that moment was stand there, shocked and hurt. But a moment was all I had. "He rose from the couch and pushed me onto the floor. I began crying from the pain while trying to wipe the food off my face, the shards were cutting into my bare legs. He stared down at me with repulsion, told me to clean up the mess, then took off toward the front door. He left. He said he needed to go shoot something. When he slammed the door behind him, I was left completely humiliated. All my acts of kindness had been turned into a shattered mess. And after all the work I had just done, he left me there, alone and crying in the mess of it all. He didn't come home that night."

"I'm so sorry, Hallie," Pastor Noah says with a softened voice. "When you say he didn't come home that night, do you think he was spending it with another woman?"

I shrug, "I really don't know. At that point, I hadn't known anything about his ex, Jessica. He may have left to see her, but he had a lot of other friends, sketchy guys—most of them were drug dealers, just like him, so he may have stayed with one of them. But I did know he was being unfaithful to a degree."

"What do you mean?"

Clearing my throat as my heart begins to race, I explain, "He was, uh, making me do some pretty gruesome things in the bedroom." I shift in my seat and turn my gaze downward, "These things made me really uncomfortable, but he didn't seem to care. It wasn't always like that, so I thought something must have changed, and I soon found out why. I . . . um," I stutter a little, heat tingling my face, "I caught him watching porn one time. But after a few moments, I realized it wasn't a recording . . . it was live. The girl in the camera was actually talking to him."

With a shake of the head and a grimace, Pastor Noah says, "These things happen in marriages, Hallie. More than you know. And what I've discovered is that the woman often feels like it's her fault. Like she isn't enough for her spouse. But that's a *lie*—the repulsiveness of this reckless habit goes far deeper than the wife's image or actions. I want you to know that this didn't happen because of you."

Struggling to meet Pastor Noah's gaze, I stare at my feet. "I guess," I reply. "It just made me feel so dirty every time he would say something or demand something that I knew was coming from this live site. I never told him I found out about it, he would have hurt me if he knew. But he really made me feel insufficient and . . . gross. It got to the point where I would try to avoid being in the bedroom with him, and for the most part, he seemed okay turning to his live feeds over me." I bite my bottom lip, "Clearly, I wasn't enough for him."

"Did you feel insufficient in other ways?" Pastor Noah asks politely, skirting over the pornography. There's nothing Pastor Noah can do to change this part of my past. My body language says it all. We're through with this topic.

"Yeah," I respond. "In little ways, I guess. He would always comment about how stupid I was. When his friends would come over to the house, he would laugh at my job and tell them how I wasn't smart enough to have a real job—that lifting weights was all I could do." I start picking at my chipped fingernail polish, desperate for a physical distraction while recounting the endless conversations he would have with his buddies as he belittled me, over and over again. "You know, sometimes," I say, focusing all the while on my nails, "when we were standing in a circle with friends or his family, he would purposely angle his body so that he was standing completely in front of me. After a few times finding myself somehow pushed out of the circle, I finally realized that he was doing it on purpose, he didn't want me to engage in conversations with *his* people. He was embarrassed by me, not physically—he didn't mind parading me around like the silent trophy wife he had proudly purchased with a big ring—but intellectually." Shaking my head and clenching my fist, I add, "He's really smart, he was top of his class at his private high school, and he graduated with a perfect GPA from university. He probably would have gotten his masters, but then he met me, and I became a burden. I guess he felt like I held him back, probably in more ways than one."

"Did he ever mention anything about leaving you, Hallie? Did he want out of the marriage, too?"

Shaking my head, I say, "No. He was always firm about our marriage. It was weird, he was embarrassed of me and he always told me how much he hated me—but then he would threaten me if I ever hinted at leaving him. I know it was, in part, his family's doing. He was brought up to believe that no matter how bad a marriage is, the vows were *till death do us part*." *Oh gosh*—I shiver. Pastor Noah inspects my involuntary reaction with a raised eyebrow. Looking out of the window, I clench my teeth together, then exhale sharply as an icy burst of fear runs the length of my body. "He told me one time after watching a horror film how he would kill me." My legs grow weak from the memory, "He tried to say it jokingly, but something about his tone and his crafty plan made me realize he had thought about it before, maybe even multiple times—that maybe there was something to it that was serious." The quaking begins to climb up my body. "He said that he would shoot me. That he would have all the cleaning products to cover it up, and that he would bury me over by Mills Pond, where that abandoned house is, way back in the field. And then he would tell everyone how I left him for another man. How he tried to fight for me but that I was too selfish, so I just disappeared one night. He said it wouldn't be too difficult to plant evidence of my affair, and that he would be so convincingly depressed that everyone would believe him. He laughed after he told me his whole plan, at how he would sit back in his recliner and drink a beer after it was all said and done." Running my tongue across my lips, I add, "He terrifies me."

Poised forward in his seat, Pastor Noah inquires without hesitation, "Are you afraid he might try to find where you live and hurt you?"

A couple blinks move me out of my trance, "No, I'm pretty sure I'm safe now. He doesn't know where I live, and he'll never guess. He's tried to follow me home once, but I've been really careful ever since. Like I said, I'm always looking over my shoulder, and I try to stay in public places when I'm out so that even if he does find me, he can't hurt me."

Pastor Noah twists his mouth, like he's going to press the matter, but he pinches his lips, then says, "Well, you've definitely been through a lot, Hallie. And I know we chatted briefly on Sunday, but how did you feel at the service with him there?"

"I only caught a glimpse of his face in the back row as I was leading worship, but I didn't react to it. Surprisingly, it was a relief knowing that you were there and that you were aware of everything that happened between us . . . of *that* night. I feel like I don't have to pretend anymore. And although it was weird not having Chip there to lead worship, that was a big relief, too."

"I'm glad. Listen, Hallie—I think you need to know that Chip has decided to step down from his position as Worship Leader at Connect Church."

My hands fly to my gaping mouth as I jump forward in the loveseat. "Oh gosh, this is my fault." Tears prickle my eyes. "I shouldn't have gotten involved. I shouldn't have told you about the issue with Becca—"

"No, no. Please don't draw any conclusion from this," Pastor Noah interrupts. "This isn't your fault. When I met with Chip and Becca, it became clear that Chip's ideas for the church and his determination to push for those ideas really didn't match what Becca had in mind for their future." He sighs, then adds, "I think they need to take some time to process what they both want for their future, and they agreed. Their marriage is fine, they will recover from this—there's no doubt in my mind. I think the issue is related to Chip's role in ministry and how Becca is feeling about that more than anything else."

With a shaky inhale, I ask, "So, they won't be attending Connect Church anymore?"

"No, last I heard, they broke the rental contract and moved out a couple of days ago to be closer to her parents. So, we've started interviewing for the job. I have this one really great connection who'll probably be our hire, and with my sabbatical coming up, I know I need to hire someone who can lead worship and preach."

I nod as the back of my throat tightens. "I still feel like this is all my fault."

"It's not. Chip made the decision to prioritize his job over the wellbeing of his wife. He may have had a vision for the worship team, but he needed to let his wife in on those plans before he tried to drag you into the mix. He broke Becca's trust, and in the midst of it all, he broke your trust too, Hallie."

With an empty exhale, I reply, "I'm starting to feel like this is becoming a pattern. When I start to place my trust in someone, it doesn't take long for them to break it." I still have Ainsley and Harrison, but it seems like the number of people I can actually trust has diminished with each passing month.

Pastor Noah and I bring our hour-long meeting to a close, and he walks to the living room to say good-bye, but movement on the beige couch just past my shoulder sends us both checking. I swivel my eyes back to Pastor Noah's twisting face as he tilts his head. "Rita," he questions looking at his wrist watch, "I wasn't expecting you for another hour."

My eyes narrow in her direction as Rita shoots me a disgusting smirk, then replies, "Yeah, I know, but you said on Sunday that you had a *new* appointment at eleven—you didn't say anything about you're twelve o'clock slot. I was on this side of town already, so I thought I would just drop in early."

Pastor Noah raises an eyebrow as he says, "Well, twelve is when I take my lunch break." With a deep breath, he claps his hands together as he rocks onto his toes and picks up his chin. "But I suppose, since you're here now, we can meet."

Rita places the book she was flipping through on the table beside the couch before she rises and hikes up her skin-tight jeans. Pastor Noah issues me a quick good-bye, and I wave just as Rita passes between us, her eyes never leaving me as her glare darkens with each stride. Once the two are finally behind the closed door, I stay a moment and focus on the muffled noises inside. Well, that confirms it—I'm unable to pick up on any of their words, so Rita couldn't have been able to hear our counseling session. I roll my eyes. Who knows how long she was there. With a shake of my head, I zip-up my jacket and brace myself for the cold.

***

Preparation for the worship practice before the Sunday service is about to begin when I enter through the front doors and run into Ainsley. "You're here early," I say.

"Miles woke me up at six this morning, so we had plenty of time to get ready for the service. Besides, I wanted to see what the new worship leader was like."

I lean in closer, dart my eyes around, and lower my voice to ask, "And?"

"He's a looker," Ainsley starts. "Tall, African American with a real artsy style. Fit, young, smells good, *and* . . . he's single," she winks at me just as I roll my eyes.

"Seriously, Ainsley—you know I don't care about that. What's his voice like? Does he play the guitar?"

Ainsley offers a sly smile, then shrugs, "Yeah, he plays. I heard him warming up a while ago, and he sounded alright." She grabs for her cell in her back pocket then adds, "Wanna go check him out? We're due in there in a few minutes anyway."

Just as we pivot to face the auditorium with the rest of the worship team still mingling by the front doors, someone hustles out of the dark auditorium and calls, "Hey everyone, if you serve on the worship team, please follow me to the stage now." This stranger then turns on the spot and struts back into the auditorium.

My head spins to Ainsley as she mouths, *that's him*. My eyebrows arch due to his sharp manner and lack of introduction. The rest of the worship team looks around at each other with twisting faces, then one-by-one, they head toward the auditorium.

We reach the stage just as the new worship leader picks up his guitar. "I'm Levi," he greets, "the new worship leader here at Connect Church." We all smile and nod, prepared to say hello, but he cuts us short. "Now, if you guys could join me on stage, we have a lot to do in a short amount of time, and I'm going to be running things differently than your *last* worship leader." Is it just me or did he over-emphasize that final bit of his curt welcome? *Does he know about what happened with Chip?* Oddly, his only concern seems to be adjusting his guitar and mic.

The group moves slowly onto the stage, as if they are about to walk the plank. The bass player, an elderly man with a consistently bad cough, says, "We usually pray before we start practicing…at least Chip would."

Without turning back to see who addressed him, Levi says over his shoulder, "We don't really have time for that today—maybe we can discuss it next week, but for now, I just want to get started."

Ainsley and I shoot each other an uneasy glance. We aren't going to pray before we start? Isn't there always time for prayer, even just a short one? Levi tunes his guitar, then briskly strums it once, placing a hand abruptly on the strings to silence the reverberating note as he says, "Good. Now, for our first song—"

The Sunday service closes with Pastor Noah's final prayer. As the noise level rises behind Ainsley and me seated in the front row, my eyes find Levi on the other side of the room. "I don't know about Levi," I confess to my best friend. Not long after Chip left, he sent an email to the entire worship team explaining his reasoning for his departure. Maybe Ainsley's skittish too. "He's so…I don't know—brusque." Levi stands, smooths his pants and adjusts the collar of his button-up shirt as he pushes his designer glasses up the bridge of his nose. Before I know it, Rita has sidled up next to the guy.

She shifts her weight while twirling a piece of her jet-black hair, eventually letting out that infamous shrieking laugh. Ainsley turns just in time to witness Levi offer a closed-lip smile.

Just then, a figure roughly the same height as Levi approaches the group. *Jonathan.* My eyes narrow. They exchange a friendly greeting. Jonathan engages with the two as if they are all good friends. *What?* My eyes bug out of my head as Rita shimmies over surprisingly close to Jonathan. My head rears. Jonathan leans over to whisper something into Rita's ear while Levi momentarily shakes the hand of a passerby, and the intimacy of the action makes my stomach lurch. As far as I know, Rita and Jonathan have never met. And yet, it certainly doesn't seem that way. Rita saunters off and Jonathan extends a hand to formally greet the new worship leader. Pastor Noah took a few moments in the service to introduce Levi to the congregation, and I can imagine Jonathan is mentioning something related to the introduction as he points to the stage, leaving Levi laughing at whatever comment Jonathan has offered. My eyes burn with focus as I study the exchange. What could they be talking about? A sour taste surges up the back of my throat. What is Jonathan saying? And why is Levi so engrossed in the conversation?

CHAPTER 14

I park in front of Pastor Noah's home for our scheduled, mid-week counseling session. Would he be put off by my appearance this morning? I yank down the visor and flip open the mirror. *Yikes.* Disheveled hair, bags under my eyes, pale skin . . . it wouldn't take a genius to see I'm not getting much sleep these days. Not like this is anything new. My lack of sleep is a pattern that was put in place long before I left Jonathan. I swipe underneath my eyes, flip the visor, and exit my car. Hugging my coat around me against the cold winter wind, I make for the entrance. Only steps away from the front door, I freeze.

My breath catches in my lungs at the sight of Jonathan's smug smile plastered across his stubbly face. He waltzes up to me. My mind goes fuzzy. I gulp and take a step back. "What are you doing here?" my voice quivers.

"Oh, I didn't expect to see *you*," Jonathan taunts. "I guess Pastor Noah counsels a lot of *people* who attend Connect Church." He takes a step closer. My muscles tense, ready to spring for the car or the front door. *What do I do?* Jonathan doesn't move, and we stand frozen in place—poised, as if waiting for a whistle to blow. Jonathan glances back at the house with a sneer. "Well, I'll be seeing you soon, Hallie."

My chest heaves as he struts to his Audi, takes one mocking look back at me, laughs, then climbs behind the wheel. *How did he know I was going to be here?* I blink and pinch my lips...Rita. Something weird is developing between them. Is she into him? I shake my head and place a hand over my beating heart as he speeds down the street. Right now, Rita doesn't matter.

What matters is that he's strategically piecing together my schedule. My stomach churns as I turn and pace toward the front door.

With a quick knock, I enter the Herald's home. "Hallie, come on back," Pastor Noah greets with a flushed face and broken eye contact. He moves through the house with surprising speed as I follow him into his office. Closing the door behind us, he pauses over his desk to shuffle some papers.

I slowly lower myself onto the blue loveseat, hesitate, then ask, "What was Jonathan doing here?"

Pastor Noah takes a deep breath and says, "So, you saw him, huh?" With a light huff, he adds, "He showed up unexpected and wanted to book an appointment with me, scheduled each week on this day, an hour before *your* appointment. I told him I couldn't do that, but that I would be willing to meet at the church another day of the week." He reaches for a stack of files on the desk, picks up a folder and makes his way over to the armchair. He takes a settling breath and smiles for the first time since I walked into the house. "I'm sorry if his presence disturbed you, I just hope it won't disrupt our session."

Shifting in my seat, I respond, "I'd be lying if I said I wasn't upset by the sight of him, but I'm more worried about his efforts to figure out my schedule. It seems like he's inching closer and closer...and that scares me."

Pastor Noah opens his mouth, closes it again, rolls his head to one side, then says, "Jonathan refused my offer to see him at a different time and place in the week. It seems that he is determined to meet the hour before your session, or not at all. And he made it clear he didn't mind if I told you about our five-minute encounter just then. The only reason I am telling you all this is for your safety."

I nod—up and down, slow and steady...taking in every word. This is all part of his plan—he's not looking for help, he's looking for every opportunity to weasel his way back into my life, and he wants me to know it. "That's Jonathan," I finally say through clenched teeth. "He knows how to work every situation to suit him best—he's always in control." *Ugh!* He's always been controlling, so why would I ever think he'd stop now? My mind filters through the many controlling acts he's forced upon me. *Time to get real.* I sigh, let my jaw go slack, then say, "This is just an example, but I bought a

Roomba to help with the cleaning around the house. When Jonathan saw it, he made me return it." I shrug one shoulder up to my ear, "And I did. He couldn't believe I would be that lazy, having a machine do the work I should be doing." I shake my head, "He had complete control over me. He even made me go to sleep when he was ready to go to sleep. If he was ready for bed, I couldn't keep my lamp on and read, or even look on my phone. Whether I was tired or not, it was lights out, no questions asked."

Pastor Noah inclines his head, his face starting to return to a normal color, then says, "He seems like a determined man."

I huff, "You can say that again. Add fear into the equation and you've got a picture of what the last three years have looked like for me."

"I can tell you're dwelling on all of it," Pastor Noah concedes, "which is natural given your past."

As I peer out the window at the bare tree branches swaying in the fierce wind, I say, "It's weird, but with my birthday coming up, I've really been thinking through my past birthdays—all of the big issues in our marriage constantly creep into my mind, but it's funny how the little things really sting, like him refusing to acknowledge our anniversary, bring home flowers on Valentine's Day, or even buy me a birthday present." I swivel my eyes around and whisper, "It's like I wasn't worth any of that."

Pastor Noah points his finger indicating his understanding as he says, "You know, it's not strange that you have to work through the minor things that Jonathan did to betray your trust rather than just the big things, like when he hit you for the first time when you returned from that trip you took with Ainsley."

I clasp my hands in my lap, "Yeah, I certainly dwell on it all, but some incidents more than others." My mind flashes to the memory of when he first hit me. The consuming terror left me cowering in the corner of our kitchen, my packed bag still sitting by the front door. I wanted to run to the door, grab my bag, and escape all over again. Instead, I stayed…for far too long. Licking my lips, I say, "It was definitely the big stuff, like him hitting me, that always made me want to escape."

Pastor Noah taps a finger against his chin, "Let's unpack that a little—your need to escape. What do you think that stems from, and how do you think you can grow from it?"

I look up at the ceiling. *Hmmm.* That's a loaded question. I press my tongue against the roof of my mouth, then say, "I guess it came from my unhappiness and loneliness," I lower my gaze, "and eventually my fear. It was like every time we arrived at the airport, I could start being myself. I didn't have to worry about him watching me and later punishing me for my actions or words. When Ainsley and I took off on a flight, I was free to be *me*, even if it was just for a short while."

"I see," Pastor Noah starts, "and do you feel that this constant need to escape hinders your ability to confront your troubles."

His words hit me like a punch to the gut. I heave a deep sigh. "Yes," I admit with my eyes squeezed tight, "that explains me exactly. When I have to face my fears, when I have to deal with the problems placed before me, my whole being crawls with the need to leave…to get out…to escape. I guess I really struggle with that *fight-or-flight* mentality."

* * *

As I drive away from my parents' home, I'm finally able to release the tension radiating through my body. The tension built from seeing Jonathan at my appointment this morning, the tension lingering from my tedious afternoon shift at work, and finally, the tension brought on by hearing my parents blabber over dinner about the successful marriages of the wonderful, young couples in *their* church. I need to talk this through. I grab my phone to call Ainsley. "Hey, are you busy? I need to vent."

Ainsley giggles, "I just put Miles down for the night, so I was going to binge watch this new reality TV show I've just started, but I have some time to hear about your problems."

I groan, "Well, I hope you have a lot of time, because I have several problems. For starters, Jonathan is now following me around town. He showed up before my counseling session trying to book the hour before I meet with Pastor Noah, probably so he could run into me every Wednesday morning, but I'm sure it's also to prove that he's trying to make some improvements in his own life. And what's up with that anyway—he should be at work by then. Does he get *special* time off because he's the boss? Oh, and also, I'm pretty sure there's something going on between him and Rita. Not only did they have that strange exchange at church this past Sunday, but it had to be Rita who told him about my appointment with Pastor Noah in the first place."

Awkward silence follows. I take the phone away from my ear and check the screen. Did I lose service? "Anything else?" Ainsley asks, her tone void of all playfulness now.

I pause, furrowing my brow for a moment, then shake my head. "Yes," I begin again, flexing my fingers around the steering wheel. "Danny followed me around work all day, and if I hadn't run to the locker room at just the right times, I'm pretty sure he would have asked me on a date. And just to add insult to injury, I also know it was Rita who told Danny about my split from Jonathan."

"Oh, man," Ainsley fumbles, but I interrupt.

"*And now for the icing on the cake*," my voice raises as I turn onto the winding road that will eventually lead me to the lake house, "I just endured an excruciating dinner with my parents talking pointedly about all the happily married couples they know who attend their church."

Ainsley slowly sucks air in before saying, "Wow, you've had a tough day."

"Uh—yeah," I say, my pulse beating against my temples. "I was supposed to stay the night at my parents' house, but I couldn't bring myself to stay past dinner." With a deep sigh, I add, "Not to mention that they canceled on us for Friday night, looks like it's just you and me for my birthday after all."

"They canceled?"

"Yeah, they said something about a local band playing at one of their favorite restaurants. They did invite us to go with them, but I told them to forget about it. It would've been a painful dinner not only having to hear that boring music all night, but my parents would have found a way to sneak in a conversation about *marriage*." Ainsley snickers. *Great.* Now I've done it. Why did I have to use a tone that might convey contempt at hearing about healthy marriages? I still firmly believe in the constitution of marriage, even if I'm frustrated now. Defeat threads my voice as I say, "They gave me a birthday card with a twenty-dollar bill in it. They told me to buy myself something *nice*. Would it be rude to tell them twenty bucks won't help pay the bills, let alone buy something nice?"

"Oh Hallie—" Ainsley begins, but again, I cut her short.

"The bills aren't too bad," I say with a half-laugh. The last thing I need to do is complain about my bills to the friend who has extended her vacation home to me, rent free. I take a steadying breath. The water and electric bills might add up, but she doesn't need to be privy to my struggles. "I'm just frustrated with my parents." I yawn, then add, "And I'm over-tired."

"Well, seven isn't too early to call it a night," she snickers. "But I know you haven't been sleeping well, and the sun always sets early this time of year, so you have your excuses."

I chuckle half-heartedly, "Yeah, I'm probably gunna jump in the shower as soon as I get home and chill on the couch for a little before calling it a night." We say our good-byes just as I pull down the long, dirt drive to the lake house. By the time I shift into park, I pause for a moment to rest my head on the steering wheel. My eyes fall shut. I could probably fall asleep right here, right now. I shake my head…there's no point in that. Ignoring my bag sitting in the back seat that was packed for an overnight stay at my parents' place, I turn off the ignition and reach for my phone.

Swaying inside, I don't even bother to turn on the lights as I toss my phone and keys on the couch and drag myself to the shower. While the warm water rushes over my aching body, I let my mind wander back to my counseling session with Pastor Noah. *Maybe this fight-or-flight thing is a serious problem.*

Once I'm toweled dry and comfortably snuggled in my sweats for the night, I turn off my bedroom light and make my way back out to the couch where my phone and keys lay. Plunking down on my keys, I grab for them and slip them into my sweatshirt pocket, then I pick up my phone and start browsing through my social media. Sitting in the darkness, I shiver. *Brrr.* It sure is cold outside, but I'm not going to turn on the fireplace. Not with my most recent bill. As I hug my knees into my chest, my browsing takes a pause. *Thump.* What was that? Did it come from outside? I shake my head.

My exhaustion is making me imagine things. I bring my phone back up to my face. *Click.* My heart stops. I didn't imagine that—it sounded like a car door clicking shut. I jump up and slink quickly over to the bay window as I blacken my phone screen. My body begins to tremble. I didn't see headlights approaching. Is there someone out there? I huddle beside the frame, and peer into the darkness. *Oh my gosh!* A silent scream slices through my mind. I slap a hand over my mouth as a tall, dark image skulks silently up the front steps. It's Jonathan—*he's found me!*

Panic surges through my entire body. *What do I do? Where do I hide?* The front porch creaks. *Ahhh!* Did I even lock the front door behind me? It's too late, his hand is on the knob. I close my eyes, crouching against the wall between the window and the door, waiting as crippling terror courses through me. The deadbolt catches ever so quietly. I soundlessly release my quaking breath. *I locked it.* Thank God all the lights are off…he can't see in.

I dart my eyes to every entranceway. What will he do next? Listening for his footsteps, I hear them leave the front porch and thud against the hard dirt that circles around the kitchen. This is it. I have moments to get out of the house before he learns how to get in. *Run!* I silently race to the side door and slip out. It's dark—so dark that maybe he won't see me make a mad dash. I hold my breath and lean into the night air. His movements place him somewhere around Miles' room. He's still on the far side of the lake house. It won't be long until he's rounding the corner. I have one shot at making this work. *Dear God, help me!* I push off the door and silently bound down the back-deck stairs. My legs shake, but I sprint to edge of the trees anyway. *Almost there!*

I scramble to the nearest trunk. Will it hide me? I fall behind its girth then look back with a shudder. There he is, emerging on the far side of the deck. *Did he see me run?* He slinks around the house like a panther in search of its prey. The stairs leading up to the door strain under his weight. I try to hold my breath. Can he hear my panting behind this tree? His focus is on the house, not the forest. *Maybe he'll think I'm not home—but what about my car?* He's definitely seen my car.

What options do I have left? Do I wait here and call the police? My chest rises and falls in rapid succession. I can risk a call to the police if he makes enough noise while trying to break in. I narrow my eyes just as his hand reaches out for the handle of the side door. It swings open. Both hands fly to my face as I stifle a cry. *I forgot to lock it!*

How could I have forgotten to lock it? My race to the tree was more important…and now I've just let the man who's here to hurt me into my hiding place. I turn my head around and let it fall back on the trunk as my breathing reaches near hyperventilation. I don't have much time before he figures out I'm hiding outside. I squeeze my eyes shut and throw both arms across my stomach. *What should I do?* My arms lock against the keys in my pocket. *That's it!* With only moments to spare, I crouch down and run for my car. My feet skid across the rough ground. I stumble just as I approach the car. *Breathe.* I silently slip the key into the lock, click open the car door, and hurl myself inside.

Vroom! The engine starts. My hands shake violently as I shift into drive, catapulting down the dirt road as I swerve dangerously around his parked car. I don't need my lights to help guide me, I just have to get out. Just as I'm about to take the first curve, the front porch light illuminates in my rearview mirror. I gasp at Jonathan's large, silhouetted frame on the top, front step… watching me flee.

My tires squeal as I take a turn onto the main road perpendicular to the lake house driveway. I catch a glimpse of his car lights moving. He's in his car. The chase is on. I hit the gas as hard as I can. *Escape, escape . . .* I need an escape. *The boating access!* The lot should be just up the road. *Yes!* The narrow entrance to the small lot is now in view. I turn the steering wheel hard as I bump down the riveted drive.

As soon as I am behind the dense patch of bare trees, I punch the car into park and shut off the engine. My breathing is heavy as I crouch in my seat. Can I watch the road and still stay hidden? Headlights shine on the road before me, and I cringe. *Oh gosh!* The Audi zooms by. I remain frozen in place, my strained breathing filling the silence. I stay like this for a few minutes. He has to be long gone by now, he has to be chasing the ghost of my car. I collapse over the steering wheel and finally let the torrent of sobs take control of my body. *He found my hiding place.*

***

"*How did he find me*?" I bluster the moment I enter through Ainsley's front door. I had to come here, Jonathan's probably circling my parents' house. At least this place is gated. I throw down the overnight bag that I had neglected earlier and begin pacing. Ainsley's eyes follow me as she pinches the skin on her throat. "I mean, somehow he figured it out, *just like he's been figuring out my appointments.* And then he's there, sneaking into the house. He probably thought I was asleep—*what would he have done if I hadn't escaped*?" A shudder starts at my neck and runs to my toes. I throw my head into my hands and stare at the floor. A smear of blood streaks across the white tiles of the entryway beneath me. "I'm bleeding," I groan, "I must have cut my foot while I was running." I pick my head up, "I'm . . . I'm sorry about the mess."

Ainsley's eyes widen. "Oh dear. Don't worry—I'll get something to clean it." As Ainsley leaves, I slide down the wall to the floor, propping my bleeding, dirt-stained foot on my knee as the tears fall again. Ainsley returns with a bottle of cleaner, a roll of paper towels, and a first-aid kit. She swipes across the tiles in silence as I clean my wound, my sniffles replacing words. Finally, she says, "Will's here. Well—you probably saw his truck in the driveway when you pulled up." Did I? Between the boating access lot and Ainsley's garage, my eyes were only searching for the Audi. "Anyway, he's in the shower right now, but if Jonathan happens to get past the security gate, he'll see the truck." She throws up both hands and shakes her head, "What am I saying—he won't get past the security system. You're safe here—Jonathan won't bother us tonight."

I nod and bite at the arm of my sweatshirt to steady my quivering chin. Eventually, I whisper, "But how did he find me?"

Ainsley pauses mid-stroke, like she's about to speculate, then returns to the cleaning, putting some unneeded muscle into it. Is she upset about the messy floor? She lifts off her knees and leaves the room with a fist-full of blood-stained paper towel. I wipe my cheek on my shoulder. Maybe I should apologize about the floor again when she gets back.

But I don't get the chance to as Ainsley re-enters the room and says, "You know what you need—*a trip.*" I groan as I reach for my overnight bag. "No, really," she says, "let's just leave tomorrow morning. There's this line-up of country singers performing in Nashville—they've been there all week. *Let's go.*"

"But Ainsley—" I start.

She raises a hand to stop me, "You told me while driving here that you can't go back to the lake house, that he might try to return again tomorrow night. Let's trick him into thinking you've left the lake house while we escape for a few days. I'm sure Jim will let you take off work, and I know my parents are just waiting around to watch Miles for a few days."

With a deep sigh, I say, "I really can't afford a trip right now."

"Don't worry about that," Ainsley replies, waving me off. "I'll pay for it—it will be a birthday present." She starts bouncing from foot to foot. "Yes, we can go for a few days, celebrate your birthday on Friday night, and be back late Saturday before worship practice on Sunday morning. *It'll be perfect.* I can book the tickets and hotel tonight, and we'll drop your car off at the lake house early tomorrow so you can pack your luggage, then go to the airport." She draws her hands together in front of her, then adds, "It might be good to have your car at the lake house so if he does come back, he'll realize just because your car's there doesn't mean you're there."

I shrug one shoulder and bite my bottom lip. It's not a bad idea. Maybe if he sees my car in the driveway of the lake house, he'll stop looking for me around town. It might confuse him long enough for me to decide what I want to do—what I need to do—to stay safe. Ainsley trots off to find her laptop. I haven't agreed yet, but she's made up her mind. My brow furrows as I look down at my overnight bag and my dirty, bare feet. It doesn't matter how hard she's trying to lighten the moment, I can't shake the near miss of tonight.

Maybe she's right though, maybe I do need to escape for a couple nights—just to throw Jonathan off. Who knows what I'll do when I return, but getting out of town for a few nights isn't the worst idea. In fact, my safety may depend on it.

* * *

The hordes of people up and down Broadway draw my attention as our shuttle pulls up to the hotel. *Wow.* Could our hotel be any better located? "Ainsley, you didn't have to book our room here—you probably paid a fortune for a hotel on Broadway," I say.

"It's for your birthday—you only turn twenty-six once."

"Well, thank you." I smile, but my stomach grips with my reality. I have only come here to escape Jonathan, a default response I was trying to leave in my past, not to practice in the present. Ainsley moseys up to the front desk, and the young man with a slick haircut and chiseled face asks for our reservations. Ainsley begins to put on a little show. She flicks her hair back, flashes a wide grin, pitches her voice just right, and before long, we've been upgraded to a suite. Ainsley collects our room cards and throws a dainty wave back at the clerk as we wheel our suitcases toward the elevators. "Um, what was that about?" I point back at the front desk.

"Oh, that? It's just a little flirting to get an upgrade," she laughs. "And it worked—now we have a room with a view of Honky Tonk Highway. I bet we can hear the music from our suite." I frown in her direction as we step into the elevator and punch our floor number. "What? A little flirting doesn't hurt anyone."

I tilt my head, "I bet Will disagrees."

"Will is working, like he always does," the resentment in her tone escalates with each word. "He doesn't have time to think of me and what I'm doing." I rock back on my heels from the intensity of her comment. My mind twists with positive comments and encouraging words, as if that would help now. I don't have it in me to rock the boat, and I don't get the chance to. *Ding.* We've reached our floor and our focus is now on finding our suite.

Our night is filled with great food, a drink here and there, and the country twang of local talent. The next morning begins with Ainsley singing happy birthday over and over as we get ready for a full day on Broadway. Ainsley wasn't lying—the country artist line-up for today is top-notch. My ears are ringing with the sound of banjos and harmonicas as the sun sets.

Ainsley glances at her Michael Kors watch. It's time to trade in our casual wear for a dress more appropriately matched for the Nashville nightlife. Ainsley drags me back to our room to get ready for a night on Honky Tonk Highway.

"What dress did you decide on?" Ainsley shouts from the bathroom as she applies the finishing touches to her make-up.

"I think I'll wear the brown one," I say as I pull the somewhat modest dress from my bag. A groan bubbles in the back of my throat. I've had my *country* fix for the day…for the year. It's not like I'm a big drinker, and I definitely don't want to parade around all night in a little dress. But Ainsley is excited for the next set of performers. I squeeze my eyes shut and massage my temples. *Was this trip for me, or for her?* Taking a deep breath, I straighten and smooth the dress against my body. What's the point of getting frustrated? Another bout of country music is better than focusing on the real reason I've had to escape.

"Well, put the dress on and let me see." I comply, and as I step through the doorway, Ainsley glances in my direction and says, "That's definitely your color—you should wear your cowboy boots, *they will go perfectly*."

My cowboy boots are a size too small, a sacrifice I was willing to make for a discounted purchase. Real leather doesn't come cheap. Why are cowboy boots a *must* in Nashville? I squeeze into the boots and rise with a groan as I wiggle my toes around. "I don't know about these, Ainsley," I shout to her. "I can't feel my toes. Seriously, I'm so used to workout shoes that I might not be able to walk by the end of the night."

Ainsley laughs as she pops her head out of the bathroom, a blush brush still in hand. "Why don't you walk around the room a little and break them in," she suggests, motioning with the end of her brush stick.

I roll my eyes playfully and smirk. You can't break in second-hand boots. "So, is that what you're wearing?"

"You don't like it?" Ainsley's face falls as she slides into full view. She smooths a hand down the black dress, her brow wrinkled. The tight material pulls across her thin torso and cuts open at the crevasse of her cleavage, meeting again at a crisscross that loops high around the neck. Would Will be okay with this dress if he were here?

"Oh no, I do," I say, my head lowered. Maybe it's just me—I have to get used to her new additions, and she probably does too. Besides, I don't want a repeat of the conversation we had on the elevator yesterday. "I was just curious. It looks great," I reassure her, raising my head and smiling.

"Thanks," Ainsley draws out slowly as she moves back into the bathroom with her blush brush. She clears her throat, "You know, Will bought me this dress for Christmas." I cringe, was that before or after her surgery? I slump down on the bed and stretch my legs out before me. "But you know what they say—what happens in Nashville, *stays in Nashville*—or is that just for Vegas?" She laughs playfully before repeating over and over that she's just kidding. Too late, a pit begins to form in my stomach.

We arrive at the first bar and the bouncer checks our IDs. Ainsley goes straight to the bar and orders two vodka tonics. *Ugh.* Could I ask the bartender to throw in a slash of juice? Ainsley thrusts the drink into my hand, and the first sip sends a bitter shiver across my shoulders. Ainsley laughs, then drags me to the dance floor.

I twist and pull at my tight dress with my free hand as I fall into a two-step behind my best friend's shadow. This is what she came here for—she's in her zone, moving to the rhythm for all to see. It seems like only minutes have passed before she chinks around her ice cubes, lifts the black straw from the glass, and motions over the loud music that she's returning to the bar. I wave her off, pointing to my nearly full glass. It'll take a while for me to stomach this one. I slink back into the corner of the dancefloor as the crowd rocks before me. I bite my lip and take another agonizing sip of my drink. Where's Ainsley? She's the life of the party, always has been, but I don't want to find her dancing on the bar. My eyes squint in the direction of the bar. *Ah.* There she is. My head tilts at the guy in a button-up shirt standing too close to Ainsley. They both lift a shot glass, clink them together, and down it. Ainsley's face contorts, then she grins as she plunks the shot glass on the bar. She leaves with a wave, a new drink in hand, and finds me again on the dance floor.

"Who was that?" I yell, inclining my head toward the bar.

Ainsley shrugs then shouts over the thumping music, "Dunno, he just came over and bought me that shot." She moves to the beat, brushing aside my concern. "Loosen up. You just turned twenty-six." Then she raises her glass in a toast-like fashion before yelling, "*Woooo!*"

The night drags on, one bar after another. She insists I get a drink at each bar we go to, but she's stopped counting, so I stopped drinking hours ago. By now, my feet are aching, and I'm ready to leave. The singer on stage leans into the microphone while swinging his guitar strap over his head. His beard tickles the mic as he announces a quick break. I tug on Ainsley's elbow. "I'm done. Are you ready to go back to the hotel?"

"Oh, no—" Ainsley contests, "*he hasn't played that one song I love so much.*" She grabs my hand and leads me to the bar. Ainsley orders a drink as my eyes widen at the guy in the button-up from the first bar who is meandering toward us. Is this coincidence, or has he been following us? With a cheap grin and wandering eyes, he orders a round of shots for Ainsley and himself. Ainsley flashes a big smile and turns to him. It's like I'm not even here…not that I want to be noticed. I wouldn't be taking a shot from a stranger anyway.

The heel of my boots bite into my skin. *Humph.* Is this night over yet? I lean in and cup my hand against Ainsley's ear, "I'm just going to the bathroom, I'll be right back." Ainsley nods, runs a hand through her hair, and turns back to face the stranger. He hands her the shot just as I leave. I drag my boots to the ladies' room positioned across from the bar. I just want my bed, that's all I want. I take a moment after using the bathroom to shift my weight from one foot to the other, gripping the sink as I roll out my ankles. My gaze lifts to the mirror over the sink. *Gross!* I look about as tired as I feel right now. I thought this trip would be more about relaxing and resting than partying. I guess not. Next to me, a group of giggling women surround the full-length mirror. With a quick shake of my head, I turn and hobble back toward the bar. My eyes scan the crowd as I search for my best friend. But Ainsley is nowhere to be found.

* * *

The flight home is a quiet one—Ainsley pretends to sleep as I mull over the argument we had when I eventually found her outside of the bar with the stranger in the button-up shirt. I was angry she had left without telling me where she was going and that she chose to go outside with the stranger in the first place. She made excuses, especially when she finally woke up, with a pounding headache no less. She protested over the bustle of the Saturday crowds and live music on Broadway during our late lunch we scarfed down before having to pack up and leave for the airport. I must've heard a half-dozen times that it's not a sin to have a private conversation with someone. But *why* did she have to have a conversation with that guy in the first place?

As I sit in the middle seat, Ainsley rests her head against the side of the plane, the raised shade providing a view of the blackening night sky. I stare past her at nothing. Why did I cave to another escape? There's the obvious reason—I didn't want Jonathan to find me. But there are other reasons, too. It's my fear that pushed me to make the decision to leave for Nashville...and my lack of finances. But really, it was the only option of escape presented at the time . . . actually, *insisted* at the time.

How much of this trip was really for me...for my birthday? Did Ainsley see a window of opportunity, using me as an excuse to get away from Will for a bit? If Will stopped working so much, would that solve some of the problems I see surfacing when I'm with Ainsley? I set my jaw and lift my chin. Either way, I don't ever want to be put in that kind of position again—by anyone—especially not my best friend.

The plane touches down and Ainsley lifts her head with an unconvincing jolt. She gathers her belongings, avoiding eye contact or conversation. As we wait to de-board, she turns on her phone and begins texting . . . to her parents, to her husband, I don't know. But she's made her point clear...she's going to ignore me as long as she can. By the time we collect our luggage and get into the Highlander, the awkward silence that follows has me shifting back and forth in my seat.

"Look," I finally say, "I don't know what happened last night, and I don't know why you thought I would be okay when I couldn't find you, but I think we should talk about it, Ainsley."

Her cold stare bears into the endless stretch of dark highway ahead of us. Ainsley eases her tone for a careless reply, "There isn't much to talk about. We just left to talk because we couldn't hear each other over the music." *That's not an excuse.* Doesn't she remember the singer was on a break when they walked outside? She huffs, "We don't need to keep bringing it up, especially now that we're home."

I rub my hands together. "I just feel like all the marriages around me are falling apart," I groan, my voice threatening to break. "It's like there's a domino effect, and I know I'm part of that group—heck, I'm leading that group with my upcoming divorce. It's just that I really do value marriage, even if mine didn't work out, and I feel like everyone around me is either accusing me or acting as if I don't respect marriage at all."

Ainsley is quiet for a moment. "Well, my marriage is fine," she retorts, her pitch hardened, "so you don't need to worry about me or deal with anything that I've done. What happened last night wasn't anything. And you *certainly* aren't the one to challenge me on where I stand in my marriage." Defense threads her retort. This isn't going how I had hoped—she wasn't supposed to take it personally. I just needed to share my feelings, I didn't mean to push her farther away. Opening my mouth to attempt a placate of sorts, she abruptly ends our conversation by saying, "It's really none of your business anyway, Hallie, so don't stick your nose where it doesn't belong. I'll drop you off at the lake house tonight, but when we meet at church tomorrow, I don't want to hear another word about last night. We're back in the real world, with real issues. My parents just texted me that there's a leak in the kitchen, Will is staying at his apartment tonight, and that new worship leader who is supposed to have everything under control is in a panic about something. So, yeah, we are back to reality, and what happened in Nashville *will* stay in Nashville. Got it?"

CHAPTER 15

The taillights of Ainsley's Highlander trail down the dirt drive of the lake house. As I stand outside the front door, my body begins to tremble. I'm completely alone out here…totally vulnerable. Why couldn't Ainsley just apologize for her actions from last night? Then maybe she'd feel better about it, and we could both go back to the safety of her secured house with the tension from our trip far behind us. But no…here I am, shaking on the front stoop of the lake house, trying to determine whether it's safer inside or out. In a flash, I unlock the door and swing it open. If he's hiding inside waiting for me, the sound of my entrance announcing my arrival is not what I need to be fearful of.

After my thorough search of the lake house, I find the windows and doors intact. He hasn't broken in. I'm safe, at least for the moment. But I can't stay here, so I hastily repack my bag. Within minutes, I'm in my car, racing away from the lake house.

I drive aimlessly around town. What next? I don't have enough money to spend on a comfortable hotel room, and I need a hotel room. There's no way I'm going to risk the unsafe confines of a dingy inn. The minutes tick by, moving me closer to midnight as I try to work through what I should do next. *Do I sleep in my car? Do I go to my parents' house?* Whatever I choose, I don't have long before my driving becomes dangerous. Another yawn stretches through the tension of my clenched jaw. I shake my head against the vibrations moving up my spine. I've got to find out where Jonathan is, that's the only way I'll really trust that I'm safe. I nod and start driving toward my old house.

As I navigate down the familiar road, heat rolls through every muscle. The mailbox that reads "McClain" comes into view, and I slow my car to a speed that starkly contrasts the racing of my heart. Turning off my headlights, I inch past the last cluster of trees hiding the house. My heart catches in my throat. There it is, everything representing my past standing before me. My eyes search for his vehicles in the dark, and I loosen my grip on the steering wheel when I find both the truck and the Audi. He's here, and hopefully, he's sleeping.

I gulp as I catch a fleeting view of the dog pens in the backyard. My heart pangs. Those poor dogs are left out in the cold. Has Jonathan given them any attention since I left? Maybe I could sneak back there and cuddle them, even just for a minute. *No!* My head snaps back to view the house. I couldn't risk it. Finding me in his backyard would be like hand-delivering a gift—allowing him to play out his darkest fantasy . . . without a witness in sight. I shiver, the movement slapping me with the memory of my life while living in that house—that prison—for three years.

The lights are off. From what I can remember, that typically means he's home for the night. It's a Saturday night. There's no doubt he's abusing some kind of substance…and probably passed out on the couch. At least he's in there alone, there's no one there for him to take his anger out on. My car rolls out of view, and the moment I'm past the house, I turn on my lights and pick up speed. My past is in the past—let's keep it that way. Time to go to my parents' place. I punch at the steering wheel, the memory of his inebriated nights stabbing at my brain. That's not what I wanted out of a marriage. That's not what I imagined it would be like with him. I would never have guessed I'd be on the run from my husband. Where did it all go wrong, or was it doomed from the beginning? A well of emotion erupts with the flood that rises from my heart, and I succumb to fierce sobs. After a few minutes of driving through my blinding tears, I punish myself for my constant need to take flight. *What has my life come to?*

"I can't handle this, God," I groan through my tears. "I thought by now I would be free from that *monster*. I prayed you would give me hope and a future. This is not the future I want—no money, nowhere to stay, no safety—*are you even listening?*" I approach a red light and drop my face into my hands as I come to a stop. My veins pulse with hot blood while my heart thumps heavily in my chest. The light turns green, and I take a deep breath. My heart drops, as if God has reached down from heaven and tugged on it himself.

Please, God—show me you're trustworthy. I don't know what I'm doing with my life, and I feel like there isn't a future here for me in Oklahoma anymore. I'll never be able to stop looking over my shoulder, always worrying about where he is and whether or not I'm safe. But I don't know where to go. Please...direct me. Lead me. Guide me. Show me I can trust you. I need to be able to trust you with my future, God.

* * *

"Hallie," my mom pauses in the doorway to the bathroom where I'm getting ready for church, "you certainly got in late last night. You gave us a fright coming in like you did." She places a hand on the frame, "But I guess now that you're here, you'll be coming to *our* church with us this morning. We're leaving in two minutes."

I cringe. She hasn't asked why I stayed here last night, neither has my dad. It's been awkwardly quiet all morning, but the unspoken truth remains . . . if I stay here, I should follow their rules and meet their expectations. But I can't go with them to their church, nor can I spill the details of why I had to stay here last night. She removes her hand and folds her arms across her chest...she's ready to be disappointed. "Actually, no," I eventually grunt. "I'm going to Connect Church this morning. I have to serve on the worship team." My mom disappears around the corner without a word, walking deliberately to the kitchen, marking her frustration with every step. As I turn back to the mirror, adjusting my long, loose sweater I paired with an old pair of low-rise jeans I rummaged out of the closet minutes ago, my heart does a little flutter. Do I have to go to church and sing beside Ainsley this morning? Jonathan will be lurking somewhere in the dark, at the back of the auditorium. Ainsley hasn't texted me or thought to check on me since she dropped me off at the lake house last night.

My mascara stick freezes mid-stroke. This is the first Sunday of Pastor Noah's sabbatical. He's not going to be in the building, but Jonathan will. My heart begins to thud hard against my ribs. *Has Jonathan pieced this all together?* My tongue runs the length of my teeth. It's fine, there is a whole congregation there, he won't do anything in front of other people. He'll put on the *good-guy* act, even if Pastor Noah isn't there. I just need to be careful after the crowd starts to clear out…I can never be too cautious.

As I drive to church, I mouth through the conversation I need to have with Ainsley this morning. She told me not to bring up the incident from Friday night, but can I honor that? Wouldn't it be better if I just address the elephant in the room? *Oh gosh*—I can't do this alone. "Lord," I pray, "please help me through this morning. After last night, I just need to connect with you. I do that best when singing on stage, and I don't want whatever's going on between me and Ainsley interfering with that. Worship is the only thing I have left." I glance down at the clock on my dash. *Ahhh!* I kick the gas pedal. How did the time get away from me? I'm late for practice. What should I say when I walk in? It's not like I can tell the worship team I spent the night dreaming about Jonathan and waking up to the nightmare of him finding me at my parents' house or at the lake house because Ainsley abandoned me to fend for myself. Maybe I'll just explain that I pressed snooze too many times. It's the truth—I needed more sleep, and now I'm paying for it.

As I skid into the church parking lot, I whip into the first available spot and exit my car in a frenzy. I jog through the front doors. The music from the auditorium is reverberating through the building…practice has started without me. As I fumble through the doors with an effort to balance my belongings, the music fades on cue. I apologize to the team through pants—sorry is all I can offer anyway as my eyes remain focused on Levi. I can't risk making eye contact with Ainsley . . . not yet.

"That's fine, Hallie," Levi says. "In fact, we are just getting started due to a small setback. Our bass player called in sick, so we have a new addition to the team this morning." In that moment, Levi steps back. A gasp gets caught in my chest. My legs stop moving. Jonathan is standing on the corner of the stage. My mouth falls open, but Levi isn't looking at me—he's looking to Jonathan who offers an amused smile as his eyes pierce my heart like an arrow shot from across the room. "I thought we were in for it, but thankfully, Ainsley suggested that Jonathan could play bass for us this morning."

I begin stepping backward, unable to rip my eyes from this gut-wrenching scene. Jonathan's grin spreads. Ainsley hangs the mic by her side—she won't lift her gaze from her feet. Levi re-adjusts his guitar with an easy smile, he's oblivious to this terrible act of betrayal. *I can't believe it.* My eyes start to sting with a thousand tiny needles. Jonathan has finally gotten his way—he's taken everything from me. And as this truth explodes in my head, rattling my entire body, I turn and run.

My tears flow as I rummage in my bag for my keys. The cool air slaps at my face while rushing to the car. I need to get in the car. I've got to get out of here. The front doors of the church open. That's got to be Ainsley. She has to have some sort of excuse as to why she would do such a thing to me. I swivel, only to find Jonathan approaching. My hands freeze as my eyes scan the parking lot. We're all alone. My stomach flips. I dig for my keys as he moves closer and closer. *Hurry! He's getting closer.* The moment my hand meets the plastic car fob, I unlock the door and dive into the driver's seat. Swinging the door shut, my hands fumble for the lock button just as Jonathan approaches the car and yanks on the handle.

"Roll down the window," he demands. I squeeze me eyes shut for a moment, then I put the keys into the ignition and comply. He doesn't deserve to speak to me, but I deserve to hear an explanation from him.

With the window partially down, I try to steady my rapid breathing. I gulp back my tears and swipe at my cheeks. With my jaw set, I yank up my head. "Haven't you taken enough from me? Did you have to take this too?"

Jonathan smirks, "I was a little upset to watch you leave that lake house the other night. So, when Ainsley suggested I serve on the worship team, I couldn't resist the chance to *reconnect*."

"How did you even find out about the lake house?"

Jonathan leans his head back and snorts, "You haven't guessed yet?" He raises one eyebrow, "Rita told me . . . when you buy that girl enough drinks, she'll spill all her little secrets."

I sputter a cough, like I've swallowed water down my windpipe. "How did Rita know where I was?"

Jonathan's lips pinch around the tip of his tongue as he tilts his head, "Wow, Hallie—you really are stupid. Ainsley told Rita at some Christmas party. I guess it's a *female* thing . . . when you girls drink too much, you'll say just about anything. She told Rita exactly where you were hiding out—right down to the name of that dirt road."

Fog fills my head. Ainsley told Rita? This final stab of betrayal is all I can stand, I've had enough. I throw my car in reverse. I don't have it in me to hear another word. *Thunk!* In a flash, Jonathan's hand is through the window. He grabs for my throat, and I punch the gas as he rocks back with the car. He lets go, but jabs again, getting hold of my sweater, taking the bulk of it with him as his arm is forced to leave through the window. With my foot moving to the break, I fumble to roll up the window. How did he move that fast? I thrash about, leaning back toward the center console. *Let me go!* But he tightens around his handful that stops the window from closing. Our eyes meet for a sickening moment. He moves his gaze slowly down my body, drinking it all in. He loves a good fight—always has, always will. His eyes stop on my exposed stomach, on my scar, and his face curls into a dangerous smile.

"Let go," I hiss.

He takes one more second before ripping his eyes from my scar, then says, "You'll never escape me, Hallie. And somehow, in the darkest corners of your mind, I don't think you really want to. That's why you haven't sent the divorce papers yet. I think you enjoy our little fights as much as I do."

A hallow, dark throttle builds in my throat, and I laugh. Now, it's my turn. "You're wrong. My parents are forcing me to wait a year before signing the papers—I'm only respecting them. I'll see you at the courthouse in October." And with that, I hit the gas again, turning the car away from him. I no longer care if he lets go of my sweater, I'll drag him alongside the car if I have to.

Jonathan stumbles for a second, then releases the material as the car surges backwards. The moment I stop to shift into drive, he charges the car. My words can sting as much as his. I'm glad I've just infuriated him. Now he knows the real reason for the delay in filing for our divorce. He pounds his fist on the roof of my car. But it's too late—I'm off.

I squeal out of the parking lot, leaving it all behind. I can never return to this church. Now, my race is with the ticking clock—I have until the end of the service to clear out of the lake house and make my escape.

CHAPTER 16

The drive back to the lake house is busied with frantic phone calls. The first one is to my brother…he's the only one I trust. I need to stay with him, not because I can't do this on my own, but because I need someone who's got my back. The conversation is easy and quick, I'm going to Ann Arbor, at least until the divorce is final. My call to Jim leaves me apologizing as I tell him I can't return to the job. A brief explanation is all he needed, he said he would send my final check to the address in Ann Arbor. My next call is to my parents…they're just leaving church. I humbly request they meet me at the lake house with my dad's truck to help me pack. Again, they refuse to ask any questions. Weird, but not abnormal—I guess ignorance is bliss.

My final call connects to Ainsley's voicemail. Just what I expected. At the sound of the beep, I blurt, "*How could you, Ainsley?* You knew exactly what you were doing when you suggested Jonathan play on the worship team." My lip quivers, "You were my best friend, and you betrayed me. You were the one who spilled the details about my separation. You were the one who told Rita about the lake house. You were the reason Jonathan found out where I was hiding. It was all you." Tears stream down my face as pain rips through my heart. "I can't trust you. And I can't stay here anymore. You can find the key to the lake house under the front porch mat—I'll be out by the time you get this message." And without the strength to say a final farewell to the one person I believed was my true friend, I hang up.

I skid into park and race from my car. There's no time to waste, I don't plan on being here by the time the service finishes. Bursting through the front door of the lake house, I begin my hasty collection as if time has unkindly thrown me back into the panic of leaving Jonathan five months ago. Luckily, some boxes were never opened. I rush to the bedroom to load up bags and rip clothes from hangers.

The front door creaks ever so quietly. I freeze. That better be my parents, but why didn't they call out? *Thump-thump.* Footsteps lead back to my bedroom. I shiver, as if a bucket of ice has been poured down my back. "Hallie?" my mom questions as my parents move into view.

My coiled muscles unwind as I nod at them then return to my packing. I say over my shoulder, "Dad, can you pack the boxes by the door in your truck?"

My father departs with heavy thuds. He's annoyed, but if there was ever a time I needed him to just stay quiet and not give his two-cents, it's now. My mother doesn't join him, instead she saunters up beside me and asks, "Why are you leaving? And where are you going?"

Forget the first question, I can't tell her why. I shove a few pairs of jeans into a trash bag with my back turned to her. "I'm going to stay with Harrison for a while. But *please* don't tell anyone where I am—I just need to get away. And don't worry," I lift both hands in surrender, "I haven't moved on the divorce yet—I'm gunna keep my promise to you and Dad."

I sidestep my mom, who's standing uselessly in the middle of the room, and move toward the dresser, but my mom puts a hand on my shoulder, halting me. "Hallie, what happened to your face?" My hands fly up to feel my skin. What is she is talking about? My tears have run dry since the moment I started packing. "Oh my, you have scratch marks all down your neck. One of them is bleeding." She turns my chin gently to the side to examine the angry welts that are now searing my skin. My fingertips slide gingerly down my neck. How could I have ignored them before?

"It was an accident that happened at church. It's not serious." But it is, and the truth of this painful reality catapults me into a frenzied rush.

My mother exhales loudly as the return of her harsh tone erases her momentary concern, "Well, maybe if you went to church with us this morning, like you should have, then you wouldn't be all scraped up." My shoulders sag, but I continue packing. Yeah, maybe I could have avoided all this if I had gone to *your* church, but then I wouldn't be my own person. I'd just be complying, like I used to when I was the fawn of the family, like I used to when I let my husband walk all over me. That's not me anymore. I lift my posture as she pulls up beside me at the dresser and starts removing my clothes from another drawer. She checks her watch, "Is your church service over this soon? Well, you young folks must not appreciate the value of a lengthy service."

Heat rises to my face and throbs at the marks Jonathan left. I turn away from her without offering any excuse. She's going to reach her own conclusions. So, just like always, we brush past the topic as if it has never been brought up in the first place. Will my mom and I ever be able to connect? *Well, not with her accusations.* I zip up one of the full bags sitting on my bed and toss it to the door. "Can you take that out to Dad, please?" She turns to exit, her eyes darting. Does she want to say anything else, to apologize? She lifts the duffle bag and swings the strap over her shoulder, hesitates in the frame, then leaves. In the welcome quiet after her exit, I bend a knee and reach under the bed, my hand thumping around. Where is it? *Ahah.* I pull out the tin box I strategically hid the first night I spent alone here in the lake house. I flip open the lid and count the bills I have left from the money I secretly stashed before leaving Jonathan. This should cover the gas it will take me to get to Ann Arbor. I fold the bills and shove them into my back pocket, then throw the empty, tin box into the only bag I have left to pack before I'm out of here for good.

My trunk and back seat are loaded with the items and clothing that I will be taking with me. I swallow my parents' disconnected farewell, and watch them bump down the dirt drive, the bed of their truck piled high with the things I won't need. I lick my lips, then turn to the lake house for one last scan. Everything's in order, just as it had been when I arrived. When will Ainsley come here to collect the key? Today? Next week? *Ah, who cares?* My time in Oklahoma is through. My safety is gone, and I'm left with one option—to take flight all over again.

* * *

TAKE FLIGHT

My eyes grow tired as the dark highway stretches before me. I shake my empty coffee cup, checking, yet again, that I've finished the last drags. *Humph.* There's no more caffeine, and my eyelids are drooping. If I stop for another latte, I may make it through the night. I yawn, for the umpteenth time. *Maybe not.* A sign flashes ahead—next rest stop, two miles away. I've got to stop and rest my eyes for a little. I pull into the parking lot, circle around the well-lit, brick building holding the bathrooms and a few vending machines, and slide into a spot, jamming my foot on the brake. I check the GPS, then power it down. I'm a few states from home…well, not home—from Oklahoma. My chin quivers, but I tighten my fists. *No.* I've done my fair share of crying this trip, I've got to give it a rest. I can't go back now, I know that. So why have I wrestled with the idea, again and again, with the passing miles? I shift into park, lock the doors, turn off the car, throw my coat over me as a blanket, and guide my seat back as far as the suitcase behind will allow. My eyes flutter closed, and thoughts of my escape become my lullaby, singing a hopeless tune of a fawn fleeing for safety until I fall into a restless sleep.

Bang-bang! I suck in a breath so sharply that my lungs freeze in the frigid air as I jolt forward. *What's happening?* I touch the dash to see if my GPS fell, but it's in place. *Bang!* My window rattles beside me, and I flinch. Someone's out there. I take the sleeve of my sweatshirt and rub against the fog on the glass. Who just woke me, and why? My groggy eyes focus on an older man who is crouched beside my car window. "You shouldn't stay here at this hour—it's not safe," he yells. I gulp, look around the grounds, then nod, and give a thumbs-up. If it's not safe, then who's to say this man is? My fingers slide down the door panel and feel for the lock. *Whew.* I'm still locked in. I twist the key to start my car and pull my seat into an upright position. The crouched man rises with the rumble of my engine. I steal a side-glance out of the frosty glass. I hope he's not waiting for me to unroll my window. I've learned my lesson with Jonathan. One hand glides down my neck, and I wince the moment I touch my collarbone. *Another bruise* . . . no surprise. I pinch my lips. I have to protect myself at all costs, even if it means being rude to this stranger. He backs slowly away from the car and watches me drive toward the highway in the muted hues that proceed the sunrise.

I shiver and crank the heat, wiggling my fingers then rubbing at the cold tip of my nose. Should I have put on another pair of socks? *Ugh.* I bend and flex my toes in my boots. I probably should have stopped over in a hotel, but there was no money for that. Besides, a few hours rest was all I needed anyway. I glance down at the empty cup in my cup holder. *Hmmm.* A coffee will do the trick, although that sudden start from sleep was like a shot of caffeine to my veins. I pull off at a convenient exit, order a latte, fill up my gas tank, and find myself on the road again just as the sun begins to rise. The gray slush along the side of the highway builds as I navigate farther north. By the time I cross the Michigan state line, I spiral again into a state of mourning. It's not that I don't appreciate Harrison's willingness to let me live with his family until I can get on my feet, it's more that my world is being flipped upside-down. I scan the dreary sky and dirty snowbanks…a perfect match for my depressing thoughts.

But I'm supposed to be a fighter now. How does this sudden move fit with the new me? Just yesterday, I was eager to spend time in worship with God at *my* church, but today I'm escaping across state lines to get far away from the abuse and betrayal I left behind. When will it ever stop? Can I ever settle down, or will I always have to flee for my safety? Will I ever be able to trust again?

CHAPTER 17

"Well, that just about sums it up, Mrs. McClain. Welcome to the gym," the woman across from me says. I flinch. She's donning exactly what I'll be when I begin my new job here: black polo shirt, khaki pants, name tag. And if she's calling me Hallie McClain, that's probably what she's going to stamp on the clip that will go on my shirt . . . for all to see.

As she rises from her desk, I clear my throat, then say, "Actually, I know my paperwork for this position indicates that my last name is McClain, but it'll soon be legally changed back to Reed, and I'm wondering if we can just stick to *Hallie Reed* for the staff and members of this gym?"

"Absolutely," my new superior says, her slow smile topped with a single wrinkle in her brow. "I'll make sure we get that detail clear for your name tag." She pulls open her desk drawer and takes out a digital camera, "The last thing we need to do for your training is get a picture of you."

As I shift uncomfortably in my seat, she asks me to smile as she points the camera at my face. *Humph.* Do I have to? My lips lift ever so slightly. *Click-click.* The shutter of the lens blinks back at me. That wasn't too painful. "What's the picture for?"

"We put it in our system so that the other trainers at the gym know who you are when you clock in. We're completely online here, so when you sign in at the front desk, the system recognizes your features and moves you through the process quickly." I nod. It won't be long before my days will be spent at this busy gym rather than sulking in Harrison and Isabel's apartment. In one, short week, I found the open position. The second week was filled with the interview and training. *Easy enough.* "Oh," she adds, "and we'll put this picture on our website so that our members can have a visual of all the trainers."

"*No!*" I blurt, my adrenaline spiking to my tingling extremities. She freezes. I blink, over and over, then lean forward in my chair. "I'm sorry, it's just that . . ." *What do I say?* I can't tell her about Jonathan. I don't even know her. Would it make sense to explain why I had to leave Oklahoma if I don't mention *him*? "Well . . . there's someone back home who would really like to know where I am, and *he* will probably be searching for me on multiple websites."

In a flash, her eyes move to the yellowing bruise on my collarbone. *Ugh.* Why hasn't that thing healed yet? And why don't they make a foundation that can really cover it up? If only scarves were appropriate at a gym. Her gaze searches the rest of my body, as if she's expecting to see broken bones. The bruise is all she'll see; the rest of the damage is on the inside. She swallows and drops her eyes to the paperwork on her desk. "Not a problem," she says in a clipped voice as she shuffles around some papers, "for now, you can be the new hire on the website without a name or picture." She lifts her head and forces a smile, stealing another glance at my neck.

I trace a fingertip across my lips and rise from my seat. "I guess I'll see you on Monday," I say, my eyes darting in every direction. I blink a few times, my face still pulsating with heat. "Thanks again for this position, I'm looking forward to getting started." She shakes my hand, and I leave her office. I take a deep breath, the mixture of sweat and cleaning solution fills my nose as I cross the upper deck of the local gym placed conveniently in the middle of downtown Ann Arbor. *Glad that's over.*

My GPS leads me back to the apartment that I now call home. I've got to figure out these roads. It's pretty easy to navigate around here, I just haven't taken the time to do it. Maybe now's the time . . . *nah.* I'd much rather crawl beneath the covers of Harrison and Isabel's guest bed—of my bed—for the remainder of this partly cloudy Saturday. This March weather is so strange, one day we'll get sunshine, the next, sleet, and every once-in-a-while, a light snowfall. It's not like Oklahoma around here…no, not at all. I'm used to people riding four-wheelers, fishing at the creek, and getting geared up to hunt turkey this time of year. Not that I'm a real *outdoorsy* gal, but there's no option for those familiar activities around these parts. I shake my head in dismay. The transition to Ann Arbor has been about as smooth as I could've hoped for. So why can't I shake the depressive state I've been drowning in these past two weeks? Is it Jonathan's intrusion, Ainsley's betrayal, or the combination of both?

I pull up to the white siding and neatly manicured lawns of the apartment building and find a vacant visitor's spot toward the far end of the complex. Usually, I have to drive around for a while. Visitor parking spots are few and far between at this complex. *Ah*—what's there to complain about? Walking the length of the street isn't the worst idea . . . especially because I haven't worked out since I arrived. There's no energy or drive for that. My tank is on empty, but at least I had enough *pep in my step* to get a job and dye my hair. *Here goes my exercise for the day.* I jog up the stairs, into the apartment, and up the second flight of stairs to the main landing of Isabel and Harrison's place. Isabel is bustling around in the kitchen, and the twins are playing in their room down the hall.

Isabel pokes her head out of the kitchen holding a container of strawberries. Did my panting give me away? Her head jerks back, "Sorry," she breathes, "I'm still trying to get used to your hair. It's so dark." She tips her head and grins, "It's beautiful, you've got that *Snow White* look going on, but it's so different." With a quick shake of her head, she asks, "Anyway, how'd it go at the gym?"

I shrug one shoulder, lifting a piece of my jet-black hair, "Fine, I start on Monday."

Isabel disappears again and turns on the tap to rinse the strawberries. "That gym is great," she calls from the kitchen. "I'm glad you could get a job so quickly—they usually have quite a few applicants there, so it says a lot that they chose you." *Chink-chink.* She drops ice-cubes into the empty blender. My stomach growls at the thought of a delicious strawberry smoothie.

"Thanks again, if it wasn't for you and Harrison putting in a good word for me, I wouldn't be starting work soon."

"No problem, we're just glad you're here," she finishes. *Vroom!* She powers up the blender, but I don't stick around. I'm not here to burden them. I've already occupied a lot of the space in this cozy apartment, so I slink back to the bedroom, close the door behind me, and collapse onto the bed in the corner of my room. There's a small dresser directly beside the door that I was able to stuff full the day I arrived. The tiny closet located just beyond the foot of the bed is flooded with some of Isabel and Harrison's storage items. They were kind enough to leave me some hanger space though. I take out my phone from my back pocket, check the screen, then place it down on the wood-finished bedside table before rolling over to face the wall.

Why hasn't Ainsley texted me? It would be nice to know that she got the key. I squeeze my eyes closed. That's not what I really want to hear…I want to hear that it was all a mistake. A simple apology is all I need. *Heck!* At this point, I'd be happy if she just said hello. Somehow, during that one, short hour, I lost my home, my job, my safety, and my best friend. My throat grows tight. A tear slides down my cheek and drops to the pillow. I thought I could trust her. She was all I had left in Oklahoma. My safety depended on her keeping my hiding place at the lake house a secret. How long before that secret was shared? And why didn't she warn me? She had so many chances to give me a heads-up, *but no*—she waited until Jonathan found out. Then, she made things worse with the worship team thing, inviting Jonathan to join. She knew how much that would crush me. How could she be so untrustworthy in the end? She was my best friend, she was all I had—and now I'm scrambling to piece together my life in a whole new place.

* * *

"Aunt Hallie?" a little voice calls out. Light floods my sight as I slide open my eyes. Nothing like a wake-up call from a child. With a lethargic roll, I meet two sets of big, blue eyes belonging to my nephew and niece who are poised beside my bed. "Um, we were wondering if you're gunna come to church with us today?" Branson questions with sweet innocence. I skipped out on church last week. He remembered, and he's going to make sure I accompany the family today.

Yawning, I smile then say, "Yes, I'll come to church with you today." Branson punches the air and runs out of the room, but Bailey stays by my side. "Hi gorgeous," I reach out and ruffle her curls. "You're all dressed and ready to go, aren't you?"

She grins shyly, then leans into the side of the bed, her smile twisting downward. She casts her gaze to my shoulder, then asks, "Did Uncle Jon hurt you?"

What? Her question jolts me out of my sleepy state. "Who told you that?"

She looks down at her tiny hands, then, without a word, crawls into bed with me and facing me, curls up by my side. She gently touches the bruise on my collarbone once she gets settled, then says, "No one—I just know that Uncle Jon is a bad man."

I'm stunned into complete silence. How much has Bailey been able to pick up from my bruises and behavior these past two weeks? *Can she really tell that Jonathan's a bad man just from me, or is there something I'm missing?*

The door creaks quietly, and Isabel pokes her head in. "Bailey," she begins with a quiet but stern tone, "I told you to let Aunt Hallie sleep."

Bailey jumps out of bed and runs to her mother, hugs her leg, then says, "I'm sorry, Mommy."

Bailey scampers out of sight, and Isabel stands in the partially cracked doorway. "Hallie, I'm so sorry they woke you, go back to sleep."

I rub at my eyes. Should I ask Isabel about what Bailey just said? I swing my legs over the side of the bed and sigh. Now's not the time. "Actually," I reply, "I'm coming to church with you today."

"Don't feel like you need to. I know this is an adjusting time for you, and we want to be sensitive to that."

"No, no—I didn't feel like I could go last week, but the feelings I have about church aren't for your church, more so for Connect Church. I'm not rejecting church all together, I just need to *get back on the horse*."

Isabel looks down at her feet as her painted toes play with the carpet, "Well, we would love to have you, but I know you're really struggling with some trust issues right now." She lifts her head, then says, "Take your time, and if you change your mind, just let us know." She exits the room, leaving me there to contemplate her words.

She's right, I don't trust anyone right now. Harrison and Isabel . . . they're different—they're family. But I don't trust my parents, so I can't really play the *family* card. I can't bring myself to trust the church, and I've lost the trust of my best friend . . . former best friend. I stretch both arms above my head and glance out the window. It's God with whom I really struggle. My eyes scan the room and fixate on the frame I received at Christmas sitting on the dresser, the only one I brought from Oklahoma. Jeremiah 29:11 has been my meditation, but how am I supposed to trust God with my future and his plans to prosper me and not to harm me when I'm bruised, friendless, and starting over in a completely new place—when I feel like I'm going to be taking flight for the rest of my life?

Shaking my head, I rise from my bed and trudge to the bathroom. I don't have the answers, but a tiny voice in the back of my mind is telling me to hold on. I can't figure out why God led me here by forcing my escape from Oklahoma, but if this verse is true, then there must be hope…somewhere, somehow.

Nations Church is upbeat, inviting, and current. The worship team closes out their last song, and although I've put up a bit of a wall, it's good to be at church again. I take a seat and sigh heavily. This is a church where no one knows my name, my past, or the darkness that lurks in the corners of my heart. I'm stiff-arming God, but that's my little secret for now.

As the worship team exits the stage, a familiar man steps up and moves toward the microphone standing in the spotlight. "Welcome to Nations Church," he says, adjusting his round, designer-framed glasses. My eyes scan the crowd and search for his flawless wife. It takes only moments to spot her long, perfectly curled locks. I bite my lip and I lower my gaze. I could've put a little more attention to my appearance. The rushed departure this morning hasn't done me any favors. I lift my shoulders and pick up my head. *Why do I always have to compare myself?* "I'm Tom Romano, and I'm here to share a few announcements before we hear from our pastor."

Tom goes through a brief list, but I miss the updates completely as I study his demeanor. It's no wonder that Sarah went after him, he's confident, well-spoken, and kind. Their marriage must be perfect. They get along so well, and *they* go to church together. "If you don't know who Harrison and Isabel

Reed are," Tom says, pinning my attention back onto the announcements, "they'll be standing at the back of the auditorium with name tags on once the service ends. A small group will be meeting in their apartment starting this week, so if you're interested, please go to them for details. My wife, Sarah, and I will also be attending and helping to lead this Bible study, so feel free to ask us questions after the service, too."

My lips pinch and I wrinkle my nose. Was this the study Harrison told me would be meeting at their home every Thursday, starting in March? Did he tell me Tom and Sarah would be attending? I mean, it would be nice to learn from them and discover what makes their marriage appear so effortless, but I don't want to sit beside Sarah, week in and week out, drowning in the truth of my broken past, failed marriage, and floundering life. If they knew all that, they would judge me…anyone would. *Heck*—I judge myself, how can expect others not to?

"Sorry, Hallie," Harrison starts just as the service ends, "we need to wait at the back of the auditorium for about ten minutes."

"No worries, I'll come with you. I mean, I guess I'll be attending this Bible study too, so it wouldn't be so bad to get to know some faces." *Better standing with Harrison and Isabel rather than waiting by myself.* We exit our row and weave our way to the back of the auditorium. Many come and introduce themselves to me, offering a warm welcome as they catch up with my brother and sister-in-law. Some express interest in their small group, and Harrison and Isabel get lost in sharing the details with those gathering around them. Re-adjusting my purse on my shoulder, a voice from behind startles me.

"Hey, I remember you," I swing around just as Sarah approaches my side. She tucks a long curl behind her ear as she leans over to give me a hug. My body stiffens. *Whoa.* This is friendly for a second introduction, but I hug her back, then gently pull away, smiling shyly.

"Yes, I'm Hallie," I offer, my eyes moving to the floor.

"Of course—*Hallie*. I didn't recognize you at first with your hair, but I have to say the color is gorgeous. It makes your eyes pop. I could see the beautiful green in them from the other side of the room." I look at her and nod my head, my smile spreading. She grins and re-adjusts her off-the-shoulder sweater. "Isabel said you'd be moving in with them, I hope you're liking Ann Arbor so far. The snow should be gone soon, and hopefully it will start to warm up in the next month. I was raised in Minnesota, so the cold is nothing new for me."

"Well, I grew up in Michigan," I shrug. "So, it's just a matter of re-adjusting, I guess."

"Oh, that's right," Sarah replies, pointing a perfectly manicured finger. "Now that you mention it, I think I remember Harrison saying something about his childhood in Michigan." Sarah taps that finger mindlessly on her porcelain cheek—her skin is evidence that she hasn't spent much time in the sun. Tom calls for Sarah to come meet a couple who's interested in joining the small group. He waves at me and I wave back. Then Sarah says, "Well, it's nice to see you again, Hallie. I guess I'll see you on Thursday night."

Offering her a short nod, I say, "Nice to see you, Sarah," as she turns and saunters to her husband's side. He slides an arm around her thin waste, and my stomach tightens. Is this how all Christian couples are around here? Back in Oklahoma, it seems like every other marriage is teetering on the verge of unhealthy. Not Isabel and Harrison's marriage, though—they're the one positive example I have in my life, they have the kind of marriage I would love to have one day. *Who knows?* Maybe I'll learn from both these couples in the coming months. Between the two of them, I'll figure out what it takes to have a successful marriage. Maybe my love life doesn't have to end with the divorce. Maybe there's hope for something better.

Turning slowly away from the mingling couples, I shake my downtrodden head. Actually, I don't need any distractions, like visualizing what a future marriage might look like. For now, I'm here to make some money and remain safe. Once I make enough to get on my own feet, I'll be moving on to the next stage of life. My stomach tightens. And that next stage better not have anything to do with Jonathan. In the meantime, I just need him to leave me alone. My throat begins to close.

CHAPTER 18

Shifting in my seat, I scan each face of the people in Harrison's small group. Maybe I'd be more comfortable had I attended their first meeting last week. I guess that's the gig though, what with my new work schedule. I'm not in a position to be requesting shifts, so I get what's handed to me. At least I'm not working now.

Tom flips through his Bible from where he's seated directly across from me, using a finger to push his circular frames higher up the bridge of his nose. "We'll end tonight's study with this verse," he says. "Proverbs seventeen verse twelve says, 'Better to meet a bear robbed of her cubs than a fool bent on folly,' isn't that interesting?" He pauses for a moment before looking up, letting us all ponder the verse. "This verse stood out to me when I read it. I don't know about you all, but I don't want to encounter an angry mama bear that's missing her cubs. In essence, I think I would much rather meet a fool bent on folly. But that's not what scripture tells us is the less dangerous of the two options."

The group immediately starts offering their various viewpoints related to Tom's statement, but I don't. Instead, I turn the verse over and over in my head. Unlike those around me, I can see what the proverb is getting at. In fact, if Jonathan was the fool, I would much rather meet a bear robbed of her cubs. Between the bear and Jonathan, I probably stand a better chance with the bear.

"Thanks for that verse, Tom," Harrison eventually concludes. "Let's close in prayer." As Harrison prays, my heart rate quickens. What kind of destruction is a fool bent on folly capable of? When will *he* finally figure out I've left Oklahoma?

Everyone begins to slowly filter out of the apartment as Isabel coaxes a few to take another brownie before leaving. Jackets are slipped on to ward off the chill of the April, evening air. Good-byes are said, and it takes a few minutes before it's just me, Harrison, Isabel, Tom, and Sarah left. Harrison and Isabel start gathering the scattered, dirty dishes and bringing them into the kitchen as I begin collecting dirty napkins. With my head bowed and focused on the task, I busy myself to avoid eye contact with Tom and Sarah. Their hands are clasped, and their shoulders are meshed together on the couch.

"It was good to see you working at the gym last week, Hallie." Tom says. "I've had a membership there for a while, so I know how awesome that place is. I'm glad they hired you."

"Yeah, I'm really liking my new job," I reply, still refusing to look up and confront their love head on.

"Well, it seems like you fit in there."

With a shy smile, I stand, tightening my grip around the waded-up bundle of used napkins, "Thanks, I used to work at a local gym in Oklahoma before I came here, so it's just a matter of learning the ways of this new gym and applying my skills." My head drops a little. If only I didn't have to leave Oklahoma, then I'd still have the comfort of familiarity.

"Their loss is our gain," Sarah chimes. "From the little I've seen, I can tell you're really good at your job. I may be coming to you for some exercise pointers." My heart lifts. I would gladly workout with Sarah. Could she be a new friend? I grin and nod at the idea, then move to the trashcan in the kitchen. Emerging into the living room again on the heels of Harrison and Isabel, they both take a seat near Tom and Sarah, so I do the same. My insides stiffen. I'm still not so sure about them just yet. They seem great, but if they get to know me, who I am, and everything about my past, I can bet they will choose to keep their distance. Can one unhealthy marriage bleed into another that easily?

"So, how did you guys feel tonight went?" Harrison asks the group.

A silent nod is all I'm willing to offer, but Isabel pipes up, "I thought it went really well—we all could use a little reminder about applying wisdom in our life. And what Tom added at the end with the verse about the bear missing her cubs—that certainly paints a picture."

"Yeah, that verse really stood out to me as I was preparing for tonight," Tom responds. His eyes slide over to his wife before he says, "I mean, I don't know what it would look like to encounter a mama-bear missing her cubs." Sarah shifts in her seat as she abruptly breaks eye contact with Tom, then he clears his throat and adds, "But the thought of it certainly is terrifying."

The tension in the room thickens and hangs between us for a moment as I witness the momentary awkwardness between Tom and Sarah. Then, Sarah quips, "But it's not nearly as dangerous as meeting a fool bent on folly." Everyone laughs, and like an evaporating mist, the tension is gone. All that's left are two loving couples, laughing together and hold onto each other… and then there's me.

My phone vibrates in my back pocket. Who could be calling me? I hope it's not work—did I mess up my schedule? I yank my phone out and stifle a gasp. Jonathan's number flashes across the screen, and my blood freezes in my veins. My gaze darts quickly to Harrison and Isabel, then I race to my room without an excuse . . . my face says it all.

"What do you want?" I bark into the phone the moment I close my bedroom door, my false bravado hopefully masking my tremors. I wish I could ignore his call. But that's just it—I *need* to know what he wants. If there are ways to placate him over the phone, then I have a better chance of keeping those I love safe.

Jonathan pauses for a moment, lapping it up. I can almost see him smiling, as if he has already recognized the affect he's having on me. "I thought I would call to see where my wife is…since she's clearly not in Oklahoma anymore."

His jeering tone is enough to make me vomit. "I'm not your wife. And it's none of your business where I am."

"Well actually, it is my business, Hallie," he retorts, the playful taunting in his voice immediately replaced with a rasp. "You see, I can't have it look as bad as it does around here, what with my wife quitting her job and leaving town. Ainsley told me at church this past Sunday that you've been out of the lake house for weeks now. This just doesn't look good on me, so it's time to stop playing this little game and come home."

I rock back, as if I've been kicked square in the chest. He knows why I've put off the divorce. All his hope is gone, now it's his time to coerce me into coming back. "That place is not my *home*," I hiss through clenched teeth. "I'm not coming back, and nothing you say can convince me, so I think this conversation is over."

"I thought you'd say something like that," he shoots back before I can hang-up, "so, I'd like to add a little incentive for your return." A shiver creeps up my back. I close my eyes and wait as he leaves me processing the possibilities, like a spider luring a fly to its death. "You remember the dogs, don't you?" My breath catches, "I know they miss you, Hallie. But I couldn't care less about them." He snorts an almost inaudible laugh, "So, here's the deal. I'm not gunna feed the dogs until you return home. And after a week, if their starvation hasn't killed them already, I'm just gunna start shootin' em."

My mouth falls open and tears rush to my eyes. "*You wouldn't!*" I cry.

"Oh yes, I would."

The sound of heavy steps pound to my room, and my door jerks open. "Is everything alright?" Harrison gushes, his protective tone reverberates through the room, but not before I can cover the speaker with my hand. I nod hurriedly, swiping at a tear. Did Jonathan just hear him?

"Who was that?" booms Jonathan.

My heart thumps hard against my chest, "It's none of your business. When will you get it through your head that I'm not yours anymore. We're getting divorced. I'm not coming back. It's over between us."

"Well, it sounds like it's over because you've found another man," he accuses. Harrison hesitates in the doorframe. I clench my eyes shut, nod my head quickly, then open them in time to see Harrison duck out of the room with a heavy sigh, closing the door quietly behind him to extend privacy. "It's true—isn't it?" Jonathan continues. "I just heard a man's voice, and he's clearly wanting to protect you, so either it's your brother or some guy you ran away with. Which is it, Hallie?"

Adrenaline spikes as I begin to pace. He's backed me into a corner; either I admit to a non-existent affair or to tell him where I'm hiding. Air barely passes through my tight throat as I blurt, "It's neither. Like I said, my life is none of your business."

His dangerous, blood curdling laugh tingles my eardrum, then he says, "Well, let's hope it's your brother then, because if not, I'll kill you, Hallie. I'll kill you, then I'll kill him—whoever *he* might be. Remember Mills Pond . . . your burial place? Well, maybe I'll start burying the dogs there first." And at that, the line goes dead.

My hand drops slowly to my side as I stand uselessly in the middle of my room, as if my feet are glued to the floor. It doesn't matter if there are hundreds of miles between us, he will follow me wherever I go.

The door behind me opens once more, and a startled swivel brings me face-to-face with my concerned sister-in-law. "I'm so sorry to intrude, Hallie," she offers from the partially opened door. With a quick glance at the phone still in my hand, she adds, "Tom and Sarah left just after you took that call, and Harrison thought I should check on you—that was . . . *him*, right?"

Offering an exhausted nod, I plop down on the side of my bed and toss my phone on the pillow. "He told me to come back to Oklahoma. That he was going to kill the dogs if I don't."

Isabel's head juts forward. She takes one exasperated glance into the hallway, then slides into the room. The moment she closes herself in, she leans back, as if the door can hold her weight and the burden of what she just heard. "He can't mean that," she says with a hint of question threading her words. "I mean, do you think he would really do that?" I shrug, nausea finding my throat. *Those poor dogs.* Isabel tips her head and adds, "You know, I bet he's out of options, and this is his last attempt to get you back. He's just trying to scare you, he wouldn't really kill the dogs—they're *his* hunting dogs."

"Well, his threat is almost working," I sigh, my chin quivering. "I want to go back just to save those dogs."

Isabel drifts over to the side of the bed and lowers herself to a seated position beside me. "Don't let him frighten you into doing anything that would put you in harm's way. He's proven just how dangerous he is, Hallie. Now that the bruises and scratch marks have healed, you don't want to place yourself anywhere near the man who won't hesitate to hurt you again."

I gulp. *Oh, he'll hurt me, alright. He'll kill me.* I grip the comforter beneath me until my knuckles turn white. "He mentioned something about killing me, too."

"*What?*" Isabel rears back, suddenly poised, as if she's squaring up for a boxing match.

I shake my head. "It's only because he heard Harrison speak to me in the background and he thought I was with another guy." With one hand massaging my temple, I explain, "A couple of years ago, he told me how he would kill me if he got the chance, and how he would make it seem like I disappeared with some guy instead. When he overheard a man's voice, he made sure to remind me of that plan."

Isabel sucks in a deep breath, "He doesn't know where we live, and he has never been to Ann Arbor, so you're safe here. But you've got to tell someone at Connect Church. Someone should know about all this—can you reach out to anyone?"

Lowering my hand and my gaze to my lap, I reply, "No, there's no one there I trust right now. Ainsley told him at church that I left the lake house, which means he's probably still serving on the worship team now that I'm not there to protest against it." I bite my bottom lip, "I just don't understand why he'd still be attending that church. Now that I'm gone, he doesn't need to keep putting on a show."

Isabel starts to bounce one knee as she twitches her pursed lips back and forth. "He's probably still there because he wants to lure you back. If you do go back in response to his threats, and he's no longer at the church, then everyone will see through his act, and that would defeat his initial reasoning as to why he returned in the first place." She breathes in slowly, "Which means that he's going to keep going to that church and keep fooling everyone in the community as long as he thinks there's a chance to get you back."

"Well, I'm not going back. And if he thinks he can use the dogs to get me back, he's wrong." A shudder straightens my slumped shoulders. This has to be my decision—and I've got to stick with it. I can't think about those precious dogs and how much I love them. *Please, Lord, don't let him hurt the dogs.*

Isabel places a hand on my knee, "I think you should block his number, Hallie. He's only going to keep playing this little game of calling and threatening you until he can find something that *works*."

I unconsciously begin biting at a hangnail. Should I block him again? She might be right—he probably will keep calling. "I can't," I finally breathe. "With the divorce coming up, I need to be able to hear from him in case anything happens. I mean, what if he goes after my parents when he figures out the dog thing won't work?" Angling my head to one side as if I've lost all my willpower, I whisper, "I just need him to sign those papers, but I know he's going to fight till the very end."

"Don't worry," Isabel encourages with a squeeze, "we'll come up with a plan to get him to sign those papers. In the meantime, I just hope these phone calls don't become a weekly thing now that he knows you've left Oklahoma."

"Yeah," I mutter in response, "I don't know what that call was for—maybe to actually get me to move back to Oklahoma or maybe to get revenge for giving him a bad name around there. Or…" my heart jumps in my throat, "maybe he called to piece together clues so he can figure out where I am."

CHAPTER 19

April quietly rolled into May without hearing from Jonathan. No word in well over a month. I guess that's all well and good, but the fear of his call remains my constant companion. Did he kill his hunting dogs? Would he do such a thing? The truth is—yes, he's capable of such a hideous act, especially in blind anger fueled by my refusal to return. If he has done something to the dogs, someone would have called or texted me about it. If there's one thing that remains consistent in my hometown, it's that small talk spreads like wildfire. I slip my phone out of the back pocket of my khaki pants and pivot to check my screen. Nothing. Turning back toward the open floor, I slide my phone into my pocket and refocus my eyes on work. I hope no one saw that.

Despite my efforts, the mundane workout routines of those surrounding me refuse to hold my attention. All I can think about is Jonathan. It's not like him to give up this easily. He's a crafty man—always planning something, so what's he planning next? He's going to try to get me back, and if the dogs aren't enough, who will he go after? Shrugging off this nagging concern, I begin circling the fitness floor. *Hmmm.* Why is it so empty in here tonight? Is it the nice weather? Maybe members are choosing outdoor activities instead of working out…I don't blame them. I glance longingly out the window as I pass by the free weights. The sun is heading toward the horizon, painting a pretty backdrop. *Please still be up when I get off in an hour.* I check my watch, but movement from the center staircase pulls my attention back inside.

A blonde ponytail bounces into view at the top of the staircase as Sarah sails up the stairs, like Pegasus. There's no question about it, she's beautiful and easy to talk to. That much has been true through all the encounters we've had at church and the study every Thursday night. Why can't I just be myself around her? She's nice enough—it shouldn't matter that her relationship with Tom is the epitome of perfection, she probably knows that not all marriages are as effortless as her and Tom's. She must see a lot of messed up marriages at work while she helps to deliver babies—but as messed up as mine was…is? A puff of air leaves my lungs. Maybe we shouldn't be friends.

Sarah catches my eye and waves from the other side of the gym. With a tight smile and a quick wave back, I stride toward the window and take in the height of the tall, neighboring buildings. *I wish she wasn't so nice. That would make all this easier.* By the time I meander toward the cardio machines, I notice Sarah sinking into a few simple stretches, her movements and appearance casting the allure of a floating cloud.

I round the squat rack, heading toward the Smith machines positioned next to the blue mats where Sarah is warming up. My loneliness radiates through my hollow chest. Maybe I'll say hello to her. A couple guys nearby are bragging about their new max reps and the heavy weight they're lifting. The two seem to be competing in an effort to draw Sarah's attention, but oblivious to their antics, she demonstrates her unusual flexibility with focused attention. She rises just as I'm about to cross her path, having completed another circuit around the weight room while making myself available to help anyone in need.

"Hey, Hallie," she greets, her tone cheerful, as if she's just bumped into her long-lost friend. "How are ya?"

"Oh, good," I reply with a smile, "just doing the rounds before I clock out in an hour."

Sarah nods, then giggles as she says, "Well, you may want to fix your nametag before you make another round—if someone needs your help, they won't know what to call you."

She crosses toward me and leans in as she unclips the magnet and rotates my nametag. *Ugh!* Has it been like that this whole time? "Wow—I can't believe I've worn it upside down this whole shift."

Sarah laughs, "It wasn't really noticeable, I'm just meticulous about things like that." She clips it back, then pats my shoulder. "There, all good—I can now tell your name is *Hallie Reed*," she finishes as if we are sharing an inside joke.

Oh gosh! Hallie Reed—that's who she knows me to be. Here she is being a friend to a girl who's deceived her into believing this is my legal name, but it won't be for another five months. I fix my eyes on my nametag and hide my cringe. With a tug on the right side to straighten it, I say, "Thanks for that."

"No problem," she replies, "I do embarrassing stuff like that all the time." I offer a grin as she moves to the squat rack. I bet she doesn't do stuff like this…ever, but her words ease the pressure building through my chest. The guys who were bragging loudly share their glances between me and Sarah as she glides toward the weights. They swing their arms about, appearing to be stretching between sets. I chew the inside of my cheek, it's not like my uniform, messy bun, and lightly applied make-up compare to Sarah. That's probably why she has the perfect marriage, not me. Could I ever have a marriage like hers? Is there someone out there who is kind, gracious, and caring enough to love someone like me, someone who's already had one go at marriage and failed miserably? I savor a long blink. Jonathan would say no.

With an abrupt turn and a quickened pace, I shove my hands into my pockets. But I'm a fighter now. *And I do deserve that!* At the very least, I deserve more than what Jonathan gave me—a crushed heart, bruised skin, and a scar that will always haunt me. For the remaining hour of my shift, I do my rounds, helping a few members with various questions and correct form, all the while avoiding Sarah.

At the end of my shift, I leave through the front doors at a quickened pace. *Phew.* Thank God that shifts over. All I need is an empty gym and a boring shift for my mind to run wild. "Hi, love," a dainty voice calls from behind. "Has it been an hour already?"

I turn to find Sarah tailing me. The breeze blows some loose strands from my bun into my face, and I tuck what I can behind an ear as I reply, "Yeah, it has. Are you just finishing your workout?"

With a quick glance at her phone while she approaches me where I wait on the sidewalk, she says, "Yeah, all done. Too bad Tom couldn't join me today." She half shrugs, "So, where are you parked?"

"A few blocks down, over in a parking garage," I point in the direction across town.

"The one on Fourth and William? Near all the outdoor patio restaurants?"

"Yeah, I think that's the one." A light giggle escapes as I say, "I'm still trying to get to know my way around here, and I usually park somewhere close, but I guess everyone's out enjoying the warmer weather, so those spots were taken."

"Well, I'm parked in that garage too, so we can walk together. Is that okay?"

"Sure," I oblige, with a hint of eagerness threading my tone. It's nice to have someone to walk with—to have a friend who will chat with me. *Wait.* I hope she doesn't start probing. Will she ask why I had to leave Oklahoma? We take a few strides in complete silence, my shoulders rising as the tension builds. *Oh gosh!* I've got to focus the attention on her. "So, you're a nurse, right?" I blurt.

"Yeah—I work at the university hospital," she says, shifting her gym bag to the opposite shoulder. "It's actually in a great location—I can workout here after my shift and see Tom at the university when he has some down time, which isn't often. Those professors are over-worked. But Tom and I both love our jobs."

"That's awesome—what led you to your job?"

Sarah starts twirling a strand of her hair as she says, "Oh, I just love babies." She bites her bottom lip as she scratches her neck for a moment, then slaps a smile on her face as she adds, "I've always loved babies, and I come from a family of nurses and doctors, so working in the labor and delivery unit was a no-brainer."

There's no question about it—Sarah adores her job, that much is evidenced in her tone. So, why doesn't she have children? Would it be rude to ask? *Ah*—it sounds like they are the career-driven couple. Besides, they both look young. They've got time. As we turn a corner, the sunlight hits my face forcing my furrowed brow into a squint. "So, you grew up in

Minnesota, then?" Reticent, I keep the conversation focused on her. Sure, she's kind and humble, but can I trust her with the details of my past…and can I put her off if she asks?

"Yeah, I loved it there. I go back to visit my family as much as I can, and it's never a dull moment with them. Although," she hesitates, "it can be a little difficult given their religious views."

"What do you mean?"

"They're all atheists. With their medical background, they just don't see how God and science can relate, and for years, I shared that same view."

I slow my pace. *I've gotta hear more.* She used to be an atheist, and now she's all in for God. How did *that* happen? I hesitate for a moment, but throw caution to the wind and ask, "What changed your mind?"

"Oh, well—that's a complicated story, probably more of a story that Tom needs to share rather than me." She grins, "You'll have to ask him some time, but let's just say that our lives were flipped upside down, and there was nowhere to turn but Christ. Our marriage was falling apart because Tom had made the decision to follow Christ before I did." My eyes bulge. *No way.* "It was killing him that I was choosing to reject Christ; thankfully, God captured my heart before things unraveled for good."

Tom and Sarah have dealt with marital problems of their own? Their marriage wasn't always this easy? *Hmmm.* Maybe they wouldn't judge me if I told them about my past after all. "Wow," I sigh as my shoes follow the slabs of pavement beneath me, "Just like that, you turned from your parents' perspective and accepted Christ as your Savior?"

"It wasn't easy," she murmurs, her lips slide into a hint of a smile. "But it was worth it. How about your parents? Did you grow up in a Christian home?"

Oh boy. My turn. "Yes and no," I sigh. "My parents have always gone to church, but that's pretty much where it ends. It's more about going to church for them than it is about having faith. When we were growing up, we had a set of super-strict rules, and that included going to church every Sunday. I didn't like church back then, it felt like a chore, not something I wanted to do. But eventually, Harrison helped me understand what it meant to be a Christian." The golden-child saved the day, yet again. My shoulders slump. It's no wonder my parents are so proud of him—he has his life intact. As for me, I'm just their train-wreck of a daughter. I'm sure in their mind, it would take one, good service at their church to sort me out . . . as if.

We cross at the stoplight leading onto South Main. As we walk by the regular Ann Arbor crowd filling the outdoor patios this time of day, I take in the beauty and bustle of it all. "That must have been difficult," Sarah replies as we continue walking. She begins to say something else, but I don't hear a word. I freeze. The sound of my heartbeat thrashes in my ears, instead, as an all-too familiar smell of smoke wafts by. *No.* I sniff again. *It can't be!*

Sarah, a few paces ahead, does a double-take when she finds I'm no longer by her side. She turns and takes a step toward me with her eyebrows drawn together. I gulp and pivot on the spot, my eyes slicing through the crowd for the source. I scan the patio, then gasp. There it is, the black and red wrapper of a Davidoff Yamasa cigar. I stumble backward as my hands fly up to my ears. The cigar sits alone, burning in an ashtray on an empty, black iron table positioned near the door of a small, red-bricked restaurant. The single chair behind the table is pulled back, but there isn't a person in sight to claim it...or the cigar.

CHAPTER 20

I blink against fuzzy spots clouding my vision, as if the adrenaline coursing through my veins is causing temporary blindness. He has to be here. Each new, smoke-filled breath quickens as I slip dangerously close to hyperventilating. *Where is he?* My eyes dart to the nearby tables like bouncing pinballs while the outdoor guests at this restaurant sitting closest to my trembling body begin to stare.

"Hallie," I hear from behind. I jump as a hand touches my shoulder. *Oh gosh—Sarah!* She steps toward me and inclines her head as her eyes narrow. But how could she understand what's happening? She wouldn't. "Are you okay? What's going on?" Unable to answer, my knees buckle as my eyes continue to scan the area. He's here. Somewhere. *He's found me again.*

"I have to go," comes my raspy reply. I can't rip my eyes from the crowded patio. I've got to find that face. He's lurking somewhere in the crowd, waiting for the perfect moment to claim the cigar and my resolve as his own.

"Yeah, okay—let's go. Isn't your car just across the road?"

My head snaps back to meet Sarah's pinched brow. "No. I can't. Not my car. He'll know."

Sarah's head juts forward, she looks in both directions at my words. Her back straightens as she nods. "Let's go to my car, then." And without another word, we flee the scene that has shattered my sense of security in this new life I've created these past two months. Taking preemptive action, almost as if she can taste the fear radiating from my pores, she leads me to the safety of her car.

We race toward an unfamiliar part of town. What am I doing? I don't even know this woman, yet I'm trusting her with my safety. I shrink into the passenger's side door. Sure, this has got to be a better option than sticking around to see what Jonathan has planned…the least of which would be another circular scar singed into my flesh. But I'm not sure I'm okay with thrusting myself into another uneasy scenario, albeit not nearly as dangerous. "Where are we going?" I blurt, my voice shaking.

Sarah's eyes are darting every which way, as if trying to locate the thing that so clearly unraveled my calm only minutes ago. "I'm taking you to Harrison and Isabel's—these back roads are faster."

My mind spins, "No, we can't go there," I spit. "The kids are there, and he can't know where I live."

Sarah hits the gas as we approach a yellow light. She flies through the intersection, then turns to me to ask, "Who can't know? Are you in trouble?"

I pinch both my lips together as tears threaten, "I don't know," I turn to look behind, "but please—just keep driving." Is he back there somewhere? Do I search for *his* car, or a rental? My face twists against my quivering chin. "What if he's following us?" I whisper, more to myself than Sarah. If he has a rental, then the game's up.

Sarah does a double-take, re-adjusts her rearview mirror, then says, "Should I drop you off somewhere downtown?"

"*No—please* . . . He'll find me there, and he doesn't care about his reputation in this town—*he's capable of anything here!*"

Sarah issues a quiet groan through her clenched jaw. Is she wondering if I'm worth the unknown risk? "Okay, I'm going to take you back to my house, Hallie. Tom should be getting there right about now, and whatever is going on, we'll at least have him around to protect us . . . protect you." My eyes flutter toward Sarah's face as she touches her cheek, an action she's done repeatedly since the moment we dove into her car. But I don't have it in me to turn down her offer. This is my best option if Jonathan really is out there looking for me . . . if that was his cigar. I offer a quiet grunt with a nod of my head, and she takes in the road ahead of us as I refocus on the road behind.

We squeal into the driveway of a two-story home just outside of Ann Arbor. Sarah rushes out of her car, leaving the gym bag behind as she speeds to the front door. We're both looking over our shoulder as we crash into the house. Tom walks out of the bedroom just as we gust into the living room. His big smile designed to welcome us immediately tilts into a grimace as he asks what's wrong. Sarah walks over to the couch, sinks down, and leans her head into her hand as her ponytail flips over her shoulder. She's probably running through the last fifteen minutes, trying to determine if I'm insane. But I know she believes me. It's hard to fake a reaction like that. I pace in the small path between the front door and the couch, trying to steady my breathing. They're both looking to me for answers, but I'm still too shaken to offer an excuse that might bring clarity.

"I'll grab you two some water," Tom finally says. He turns from the living room, walks toward the other side of the house and disappears behind the wall into the kitchen. The fridge rattles open the moment I sink into the sea-green armchair opposite Sarah. With my legs still quaking, I take in a long, shaky breath, then release it. "Here you are," Tom says, returning to the living room and handing me a bottle of water. He crosses over to sit beside his wife, handing her a bottle as well.

I take a sip. The pulse beating against my temple begins to slow. How do I explain this? Will Tom and Sarah understand that all it took was a little red and black cigar wrapper to unnerve me? Their staring eyes bear down on me. I've got to say something. I slowly screw the top back onto my bottle. "I'm married," I blurt. Both of their heads fall slightly forward. "And it's complicated, if you can't already tell." I clear my throat, waiting for someone to throw in some offhand remark, but they respect my words while extending me the time I need to process through them appropriately. "I had to move to Ann Arbor because, after I left him, last October, I needed a safe place to live, and eventually," my head drops as my eyes flutter closed, "he found me."

My brain spirals out of control. *Ugh!* They're never going to understand if I don't tell them everything. All the shameful details of my past hit me like a crashing wave, and before I know it, I find myself ready to unleash, as if the fiercely shaken bottle of these past eight months has been uncorked right here in the living room of two people who will either be my true friends or reject me after learning about my broken past. An hour passes before my eyes as I explain everything. Somehow, a numbness covers me like a blanket, almost as if I'm telling someone else's horror story, not mine. Tom and Sarah remain silent as they work through my recount of betrayal and abuse. I tell them everything—my broken relationship with my parents, the betrayal from Ainsley, and the extensive abuse with Jonathan.

"Now, you both know it all," I sigh. A weight is lifted off my chest. That wasn't as difficult as I expected. Silent seconds linger between the three of us. I look down at my empty water bottle. If they were going to judge me, I would have already seen it in their faces, especially during the difficult parts of my story.

"Hallie," Tom begins slowly—the first words spoken since I spilled it all. "We had no idea you'd been through so much." He drops his head, "No one should have to endure that kind of hatred, and I'm so sorry that you faced such horrible things in your marriage. That's not how God designed marriage," he says as he reaches over and grabs hold of Sarah's hand, "and that's not what someone like you deserves. It's not what anyone deserves." With his head still hanging, he asks, "So, you thought you saw him today?"

I rise from the armchair, my legs screaming to be stretched. "Not *him*." I confess, "But I walked by a table in the corner of the patio, and there was a cigar burning." Tom and Sarah both lift their head and wrinkle their brow. I begin to pace again. "It was *his* cigar, the one he always smoked." I bite my lip. "It's a Davidoff Yamasa, it's the only cigar he smokes." They still don't get it. I stop, mid-stride, and yank up my shirt. "It's the cigar that gave me this scar years ago."

Staring at the burn mark on my stomach, Sarah's mouth drops, "He gave you that?"

I nod, drop my shirt, and melt back into the armchair. "I just have this feeling that Jonathan was there tonight, and that he left the cigar, burning there, marking his presence. It would be just like him to do something like that…to remind me that he's looking for me. He doesn't know anything about Ann Arbor—he's never been—so it makes sense for him to pick a public place nearby all the local gyms, just hoping I would walk by." Groaning, I add, "He may have even searched the gym floors for me."

Tom stretches his legs as he leans back on the couch, "He would do all that just to find you?"

A small whimper escapes, "Yes, I haven't heard from him in a while. He called just over a month ago to tell me he was looking for me. He tried to threaten me, hoping to get me to return to Oklahoma. While I was on the phone, Harrison spoke in the background, and although he couldn't tell it was Harrison's voice, he probably guessed as much. I'm not on the gym's website, so there was no way of really knowing if I was here." I chew the inside of my cheek. "It wouldn't surprise me if he flew here to look around for me. He'll stop at nothing, and he has the freedom in his job to take off all the time he needs to find me."

Sarah looks to the ceiling while shaking her head, "Now I know why you were so scared. I just hope he didn't try following us. If he did, I'm glad I brought you here and not back to Harrison and Isabel's."

Exhaling slowly, I slump my shoulders and say, "Maybe I'm wrong." Silence, then I clear my throat. "I just hope I'm still safe here."

Tom brings his knees back in and rests his elbows on them, then says, "You probably are wrong, Hallie. That cigar could've been anyone's, and in a population of over a hundred thousand people, I doubt it would be him."

I wobble my head with a half-nod. He's right…this is ridiculous. That could've been anyone's cigar. "I'm sorry if I ruined your evening with my overreaction. You've both been so kind to let me stay here and unload all this on you."

Sarah exhales slowly, then smiles a mother-like smile. "Anytime," she offers, "you've got a friend in me . . . in us." My heart swells to the point it might burst. That's exactly what I need right now—friendship.

***

In the weeks that followed my scare, Sarah and Tom proved to be good friends, dragging me along to university events, going out downtown, and finding one-off excuses to pull me out of the apartment. Yet, if they're so great, why do I still follow Ainsley on social media to see what she's up to? My heart thuds dully in my chest. I want reconciliation between us, but the way I left it in my final voicemail hitches Ainsley to the sole option of offering a humble apology. It's been nearly three months since my frantic departure from the lake house, and she still hasn't made any effort to acknowledge her mistakes.

With my phone in my hand and my gym bag slung over my shoulder, my sore muscles carry me to my parallel-parked car while my heavy breathing marks my struggled return to my regular workout routine. My finger scrolls down the screen, then stops. It's one of Ainsley's recently posted videos. My eyes narrow. Is it of Connect Church's Vacation Bible School program? *Hmmm.* That's right, Miles is old enough to attend now. And I guess Ainsley volunteered again this year, she and a ton of other volunteers...it takes an immense team to pull it off. I bite my lip and hover over the play icon. Should I watch it? My chest tightens. I've got to watch it...I used to be a part of it.

I click on the link and slide into the front seat of my car. The video jumps to the stage, the same stage where I used to sing with my best friend each night for VBS worship. My tongue slides across my teeth. Jonathan should've been serving alongside us too . . . *Heck,* I begged him to volunteer with me every year. They needed him for bass, and I had hoped VBS might somehow get him back involved with church, but he made it very clear that he would not sacrifice any of his time to deal with kids for an entire week. *Of course not.* Why would he when he could make *better* use of his post-work hours by lounging on the couch, drinking and smoking the nights away? Colorful images dance across my screen. It must have been a fun week. Something new flashes. I blink, my head drawing back. My finger jumps to rewind the time on the clip. Am I hallucinating? There's no way I saw what I think I just saw. As the scene replays, I hit pause at precisely the right moment, and stare at the screen with my lips parted. It's Jonathan, playing the bass guitar on stage as the children below are paused in their jumping to the worship music produced by the team of volunteers in bright orange t-shirts. The team I used to be a part of, and now, he's one of them.

Wow. I lift my chin and tighten my grip on the phone, although I wish I could throw it across the car. My eyes glue to the screen as I hit resume. How could this be true? There has to be an explanation as to why this monster has actually chosen to do something he refused to do so many times before.

As the video continues, my heart falls to my stomach. *Oh gosh.* Jonathan fills the screen, and he's holding Miles. Ainsley stands near them, and they laugh together at the kids playing tag all around them on the front lawn of the church building. My eyes bulge. Then, Ainsley shuffles closer to high-five Jonathan. I stop breathing. She has actually befriended the man who has stolen my safety, security, and sanity over the years. How could she do this? The remaining two minutes of the video flash image after image of Jonathan participating in the children's study groups and praying into the mic on stage. I swallow again and again against the lump stuck in my throat. But I watch on as the camera man catches the partially concealed act of flirting between Rita and Jonathan during pizza night. Maybe that's why he's there . . . volunteering his *precious* time. Rita's shrieking laugh plagues this entire video. She was there all week, and so was he. The video ends, and my stomach rolls. In the course of three months, Jonathan has become the face of Connect Church.

I punch my car into drive and race home, my stomach in knots. I shouldn't have watched that video. The amalgamation of Ainsley's vengeance, Rita's persistent flirting, and Jonathan's manipulation is more than I can handle. I hit my fist on my steering wheel as I take another turn. I've not only been forced to leave the worship team, my hiding place at the lake house, and my safety net, but I'm now having it all thrown back in my face as Jonathan steps triumphantly into the limelight.

By the time I park, grab for my gym bag, and exit the car, I find myself climbing the apartment steps with other group members of Nations Church. I shake my head. How did I forget about group tonight? Has the betrayal seen in the video—seen all throughout the church that was once a trustworthy place—really bothered me that much? The moment I reach the top landing of the apartment, I slink past those gathered around the dining room table for refreshments, toss my gym bag into the corner of my room, and grab for a light, zip-up hoody to throw over my workout top. Taking one, quick scan of the room, I lunge for my Bible on my bedside table and close the door behind me, moving to claim a seat in the living room. Sarah is already settled in a seat next to the fireplace, so I meander toward the chair beside her.

"Hey," she greets, standing to give me a hug. "How are you?" But the second she catches sight of my furrowed brow, her grin fades. "Uh-oh, something's wrong," she adds. I return the hug, then slump down in the chair next to her.

"It's nothing," I mumble, but the heat pulsing across my forehead suggests otherwise.

Sarah's eyes don't leave my face. She goes to respond when Harrison announces, "Alright folks, let's get settled in the living room and we'll get started." Everyone moves to find a seat, then Harrison opens our study with prayer. We pick-up where we left-off in our study through Proverbs as Harrison points out concepts of wisdom and foolishness that resurface in each new, profound line of the passage we are analyzing tonight. Harrison reads through Proverbs, chapter twenty-six, and although my muddled thoughts, affected by the video I watched earlier, distract me from much of what my wise brother is sharing, a verse catches my attention: "As a dog returns to its vomit, so fools repeat their folly." This analogy from verse eleven leaves most of the group cringing, but their comments are pushed to the back of my mind. This is Jonathan and his foolish acts of manipulation. I press my tongue to the roof of my mouth. It won't be long until he returns to his folly, like he always does. Whether he's taking a break from the drugs or being discreet, everyone will see through his façade sooner or later.

My memory stings with the words Ainsley offered several months back, when she showed nothing but support for my departure from that abusive marriage. *She* was the one who told me his victimizing act will run thin with time. So how is it that now, she is the one high-fiving him, serving on the worship team beside him, and letting him hold her son? *Her son.* Why would she do that when she knows how awful Jonathan truly is? Is she in denial? Maybe she thinks I was lying about how dangerous he is . . . how manipulative he can be when he wants to win someone over.

"Hallie?" The sound of Harrison repeating my name swings me back to the present. *Oh dear.* Everyone's eyes are fixed on me. Harrison raises one eyebrow, as if he's waiting to hear my response. "Wouldn't you agree?" he prompts.

Heat rises to my face. "Sorry, could you repeat what you said?" I cringe, but breathe a sigh of relief as everyone's eyes return to their Bible.

Harrison smiles, "Oh, I was just saying how prevalent gossip is in small towns, especially small-town Oklahoma. Check out verse twenty, 'Without wood a fire goes out; without a gossip a quarrel dies down.' We constantly have to fight to withdraw from gossip in our hometown, so we know this truth all too well."

I nod, "Oh, yeah. Gossip definitely adds fuel to the fire," and at that, my thoughts return to Ainsley, as if I could shake this whole ordeal anyway. If it weren't for her gossip, partnered with Rita's big mouth, I might still be in Oklahoma right now.

Harrison continues reading, and yet another verse sinks me deeper into the darkened corners of my mind. "Enemies disguise themselves with their lips, but in their hearts, they harbor deceit," he reads from verse twenty-four. Was Ainsley just putting on a show that whole time? Or was she so blinded from guilt that she refused to accept responsibility for her actions in Nashville, and instead, turned it on me?

For the remainder of the study, my attention slips in and out of the conversations taking place within our group as I position the words found in scripture alongside the actions that have been taken against me. There is such truth found in these passages, and I've experienced it first-hand. I can't seem to come to grips with all that I've lost and all that I've had to give up these last several months. My breathing grows shallow. Is God really worthy of my trust? Does God have my back, even now? Tom interrupts my spiraling thoughts as he closes our group in prayer, and with a quick shake of my bowed head, I focus on staying in the present instead of painfully analyzing my past.

By the time everyone has said good-bye, we slip into the familiar pattern of this post-study meeting: me, Tom, Sarah, Harrison, and Isabel sitting around the living room. This routine ending our Thursday nights has become my highlight of each week. We discuss scripture, talk through the dynamics of the study and what Harrison and Tom want to study for the next week, but most importantly, we laugh. Tonight, our conversation takes a bit of a turn.

"You alright, Hallie?" Harrison asks, his forehead wrinkling. "You seemed pretty distracted most of the night, and I didn't mean to put you on the spot earlier."

I wave him off, "No, you're fine. I just saw this video from Connect Church and it really has me thinking through some things."

"What kind of video?" Isabel asks.

Sighing heavily, I say, "It's the church's VBS video from this year, and Jonathan is in it." Everyone's eyes register my words as they widen, forcing them all to shift in my direction. In the chaos that followed my panicked reaction to the patio scene a few weeks back, we've discussed these matters together, Jonathan being a consistent focus, although we all agreed we wouldn't be calling him by name. A groan throttles from my chest. I need to use his name tonight and these people sitting here before me are my safety net. They understand. And I guess God does too. No matter how angry I am, God's proven he's never too far from me.

"Can we see it?" Sarah asks, her tone piqued with curiosity. I nod slowly, reach over to pick up my phone resting on top of my Bible, and find the video still loaded on the screen. I hit play.

At the first sight of Jonathan's image, Isabel inhales sharply. Her gasp tells it all…Tom and Sarah have identified the monster. "Wasn't that Ainsley that high-fived him?" Harrison asks as soon as the video ends. With a nod, his grunt marks his matched frustration with her betrayal.

My eyes swivel around the group, but no one is as flustered as Isabel. Her cheeks flame red, ten shades darker than her hair. "How can the church do that?" she eventually sputters. "I mean, that terrible, terrible man is now the face of Connect Church. It's like his history with the church has been erased in a heartbeat. They're all treating him like their long-lost friend who has finally returned, and they have welcomed him with open arms." Struck by the absurdity of it all, Isabel gathers her curls to one side and gives them a twist. "I mean, it's bad enough that they eventually pushed you out, but it honestly looks as if they're happier to have him around than they were to have you. How is your pastor even dealing with all of this?"

I place my phone down, my hand growing limp. "He doesn't know, he's on sabbatical. And the new worship leader, Levi—who replaced Chip Catcher when he left—has taken over." My posture folds over as I add, "Levi seems to like Jonathan, and because he's pretty much running the church in Pastor Noah's absence, he's just eating out of Jonathan's hand." My voice drops with my next, sorrow-filled thought, "And Ainsley's probably encouraging it all—I mean, she and Jonathan look like best friends in that video." Sarah nods, her eyes softening with each of my comments. "But what does it matter?" I finish, "I can't return, and I knew that when I left. Pastor Noah doesn't know a thing, and I'm not going to bother him. There's no future for me there."

"Well," Harrison starts, "that church has always been about extending grace, so maybe that's what this Levi guy's doing."

"No," I reply, "he's really just oblivious to it all. You know Jonathan can put on a good show, and for the most part, he can be very convincing. Levi must think Jonathan is awesome, especially if he's willing to step in when Levi needs him—whether that's playing the bass on Sunday morning or serving as a volunteer at VBS." My throat tightens, "I just can't believe they would let him around all those children. Ainsley *knows* he shouldn't be around children. But it doesn't look like she told Levi about his past, and I bet she didn't mention anything about the *live feeds* he used to watch of those poor children." I gulp, bile rising in the back of my throat. "If they knew that, they'd never let him around those kids." Harrison and Isabel lock eyes for a moment. In a flash, they break eye contact. Isabel begins collecting dishes while Harrison rubs both hands down his face. My head tilts and my eyes narrow.

"If you ask me," Tom says, drawing my attention back, "that church and your old friends might not be handling this situation well. Bringing it back to our passage we read tonight, verse four says, 'Do not answer a fool according to his folly, or you yourself will be just like him' . . . and that's the truth." With a turn of his head, he looks at me, then adds, "I'm just glad you're free from all the gossip, betrayal, and foolishness of your past. This may not be your first choice of where you want to live, but we're all thankful you're here in Ann Arbor." And although I smile in response, my gaze falls. What was Harrison and Isabel's earlier glance all about?

CHAPTER 21

"Hello everyone," Tom greets from the church stage as his eyes roam the congregation, "I hope you've had a good week and that you're staying cool, despite this blazing, July sun." He throws in a tug on the neckline of his button-up shirt, and the crowd laughs quietly. "Anyway, for this Sunday's announcements, I wanted to remind you all that we will be caring for the community through our outreach program by serving the lost and needy in downtown Ann Arbor. If you're planning to serve alongside us this Friday, please meet us at the corner of Liberty and South Main at 11:00 a.m. wearing your Nations Church t-shirt, and if you don't already have one, come see me at the back after the service." He points to the back of the auditorium, then drops his arm as a humble smile begins to form, "I've seen what a difference we can do in the community by caring for the people in this city and reaching out to those in need. So, I encourage you all to consider serving with us this Friday. Your actions will be seen, and you never know how God will use you." He flips over the sheet in his hand as he glances down, then adds, "Also, don't forget—" but his list of announcements blur in the back of my mind. I grab a pen wedged in my Bible and start fiddling with it. It's been a while since I've served. Maybe this is what I need to get my foot in the door here at Nations Church.

I chew on my bottom lip and mindlessly trace a heart on the bulletin. *Humph.* What is the point of stiff-arming Nations Church? This is a good church, and the people here are caring. They make God a priority in everything they do, so why can't I get with that? I draw another heart and start shading it in. Connect Church hurt me, but should I punish *this* church because of that pain? And was it really an issue with Connect Church, or just the result of a brewing perfect storm? I run one hand through my hair and wrinkle my nose. The problem is me. I don't want to let people get close to me . . . to learn about my life . . . to discover the shameful secret of my upcoming divorce. As far as anyone knows in this church, I'm Hallie Reed. Hallie McClain never existed in their eyes. I'd like to keep it that way.

Sarah leans over and whispers, "I don't know what your plans are on Friday, but I would really love it if you could come to the outreach event and serve with me and Tom." She sits back and raises one eyebrow as Tom exits the stage and moves to the seat beside her. My gaze flits between the doodled bulletin and the sparkle in my friend's eyes. I smile at her and nod right as the pastor steps onto the stage and asks us to bow our heads in prayer.

* * *

"Wow, it's really hot," I say as I air out my newly acquired Nations Church t-shirt. Tom laughs, and I add, "Why do the t-shirts have to be black?" Tom's response is lost to the distraction from the group. My eyes travel down my body. At least I wore white pants to pair with the outfit. As I lift my head, I notice someone approaching Tom to say hi, and I melt back into the sea of matching t-shirts as we wait for further instructions. Harrison is at the far end of the group, greeting a passing couple whose interest is piqued. I smile as I turn my head. *Ah—Harrison.* I'd bet money that he already mentioned something profound about a relationship with Christ. His evangelistic skills never cease to amaze me.

I roll my eyes and turn. My smile fades as I scan the outdoor patio currently being set up for lunch; the same patio that haunts me. My stomach grips. One little cigar label and I go crazy. I slowly release a sigh and start biting on a hangnail. That was a month ago, and I haven't heard a word from Jonathan. If that was his cigar, he would've called to taunt me. Sarah thinks his silence could be good news, and the more we talk about it, the more I'm inclined to agree.

All signs point to the idea that Jonathan has given up . . . he's accepted I've moved on. Could she be right? I search for Sarah, my listening ear, my advice giver, my friend. It takes me a moment to find her long ponytail as she leaves a group of women to move closer to Tom. The two are left alone. Tom kisses the top of Sarah's forehead and gently lifts her chin to meet his face. They stare into each other's eyes, lost in a moment. They have no idea I'm watching. My eyes lower as I shift my weight. My heart thuds as I press my lips together. By now, I'm used to being the third-wheel, so why does my heart ache? I shake my head. I'm glad they have each other, and when I'm around them, it's hard to believe they ever dealt with any marital issues.

"Hey—thanks for joining us today," the pastor announces across the crowd, his voice drawing me back to our task at hand. "It's time to get started, so if you all want to grab some care bags in the plastic bins positioned behind you, then you can follow Tom and Sarah to the east as they navigate more toward the university, or Harrison to the west as he targets the more professional side of town. Or," he continues, pointing both thumbs to his chest, "you can stay with me in this general region as we cover this area in the direction of Kerrytown. If you have questions, feel free to ask." At that, the bustling group begins moving toward the black bags that match our t-shirts, each filled with our church flyer tied to the hygiene kits, water bottles, and snacks that we'll be handing out to those we come in contact with over the next three hours. I clench my teeth. *Oh dear.* Do I go with Tom and Sarah or my brother?

"You're coming to the university with me, right?" Sarah asks as she sidles up next to me.

"Uh, well, I was just thinking about that, actually. I'm not sure I'm prepared for an intellectual debate about Christianity with *those* students."

"Don't worry about that, you'll be great. Besides, we'd really appreciate someone younger and a little more *fashionable* on that side of town. University students can be hard to approach, and some people are a better fit there than others."

She nudges me playfully. I giggle, "Well, if I'm needed, I guess I can give it a try."

"Yes," she interrupts, "you're *desperately* needed." With a laugh, we both grab a couple of bags and sling the long straps over our shoulders, turning for the walk down Liberty to the other side of downtown. Tom, who's just ahead of us, pivots, cups his hands, and calls, "If you're heading to the university, follow me." As he turns and starts walking, I follow, but somewhat reluctantly as I usher Sarah ahead of me. I'm not about to look like a ringleader alongside Tom and Sarah. They are the ones with all the answers . . . not me.

Dropping to the back of the crowd heading toward the university, I fall behind a group of younger women, chattering and laughing only a few paces ahead. As my shoes slap the pavement, I take one last glance over my shoulder to see if anyone is seated in that outdoor patio. *Ah, empty.* What else did I expect, it's still early. I lift my gaze and ball-up my fists. Why is there a pit forming in my stomach? Jonathan's probably not looking for me, he's probably given up all hope that I'll return to Oklahoma. But a small voice in the back of my head insists on harassing me. If he doesn't think he'll get me back, then why is he still serving at Connect Church? *Why is he still trying to fool everyone?*

The next three hours fly by as conversations spark, needs of the homeless scattered in this area of town are met, and questions about our church and the service we're doing in the community are asked. My heart lifts with each encouraging conversation, and a group that I was chatting with actually said they were looking for a church in the area, and that they would consider checking out Nations Church this Sunday. Exhausted and overheated, I check the time on my phone. *Jeez.* How is it that we are only minutes away from meeting Tom and Sarah? They told us to meet on this side of town before we head back to the corner of Liberty and South Main.

Navigating to the *Diag*, my eyes wander the diagonal sidewalks that mark this green space. What a great name for it…it's easy to remember and trendy. My gaze lifts to the white stone and gothic style architecture of the many buildings surrounding me. This campus really is quite breath-taking. What if I was smart enough to attend here? I laugh at myself. *Where did that come from?* I never had a shot at attending a big university, Jonathan made that very clear. The echo of his deep voice repeats in my mind . . . *Community College is all you can handle; a mid-level trainer is all you'll ever be.*

"Hey," comes Tom and Sarah's unified greeting from behind. I spin in their direction, then snicker. It's not the first time they've said the same thing at the same time.

"Hey guys," I reply.

"How was your afternoon?" Sarah asks.

"Great—it went really well. I saw you guys a few times, but you looked like you were deep in conversation, and I didn't want to bother you."

"Oh, I wish you would've. It's always great to have someone join the conversation," Tom offers.

"Yeah, well," I start, diverting my gaze, "you were both talking with some university students, and I didn't want to dumb down the conversation by joining." Tom and Sarah have the brains to engage in seriously intellectual conversations with these students.

I shift my weight in the silence that follows, then lift my head and force a smile. Sarah locks her head forward and Tom tilts his face to the side in a *professor* sort of way, like he's analyzing a petri dish. *Oh come-on.* They know me by now, it didn't take Jonathan long to figure out I was dumb, and these two are way more academically advanced than Jonathan. "What are you talking about?" Tom asks. "You could never dumb down a conversation. You're very intelligent, and you offer tons of insight."

With a roll of my eyes and a snort of laughter, I reply, "Not to these students. They're so smart, and I'm just a small-town girl who doesn't know anything."

Tom rocks back, "That's not true at all," he declares, "and I would know. I teach these students."

Sarah shakes her head and says, "Hallie, you've been through a lot, and I can only imagine these are lies that *he* has fed to you over the years," I grimace. How is it that she goes straight to the heart of the issue every time? "But it's time to put the past behind you. These students are no better than you. In fact, you could enroll here tomorrow and experience just as much success as any one of them."

I lower my head, then Tom chimes in, "She's serious, Hallie. You're quite capable. You can do anything you put your mind to. You should know that by now, what with all that you've overcome in your past." My friends' voices remain confident, and the moment I lift my face, their bright eyes and smiles serve as my cheering squad. *Hmmm.* Maybe I *am* capable. I don't have to be tied down to what I've been told in the past. I'm a *fighter*. Who's to say I can't enroll here?

Tom and Sarah turn and greet the others as they bustle up beside us. Tom sends them back down Liberty where we're to meet up with the rest of our group while Sarah lingers by his side. Sarah's face twists as she says, "Actually, I better go with those girls up there. They said they wanted to chat with me about something personal, and this might be the right time to do that." She plants a quick kiss on Tom's stubbly cheek than jogs to meet them.

A few more arrive, and they look just about as tired and sweaty as I imagine I do, but their spirits are high, and they're eager to hear about each other's experiences. "I think that's all of 'em," Tom concludes, "I guess we should head over, too."

I nod, and we bring up the rear of the group, our empty bags marking the productivity of our day serving the community. "So," I start. Now's the time to get to know a bit more about Tom, even after all Sarah's shared. "Sarah mentioned a while back that you guys weren't Christians when you got married."

"Oh, yeah—she told you that, huh?" He laughs, then adds, "Actually, our story is kind of awesome. When we met ten years ago, I had just finished my PhD. She was working as a nurse for a while, and I fell in love with her at first glance. I knew I was going to move for my job, so after our second date, I asked her to marry me." He chuckles and shakes his head, "I was shocked when she agreed, and we eloped later that month."

"Wow—that's pretty crazy. You guys barely knew each other . . . how did that work out?"

With a big grin, his dazed eyes stay locked on the sidewalk in front of us, as if remembering that time. "Honestly, it was great. We were so in love that we were willing to work through anything. Our parents were upset we eloped—and I come from an Italian family, so they were furious we didn't have this big ceremony with our extended family, but we knew we made the right decision to elope. Family connections at that time were strained at best."

We wait at a stoplight, then cross the road with the small group in front of us, dotting the sidewalk with our black t-shirts. People bustle by us and head to their shop of choice from the options that line this side of the street. The crowd thins a bit, so I ask, "I know Sarah's family don't believe, but what about yours? Are they Christians?"

"When we got married, they weren't." He scratches at the stubble on his face, then says, "In fact, my dad was an alcoholic, and my mother just barely put up with him. I grew up in an angry home. My parents were always fighting. I was an only child—I guess my parents had enough to deal with, so they broke the Italian tradition of having a big family. Finally, my little brother came along when I was twelve." He chuckles, "I think Vincent was just as much a surprise to my parents as he was to me, but I was so happy to have a brother."

"So, you're a lot older than your brother, then."

"Yes, he's actually around your age—he's twenty-five now, I think."

My head tilts, "I just turned twenty-six, but that would make you—"

"Thirty-seven."

My face turns to study Tom as I say, "You really don't look that old—I never would've guessed you're almost forty. Is Sarah that old as well?"

Tom grins, "No, Sarah is a couple years younger than I am, but we seem to fool a lot of people with our age. I guess we hold tight to our youthful features."

"No kidding," I chuckle. "I would never have guessed you both were that age. But I guess that makes sense, what with your careers."

"Yes, that—and I had to grow up pretty quickly. It became clear that my parents were not able to cope with a baby, so I took it upon myself to help raise Vincent." A light groan creeps out of his pinched mouth, "My father wasn't exactly a good representation of how a respectable man should act, so I decided to be the kind of guy that my brother could learn from. It wasn't that my dad was a horrible man," Tom corrects, rubbing at his forehead, "it's more that his alcoholism meant he was pretty absent for most of our lives. It really felt like my mom was a single mother, working to keep the family together. You could tell she held a grudge against my dad—they weren't happy. Until . . ." he sighs heavily, "until it all changed."

Approaching another stoplight, silence ensues. Again, we're surrounded by others, but the crowd eventually dissipates as we cross the road. He offers a thin smile, then continues. "It was my brother's senior year of high school, and he was very busy. He was the all-star athlete of his high school, and we were expecting him to get a scholarship. Vincent is such a talented athlete, unlike his book-worm of an older brother." I laugh along with Tom, then he adds, "He came home from practice one evening and collapsed. Honestly, he was probably dehydrated and stressed—it was the middle of basketball season, and he was feeling the pressure of carrying his team through the season. My mom was at work, and my dad was at home, but he had already had quite a lot to drink that day. Unable to reach my mom, my dad decided to take Vincent to the hospital." With a shrug of his shoulder, Tom shoves his hands into his pockets, "It was the middle of winter in Massachusetts, and my dad was drunk. Not the best conditions to be driving frantically to the hospital. As fate would have it, Dad hit a patch of black ice and flipped the vehicle. The vehicle rolled and eventually crashed the passenger's side into a tree. Dad thought Vincent had died instantly. He doesn't remember much, but he remembers his son's limp body lifted out and transported immediately to the hospital. They had to cut a gash in Vincent's throat in the ambulance for an emergency tracheotomy." My tongue clicks against my teeth, making a quiet *tsking* sound, and Tom jumps a little. He must have been caught up in the memory of it and almost forgot I was here. "Vincent was in the hospital on life support for a long time. He was in a coma, and we thought that would've sent my dad into a drinking frenzy far worse than before, but it had the opposite effect. My dad swore he was never going to have another drink again, and although it was hard—and it's been a journey—to this day, he has kept that promise. In my parents' misery, they had to turn to something, and surprisingly, they turned to each other, and then they turned to God." My head swivels in his direction. "I know—I didn't expect that either, and I honestly thought it was some kind of ridiculous trick . . . that maybe they thought if they could pray enough, God would deliver their son out of a coma."

What a story. He's got me hooked. "Did he ever come out of the coma?" I ask. "Is Vincent alright?"

Tom somewhat snickers, "Yes, he did." I breathe a sigh of relief. "And it was definitely a miracle that he fully recovered. But before he came out of the coma, my dad—of all people—challenged me to turn to God, too. I was so angry . . . my dad had done this to my brother. I was the one who raised Vincent, I was the one who cared for him, but my dad was sitting there challenging *me* to pray for a miracle that would fix the mistake my dad had caused in the first place. Instead, I chose to hold a grudge for a while, but Vincent wasn't getting any better. So, eventually, I thought I might as well try this game with God that my parents appeared to be playing."

We snake down the sidewalk, following the church group ahead of us. My feet shuffle along as he continues, "I didn't know where to start, so I flipped to Genesis—I mean, it makes sense to start at the beginning of a book, doesn't it?" We both chuckle quietly. "Well, I came across the story of Noah." Tom leans down to adjust his shoe, fishing out a pebble, and the mention of Noah's name makes me purse my lips—I miss my pastor. He helped me work through so much concerning my failed marriage before he went away on sabbatical. Randomly hearing his name used makes me realize how much I miss his guidance. Sure…he needs this time of rest, but a little part of me wishes he would return to the church to see how Jonathan is being accepted, even promoted, during his absence. My shoulders become rigid. *It doesn't matter.* He won't return until after the divorce papers are signed, and there's nothing I can do about it.

"Anyway," Tom says, standing up tall and pulling me back in, "I read about the ways God tested Noah's faith by building the ark, preparing for the animals that God would send, getting them all on the ark, and then waiting as the rain poured for forty days and forty nights. It felt exactly like what I was going through—waiting out the storm, hoping my brother would recover." We cross another street, "But, as I continued to read, I felt prompted to ask God to give me a sign in forty days, a sign that he was listening to me after all. I prayed that prayer every day, and just as Noah sent out a dove to find dry land and bring back an olive branch signifying the good news, God also sent me my *dove*. My brother woke up." I hold back the tears as I gulp against my constricting throat. What a shock that must have been—a family choosing to cling to a God they didn't know during a troubling time. "And through that whole process," Tom continues, "I finally learned that I could place all of my trust in him. And now, every time I see a rainbow, like from Noah's story, I'm reminded of how I placed my trust in God during that unpredictable and testing time in my life, and how God came through, even when it all seemed impossible."

"That's amazing," I say. "And Sarah was with you through it all?"

Tom starts cracking some knuckles as he smiles over at me. "Sarah was a bit of a different story. Honestly, her family members are in the field of medicine, so she went to them to get some answers as to why Vincent finally came out of the coma. But she couldn't get a scientific answer—because as you know, miracles can't be explained by science. She really grappled with the fact that everyone in my family had given their lives over to Christ, and I think, in a way, she was still trying to find some scientific answer to explain the whole ordeal. That is," he smirks, "until she talked to my brother. Vincent told her that he heard my father and mother's—and eventually my—prayers spoken at his bedside. He said that he felt this sense of warmth, peace, and love that he's never known before while he was in his coma. He knew it was God, so when he came out of the coma, there was no question that God existed. He stayed in the hospital for a while longer to recover, then he had to go back and complete his senior year. His educational path had been put on hold for so long, he knew his life had changed forever. Any chance of a scholarship was out the door, and he had to figure out what he was going to do with his life. But one thing was for sure, he wanted to follow God."

"So, Sarah heard all this, then decided to believe as well?"

"Well," he clarifies as we approach the swarm of black t-shirts, "it wasn't that easy. For a while, she considered leaving me. She said I had changed so much, and she wasn't sure if she could just reject her whole upbringing to go down the same path that my family had chosen. We had a lot of heated discussions, and it was rocky there for a while. But eventually, God won—she surrendered. Let's just say, our marriage wasn't perfect," he draws up a shoulder and sighs, "it's still not perfect." With a brief nod, he lifts his tone to say, "but God's working in our hearts, and we just have to take things one day at a time as we place our trust in Christ."

We approach the group, and just like that, our conversation is over. Tom waves a quick good-bye as he weaves around the people to find his wife. My heart fizzles. What did Tom's last comment mean? Are they working through something now? They seem so happy, but maybe that's every marriage. Maybe I'm not the only one facing hardships—although I hope and pray I don't see anyone else getting divorced. *What am I thinking?* Tom and Sarah aren't *there.* They've already overcome that hurdle, even if they are wrestling through something right now.

I rub at my neck and toss my hair over to one side as I weave through the crowd. Tom's story is something special...but it probably didn't seem special when he was in the thick of it. Could that be the case for me, too? Of course, I can't predict the future, but will I look back at this storm and eventually find *my* dove? Can I trust that at the end of this trial, when I finally sign those divorce papers, there will be a rainbow waiting for me? I reach the clear bin and return the empty care bag as those around me begin saying their good-byes. With the late afternoon sun still blazing down, I shield my eyes as my brother approaches. "Did you have a good time?" he asks.

"Yeah—for sure," I offer. "How about you?"

"Oh yeah—I had a great time. Isabel is going to be sad she missed it this year. We usually get a babysitter, but I guess all the people who watch the twins are serving here today." He throws up both hands in defeat, then chuckles. "Oh well. Anyway—I'm heading back to my car parked on the other side of town, near the campus." He looks at his watch, then adds, "What are your plans?"

"I gotta slip back to the apartment for a bit and change. I work the evening shift tonight, so I'll get some down time before I go in, which should be nice."

Harrison says good-bye and walks back down Liberty. Sarah prances to my side, drops her empty care bag in one of the plastic bins and says, "I heard Tom told you all about *our* story. Pretty crazy, huh?"

"You could say that again." I grin, "I'm glad you chose Christ in the end. And I'm glad Vincent is okay. How's his health now?"

"Oh, he's great—he's finishing up his masters at Harvard this upcoming year, then he'll be applying to med schools."

"So, he's going into medicine then?"

With a smirk, Sarah says, "Yeah—ever since the accident, he's been dedicated to helping other people. He wants to be a doctor, and he says that when science and medicine can't do the trick, he—of all people—knows the power of praying for a miracle."

"That's awesome, I'm so happy for him. Maybe one day I'll get to meet him."

"Absolutely. Just when you do, don't stare at his scar." She ducks her head and lowers her voice, "The scar on his throat, the one from the tracheotomy, is pretty nasty. He isn't really that bothered by it, but it can't be comfortable having people stare at it all the time and question what happened."

My gut tightens, "I know the feeling all-too well."

Sarah reaches for my hand and squeezes it, as if she knew I would be able to relate. Then, she changes the subject with ease. "Are you parked in the garage?"

"No, actually—I found a spot on South Main, so I decided to use the meter."

"Nice, well I'm in the parking garage over there. So, I guess I'll see you on Sunday?"

"Okay," I offer. Sarah's so easy to talk to—she's honest and real. We smile as we both wave and begin walking in opposite directions. I fan my neck as I quicken my pace. *Gross.* I can't wait to get back to the apartment and shower. My clothes are melting into my skin. Blinded by the sunlight and zapped from the heat, I fall into my car, swing my door shut, and start the engine. Cranking the AC, I sit there with my eyes closed and my head back against the neck rest. *Ah…finally,* some cold air. The cool air blows on me for a while, then I eventually lean forward to put my car into drive. *What's that?* Something fluttering in the wind on the other side of my windshield catches my eye. I peer harder, then gasp. A Davidoff Yamasa cigar, complete with the red and black wrapper, is tucked under my windshield wiper. But this time, it's not burning.

CHAPTER 22

All the synapses in my brain ignite as my eyes fight through the crowd to find the outdoor patio. I'm too far away, even if he's over there, I can't identify his face. My hands quake with the surge of blood pumping from the thudding of my heart. This is not a coincidence—Jonathan's here, in Ann Arbor. He's trying to find me, and he's close. Too close. My head turns, craning to get a panoramic view as my clammy hands grip the steering wheel. *Is he watching me now? Is he waiting for me to get out of my car and remove the cigar?* My jaw tightens. I won't give him that satisfaction. He's going to have to chase me. I lock my doors and pull slowly out of the parking space. *Nice and easy.* There's no need to draw any attention—he could be distracted. My heart races as my foot quivers. *Dear God!* I want to pound on the gas pedal, to flee the scene as quickly as possible, to get out of here before he can wreak anymore havoc. My chest caves and I swallow. The damage is done. His message has been sent. *He's not giving up*.

As I agonizingly creep along with the Friday afternoon traffic, my eyes dart. Where is he? I peer through the windows, trying to catch a glimpse of that all too familiar, dangerous face that still haunts me, but he's nowhere in sight. If he had been close, he would've approached me while I was cooling off in the car. He had the chance to do whatever he wanted without a friend around to protect me. I clutch at my chest. He doesn't have to keep up his reputation in this city. What is there to stop him? He's a reckless man on a mission to get me back—to get me back, or to get back at me. A chill rises like a knife point sliding up my back.

I crank the AC even higher, as if the cool air can counteract my sweaty palms. *I knew I wasn't going crazy last month.* He was here—probably keeping his distance to figure out where I live. *Oh my gosh—Harrison!* What if Jonathan saw me talking with Harrison just then? What if the reason he's not banging on my car window right now is because he's following Harrison—expecting Harrison to lead him back to my new hiding place? My throat swallows a harsh gasp. What if he got to Harrison? Caught him off guard? Would he hurt my brother to get to me?

The sound of a loud horn snaps me back, and I slam on the breaks. I exhale sharply. *Red light.* I've got to pay better attention. A car crawls through the intersection, and the driver turns to stare me down. *So what?* I slap one hand to my forehead and reach for my phone. There are more important things at hand . . . I've got to contact Harrison. It rings—one time, two . . . three. *Is he going to answer?*

"Hello?"

"Oh, thank God—are you okay?"

My heart plummets with the momentary silence that follows. Harrison finally says, "Yeah, I'm fine. Why, what's up?"

With a quick exhale, my eyes land on the cigar still tucked under the windshield wiper. The red and black wrapper, now partially unraveled and blowing in the breeze, makes my stomach flop. In the time I've spent searching for Jonathan, my eyes have avoided the planted evidence of *his* presence. "He's back," I cry, "and I *know* it's him this time."

Harrison doesn't skip a beat, "Okay—where are you? I can come get you…we can go wherever you want so you feel safe. We don't have to go back to the apartment."

A horn from behind makes me jump, and I look up to find a green light beckoning my idling car. "I don't know what to do," I whimper as I tap the gas only to slow down again as I approach another long line of cars at the next stoplight. "I'm so distracted, I keep trying to find him, and I feel like I'm gunna get in an accident. But I'm terrified, I feel like he's gunna jump out at me while I'm waiting at these stupid, long lights." My head swivels in all directions the moment I come to a complete stop. With my eyes inspecting the moving bodies on the sidewalk beside me, I add, "And I thought he got to you on your way to your car. I thought he might've hurt you."

"He didn't get to me—I'm fine," Harrison reassures me, "but I want to make sure you're fine too. Where are you going now?"

The line of cars begins to move, but I can't speed above a slow crawl. My heart feels like it's going to pound out of my chest. "I'm still on South Main—but I *have* to go back to the apartment. I gotta work tonight. I can't skip work, I *need* that money." My chin quivers as my breath catches. How is it that my whole world can unravel from the sight of this red and black wrapper, still waving in the wind, as if it's a flag used to signify the start of a war?

"Okay," Harrison responds, his voice steady. "Here's the plan. You go back to the apartment, and I'm going to follow. As soon as you get there, get into the apartment as fast as you can, and I'll wait outside in case *he* follows us there."

A tear slides down my face, "But what if he does follow us, and then he'll know where I am—where the twins are?"

Harrison grunts. "I'm navigating to South State right now, so as soon as you can, cross over to meet me. It's the long way back to the apartment complex, but I'll pull in behind you to see if anyone's following."

Good idea. I turn on the windshield wipers. One quick *swish,* and the cigar flies away. Why can't my fear disappear with it? I keep the phone glued to my ear, throwing all caution to the wind. All I want to hear is my brother's reassuring voice helping me navigate safely home. I don't care if it's not safe, or if it's illegal—I just need to get home without cementing my sight on the rearview mirror. By the time I get to the apartment complex, it appears as if the coast is clear. I park right next to the handicap spot directly in front of our building and storm up the stairs. The moment I'm through the front door, I lock the handle, slide the deadbolt, and fly up the second flight of stairs, taking them two at a time.

I bolt to the kitchen and lean over the counter in an effort to see out the window. The taillights of Harrison's SUV idle directly behind my parked car. I let my eyes roam for a full minute. Finally, my shoulders drop. There's nothing going on out there. I guess we weren't followed, and if we were, that's up to Harrison to handle. I've got to get ready for work. I back away from the window, my breathing becoming more even. I pivot slowly, then jump as Isabel enters the kitchen.

"You alright?" Her head tilts to one side.

My chest rises and falls as my eyes drop to the kitchen floor. "No, not really. I found a cigar under my windshield wiper today when I was parked downtown . . . *his* cigar."

My eyes lift, and Isabel's head cocks to the other side, as if she's deciphering a code she can't quite crack. "You mean, he's in Ann Arbor—like, looking for you, right now?" I nod slowly. "What? He's trying to follow you around downtown or something?"

I rub my face as I walk past her and into the living room. She follows in my wake, waiting for my response. "I guess," I slump down on the couch. "I thought the burning cigar from last month was a coincidence, but now I know he was here, and he was sending a message. I haven't changed my plates, and he knows what my car looks like—I mean, he paid for it. Maybe that's *why* he paid for it, so he feels like he has a right to it . . . I dunno. But downtown isn't that big, so he probably just thought he would plant himself in the most populated area and wait until he caught a glimpse of something familiar." I curl my knees into my chest and shudder. "I honestly didn't think he would be that determined to find me, and I didn't think I would be that easy to find. He's never even been to Ann Arbor—so it was a shot in the dark." I throw my head back and close my eyes for a second, then say, "That must be what he's been up to these past couple of months. I thought his silence was weird, but I hoped it was a sign he was giving up—not a sign he was trying to find me, again."

With a tentative glance down the hall, Isabel moves closer, then perches herself in the recliner next to me, "Do you think he knows where you're staying now? Should I be worried?" and she looks down the hall again.

"I don't think so. Harrison's downstairs right now, keeping a look out and waiting for me to get changed into my work clothes—then he's going to drive me to work, even though I don't have to be there for a while."

"And then what, Hallie? I mean, it's July—you still have three months until you sign those divorce papers and meet up in court. Now that he knows you're in Ann Arbor, he probably won't leave you alone."

A sour taste fills my mouth. I hadn't thought about that. I've been so focused on escaping from him and getting here without him following me that I haven't had time to think about what the next three months are going to be like. And what about after that? What happens if he doesn't leave me alone, even after we sign the divorce papers and finalize this in court? "Maybe we end this early. I mean—who are my parents to demand that I wait a *whole* year to finally be free from that monster?" I cringe as the words leave my mouth. I can't do that to my parents. The last thing I told them when I left Oklahoma was that I'll hold to the promise I made them. I squeeze my eyes shut. I would give *anything* to end it all right now, but I've come this far, and I need to show them I can honor their wishes. My eyes flutter open and I clench my teeth. I can still be a fighter. It doesn't matter if I don't feel like one . . . I *am* one. I plant my feet back on the carpet, holding my posture for a second, then hunch my shoulders over. "What does *free* even mean—what if he's always trying to find me? What if I lead him back here to the twins?"

As if on cue, Isabel's eyes float over to the hall again, "Well, they're napping now, but we'll do what we must to protect you *and* the twins. Don't you worry about that." My face contorts with the apology that's playing on my lips. Isabel reads me like a book. "It's fine, Hallie. We've always been fine, and we'll lock the doors at all times. Harrison spends a lot of time at home, so he'll be here to protect us. And we'll pray Jonathan manages to stay away—I mean, he's gotta work sometime, doesn't he? He can't be taking all this time off work, so there's hope there." She lifts her eyebrows so that her features match her even tone.

"I just dunno, Isabel. I really thought I was safe here—and things are starting to look up. I've got friends now, and you know how helpful Tom and Sarah are. But when will this all be over? I mean, now that I'm aware of what lengths he'll go to, I can't be naïve enough to think he'll leave me alone after the divorce is final." A groan starts in my belly and slips out of my mouth, "I just need something to hold against him—something that will force him to leave me alone. I need a way to blackmail him."

Isabel runs a finger across her lips as she sinks back into the recliner. "What if," she starts slowly, "you called him and recorded him. You could try to get him to confess to all the things he did to you while you were married. If you have it recorded, then you could tell him to leave you alone, or you'll press charges. And then, if you needed to, you could use that recording as evidence against him in court."

"Do you think the evidence will be admissible?"

Isabel hesitates, then replies, "I'm not sure, but even if it isn't, *he* doesn't have to know that. He doesn't even have to know what the evidence is that you claim to have, he just needs to feel threatened by it."

My eyes wander aimlessly around the room. *Hmmm.* This could work. "Yeah, I think if I got him angry enough over the phone, he would confess to a lot. He really likes to taunt me with threats from our past."

Isabel nods, "I think you should do it, Hallie. It may not be the best plan, but at least it's something. You'll have to wait a little while until we know he's left Ann Arbor, but when you call him, be sure to set up the recording so you can get it all. I think you should take him to court *anyway* for all those terrible things he did to you. If he were in prison, where he belongs, Jonathan McClain wouldn't be able to hurt anyone."

"Mama?" comes a little voice from behind the recliner. Isabel squeezes her eyes shut and pinches her lips. *How long has Bailey been listening?* Does she know what prison is? Bailey tiptoes around the chair and stands—her toes pointing inward—before the two of us. Her eyes darting back and forth from one worried face to the other. "Are you guys talking about Uncle Jon again?"

"Again?" Isabel questions as she leans forward, sliding a hand down her cheek. "What do you mean *again*, sweetie?"

Bailey shuffles sideways to the arm of the recliner, then looks down to her feet as they slide back and forth across the carpet. "Well . . . um," she steals a quick glance up at me, then says, "Because we talked about how Uncle Jon had hurt me that one time. Remember, Mama—how when I told you he was a bad man?"

My heart falls to the pit of my stomach, the crash from these words pummeling straight through me. I look to Isabel, my eyes pleading. *Oh, dear God—not my niece too.* Isabel casts her eyes downward as she rubs at her neck and leans over, asking Bailey to go back to her bedroom so she and Aunt Hallie can talk. Deafening silence fills the room as my soul begs for an acquittal. My eyes flutter closed. A tear splashes on my shaking hand. "Please tell me it's not true," I beg. Isabel's silence isn't the response I need, and I fall to my knees sobbing. I married a man who not only put me at risk, but also those most precious to me. My heart bangs so hard against my body that I think it might stop. I wish it would. As I cry without restraint, my mind floods with the many memories of fear and agony that I endured as an adult . . . as a grown woman who has the capability to process my unwarranted pain. But that little girl wouldn't understand his violence. She wouldn't understand why someone would lash out at her for reasons unknown, and yet, she's experienced it. To what extent, who knows. But she's faced the kind of ugliness that no person should *ever* have to bear. At the thought, I weep with renewed anguish as I lean against the couch. The acts felt from the unrelenting hands of that monster terrorize me on my best day, but now I'm stuck here, reliving it through the eyes of a child. Isabel sniffles in the background. My heart throbs, like I've been punched in the chest. How could I have placed Bailey in *his* dangerous presence? If only I had spoken up sooner about what I was enduring. *How selfish can I be?* My mind searches for answers that might not be true if I could just turn back time. "What happened?" I whisper.

Isabel sniffles again, then clears her throat. "We don't know, exactly. She only brought it up recently—and she really caught us off guard with it all. We told her she wasn't in trouble, but she needed to tell us everything that happened. We think he hit her across the face, but she hasn't hinted toward anything worse. We don't know how often—honestly, I'm surprised it even happened once—it's not like we left the twins alone with him. So, it's a bit of a mystery. But," she takes in a shaky breath, "red flags were raising when she kept telling us how he was a bad man and that she was scared of him."

My heart rips down the center, sending me tumbling into another bout of sobs. "I'm so sorry," is the only muffled response I can offer, so I say it over and over again. But it doesn't matter, nothing can lift this weight off my heart, not even these repeated apologies.

After a moment, light fingertips touch the small of my back, and Isabel kneels beside me to say, "It's not your fault, Hallie. We never blamed you and we never will. That man is sick—he's sick in his mind and in his soul." Isabel starts patting my back, then adds, "Call him, Hallie. Get the evidence you need to blackmail him. The sooner he leaves you alone, the better we'll *all* be."

CHAPTER 23

My shoes hit the welcome mat in Tom and Sarah's house and I let out a long sigh. This is where I need to be for this phone call. Now's my time to collect my evidence, and Sarah is willing to walk me through it. "Thanks for letting me do this here," I say to Sarah. "I don't want to put Harrison and Isabel through this, but I also don't want to be alone."

"No problem," Sarah says as she closes the door behind me. "Tom's at work today, so it's just you and me."

I lift my chest and inhale deeply through my nose. "Perfect. I saw from social media that *he* is back in Oklahoma. So, today's the day I get him to confess to everything. I installed an audio recorder on my laptop, and I'm going to record our conversation as we talk on speaker phone."

"Good." Sarah offers a closed-lip smile with one small punch in the air to cheer me on. She walks past the couch toward the kitchen and I follow on her heels. "Let's set up on the kitchen table, I think that's probably the best place." I head toward the large, square table and begin setting up the recorder when my hands start to shake. Sarah freezes, then reaches over to place a steady hand over mine, "It's gunna be fine, Hallie. Just like you said, get the evidence you need and end the call." She gives me a quick squeeze, then moves her arm across the table as she sinks into one of the kitchen chairs. "He knows your calling him, right?"

I gulp, then give one, long blink. "Yes. I texted him to tell him we needed to talk. He's at work, but he said he'd take my call—Lord knows he's done a lot worse at work than taking a personal call." Sighing, I add, "And

I'm sure he was just waiting for me to contact him after the whole *cigar-on-my-windshield* episode last week."

"Well, at least he doesn't know what's up your sleeve."

I cast a long side-glance at nothing, then lower into the chair across from Sarah and add, "Yeah, Jonathan would never expect this. He thinks I'm too dumb to do something like record him, and I know he will spill the gory details if I can get him riled up enough." I run an unsteady hand through my hair and shift to remove my phone from the back pocket of my jeans. With the laptop open, the recorder up, and my phone out, all that's left is to dial the number. I chew on the inside of my cheek. Am I really prepared to race down memory lane with the man that created a life I'm so desperate to forget?

As I stare down at the phone, my hand poised as if ready to draw a sword, Sarah reaches over the table and presses her fingertips against the surface before me. "Hallie," she starts, and my eyes raise to meet her unwavering gaze, "I've been praying about this call. Be strong. God's here with us, and he'll get you through this. Just stay calm, follow through with the plan, and remember that if it gets to be too much, you can always hang-up and try again later . . . either way, I'll be here to help."

"Thank you," I manage through the lump forming in my throat. *I can do this—I'm strong . . . I'm a fighter.* I nod my head and raise the phone to my mouth. *Please, God—let me get what I need to end this battle.*

The recorder begins counting the seconds as the ringing echoes loudly over the speaker phone. The sound waves jump on the audio record icon—it's picking up the ringing tone. Everything's working, I just need him to answer with the right greeting. I hold my breath as the line connects, and my stomach does a somersault. "Jonathan McClain."

My heart soars. I took a risk calling his work phone, but I got what I needed—he's identified himself. Sarah gives me a silent nod from the other side of the kitchen table, and I take a deep breath, "It's Hallie."

Papers ruffle and the wheels of a rolling office chair screech. "What are you doing calling me on my work phone?" comes his hushed tone.

I ignore the question. "You've been to Ann Arbor. You're looking for me."

Jonathan laughs quietly. *Click.* His office door closes shut, "That's what this call is about? Didn't the cigar left on your windshield provide enough evidence? Yeah, Hallie—I've been to Ann Arbor. I knew that was your brother's voice I heard in the background of our last phone call, so I thought I would come scope out your new *home*," he jeers.

"You're not welcome here, Jonathan. Don't come back." My voice trembles just a little, so I straighten my back and sit up taller. I have a job to do, and I can't let my emotions get the better of me. "Seriously, Jonathan. This marriage is over, and there's nothing you can do to make me change my mind. You can't scare me into coming back to Oklahoma, I'm only coming back for the court date in October."

"Give it up, Hallie," comes his vindictive retort. "Whatever you're doing in Ann Arbor is a waste. You're too stupid to get a real job, and when you finally stop living off your *brother*, you'll run back to me."

His words slice through me. *How dare he*—I don't live off my brother. I'm only here because Harrison is the last person I trust with my safety. *And stupid, huh?* How's this for stupid . . . time to dig-up some dirt. "I'll never come back to you, you know why? Because you *beat* me . . . all the time, and all my bruises proved that. And you controlled me, burning me with your cigar…giving me that scar on my stomach, as if that could ruin my chances of ever having children." I pound my free fist against my thigh. "Then, that one night, when I was just trying to help you…you really tried to kill me. You *forced* yourself on me, nearly ripping off my nightgown, and tried to strangle me. You locked your grip around my neck and you wouldn't have let go if I hadn't hit you with the lamp in self-defense." The rush of my words keep pace with my racing heart, *I have to get him to admit to all this.* "You know all of this is true."

Another mirthless laugh, "So what if it's true?" His tone takes a nasty dive with his next words, "You're my wife, I'll hit you anytime I want. I'll burn you with a thousand cigars if I have to. I'll *take* you when I feel like it, even if you try to refuse me. And I could kill you in a heartbeat . . . if I *feel* like it. I *own* you, Hallie. When will you figure out that you can never escape me? You deserved everything I did to you, and I'm not the only one who thinks that."

My mind reels. I'm done—he's confessed to it all. But now I need to know more. "What do you mean?"

His tone returns to his even, deep voice. "Ainsley told me just the other week that she thinks you deserved what you got. And if your best friend's saying that, then what more do you need? You're mine, and I'll treat you the way you deserve."

My heart drops to my stomach. *How could she say such a thing?* I wouldn't wish Jonathan's violence on my worst enemy, let alone someone I used to call my best friend. "No one deserves to be abused," I throw back, my gumption lifting with the heat that rises from my gut, "*Especially not Bailey.*" Angry tears threaten, but I can't stop yet, "Yeah, Jonathan, my niece told us what you did to her. *How could you hit a child?*"

"Easy," he retorts in a dangerous voice, "she got out of bed that last time we stayed at your parents', when Harrison and Isabel came to visit in the summer. She started crying for her mom. She wouldn't stop, so I slapped her across the face and told her to go back to sleep. That's called showing a kid who's boss. Someone needs to teach her to be seen and not heard."

"*How dare you,*" I shriek. We're past the point of no return, now I'm seeing red. "You had no right to put a hand on her like that, *or any other child for that matter.*"

"Your brother would never do it, and someone needs to show that kid how a real man deals with that kinda mess," and he throws in a few cuss words to make his point.

"You're not a real man. You're a monster."

"*Rita* would disagree," he snickers as he fires back with the kind of ammunition he thinks will hurt, but I don't care who Jonathan *cozies* up with.

"I don't care what *Rita* thinks. What you do, *or who you do*, in your spare time—that is your business." I grit my teeth. How dare he compare me to Rita…we have nothing in common.

"Don't start accusing me of an affair, Hallie. Rita told me all about your flirting with Andrew and how you were going to meet up with him for coffee or *something*. So, don't you start pointing fingers at me." My jaw drops, and my wide eyes meet Sarah's behind the laptop that's still recording.

She tips her head forward with a look that says, *clear your name*, then she moves her eyes purposefully to the laptop. *Oh gosh*—this false accusation needs to be denied.

"There was never anything going on between me and Andrew." I sputter as my thighs flex, wanting to jump from the chair. "Pastor Noah can attest to that. Andrew texted me once, and I never replied. You can check my phone records. I've never cheated on you, Jonathan."

He breathes heavily into the phone, "Don't play dumb with me, Hallie. You said it yourself, you knew I was in Ann Arbor, watching you. It doesn't matter if you changed the color of your hair, I can recognize you a mile away. And I saw you walking down the street with that *guy*. You both looked cute, with your matching, black t-shirts." My lips part as my gaze finds Sarah again. Our eyes lock. *He saw Tom.* "You want to tell me you're not sleeping with him, too?"

Heat pulses against my temples as my eyes drop to the recorder. "I'm not. I—" I stutter, my heart catching in my throat. He can't know about Tom and Sarah. I clench my stomach and jut my chin out. "Just because you've been keeping yourself busy with Rita doesn't mean that I'm sleeping with someone, too. I've never had an affair, and that guy you saw me with is just a guy from church. That's why we had matching t-shirts—we were doing something for the church." From the corner of my eye, I see Sarah shift uncomfortably. "Not that it's any of your business who I talk to," I add.

"It is my business. Like I said, you're my wife, and your actions have been dragging my name through the mud for far too long now," he grunts. "Don't you know what I'm capable of? I can find you *and* him. I can make this all disappear with two slugs from my shotgun."

My skin crawls. I do know what he's capable of, and if I have to, the courts will too. Without any acknowledgement of the threat, I move past it and say, "We're getting a divorce in two months, it's not your concern who I spend time with here in Ann Arbor. It's none of your business now, when you sign those papers, or after the divorce is finalized in court."

"Give it up, Hallie. You know I'm not signing those papers," he spits. "You're gunna be my wife. I don't care how many affairs you've had, you're gunna learn what it means to be an obedient and submissive wife."

"No—I'm not." I steady my breathing, like a fighter about to deliver the final punch. "You *will* sign those papers, Jonathan—the moment they're served to you. And you won't return to Ann Arbor. If you refuse to listen, I'll take you to court for all the terrible things you did to me while we were married. I'll press charges."

"You don't have any money to take me to court. And, even if you tried, no one would believe you . . . don't forget, everyone loves me around here. I'm well-known and well-respected, you couldn't convince anyone otherwise if your life depended on it."

My nostrils flare, "*I'll find the money if I have to, and then everyone will know who you really are!*"

"And then what, Hallie?" He chuckles, like I've just told him a joke. "You're gunna ride off into the sunset with that *guy* when it's all said and done? You think your life will be perfect the moment we leave the courthouse? I know where you live now, and I'll find you—no matter what." His voice drops to a hushed whisper that pricks my skin with every syllable, "If I can't have you, Hallie, then no one can." And with that, the line goes dead.

I stop the recorder, place my phone down, and drop my head into my hands. Sarah's still sitting across from me, but I can't keep it together anymore . . . the dam breaks, and, as if a tidal wave crashes against my heart, I sob. Sarah leans across the table and places a hand on my arm while silently respecting my need to cry. Eventually, I reign in my tears. "You did great, Hallie," she whispers. "You got what you were looking for, and you held it together the whole time."

I lift my head, my eyes burning, and she rises for the tissue box perched on top of the fridge. Gently handing me the box, she rests in the seat beside me. "I just don't know if my threat is going to work," I gulp. "I don't think he's gunna leave me alone."

Sarah drops her chin to her neck, then says, "Give it a couple weeks, and then just send him a text that you're going to press charges if he returns to Ann Arbor or refuses to sign the divorce papers."

"But he knows how vulnerable I am. I haven't fooled him. He'll just keep coming after me."

"Then send him a copy of the evidence as proof of what you need to take him to court." Sarah's fist drops to the table like a gentle gavel, "You told me he was worried about his reputation. He even made that clear over the phone. If he realizes you have something that will completely ruin him, then he'll be forced to leave you alone."

With a slow nod, I take a steadying breath and say, "If there's one thing he's more worried about than revenge, it's his reputation."

"Good—well, let's use it against him. Keep a copy of this recording safe, and if you need to use it to protect yourself, then do it."

I run my fingers over the mousepad to save the recording, then ask, "Will you keep a copy of it too?" My eyes widen in her direction. "I would give it to Harrison and Isabel," I start, "but I don't want them listening to what he said about Bailey." And with a huff and a small smile playing in the corner of my mouth, I add, "Besides, I think Isabel might just press charges herself with that kind of ammunition in her hands."

With the hint of a grin, Sarah says, "Sure, you can send me a copy."

As I continue working on the laptop, I reply, "Technically speaking, it involves you too. I mean, he never mentioned Tom's name, but—" and I trail off.

Sarah tilts her head and pinches her eyebrows together. "You should've just explained that Tom's married to a friend. You should've told him about Tom and me. Then, he would've gotten off your case about the affair."

I shake my head in dismay. "I couldn't do that, Sarah. You have no idea how powerful and manipulative he is. He already knows too much about my life and the people I care for. I don't want to put you and Tom at risk—I'd rather have him think I'm having an affair." I raise one eyebrow and click away at the mousepad. "Although, I would never cheat, not even on *him*."

Sarah leans back in her chair and says, "Well that's good, because cheating is such an ugly thing." My eyes widen and my forehead wrinkles as my hands freeze over the mousepad. *Oh my gosh—please don't tell me this is what Tom and Sarah are going through.* "Oh no," she throws both hands across her heart, "not me and Tom. No, no—there's never been an issue like that with us. Although, we have our struggles," she mutters, but then clasps her hands together on the table. "No, we just learned about Vincent—Tom's brother—he just found out his girlfriend since high school has been cheating on him for years."

"Oh my gosh—since high school? But that was like ten years ago."

"Yeah," she sighs. "He thought he was going to marry her, but every time he brought up the idea, she just kept saying she's not in a rush, or that she doesn't really believe in marriage." One corner of Sarah's mouth turns downward as she shrugs. "She's definitely not the right girl for him anyway, but they were dating before his accident. She stuck by his side through the coma, so I think Vincent felt he owed her. It eventually came out why she was so opposed to marrying Vincent. It was because she was on and off with Vincent's best friend."

I inhale sharply, "So, he lost his girlfriend and his best friend all in one discovery?"

"Yep," Sarah says matter-of-factly. My heart drops—I know what it's like to lose everything in one moment. "I mean, she's a pretty girl, so I'm not surprised that she used that to her advantage. But she started cheating on him while he was in the coma, and apparently it didn't stop there. It's been going on for years, and now, Vincent is really struggling with this betrayal—he was on the phone with Tom all last night talking it through." She yawns. If Tom was up last night, she must have been too.

"Poor Vincent," I offer. "I'm glad he's got family like you and Tom to help him work through this kind of stuff."

"Yeah, and I'm glad we've been able to be there for him." She clears her throat, then adds, "But you know all about betrayal, Hallie. If Ainsley really did say you deserved everything you got in that marriage, then that might be the worst thing I've ever heard."

My head turns with her words as if I've been slapped across the face with the reality of it all. "I hope she didn't actually say that. Jonathan lies a lot, so he could've been lying about that, too," but my hollow excuses amplify my empty words. Yes, Jonathan does lie, but isn't Ainsley looking for a way to defend her choice of dropping our friendship?

As if she's rummaging through the thoughts in my head, Sarah says, "Yeah, well from what you've told me, I wouldn't be surprised to learn that

Ainsley was willing to stoop that low, especially if she's still bitter toward you," and at that, my heart sinks.

* * *

It's been weeks since I've heard anything from Jonathan, all the while I'm living daily with the question of whether he's listening to my threat or planning something far worse than lurking in downtown Ann Arbor and marking his territory with his infamous cigar. I roll over in bed and check the time on my phone. *Ugh*! One hour until I have to be at work. I tug on my pillow, then pull the quilt closer. *How about my nightmare last night?*

In this dream, Jonathan found me at the apartment. He was threatening the twins in an effort to get me to obey him. He demanded I bring Tom and Sarah to him, and the moment they showed, he pulled out his shotgun. I woke before any blood was spilled, but I'm stuck with those vivid images seared into my psyche. It's like Jonathan's holding me in his claws, and he's ready to hurt the people who I care about just to get to me. I rock deeper into the mattress, as if it could swallow me whole. Will anything I say or do get that monster out of my head? My eyes dart around the room. Maybe I should leave, then everyone would be safe…even if I didn't have anyone I could trust by my side. But where would I go? Would I really be protecting those I care for by fleeing if Jonathan knows they are here anyway? *No, I'm going to fight this to the very end.*

My gaze lands on the verse from Jeremiah 29:11 that still serves as my comfort in all of this. I'm counting down the days until we're given a date at the courthouse. But is there any hope for a future? My blood starts to pulse in my ears. I take a deep breath, roll over, and repeat the words over and over in my head. *"For I know the plans I have for you," declares the Lord, "plans to prosper you and not to harm you, plans to give you a hope and a future."* Can God be trusted, even when things look as dark as they do? I press my elbows into my side, making my body as small as possible. Sarah trusted God—and before she chose to do that, Tom trusted that Christ would save his dying brother and redeem his marriage. But Tom got his *dove*, and his storm ended with a *rainbow*. For me, there is only a storm . . . ahead and behind. Maybe

Jonathan has left me alone for a while, but that doesn't mean he'll leave me alone forever.

I grab for my phone and bring it to my face. The screen flashes as the light causes me to wince. I blink a few times, adjusting my sight, then freeze. The date on the screen snatches my breath. Exactly a year ago, Jonathan tried to strangle me. On this day last year, I thought my life was going to end. I gulp and take in a breath. I knew it was time to leave the moment his grip tightened around my throat, but I didn't know how I was going to manage it all. Since that day, I've told people about my story, not many—but I did muster up the strength to share that living nightmare. And what's more, I had the strength to leave him—to get out, to make it on my own. Now, a whole year later, I'm stronger than I ever imagined I could be. I left town when my world unraveled, something that this little fawn would have never done in a million years. I fought back when Jonathan tried to force me to return to Oklahoma. I found a job, I didn't give into my fear, I took action to collect evidence. And now, I'm not going to waver.

Using my elbows to hoist myself into an upright position, I open my text messages and begin typing:

> Just so you know, I have all the evidence I need to take you to court. I never wanna see you in Ann Arbor again. Once you sign those papers I served you with last week, they'll issue a court date. If you don't sign those papers or if you miss showing up in court, I'll press charges.

I hit send and wait for his reply. This is what he gets when he messes with a fighter. I've fought through so much, and now the end is near. My phone buzzes with his reply.

"K," is his simple response.

My heart thumps. He better sign those papers. I lean my head back and place my phone down beside me. *Lord, please let this be the end of me and him. I remember how I desperately prayed for my escape on this day last year. I remember how long it felt waiting until Harrison showed up to move me out. I remember the fear I felt every night, wondering if he was going to hurt me again. Please, keep me safe now. I pray October will be here before I know it. Let him sign those papers without a fight.*

CHAPTER 24

"Hallie, could you come in here before you clock out, please?" my floor manager calls as I'm poised to bound down the stairs after a long shift. My throat tightens—*uh-oh*. A yawn plays at the base of my jaw, but I stifle it. It doesn't matter how exhausted I've been from working extended hours lately, I have to hold it together a bit longer. This initiative to add on several summer programs has made work crazy. Thankfully, summer is ending. With a longing glance at the exit, I pivot and head in the direction of her office, my chest tightening with every step I take. What would warrant this impromptu meeting? "Thanks, Hallie," she offers from a seated position behind her desk as I step inside her office, close the door, and tiptoe toward her.

She gestures to the seat in front of her desk. As I lower my body, my heart starts to beat faster. *Am I in trouble?* I look around the office. It wasn't too long ago that I had begged this woman not to put my name or face on their website. *Is that why I'm here?* Is she going to demand that I make my presence known to the online world? Does it even really matter at this point, now that Jonathan knows where I am? Her focus is hitched to the computer screen, so I clasp my hands together on my lap, my knuckles turning white with the tension that builds from the silence that stretches between us. Then, she turns to me and says, "Sorry I dragged you in here before you left, but I wanted to catch you for a quick chat."

"No problem," I reply, my blood coursing through my veins.

"We just wanted to thank you for all the hard work you've done on this floor during the past several months." I breathe a sigh of relief. "Our summer programs take up a lot of our time and manpower, and we recognize the amount of work that's left you with up here. The truth is, you're incredibly valuable to our team. You never complain, you always have a smile on your face, you know what you're doing in the gym, and the members have nothing but positive things to say about you."

A shy grin spreads across my face. "Well, that's what you pay me for—to do my job," I say with a light shrug.

"That's true," she responds, "but when things got busy over Labor Day weekend, while we were bringing our summer programs to an end and trying to finish up with all the final details, you really took over up here. I saw how hard you were working, and I really appreciate it."

With a short chuckle, I say, "Yeah, Labor Day weekend was crazy, but I knew how hard everyone else was working—it wasn't just me."

The floor manager rolls her chair closer to the desk and locks eyes with me, "Well, now that we are well into September, things should start to slow down. Summer is always crazy around here, and it tends to bleed into the *back-to-school* phase just a bit. But I wanted to thank you for your hard work and reassure you that you'll be getting more assistance up here on the second floor." She smiles, ending our short, yet rewarding meeting. We shake hands, and I leave her office unable to hide the smile plastered across my face.

The setting sun paints a pink and purple backdrop behind the tall, downtown buildings on this mildly warm, autumn day. As I walk to my car, I push my shoulders back. Sure, I've endured long hours and busy shifts at the gym . . . but what else would I be doing? Besides, I want to be a help, and it sounds like I have been. The corners of my mouth begin to fall as I draw closer and closer to the *infamous* outdoor patio. *Ugh.* It didn't matter how many times I circled around the gym before work, all those spots were taken. I was left with no other option but to park over here.

My skin prickles as I approach the busy street lined with outdoor seating. It won't be long before they start packing up the patios . . . I'd give it a couple weeks. The cold, fall temperatures are around the corner, but for now, there are still people choosing to eat outside. Why wouldn't they, what with the painted sunset and pleasant temperature? I cross another street. I'm steering clear of the patio that still haunts me with the smell of that cigar. But I can't rip my eyes from the scene, as if I'm trapped in a game of "Where's Waldo." *He's not here. He hasn't been here since he put the cigar under my windshield wiper.* My chest rises and falls in rhythm with my footsteps, and as soon as I turn the corner toward the parking garage, I quicken my pace.

All it took was my threat from last month. Since then, the streets of Ann Arbor have been voided of *his* presence. I'm guessing he must have signed those papers, or we wouldn't have been issued a God-ordained court date on the year anniversary of when I left him. *Hmmm.* Does his current silence mean he's scared of the damage I can do in court? Or does he have one last trick to play . . . an idea to call my bluff? I bite my thumbnail. *It's not a bluff.* If I have to, I will take him to court, even if it costs me every penny I've earned at this new job. I jump behind the wheel and go through my routine: lock doors, check wipers, scan interior, and search the landscape for any signs of him. I press my lips together . . . *all's good.* Everything inside the car looks like it did when I parked it here this morning, there's nothing out of place. So, I turn on the engine, and navigate out of the parking garage. As I turn down the busy streets, waiting at each light, my eyes start to dance. I can't help it. Something inside of me has to look for him. This is what he's done to me. But that will end in a month with our upcoming court date… it better end. I chew on the inside of my lip. *Will he finally give up all hope and leave me alone forever?*

* * *

"Only one week left till it's finally over," Isabel cheers in a hushed voice as I fly up the apartment staircase. She hasn't seen me all day, and her eyes spark when we come face-to-face. She's as eager for the court date as I am. I pat her arm and motion with one hand for her to follow me. Many small group members are mingling around the dining room table. It doesn't matter that I worked another long shift today, I have a renewed strength for our Bible study tonight.

"Yeah," I reply, "I can hardly believe it." I move to my room as she follows on my heels.

"Harrison spoke to your parents, and they are good to pick you up from the airport."

"Oh, good," I say as I drop my gym bag in the corner of the bedroom, "I've been dreading that phone call, so I'm glad he talked to them."

"Well, they didn't seem happy about it," Isabel confesses from the doorway, "but they'll be there—I just wish we could be there for you, too."

I replace my jacket with a comfortable sweatshirt as I offer a gentle smile. "I know, I wish you guys could be there, but you've already done so much for me."

Sighing deeply, Isabel says, "You've always been welcome here, I just can't believe *he* found you in Ann Arbor. You still haven't heard from him or seen any sign of him, have you?"

Pulling off my workout shoes and sliding my feet into a pair of slippers, I answer with a shrug, "Nope, but it would be just like him to try one last thing before we go to the courthouse. This divorce is uncontested, so they simply make sure we're both there, then they grant the divorce, but something could still go wrong, and his silence kinda makes me worry. So, I'm preparing myself for whatever trick he might throw at me, just in case." Reaching for my Bible on my bedside table, I add, "I just hope it doesn't involve a return visit to Ann Arbor or anything to do with my parents."

Isabel offers a quiet, lip-twisting grunt in response as we both move to the hallway and join the growing group in the living room. I approach Sarah and settle in the chair beside her as she offers a lively hello paired with a big hug. The group begins as Harrison explains we'll be taking a momentary break in our study to discuss the upcoming baptism. "We typically like to do baptisms outside, if we can manage," Harrison says to the group, "but we figured that the flurry of snow we're supposed to get on Sunday will be a bit of a deterrent." Everyone laughs, then he continues, "Our baptism went so well over the summer that we've had several people ask to do another one. As we work through our passage tonight, I want you all to consider what baptism means to you. And if you haven't been baptized before, maybe you can think through the possibility of getting baptized on Sunday." As he tells us to turn in our Bibles to the book of Acts, my enthusiasm fizzles. This whole lesson is for me, and Harrison knows it. *I'm the only one in this room who hasn't been baptized yet.*

The next hour passes awkwardly as my guilt is fueled by the passage we're analyzing in Acts. Tom isn't taking much of a lead in the study tonight, and I keep glancing at him, waiting for him to jump in. As Harrison closes in prayer, my throat tightens. I'm one week short of getting my divorce, and I'm still unwilling to completely surrender to God and trust him with my life.

As the group filters out, saying their typical good-byes and reaching for their jackets, I wait where I'm seated. I lick my lips with the imminent conversation. Before I know it, the room is empty of everyone but the usual five of us, just like every other Thursday night. I sit in silence, waiting to hear Harrison ask what I thought of the passage we studied tonight, but instead, Sarah speaks up first.

"This study really hit me hard," Sarah says as she places a hand over her heart. My head inclines, and I purse my lips. "When we did the baptism this past summer, I convinced myself I'd be able to get baptized at the next one. But now that we're only a few days away from it, I still don't think I'm ready." My body starts to rock back, but I tighten my abs, cushioning this blow by re-crossing my legs.

"You're not alone," Isabel offers. "It's a big step to take, and there are a lot of people who hesitate to publicly declare their faith in front of a large crowd."

"Yeah," Sarah starts as she flips in her Bible to the passage mentioned earlier in the study, "but I really thought I would be ready by now. I mean, when Harrison read, 'And now what are you waiting for? Get up, be baptized and wash your sins away, calling on his name,' I felt like God was talking directly to me." I press my tongue to the roof of my mouth in order to keep my mouth from gaping—Sarah is saying *exactly* what I'm feeling. "So, I asked myself—what *am* I waiting for? And the truth is, I don't feel like I have a good enough excuse." Tom stands from the couch and moves behind Sarah, who's still seated beside me. He places both hands on her shoulders, and she starts to cry.

A few blustering remarks are uttered through her tears, but Tom takes over, patting her shoulder, as if to say that the burden isn't just hers to carry. "The truth is, we can't get pregnant, although we've been trying for years." The group is stunned into silence, but I reach over and touch Sarah's leg, her tears splashing down on my hand. *This* is what they're struggling through. Tom's shoulders fall, "My beautiful wife has wanted children since the moment we eloped, and I can't give her that. We've been to doctors appointments, we've tried lots of things, but nothing has worked."

Sarah wipes the tears from her cheek and puts a hand on top of one of Tom's hands, then adds, "It's not just you, Tom. The doctors have said that it's a combination of a few things, my problems included." She sniffles and swipes the other side of her tear-streaked face. "I guess I just thought that life after becoming a Christian would be easy—that I wouldn't be challenged. And yet, when we started trying for children, we experienced the biggest trial of all. I want to place my trust in God and get baptized—I mean, Tom has been baptized, so why can't I bring myself to trust God and do the same?"

Quiet fills the room, and my heart plays an emotional tug-of-war within my chest. "I know what you mean," I eventually offer. All heads move in my direction. "My circumstances still haunt me too—in a different way," I say as I direct my gaze toward Sarah for a second. "But I can't seem to shake my reality in order to move forward with getting baptized."

Sarah nods, "Almost like you wouldn't be giving your all to God if you got baptized now? Like you'd be resistant, even though you still have faith that you know will never leave you?"

"Exactly." Harrison and Isabel are still there, but the walls close in on me, Tom, and Sarah, who've become like family. It's as if there's nothing off limits—we can challenge each other and walk through life together without feeling betrayed. Was it ever like this with Ainsley? *Gosh—how different could they be?* Ainsley had a child, and she struggled with being a young mother…Sarah is getting older and watching her window of opportunity to have children dwindle. I guess it's not all that different. Everyone struggles, it's just a matter of how we react to that struggle. Sarah and I both need to heal, and there is a real freedom that comes in a friendship when we can both acknowledge that reality.

A startling buzz from my phone in my back pocket catapults me back to the present. Rita's name appears on the screen. *What the—?* I open the message with a shaky hand. *Ahah.* This is the trick *he* has been keeping up his sleeve.

> I heard you'll be coming back to town next week.
> When do you arrive?

I nearly spit at the screen as I read her words, my eyes running across the lines several times as my brow furrows. *They can't really think I'm that stupid.*

"You okay, Hallie?" Harrison asks from across the room.

I raise my eyes and lower my phone with a frustrated shake of my head. "Rita just sent me a message asking when I'll be arriving next week. Jonathan made her send it, I know he did. I knew he was gunna try something, I just didn't think it would be this lame. I mean, do they think I'll send them my itinerary with all my flight details so that he can easily track me down?"

"That's ridiculous," Isabel huffs as Sarah sits up straighter in her seat and Tom returns to the couch. "Obviously, you're not going to respond."

Hmmm. "What if I do?" I pose, all heads jutting with my words. "Yeah, I mean, if they think I'm dumb enough to tell Rita about my flight plans, then that's exactly what I should do."

"Uh, Hallie," Sarah says in a high-pitched voice, her eyes widening to reveal the white around her irises, "I really don't think that's a good idea. You just said—"

"No, I know," I interrupt, "but what if I give them the *wrong* details? I mean, our court time is on Friday at four, so if I told them I will arrive just before we have to meet at the courthouse, then I may be able to ensure a little more safety when I spend Thursday night at my parents' house." The four of them contemplate my words for a moment, then the nods begin. I reply to Rita with a bit of attitude, explaining that it's none of her business when I arrive, but relaying the false time anyway in an effort to play into their scheme with the kind of stupid response they're expecting. We wait around a little, filling our time with aimless conversation until I finally accept that she isn't going to reply. As far as I know, they now think I'm arriving on Friday. My shoulders relax. I may have just bought myself some safety during my return trip to Oklahoma.

Sarah rises to leave, then says, "Can I take you to the airport next week, Hallie? I know you need to be there around the time our group starts, so I can run you to Detroit and be back here shortly after we begin—I shouldn't miss much."

I look to Isabel, who was supposed to drop me off, and motion to her with one raised shoulder. Isabel tilts her head and says, "Actually, that would be really helpful, Sarah. There's this new cake recipe I've been wanting to try for group, so that would give me the time I need to do it after I pick the twins up from school."

"Great, then it's settled," she says. "I'll text you when I'm on my way over."

The corner of my mouth turns up in a half-grin, "Perfect, thanks Sarah." We all say a quick good-bye before she and Tom disappear down the staircase. After a full-day of work, Harrison shoos me to bed, refusing to accept my assistance with cleaning. As I settle under the covers for the night, I check my phone one last time. Rita still hasn't responded, and at this point, she won't—I just pray they bought my lie.

* * *

Tom offers to carry my luggage down to the car where Sarah is waiting for me as I say my good-byes to Isabel, the twins, and Harrison. "I'll be praying for you, Hallie," Harrison says. "You're so strong, and as much as you have panicked over this whole ordeal, this is what you have to do . . . this is right, no matter what Mom and Dad say." A weak smile forms as I wave and tell the twins I'll be back on Saturday. While trudging down the stairs to Sarah's car, my stomach grips. As much as I've dreamt about Oklahoma and returning to my *home*, now that I'm about to, my heart aches. Oh sure, I don't really have anyone left in Oklahoma, but I've wondered what it would be like to return. *How things have changed.* Now, my torn heart is left grappling with my sorrow over being absent from Ann Arbor for a few days. And the question still remains…what will be waiting for me at the courthouse on Friday?

Once settled in the passenger's seat, I smile at Sarah, who's just kissed Tom good-bye through the window. "Thanks again for offering to take me to the airport. I really appreciate it, and I know Harrison and Isabel do too—they're pretty busy today."

"Not a problem—you got everything you need? All the paperwork or whatever else?"

"Yep," I reply. "I'm good to go . . ." But am I, really? This time tomorrow, I'll be a free woman. My toes curl under. What does it mean to be *free*?

As Sarah navigates to the highway, we chat a little about our work week. Eventually, the conversation turns back to the trip I'm about to make. "How are you feeling about all this?" she asks.

I twist my mouth back and forth while the highway before us blurs. What's really dancing in the distant corners of my mind? "I dunno, really. When things took a turn for the worse last summer—that time in August," Sarah nods, "I was so ready to be over it all. I thought once Harrison arrived to help me move out, I would wait ten days, and then file for a divorce. My parents really hit me hard with their request—their demand—that I wait a year to sign the papers." I sigh, "When I agreed, I wondered why I was willing to do that. I mean, all I wanted to do was to be rid of him and to be free from his abuse, but for some reason, I listened to my parents and waited a year, even though I knew I was still gunna go through with the divorce at the end of it." My hands begin fiddling with the bottom hem of my jacket, then I add, "If I had divorced him when I could, then I wouldn't have had to deal with the gossip about the *affair* I supposedly had, I wouldn't have had to deal with Rita and all her mess—following me around town and trying to get under my skin." My heart takes a slight dip. "I wouldn't have had to deal with losing Ainsley as a best friend or leaving Jim's Gym. If I hadn't listened to my parents, maybe by now things would be normal in Oklahoma. Instead, this wait gave Jonathan some sense of hope and forced him to come find me, wherever I was . . . to torment me for an entire year."

My stomach flips. My life would be completely different right now if I had just waved my parents off and done what I wanted with the divorce.

"Maybe God knew it would be good for you to go through all this," Sarah offers, interrupting my thoughts. I turn to her, my eyebrows lifting in question. "That sounded a bit harsh, and I'm definitely not saying that you *deserved* to go through any of this. But God puts us through hardships to grow our character. And as much as it *sucks*," she emphasizes—she knows . . . what with not being able to get pregnant, "we really learn so much about our faith when we have to deal with the turmoil." I sink deeper into my seat, her words ringing undeniably true in my ears. This year, I've not only learned more about who I am and what I'm capable of, but I've learned that God provides even when it seems like my whole world is unraveling. I left Oklahoma, but I settled in Ann Arbor. I left Jim's Gym, but I found a job within a week of my arrival here. I lost Ainsley, but I gained Sarah. Yes, I've been through some serious messes, but God's been there with me through it all.

"You know," I start, "I think you might be right. I honestly didn't know what I was agreeing to a year ago, but I will say that God has used this year to teach me some things. Maybe if I had gotten the divorce ten days after I left him, I wouldn't have figured out just how strong I really am. I wouldn't have fought my way through so many things…I wouldn't have met you and Tom." We sit in silence for a moment, and my gaze shifts to the window as we blur past the barren trees that line the highway. "It seems like God knew what he was doing, even if it was hard on me."

We chat a little more about our personal walks with God, what he's teaching us through scripture, and how he's growing our character in different ways as the highway stretches on. At the first sight of the airport sign, my muscles tense as I recoil into the passenger's side of the car. "You okay?" Sarah asks.

I gulp. Here it is, again—the whole fight-or-flight battle that hits me without fail at this point in every trip I take to an airport. "Yeah," I reply. "It's just that it's been a while since I've flown, and for the most part, I would usually be flying to escape *him*. But now I'm flying to return to him, and that makes me a little uncomfortable."

"That's true," Sarah offers, "but your return is for a good cause . . . once you leave the courthouse, you won't have to escape from him anymore. That's gotta give you some hope."

"You'd think," I say with a hollow chuckle. "But I know what it feels like to approach an airport with hope filling my heart, and right now, it doesn't feel that way at all."

"Well, I know when I'm feeling miserable, especially as I help all these women deliver babies when I still don't have a baby of my own, I meditate on this verse: 'For I know the plans I have for you—"

"Declares the Lord," I chime in.

She turns to me briefly and grins, then we finish the verse in unison, "Plans to prosper you and not to harm you, plans to give you hope and a future."

Her smile widens, "So, you've heard it before," she adds with a tickle of laughter edging her voice.

"Once or twice," I laugh back. "Actually, Harrison and Isabel gifted that verse to me in a frame this past Christmas." With a light shrug, I add, "It's kinda been my lifeline ever since."

"I know what you mean . . . mine too," Sarah replies. "You know, Hallie—you've gone through so much, but I know God's going to give you a hope and a future. Your story is crazy, but it's not over yet. God's going to use your story one day."

My shoulders relax just a little at the sound of her words. I nod, "And I've got a recording in case anybody wants to hear just how *crazy* this journey has been."

"Yep," Sarah replies, "and I have a copy of that recording just in case you need me to do anything with it."

"Thanks," I offer, "but I don't think it will come to that. Who knows why Rita messaged me last week, but it seems like Jonathan is going to show up at the courthouse when he needs to. He must know how serious I am about the threat of evidence, otherwise he would've returned to Ann Arbor. So, I doubt he's gunna try to push me. Deep down, he knows I wouldn't threaten him with something I don't have."

As Sarah pulls up to the airport drop-off, she adds, "Well, at any rate, I'm here for you. And I hope you don't run into Ainsley—it honestly makes me so mad that you had a friend who would just betray you like that." With a grateful smile, we both exit the car. I grab my suitcase from the trunk as she asks, "Will you text me when you land?"

"Sure, it might be a little late," I say.

"No worries, I'll probably still be at your brother's place by the time you land, anyway." With the automatic, glass doors awaiting my entrance, Sarah adds, "We'll miss you tonight at group, but I'm glad this year of waiting is finally up. I just hope the worst of it is over." Nodding and offering a quick wave, I pivot toward the doors of the airport and heave one, long breath. *Yes, I hope so too.*

* * *

"How was your flight," my mother asks in a flat tone. My dad takes my suitcase and hauls it into the back of my mom's SUV.

"It was fine, I'm just really tired," I say as I slip into the backseat. My dad walks around to the driver's seat . . . he still hasn't greeted me.

"And how is everyone in Ann Arbor? Things going well there?" She pulls the seatbelt across her torso while my dad puts on his blinker and starts inching his way into traffic.

"Yeah," I sigh, "everyone's good." My dad pretends to study the vehicles moving along at a steady pace.

"The twins doing well in school? I know they just started, but they're already so smart."

"Yep. They're doing great," I half grunt as I take out my phone to text Sarah that I landed. If she's still with Harrison and Isabel, she can pass the word along.

"Well, that's good," she continues, "I mean, they have to do well in school. They'll probably be our only grandbabies, so they need to be successful."

There it is, the demeaning comment I've been waiting for. "Mom," I say with a roll of my eyes, "I'm getting divorced, I'm not barren." And with the comment, my mind flits to Tom and Sarah. I say a quick prayer that God will give them a baby, but my heaven-bound plea is interrupted.

"You might as well be," my mother retorts under her breath. My fingers freeze as I blink. *Message received, Mother.* I bite my tongue and slump back against the headrest, closing my eyes. Is she trying to say I'm all used up and no one will want me? My nose wrinkles . . . it doesn't matter. I'm not going to get into it tonight.

Not that I could if I wanted to, because my dad finally decides to chime in. "You know, Hallie, we really thought you would come around this year. A year seemed like a good amount of time for you to come to your senses, but you still insist on embarrassing us by going through with this."

"Dad, it's so much more complicated than you think," comes my mumbled response as my eyes flutter open and my head leans on the window.

"How can it be complicated, Hallie? You married the guy, you said the vows, now it's your job to follow through." With one hand still on the steering wheel, he throws up the other, "That's what's the matter with society today, they treat marriage like a dating relationship—when they're through with their spouse, they just get divorced. As if it's no big deal."

My chin begins to quiver. He has no clue, and he wouldn't even hear me out if I thought I had it in me to tell him. "It's not like that," I respond. "Look, I don't want to get into it, but I'm getting a divorce tomorrow, and I would really appreciate your support, just for the day."

My parents look at each other for a second as the car gets awkwardly silent. No one says another word. I blink back tears. Why are the two of them being so weird? My phone buzzes on the seat beside me. I open Sarah's reply to my text, and my heart soars at the selfie she took with Tom, Harrison, and Isabel. Their smiles are exactly what I needed to see, and I keep the photo up on my screen until we pull into the driveway.

My dad returns to the back of the vehicle to grab my suitcase as my mom and I step up to the small, covered, cement porch. She opens the screen door and takes out her keys to unlock the front door, but she leaves them hanging in the lock. With a slight frown, I follow her inside. *Oh no!* I step back, like I've been body-checked. This is why my parents are acting so strange. My eyes widen at the two packed bags sitting beside their bedroom door. I take a few steps toward the bags, my eyes falling to the ugly, shag carpet. I tighten my fists and pierce daggers back at these items…as if they are responsible for this betrayal, not my parents. My dad opens the screen door behind me.

He sets my suitcase down in the den to our left, then says, "We are leaving for the nursing home tonight. Grannie's health has been declining, and I know she would really like to see us."

I rip my eyes from their packed bags and look back at the two of them, poised next to the screen door, ready to leave. A knife stabs at my heart. My mother avoids my eyes as she offers a feeble explanation, "They're doing some sort of special dinner tomorrow night at the home." She shifts her weight from one foot to the other, "We haven't been to visit in a while, and now just seems like the right time."

"We'll be back on Saturday to take you to the airport," is my father's final remark as he walks over to pick up their packed bags. Everything in me wants to scream *you can't leave me here alone!* But nothing comes out. I just stand there, with my mouth ajar, unable to produce a word or a tear that would explain what's racing through my mind.

"We'll leave the keys with you," my mother says, still unwilling to lift her gaze as my dad removes the key from the lock and places the keyring on the table beside the door. "We'll leave you the SUV so you can go where you need to tomorrow."

"*No*," I nearly shout, then I clear my throat, steadying my quivering voice. Now that I have both my parents' startled attention, I add, "Leave the truck instead…please." Their eyes narrow, but they nod, then leave without another word. They may not understand it, but if Jonathan comes by the house at any point, he needs to believe that my father is here, and the truck will be evidence of that.

I lock the door behind them and move to the window in the den. Maybe they'll change their minds. Headlights leave the driveway, and my heart plummets once again. My mouth waters, like I'm going to be sick. I swallow. They have no idea what kind of danger they've put me in by leaving me here alone until Saturday. The house is eerily silent as I step back from the window and grab my suitcase. I trudge down the hall, past my parents' room and Harrison's old room, until I reach my bedroom, just before the bend in the hallway. I open the door and flick on the light. *Oh my gosh!* My eyes sting and my face builds with heat. There, sitting on my bed, are all my belongings. My parents left everything that we packed from the lake house piled high on the mattress, right where I was supposed to sleep tonight. I bang the lights off and slam the door shut. *Oh sure...*they knew I was coming, but did they bother to help me out? I cross over to the hall closet beside the bathroom and yank out a blanket and pillow. My stomach falters, like I've been punched in the gut. I turn down the hall, pass through the dining room, and slump over to the couch in the family room. This will have to be my bed for the next two nights. I'm not going to clear out my room. It's like they left the stack on my bed as a punishment for my decision to file for a divorce. *Humph.* Maybe not . . . maybe they left all that stuff because they thought I'd eventually collect it to move back in with Jonathan. Wouldn't that be just *peachy*, granting their only wish? I didn't think I could sink any lower after seeing my parents' packed bags. *Man, was I wrong.*

I set up my bed and unpack my pajamas. My eyes flit to the corners of the large room. Good—the blinds are closed. I change out of my clothes then meander into the kitchen, passing the dining room table. My hand fumbles to grab a bottle of water from the fridge. Turning off all the lights, I use my flashlight on my phone to find my way back to the couch. As I curl into the narrow, suede sofa, my heart rate begins to climb, coursing through my muscles and snapping my mind to attention. Each creak of the old house sends me jumping. This place is so old and creepy. Why didn't I just fly in tomorrow, like I had lied to Rita . . . to Jonathan? *Oh God—please let him believe what I told him last week.* He can't know I'm in town tonight. The wind whistles outside, and I force my eyes closed, but every sound serves as a siren going off in my head. I lay still, with my heart pounding and my ears ringing. How will I ever sleep tonight?

CHAPTER 25

Yawning, I stretch my arms over my head and dangle my feet off the side of the couch. The day has finally come. It's not like last year, when I was waiting for Harrison to help me escape. No…today is a whole new ballgame. Today is the day I end my marriage for good. I kick off the blanket with a grunt. So much for a good night's sleep to get me through the events of the day. But at least it was only my racing heart that kept me awake . . . it could have been much worse.

I grab for my phone on the glass coffee table, blinking at the early morning light peering through the closed blinds. I fold one arm over my stomach as I lean forward to text a threatening reminder to Jonathan. This is it—I didn't fly all the way here to be deserted by my parents and played by *him.* I don't expect a response, but I do expect his full cooperation . . . *or else*. Placing my phone down, my weak legs carry me to the kitchen. *Coffee,* that's the answer. With a quick glance in my parents' fridge, I groan. *Wow.* No creamer. My eyes scan the empty racks. Well, thanks for the hospitality, Mom and Dad. I shut the fridge and lumber out of the kitchen. I guess I'll be eating out today. I should call Harrison, he would be outraged at my parents' decision to travel an hour and a half away at such a critical time. *No.* I can't. I lift my chin and curl my lips inward. I'm a fighter, and I don't need my parents holding my hand through this day anyway.

I change clothes, brush my teeth, grab for my purse and phone, and head toward the front door. Time to get out of this wretched house. At least they left me the truck. If it weren't for that and the lie I fed Rita last week, I wouldn't have stayed here last night.

As I swing open the front door, the sun shines through the screen door and leaves me squinting in the heat. *Jeez.* Why is it so hot in October? I wrinkle my nose and remove my jacket, placing it on the hallway table and picking up the keys in return. I lock the door behind me. *Bang!* I jerk back, one leg frozen mid-air as I'm about to descend the steps. *Oh gosh.* I forgot about that creaky, screen door. Dad was supposed to have fixed that. My quarter-length, black shirt, complimented with a pair of gray dress pants, has me blasting the AC the moment I rumble my dad's old truck to life. I rummage through my purse, past all the paperwork I'll be bringing with me to the courthouse, and find my sunglasses. My hand pauses on the gear-shift, and I scan the interior of the truck. If Jonathan suspected I stayed here last night, he would've left something to scare me . . . something my parents wouldn't think twice about. I take one last look around and shrug. The truck looks as normal as ever. I pick at some cotton coming through the tear in the single bench. That was my doing, years ago, when my dad had rushed me to school. I had to present a school project in my biology class, and when I yanked it from the truck in a rush, the sharp edge ripped the seat. My dad wasn't happy. I groan. Here I am, older and more mature, but still causing him grief.

I sigh heavily, hit reverse, and back down the short driveway. *Here's to a day out on the town.* First, I head to Java for an iced latte. There's no way I'm ordering a hot drink today. I scan the parking lot of Jim's Gym as I walk down to say hello. *Phew.* Rita's jeep is nowhere in sight. That would be just my luck…running into her as I say hello to all the trainers so she can run back to tell Jonathan I lied. Everyone offers warm greetings, and Jim has some kind words to share about how much he misses me. Danny catches me just as I'm leaving, and although he spends a good amount of time bragging about how he's *transformed* the bodies of all my old clients he took once I left, at least he doesn't hit on me. My stomach growls. I should've gotten a muffin or something at Java. *Oh well . . .* just another excuse to hit up my favorite restaurant. As I drive over to the other side of town, the courthouse appointment lurks in the corner of my mind. I drive down the familiar streets, turning at the second-hand shop where I purchased my cowboy boots, then turning again at the little, white church that always looks empty. It doesn't seem to matter how I distract myself today, the courthouse awaits, constantly nagging at me, reminding me that something dreadful is around the corner. *Don't dwell on it.* I throw the truck into park and hop out, ready to order the same lunch special I get every time I come here.

I smooth a hand down my full stomach as I walk to the truck. Settling behind the wheel, I turn on the engine and start to inch out into the traffic. *Thunk.* I slam on my breaks, missing the bumper of a Highlander by a hair. *Oh gosh!* That's Ainsley's Highlander. I freeze, watching as she pulls into a parking spot. I duck in the front seat, just low enough to remain hidden yet still able to peek out the window. Did she see that near miss? Will she recognize the truck and come over?

I unroll the window a crack. If she's going to approach me, I need to be prepared. She exits the driver's seat and turns for a moment to get Miles out of the back, her phone wedged between her shoulder and ear. I strain to hear through the cracked window.

"No, Mom. I'm not going to the courthouse," she groans into the phone. I hold my breath as my eyes narrow. "Well, Hallie isn't the friend I thought she was. Jonathan was texting me the whole night after we got back from Nashville, and he told me I only knew half the story." She plunks Miles on the ground, moves her phone to her other ear, and rubs the back of her neck. "She *lied* to me about Jonathan, and I should've known . . . the way she was acting in Nashville just confirmed that she's judgmental and *chooses* to be the victim rather than telling the whole story." Miles runs for the door of the restaurant. He knows the routine. She pauses just outside of the door beside Miles and puts her hand on her hip. "Jonathan asked to meet with me so he could tell me the whole story, and now that I know *everything,* I feel bad for *him.*" She throws up her free hand and disappears into the restaurant.

I grip my stomach as I sit up straight. *There it is.* I should've known Jonathan would get to her too. He knows what people want to hear, and it seems my last conversation with Ainsley was all she needed to lend a listening ear. As I drive off, I gulp back tears. *No, I'm not going to cry for this.* The rumors around here haven't stopped, and now's not the time to give into them. The problems of this place and the people here are not mine to handle anymore. I don't have to make my case in front of my pastor because someone has been spreading rumors about me. I don't have to explain my way out of any alleged affairs. *I'm done with it all.*

My heart falls to my stomach. But I still have to look over my shoulder for Jonathan. Did he mean it when he said he would never give up trying to find me? Will I ever really be free from him? Maybe I'll get a better feel for all that when I leave the courthouse. Maybe my *mysterious evidence* is enough to keep him away for good.

I spend the rest of the afternoon sauntering mindlessly through various stores, biding my time. My belly gurgles. Only an hour left until I have to be at the courthouse. Fighting back nausea, I distract myself in the local library, browsing book covers about various heroines. *Can't I just be like these women?* My phone buzzes from my purse. It's Sarah with a text saying she wishes me luck and that she's praying for me. Within the next thirty minutes, I receive similar texts from Harrison and Isabel, and with each new message, my heart lifts just a little. Maybe I am like the women who stand strong on the covers of these books. Maybe I am just as fierce—maybe I can fight against all odds, just like them. As I drive to this final encounter with the man who once stole all my sense of hope, drive, and strength, I cling to the fighter in me that I've adopted over the past year. *Here it comes, the final test of my fight-or-flight battle.*

By the time I pull up to the courthouse, my fingers are trembling. A dark cloud starts to roll in, and the sun disappears behind it. *Humph.* Why did I have to leave my jacket behind? I glance quickly at the clock on the dash, then kill the engine of the truck. Only fifteen minutes left . . . I've got to pray. *God, be with me. If I've ever needed your strength, it's now. I know you didn't design marriage to end in divorce, but I also know that you've been with me through every step of this disaster, and you have a plan for my future. Please, give me hope, right here . . . right now.*

The moment I step out from the truck, a fierce wind whips my hair away from my face and tugs at my purse. I shiver. *Oh dear.* It must have dropped at least ten degrees on my ride over. Folding both arms across my chest, I plunge a shoulder into the wind and march toward the courthouse.

My eyes scan the parking lot for Jonathan's car. My mouth falls open, and I take a quick step back as my eyes narrow. *He's here already?* I turn my back to the wind that's still picking up speed and sidestep between two cars only a few spots down from his. I peer over the hood of one car. His driver's seat is empty. Not only did he get here early, he's already inside. My skin crawls. It's not like him to get here early. A lump forms in my throat. *What's he planning?* I approach the glass door and pull it open against the wind. There he is, turned away from the door, chatting to one of the security guards behind the metal detector in this large entrance hall. Bile creeps into the back of my throat...he's engaged in a friendly exchange with a man in a police uniform.

"It was really good to see you," Jonathan says. I lick my lips. His clothes are neatly pressed, almost hiding his thin frame. His buzzed hair is tidied-up, unlike my windblown tangles, and his face is clean-shaven. I move wordlessly through the metal detector on the other side. Can I sneak by and into the courtroom without being seen...and without throwing-up?

"Yeah, man," the security guard replies, "you too. You look fit, and it seems like you're doin' good. So glad to hear that the family is well, and that business is good—as always." They shake hands, then he adds, "Man, the McClains are still doin' things right 'round here, and I respect that. Now you make sure to hunker down tonight. A nasty storm's brewin'—it's gunna get ugly."

With a courteous nod, Jonathan pivots just in time. We lock eyes, and his pleasant smile drops instantly. A shiver runs up my spine...he's got everyone in this town right where he wants them. With a nervous twitch, I flee from his burning glare, enter the large courtroom, and find my seat. My knees bounce relentlessly during the next thirty minutes, matching the rapid beat of my heart. When the judge finally grants the divorce, the tension begins to leave my shoulders. I rise when excused. Is it acceptable to run from a courtroom? *My marriage is finally over.* He signed the papers without a problem, and our divorce is now finalized. I take a deep breath as my heart soars. I'm finally Hallie Reed again. The courtroom doors thud shut behind me, and I beeline for the exit doors as the tiniest smile lifts the corners of my mouth. *I did it!* This agonizing year is finally over. I can start living my life now.

"Hallie," comes a bark from behind. I spin around, my smile fading instantly. "Guess you got what you wanted," he growls as he approaches me.

"Yes, I did," I spit. "Now it's over, and you can leave me alone."

His black eyes seem to burn red, "I guess so." He lowers his voice, "I mean, you probably still have that *evidence* against me."

My legs begin to tremble, but I stand tall. "I do, and I can use it whenever I need to, just so you know."

"It almost makes me curious what you got—but it's not a problem. Like you said, it's over now." His eyes narrow, "I'm just surprised your parents weren't here."

My limbs begin to shake at the mention of my absent parents, but I hold his gaze and force the strongest voice I can muster as I say, "They're here. Just not *in* here. I don't need my parents to get a divorce, but they *are* here." My head spins with this lie. *I hope I didn't over-do it.*

A shadow passes over his face, darkening his features to match the gray and black clouds outside. But in a flash, it's gone, convincing me that the look might not have been there to begin with. "Well, I guess this is good-bye then," he states, and without another word, he brushes past me and out the door. The wind catches the glass for a second, and I wait back, long enough to watch his car leave the lot. The moment his vehicle is out of sight, I let out a long breath and lean against the door. *He's gone.*

I stop at one of the nearby, family-owned diners for a quick dinner. As I pick at my salad, the owners are nervously watching through the windows at the approaching storm. They eventually tell the few guests still here that they are closing early tonight. *So much for a celebratory, Friday night dinner.* I text Harrison, Isabel, and Sarah to let them know my marriage is finally over. Who is Jonathan celebrating his freedom with? I shake my head and rise to pay the bill, leaving behind my half-eaten salad then clambering back into the truck.

The whole drive home has me fighting the gusty winds. The moment I'm parked in the driveway, I run to the house through heavy raindrops. I slam the door closed behind me, lock up, and fling the keys on the hallway table. As I trudge down the hall, carrying my unused jacket with me, my eyes flicker toward my parents' bedroom, then to Harrison's old room. *I wish someone was here. I wish I wasn't alone.* I could just stand here and sulk, but that wouldn't change my circumstances, so I meander into living room. Slumping on the couch, I toss my belongings on the floor, then place my phone on the coffee table. I slide off my flats, curl my legs up, and flick on the TV. It's kind of weird, sitting here, clicking through the channels, as if the sound of the TV can keep me company. An hour passes as the house rattles with each roll of thunder. I rise from the couch and march to the window. If there's thunder, then there's got to be lightening. That police officer at the courthouse was right, it's probably going to get ugly out there. Shivering, I reach into my suitcase and find a pair of sweats and a hoody. Once I'm changed, I sink back into the couch, hug the pillow, and yank the bundled blanket up to my chin.

Bang-bang! My heart leaps as I jump off the couch. Is someone knocking on the front door? My heart drums against my ribs as I tiptoe down the hall. With each turn, I pause to flick on the lights. Who would be calling on my parents now? As I reach the end of the hall, I turn toward the den and peak through the blinds. A white van is parked in the driveway, the headlights still on. Squinting through the darkness, a flash of lightening highlights a florist logo on the side of the van. *Bang-bang!* Another loud knock rattles the door, and my brow furrows as I slide over and twist the lock. I open the door a crack and breathe a sigh of relief. It's a complete stranger holding a vase of flowers. I flick on the porch lights as I open the door wider.

"Delivery for Hallie Reed," he calls over the rain and wind, his back holding the screen door open.

"That's me," I reply with a tilt of my head. "Who are they from?"

"Uh," he starts, looking down at a stapled mess of folded papers threatening to fly away, "Harrison and Isabel Reed. Can you sign here?"

He hands me the folded papers and indicates with the pen where I should sign. A smile spreads as I scribble my signature and take the glass vase. The delivery guy jogs to his van as I use my backside to close the door. While taking out the card to read, I walk down the hall:

> We're so proud of you! Wish we could be there to celebrate. God is in control!
>
> Love, Harrison and Isabel

My grin widens as I slip the card into the front pocket of my hoody and gaze at the beautiful bouquet, accented with vibrant colors of lavender. I place the vase on the dining room table and move to the coffee table to grab my phone. "Thank you for my beautiful flowers," I say the moment our call connects.

Harrison laughs, "You're welcome. I thought I would send something your way on this monumental day, so I asked Isabel what would be best. The flowers were her idea."

"Honestly—these flowers have been the highlight of my day, despite the fact that I'm now free from *him*."

"Well, good, I'm glad." Harrison clears his throat, "Listen, I don't want to steal you away from Mom and Dad, I'm sure they're soaking up as much time as they possibly can with you before you return to Ann Arbor tomorrow. But, uh—"

"Actually," I interrupt. I run a tongue across my lips, "I'm all alone."

A pause, then Harrison says, "*What?* You're joking. Mom and Dad left you? Where did they go?"

I groan, "They went to see Grannie. She's got some kinda special dinner tonight at the nursing home. I dunno—they said her health was declining, but—"

"So, were they with you at the courthouse?" I search for words. What can I say that won't make Harrison angry? "*Hallie?*"

"No," I finally mutter. "They left last night after they picked me up from the airport."

"I don't believe it—"

"Don't worry," I interrupt, "I'm safe, and things went smoothly at the courthouse. Honestly, I don't need them holding my hand through this divorce, and it shows them that I'm strong when I can do things like this on my own."

"Wow, Hallie." Harrison sighs, "I'm so sorry. Now I really do wish I was there."

With a small chuckle, I walk up to the blinds in the living room, peek through, and say, "I do too. We've got a serious storm brewing, and it's only supposed to get worse. The rain's been pretty heavy, on and off, but the winds are crazy. It was really hot all day until later this afternoon, around the time I showed up to the courthouse, and then the temperature dropped."

"Oh, that's not good."

"Yeah, I was eating dinner when—" and just then, the lights go out and the TV cuts off, plunging my surroundings into immediate quiet.

"Hallie, you alright?"

My heart thumps, "Uh, we just lost power," I whisper. Shuffling over to the other side of the room, I check through the blinds. "Yep," I confirm in a hushed voice, as if Harrison is right here beside me, "no one has power. I'm just glad I haven't lost cell service." My stomach tightens. "And I hope I don't."

Creak! My head snaps away from the window. *What was that?* I remain frozen on the spot as Harrison says, "Hello, you still there?"

"Hold on," I whisper behind a cupped hand, and I move down the hall. Is that the screen door banging in the wind? Did I lock the front door after I got my flowers? *I must have.* My free hand feels down the wall as my quivering body carries me past the hallway table. I lean into the door and twist the handle. *It's not locked.* My breath catches in my throat. With Harrison still on the phone, I twist the lock and back away slowly. Every muscle of my body is wound as tight as a spring while my eyes strain to see the objects in my immediate surroundings. I crouch low into the shadows of the hall, my breath returning with heavy gasps echoing in the eerie silence. *Is anyone here?* Just then, a flash of lightening reveals the murderous silhouette of a man in the den, but the thunder that follows belongs to Jonathan's treacherous voice, "Hello, again."

A scream sounds from miles away, yet it's coming from my mouth. I race down the hall. "*He's here! He's here!*" I shriek as I fumble around the corner.

Pow! A hit from behind crashes me into the wall. My cell phone is thrown out of my hands from the thrust of Jonathan's contact, and I cry out from the blow to my head.

Tumbling to the floor, my brain rattles for a split second, then instinct ignites my body, and I kick at whatever comes at me next. Through the ringing in my ears, my foot makes contact. *Thump!* Jonathan groans. In a flash, I rise, my body pulsing with such a fierce flood of terror that I can barely control my limbs. With a quick dash, I round the corner of the living room and duck behind the bookshelf. It's dark . . . he won't see me—he can't. My heavy gasps punch through my lungs, and my brain falters from the blow to my head as I whip my hand over my mouth. I wait, my head vibrating from a surge that threatens my consciousness.

"Now look, Hallie. There's nowhere for you to go," comes Jonathan's jeering voice. His footsteps mark his movement as he rounds the corner of the hall. "Don't forget, I know this house too," he says, his voice accompanying him into the kitchen. *Here's my chance!* I bolt for the closet on the far side of the room. I whip around the TV stand, using its bulk to hide me. "And I have your phone, too," he taunts, still near the kitchen. I click the door handle open and flail my hands about. Where's the shotgun? *Dad used to keep it in here—where is it?* "But it's too bad," he growls as another flash of lightening sparks behind the blinds, "*whoever* you were talking to is no longer on the phone." My hands stop. That was it, my brother was my chance of making it out of this alive. *Please, Harrison, call for help*. My hands start thrashing around to find the one thing that could save me. *Please be here.*

Crash! The shattering of glass sets my muscles on fire as I startle so harshly that my flesh pricks with a million needles. "I'm guessing those flowers were from your secret lover in Ann Arbor." With a couple of belittling tuts, he drawls, "Hope you didn't like that vase." Glass clatters across the dining room table, as if he's dragging his hand through the shards. He's moving closer. "Didn't I tell you that if I can't have you, no one can?" His ridiculing voice is now heading in my direction. He's loving this slow hunt, like a lion playing with its food. I bash through the closet as his movements carry him closer. *I've got to find that gun!* Blind, I turn and dive in as I can hear his lethal laugh getting closer and closer. Then, it stops. I swing back around, blinded by the light of my phone screen shining on my face. Cold iron brushes across my fingertips. *Swoosh!* My body is hurled off the wall, but I manage to grip the gun and drag it with me.

Jonathan flings me to the floor. *Ahhh!* Something slices down my free arm and hot blood pours from the wound. The piece of glass in Jonathan's hand comes at me again. I swing the gun as hard as I can at his head, and the *crack* of contact tingles through my arm. He stumbles back, the glass flying from his hand and clattering across the coffee table. A lightning bolt from outside illuminates the room just long enough to see his bloodthirsty snarl. He's no longer enjoying the brutal circling of his prey, he's coming in for the angry kill. But every ounce of my shaking body is ready to show this man that I'm a fighter now. I hoist the gun up the second he lunges at me as I fumble desperately for the trigger. He plows into me, driving my head into the carpet. *Crunch!* My ribs crack, and I scream. My cry reverberates through the room, louder than the thunder that rattles the house. He rips the gun from my grip and hurls it to the side. "I don't need a gun," he roars over the storm, "I'll finish this the way I should have a year ago." And in a flash, he hammers into me again. My body thrashes about as I fight back, launching every possible blow at the man smothering me. *I must fight! Where's the gun? I need the gun!* But it's too late, his hands are around my throat. I throw kicks and blows, thrusting my body off the ground and twisting viciously. His grip locks into a deadly hold. My breath leaves me. I beat on his arms as I try to reach for his face. He's so close, yet so far away. I can't reach his face hovering above me, his menacing, drug-crazed eyes thirsty for revenge while his hands remain triumphantly latched around my neck. My vision begins to fade. This is the end. He's finally going to take my life.

He laughs and moves to straddle my body that can no longer thrash. He's made a mistake. *Bam!* My foot kicks at his groin with all the might I have left. He falls back, his hands releasing as he rolls over and groans. My raspy breath returns with fierce drags. I roll over, one hand on my throat as I reach for the gun. Jonathan rises slowly from his knees. I push myself up to my feet, take a wide, steadying stance, grip the barrel with both hands, and swing with all my might. The stock connects with Jonathan's face just as he's reaching full height. He stumbles, then falls backward. *Crash!* His body smashes down on the coffee table and shatters the glass. I force another raspy breath as I secure my stance, but he's not moving.

My vision begins to grow dark. I collapse back on the floor. Just then, a woman screams, sending my mind reeling with the dissipating fog as I pull an anguished breath frantically into my lungs. *Mom?* Flashing blue lights from somewhere outside skirt my dimming consciousness. With the commotion that follows, my mind slips away to a sweet oblivion as my throbbing head sinks back into the sticky wetness of my blood spattered across the shag carpet.

Epilogue

The events from that night are still a blur. But I survived. God sent the storm so my parents would return home at just the right moment. It didn't matter that they came back for the safety of the house, what they found was the real reason why I had to leave *him*. And that realization has made all the difference. God prompted Harrison to call the cops when our call was disconnected. Watching Jonathan being carried away in handcuffs was the reassurance I ultimately needed. I now know that God does have a plan for me, a plan to prosper me and not to harm me, a plan to give me hope and a future. When I eventually boarded my return flight to Ann Arbor—stitched up, bruised, and battered—I knew I would no longer be afraid. I knew I wouldn't need to be looking over my shoulder for Jonathan anymore. And when the airplane took off, it was the first time in my life I was finally flying toward something and not away from it.

* * *

The mid-August sun disappears behind a cloud as I close my car door and smile. Nations Church has gathered on this Saturday afternoon for an outdoor baptism at Harrison and Isabel's new, two-story home, complete with four bedrooms and a pool. With a quick glance at the time on my phone, I run a hand through my newly dyed hair. *Ah, finally*—back to blonde. My jet-black hair only reminded me of my fear. I breathe a sigh of relief at my freedom. It's something I've become accustomed to over the past ten months, but I will never take it for granted.

As I stroll toward the backyard, Sarah pulls up in her car, emerges from the driver's side, and gives me a tight hug…or at least *tries*. "There's still plenty of time before the baptism, right?" I nod. "Good—it's just that Tom is picking up his brother, Vincent, so he can be here too." She reaches over and squeezes my hand, "We're finally doing this—we're getting baptized today."

"It's perfect timing, isn't it?" I reply, reaching over to rub Sarah's protruding belly, "I mean, *Baby Romano* will be here before we know it."

"Isn't that the truth," Sarah says, looking down at her swollen stomach with watery eyes. That look in her gaze is one I've learned over the last ten months, it's the look of a mother's love. "So, how about you? Other than Harrison and Isabel, do you have family coming?"

"Oh yeah—I forgot to tell you. My parents decided to come after all. They flew in last night. They asked their neighbor to feed the dogs while they're gone." I heave a visible sigh of relief. Who would've thought my parents would be the ones to take the dogs? All it took was Jonathan behind bars, and those dogs finally got the lucky break they needed. "And I'm shocked, but they're actually looking forward to being here for my baptism."

I push open the backyard gate with a smile and beckon Sarah through. Just then, a pound of thunder rumbles in the distance. We both glance up at the black clouds, then exchange a grimaced look. "This might be over before it begins," Sarah says. "Those clouds don't look good." We walk past all the people mingling around the pool, some of them turning their gaze upward with similar twisted faces.

Sarah and I climb the stairs to the screened-in porch. I inhale deeply. *Hmmm.* Do I smell jalapeño poppers? My mouth waters at the sight of the fold-up table covered in a yellow tablecloth. The twins run past, helping Isabel unwrap the plastic covering on a few of the dishes, and Bailey's eyes light up at the sight of the mini cupcakes. She and Branson giggle with glee, and I can't help but laugh as we enter the house. Harrison pivots in the kitchen at the sound of the door closing behind us. "Hey, you made it," he gibes, "we were starting to get worried." My parents, who are standing beside Harrison, move toward me.

"Hi Mom and Dad," comes my muffled greeting from their awkward hugs. They've started doing this, acting as if every time they see me it could be the last. "How was your flight?"

"Good," my dad starts, "Harrison picked us up last night, and we went straight to sleep as soon as we got back here."

"Yeah," my mother says, "we wanted to come by and see your new apartment, but we were a bit tired. Maybe we can come and see it after the baptism. Oh—I forgot to say," she adds, "congratulations on your promotion at work. You're doing so well, and your father and I are so proud of you."

"Thank you," I say, the edges of my face tingling with heat. "Oh, Mom and Dad," I turn to Sarah, who is standing behind me, "This is my friend, Sarah. She's married to Tom and they've been helping lead the Bible study that meets here mid-week. I think you'll be around for it this week—so you'll get to know them a little better."

Sarah extends a soft hand in greeting as my mother says, "You've got such a beautiful glow about you, Sarah."

"That must be this little one," Sarah says with a laugh as she pats her stomach. I smirk. Sarah glows whether she's pregnant or not.

"Is it a boy or a girl?" my dad asks.

"Actually," Sarah begins, with a sideways grin, "we were so surprised with the pregnancy we thought we might as well stick with this idea of being surprised. We haven't found out the gender, but we look forward to finding out in November."

"Oh, well that's nice," my mom replies, then her eyes move back on me, "babies are always such a blessing, and we're hoping to one day have more grandchildren." Her voice lifts with this comment, and I smile. My parents have definitely changed their tune.

"Not from us," Harrison adds with a laugh. "Isabel and I are *done.* She loves her work now that she's back teaching, and I don't think I could convince her to have any more children even if I tried. So, the pressure is on you, Hallie."

We all laugh as my mother interjects, "No, no—there's no pressure. It's just something to think about when the timing is right and when you've found the right guy to marry."

"And we hope you do find the right guy," my dad adds. He clears his throat, almost as if he's preparing to defend in court. "We now understand just how destructive it is when you're with the wrong guy."

My father's eyes get misty, so my mom redirects our attention as she nods, pats me on the shoulder, then asks my dad, "Should we get some lemonade?"

As the two of them walk out of the back door, Harrison turns toward Sarah and me to say, "You know, Hallie—Mom and Dad are coming around. Their conversations lately haven't been just about going to church, like they're ticking the box." He tips his head forward, his eyes almost twinkling. "They're starting to understand what it means to have a personal relationship with Christ. Last night, they told me that you have a lot to do with that. They said your humility about their confusion with Jonathan really caused them to see that there was something different with you." His mouth turns up in a half-grin, "Your story and how you handled that whole year of waiting to get the divorce has ultimately led them to believe that there are some holes in their church-going ritual that can only be filled by actually getting to know who Christ really is, not by just showing up at church each Sunday. I mean, look," he throws a hand up in the direction of the door, "they actually flew to watch you get baptized. *That's huge*. They aren't there yet, but they're moving in the right direction."

With a small grin, my eyes move to the door, then back to Harrison. "They were pretty shaken up with what happened last October. Once I finally recovered, they didn't want me to get on that flight, but I knew there was nothing left for me in Oklahoma—everything I had was waiting for me here in Ann Arbor." I lower my head with a smile. My heart flutters. Next week is going to be an exciting start to a whole new journey. I nod, then add, "Their testimony is what helped put Jonathan away, and they stood by my side through that whole trial. I never thought it would end that way, but thankfully, God knew that was exactly what I needed for closure. Now, there's no doubt in my heart that God can be trusted. He's been with me through these last two years—guiding, protecting, and helping me. I can see that now, and that's why I'm making the decision to get baptized today."

"On that note," Harrison replies, "you guys brought a change of clothes, right?" We both nod in unison. "Good—there are a few others getting baptized first, but when I jump in the pool, Hallie, that'll be your cue to get in as well. I'll ask you a few questions about your faith, then I'll dunk you."

We laugh, just as a flash of lightening sends people piling into the kitchen. "Hi folks," our pastor says once everyone settles inside, "I've checked my weather app, and although it's starting to rain outside, the lightening should pass very soon. Once we see it clearing, we'll head back out and immediately start with the baptisms."

The volume in the kitchen rises as Harrison saunters off to speak with the pastor. Tom clambers through the back door, and my heart catches in my throat. He's followed by the most handsome guy I have ever seen. Tall and muscular, this stranger runs a hand through his wet, dark hair, then moves it to his clean-shaven face as the raindrops fall onto his slightly exposed chest, easily noticed at the neckline of his button-up t-shirt. His tailored shorts bring the outfit together, right down to his soaked-through, leather flip flops. *Expensive taste.* As they start to move closer, my eyes narrow. This stranger looks a lot like Tom, only tidier…and prettier. The two turn in my direction, and my heart skips a beat. It's Tom's brother. *It's Vincent.*

Tom and Vincent approach our side, and Tom leans in to kiss his wife, then moves aside so Vincent can greet her with a hug. As I stand in Vincent's presence, the chatter from the room fades to a dull buzz. My heart pounds erratically within my chest. Is the uneven rise and fall of my breathing visible? They turn to me, standing there, trying to find my breath as a shy smile creeps into the corners of my mouth. "Hallie, this is my brother, Vincent," Tom says. Vincent's smile slowly spreads across his face as he reaches out to shake my hand. His gaze remains steady as our hands meet. Heat rises as I whisper a greeting, and my eyes drop ever so slightly from the penetrating stare of his chocolate brown eyes. The scar on his neck pummels my mind. But I don't recoil…quite the opposite—I grin. It's perfect. I release a short breath. We all have scars that tell our story, and his is beautiful.

"I already feel like I know you," I offer the moment our hands part.

"That's funny," he says, his voice warm and strong, "I was going to say the same thing." Sarah and Tom steal a guilty glance at one another, then Tom says, "Well, you two might be seeing a little more of each other on campus. Vincent's been accepted to the U of M med school," he says to me, then turns to Vincent and adds, "and Hallie's just been admitted to the kinesiology department to complete her bachelor's degree. Her classes start next week."

"That's amazing," Vincent offers. His wide smile seems to grow, and his bright eyes haven't left my face.

"Not nearly as amazing as becoming a doctor," I reply then turn to Tom. "Although I'm so happy I got in. Honestly, I don't think I could've done it without your brother's glowing recommendation letter."

"This guy gave you a recommendation?" Vincent asks, his high tone accusatory. He wraps an arm around Tom's shoulder, his bicep bulging with the playful movement, "He didn't write me a recommendation letter."

Tom wrestles with Vincent for a second as he jabs a few benign right-hooks at Vincent's torso. "That's because you don't need my recommendation. You've got a master's from Harvard. You're all set, man."

The two guys settle after a good laugh, and Sarah drops a gentle hand on her stomach as she laughs along with them. "Nah," Vincent eventually replies, his voice lowering, "I'm just glad that God's given me the brains and the willpower to continue in my education. And with a friend already on campus," he gestures at me, "I'm looking forward to the start of classes next week."

The conversation continues with ease. My mind takes a step back to survey the three in front of me. They're so beautiful and intelligent. And yet, I don't feel ostracized—pushed outside of the circle. It's almost as if I fit perfectly here, with them.

Eventually, our attention is pulled back toward the door as the pastor announces that it's safe to venture outside for the baptism. Vincent turns with Sarah and they start edging toward the door. My heart fills with a warmth that radiates to my fingers and toes. He leads his pregnant sister-in-law through the crowd, like a body guard protecting the Queen of England. *Can a man that strong really be that gentle and kind?*

"I'm glad you've finally met my brother," Tom says, startling me out of my reverie. He smiles, then runs a hand mischievously over his mouth as he adds, "You know, I've got a feeling about you two. Maybe it's God, but now that you're through your *storm,* I think Vincent could be your *dove.*" With a grin, he turns and looks at me as I stop, mid-stride. He raises an eyebrow, clearly remembering our conversation on our walk across town. He shrugs one shoulder and blends into the crowd heading outdoors.

Within minutes, everyone is crowded around the pool. When it's Sarah's turn to be baptized, Tom helps her into the pool and watches with teary eyes as she shares how she prayed through her trust issues with God and knew this was a decision she needed to make even before she got pregnant. It didn't matter whether or not God was going to give her what she wanted most…a baby. As her testimony draws to a close, she rubs her stomach in a circular motion. She and Tom were surprised with a positive pregnancy test not long after she made the decision to get baptized. A few more people are baptized after Sarah, and when Harrison jumps in, I take my cue and wade out to him and the pastor.

Now, it's time I share a few words about how I've grown over the past two years. My *fight-or-flight* battle has come to an end, and there is no doubt in my mind that I can trust God with my future. My testimony ends as I share Jeremiah 29:11 with the crowd, then Harrison asks, "Hallie, do you believe that Jesus Christ died on the cross for your sins?"

"Yes," I say with confidence.

"Do you believe that Christ rose from the grave, and that he has redeemed you from your former life?"

"Yes."

"Do you claim Jesus Christ as your Savior?"

"Yes."

"Upon this profession of faith, I baptize you in the name of the Father, the Son, and the Holy Spirit." Harrison lowers my body under the water. The moment I'm lifted up, the crowd roars with celebration along with the angels cheering in heaven. Tears fill my eyes as I lean over and hug Harrison. "I'm so proud of you, Hallie. You'll always be my little fawn, but you're so much stronger now, and I'm so glad you've placed your faith and trust completely in God." He releases me as I nod and wipe at my face, my tears intermingling with the pool water. "Now, let's get some grub," Harrison yells to the crowd.

Harrison gives me another quick hug, then he and the pastor climb out of the pool, their towels waiting in a chair. I wring out my hair as I wade toward the shallow end. I pause on the top stair of the pool just as Vincent approaches my side.

"You know, I love Jeremiah twenty-nine eleven—it's such a great verse." I nod unable to speak just yet. As if sensing that I need to be alone, Vincent asks, "Why don't I grab us some juice?" He turns toward the back porch, then pauses and pivots for a moment to say, "You know, I'd love to hear more about your story. I think you and I have a lot in common."

With a brief laugh, I shake my head and say, "I think you're reading my mind." He smiles, a twinkle catching his eye as he lowers his gaze, then saunters off. I turn back to the pool, standing there, my feet still immerged in water, gripping the railing, and my mind wanders to my journey these past two years. After all that I endured, I did it. I finally got baptized.

As another tear slips down my smiling face, I spot a rainbow forming through the dark clouds moving off into the distance. I utter a sound somewhere between a gasp and a laugh. There's my rainbow—a real promise I can cling to forever; that through it all, God *can* be trusted.

About the Author

Tiffany Price has completed her graduate studies in Technical and Professional Communication with a focus on Multicultural and Transnational Literatures. Tiffany is employed as an online English, Literature, and Communications instructor at various universities. Tiffany also works alongside her husband in church ministry through the Acts29 church planting network. Tiffany was born and raised in Canada, spent her adolescent and early adulthood years in North Carolina, then transitioned to Manchester, England for a two-year missional post, which is where Tiffany penned her first novel, *Love's True Colors*, published by Ark House Press in 2016. Tiffany currently lives in Brisbane, Australia with her husband, Matt.

CPSIA information can be obtained
at www.ICGtesting.com
Printed in the USA
JSHW031309140521
14757JS00002B/136

9 781631 952906